THE JERICHO ITERATION

THE JERICHO ITERATION

ALLEN STEELE

ACE BOOKS, NEW YORK

THE JERICHO ITERATION

An Ace Book
Published by The Berkley Publishing Group
200 Madison Avenue, New York, NY 10016

Book design by Arnold Vila.

First Edition: November 1994

Library of Congress Cataloging-in-Publication Data

Steele, Allen M.
    The Jericho Iteration / Allen Steele.—1st ed.
        p.   cm.
    ISBN 0-441-00097-5 (hard) : $19.95
    I. Title.
    PS3569. T338425J47 1994
    813'.54—dc20   94-6721
                                                         CIP

PRINTED IN THE UNITED STATES OF AMERICA

10   9   8   7   6   5   4   3   2   1

for Kent, Lisa, and Megan Orlando

Acknowledgments

Many people assisted in the development of this novel, most of them St. Louis residents I met during everyday life: police officers, firemen, city officials and bureaucrats, businesspeople, and not a few ordinary folks who just happened to be at the right place at the right time. Some were aware that they were being questioned by an author researching a novel and some were not, but all of them gave me invaluable insights and firsthand knowledge.

To these folks I give my most sincere thanks. This novel could not have been written without their help.

I'm also grateful to Steve Bolhafner, Liz Caplan, Sonny and Carol Denbow, John Furland, Ed Graham, Dot Hill, Frank and Joyce Jacobs, Chris Merseal, Frank M. Robinson, Mike Rosenfeld, Donna Schultz, Mark Tiedemann, Harry Turtledove, and Mark Zeising for encouragement, useful information, and many small favors rendered during the course of this work. As always, particular thanks go to my wife, Linda, who drove me around her hometown, suggested places I ought to visit, and told me when I was going wrong.

Most of all, I wish to thank my editors, Ginjer Buchanan and Susan Allison, and my agent, Martha Millard, for remaining faithful when the going got tough.

—St. Louis, Missouri
September 1991–February 1993

Let's talk about Jericho.

According to the Book of Joshua, the Canaanite city of Jericho was destroyed after Joshua marched his army around the city's walls for six days. On the seventh day, upon his command, the Israelites blew their ram's horns and began to shout. The walls collapsed, thus allowing Joshua and his followers to overrun the Canaanites and claim the city as their own.

That's how the legend goes, at any rate. About twenty years ago, archaeologists studying the ruins of Jericho in Israel, just outside Jerusalem, arrived at a different conclusion. They uncovered evidence suggesting that Jericho had been destroyed not by ram's horns but by a major earthquake caused by a geological fault line running through the Jordan Valley. Furthermore, the city was destroyed at least a hundred and fifty years before the reported date of the Battle of Jericho. Hence, the Talmudic account differs considerably from modern interpretations of the same evidence: in short, people took credit for something nature had already done.

And now it's Friday, April 19, 11:32 P.M. About three and a half millennia since the fall of Jericho, give or take a few hundred years, but who's counting? It doesn't make much difference in the long run. The more things change, the more they remain the same.

I'm sitting cross-legged on the living room floor of an abandoned, half-collapsed house in south St. Louis. It's the middle of the night, and I'm dictating these notes into my pocket computer. Joker's nicad is still fully charged, but I'm nonetheless keeping an eye on the battery LED. If it runs low . . .

Well, I'm sure I can find another. They're not as hard to find on this side of town as, say, an unclaimed can of Vienna sausage. On my way here I passed a scavenged 7-Eleven about four blocks away; southside looters normally don't go after batteries, although you never know.

I heard recently about a teenager who was killed scrounging through a video rental shop; seems he had been trying to make out with an armload of movies when a street gang that had claimed the store as their turf caught him. The story that made its way to the *Big Muddy Inquirer* was that they had strung him up from a telephone pole; when he was found the next morning, he had a copy of *Hang 'Em High* wrapped around his purpled neck. A touch of irony, if you like that sort of thing, although I doubt the guys who murdered him would know irony if it shot 'em in the ass with a Smith & Wesson.

Of course, this could be only another rumor. We've heard a hundred of them since the quake, and since it was never substantiated, we never ran it in the paper. Nonetheless, I think I'll keep talking only until the low-battery light begins to blink. Bopping on down to the 7-Eleven ain't what it used to be.

When the family who once lived here moved out of the city, as have so many others since New Madrid, they took with them whatever they could salvage. What little furniture they left behind is mostly buried beneath the rubble of what used to be their bedrooms; there's also a bad stink from that part of the house. I hope it's only a cat. Dead cats don't bother me, but dead children do.

The former residents left behind the refrigerator and the stove, but since there's no electricity in this neighborhood, they don't work. Union Electric must have determined that this is a vacant block, because even the streetlights are inoperative. There's also a filthy couch infested with insects, a mildewed Mickey Mouse shower curtain, which is the sole clue that there were once kids living here—like I said, I hope it's only a dead cat I smell—and, on the top shelf of the kitchen pantry, a half-empty box of Little Friskies.

Got to be a dead cat.

I'll have to ask the dog if he knows.

The dog who discovered me in the house was glad to have the Little Friskies. I found a forgotten spare key tucked beneath the back-door welcome mat—whoever once lived here didn't have much sense of originality when it came to hiding places, but then again, St. Louis used to be a much safer place—and had invited myself in when I heard something panting behind me. I turned around to find, in the last weak light of day, a full-grown golden retriever who had followed me into the backyard. His big red tongue was hanging out of his mouth, his fur was as wet as my leather jacket, but unlike so many other strays I've seen recently he didn't appear to be feral. Just a big old chow dog, living by his means in what used to be a middle-class neighborhood.

He sniffed me and wagged his tail, and didn't mind when I patted him on the head, so I let him into the house with me. What the hell; we both needed company. As luck would have it—for the dog, at least—there was the box of cat food. He didn't seem to mind the moldy taste. I only wish I could have eaten so well.

Friendly pooch. He decided to stay the night. I warned him that he was accompanying a federal fugitive and was thereby subject to prosecution to the full extent of the law, but the mutt didn't give a shit. I had given him a bite to eat, so I was square in his book, and he paid me back by warning me about the helicopter.

Several hours later: the sun was down, I was exhausted from running. Lying on the couch, idly scratching at the fleas that had come crawling out of the upholstery, listening to the cold, hard rain that pattered on the roof and dribbled through the cracks in the ceiling. Eyes beginning to close. It had been a hell of a day.

The dog was curled up on the bare floor next to the couch, dead to the world, when he abruptly leaped to his feet and began to bark. I opened my eyes, glanced at him, saw that he was looking out the wide picture window on the other side of the room.

I couldn't see anything through the darkness, but I could hear a low drone from somewhere outside the house. . . .

Chopper.

I rolled off the couch and fell to the floor, then scurried across the living room and through the kitchen door, out of sight from the window. By now the sound of rotor blades was very loud.

While I cowered in the kitchen, hugging the wall and sweating rain, the dog fearlessly advanced to the window and stood there, barking in defiance as the clatter grew louder. Then the helicopter was above the front lawn, invisible except for its running lights.

Captured by the Apaches.

One, at least: an AH-64 gunship, twenty-one thousand pounds of sudden death. Maybe it was an antique, but I remembered when I was a kid back in '89 and saw the TV news footage of those things circling the skies above Panama City, hunting for PDF holdouts and some pimple-faced cokehead named Noriega. Now one of them was hunting for a journalist named Gerry Rosen.

By the way, did I mention my name?

For several long minutes the Apache hovered outside the window. I could imagine its front-mounted TADS infrared turret peering into the house, the copilot in the chopper's back seat trying to get a clear fix through the downpour. The helicopter was close enough for me to make out the shadowed forms of the pilot and copilot within its narrow cockpit. The picture window shuddered in its tortured frame from the propwash.

It occurred to me that, if the 30-mm chain gun beneath the forward fuselage were to let go, the plaster wall in front of me wouldn't protect me more than would a sheet of Kleenex . . . and if I ran for the back door, the IR sensors would lock onto me before I could make it through the backyard. Anyone seen on the streets by ERA patrols after the nine o'clock curfew was assumed to be a looter, and in this side of town they didn't bother to make arrests anymore. In fact, they didn't even give you the dignity of slinging an old Clint Eastwood flick around your neck.

I clenched Joker against my chest and waited for the bullets to come through the window. They had found my best friend, they had found the poor bastards from the Tiptree Corporation, and now they had found me. . . .

And yet, despite all the noise, locked in the center of a crosshairs, the dog stood his ground. With his paws jammed against the windowsill, his lips pulled back from decayed brown teeth, his tail down but not tucked between his rear legs, this scrawny, matted stray dog angrily snarled and snapped and barked ferociously at the flying machine on the other side of the window, and in a brief, sudden, very clear moment of understanding, I knew what he was saying—

Get out of here, get out of here, this is my house, my house, MY HOUSE, GET THE FUCK OUT OF HERE THIS IS MY HOUSE!

—and then, in that moment between life and death, the copilot studied the image on his night-vision screen and reached a decision.

Ain't nothing here except a damn dog.

The ERA chopper rose upward, then angled away into the wet night, its lights following the ghostly strip of the ruined street until it vanished from sight.

The dog got some more Little Friskies for his smooth move, and I haven't slept since then.

Perhaps you may feel secure, hiding behind whatever walls you've erected around yourself, but I tell you now, as solid fact, that what happened to me and my city is not far removed from you. None of us is safe, and any sense of security you may have now is a lie.

My name is Gerry Rosen. I'm a reporter, and this is what happened to me during two days and three nights in Jericho, now better known as St. Louis, Missouri.

From the Associated Press (on-line edition): May 17, 2012

ST. LOUIS, MO. (AP)—A major earthquake, registering 7.5 on the Richter scale, struck St. Louis today, devastating large areas of the city and surrounding area and killing hundreds of people.

The quake, which began at 1:55 P.M. and lasted approximately 45 seconds, was epicentered in the town of New Madrid, about 130 miles southeast of the city. The quake caused high-rise buildings in the downtown area to sway, destroyed scores of smaller buildings and countless homes across the county, and led to the collapse of a light-rail bridge spanning the Mississippi River.

The exact number of people in St. Louis killed or injured by the quake is not known at this time. However, local police and fire officials say that at least two hundred fatalities have been reported so far and city hospitals are overwhelmed by people seeking medical assistance.

Particularly hard hit by the quake was the downtown business district, where many older buildings suffered extensive damage. Although no high-rise buildings collapsed during the quake, many interior walls fell. Dozens of smaller buildings were completely demolished, burying their occupants under tons of rubble. These included the old St. Louis City Jail, where at least 35 prisoners were instantly killed, and the nearby City Hall, where at least 10 office workers are reported missing.

Two local schools were also leveled during the quake. One city fire official said that there were "hardly any survivors" among the elementary schoolchildren who were attending classes at one of them, a Catholic private school in the city's prosperous west side.

Many streets in the downtown area have been ripped up by the collapse of underground caverns beneath the city, causing dozens of vehicles to fall into the gaping crevasses. Underground sewage pipes and electrical conduits were torn apart by the quake, causing the downtown area to be flooded with raw sewage. At least one chemical storage tank has been ruptured, and hazardous toxins are reported to be flowing through storm drains into the Mississippi.

Electrical power has been lost to most of the city, along with telephone lines and cable communications systems. Scattered fires in various neighborhoods have been reported by utility officials, largely caused by severed gas lines. Efforts to control the fires have been hindered by breakage of municipal water lines to much of the city and the loss of firehouses in at least three wards.

The William Eads Bridge, a major conduit for the city's light-rail system, collapsed into the Mississippi River, and eyewitnesses say that a westbound commuter train was crossing the bridge from East St. Louis, Ill., at the time of the quake. No official statement has yet been issued regarding the number of casualties, but officials at the scene say that dozens of people who were riding the MetroLink train may have fallen to their deaths.

The Gateway Arch, the national landmark on the west bank of the Mississippi that is the city's symbol, survived the quake intact, although roof sections of the underground visitors' center beneath the Arch fell during the quake, killing at least five people and injuring dozens of others. Witnesses report that the Arch itself swayed during the tremors.

Missouri Gov. Andre Tyrell, who was attending the National Governors Convention in Las Vegas at the time of the disaster, has phoned the President to ask for fed-

eral assistance, says spokesman Clyde Thomson at the
state capital in Jefferson City, itself rocked by the quake.
Thomson said that Tyrell is flying back to the state,
although commercial air traffic in and out of St. Louis
International Airport has been suspended by the Federal
Aviation Administration because of hazardous runway
conditions.

Although the local Emergency Broadcast System was
crippled by the loss of the KMOX-AM radio tower, St.
Louis Mayor Elizabeth Boucher went on the air from
radio station KZAK-AM at 2:30 P.M. to plead for calm
and cooperation from the city's residents. "Please help
our police and firemen do their jobs," she said, "and
assist your neighbors in whatever way you can.

"May God help us in this time of crisis," Boucher said,
her voice shaking.

Several small towns in eastern Missouri and south-
western Illinois were also devastated by the earthquake,
the force of which has been estimated to be equivalent to
the detonation of 900,000 tons of TNT, or a nine-kiloton
nuclear explosion. Significant damage was also reported
in Evansville, Ill., and Memphis, Tenn., and tremors were
felt as far west as Kansas City, where a church bell was
reported to have rung twelve times during the quake.

Hundreds of National Guard troops from across the
midwestern region are being sent to Missouri to aid local
relief efforts. Spokesmen at the Washington, D.C., headquarters of the Emergency Relief Agency say that ERA
troops are being mobilized at this time . . .

Excerpt from *The Big Muddy Inquirer*:
December 18, 2012

Christmas In Squat City:
"Santa Will Still Find Our Tent."
Seven months ago, Jean Moran lived in a two-bedroom
ranch house in suburban Frontenac. Each morning she

packed sack lunches for her two children and sent them off to meet the school bus, while her husband, Rob, skimmed the paper and had one last cup of coffee before driving downtown to the insurance brokerage where he worked. Jean then spent the rest of the day doing housework, paying bills, shopping for groceries, chatting on Compuserve with friends around the country . . . the daily affairs of a slightly bored young housewife who believed that her life was as solid as the ground beneath her feet.

Then, one day last May, the ground was no longer solid.

Now Jean Moran and her kids, Ellen and Daniel, are only three of some 75,000 residents of the vast tent city that is still in place in Forest Park seven months after the New Madrid earthquake.

She still does housework—or rather, tentwork, the day-to-day housekeeping responsibilities shared by the four homeless families who occupy tent G-12—but gone are all the material things she once took for granted, except for a few family pictures she salvaged from the wreckage of her house.

For a while after they moved into the park, Ellen and Danny went to school three days a week, attending one-room elementary classes conducted in the mess tent by volunteer teachers from the Urban Education Project, until government cutbacks closed the school last November. Now, while Jean fills plastic bottles from the water buffalo parked nearby, her children are two more kids playing in the frozen mud between the olive drab tents of Squat City.

"I'm just grateful I didn't lose them, too," Jean says quietly, watching her kids as she hauls the two-gallon jugs back to her tent and stows them on the plywood floor beneath her metal bed. "They were both out in the playground for recess when it happened . . . thank God I was in the carport and managed to get out in the open, or they would have lost both their parents."

Her husband had also been out in the open during the

quake, but he wasn't as lucky as his wife and children. Rob Moran was killed when a cornice stone fell ten stories from a downtown office building while he was on his way back to work from a late lunch. He had a life insurance policy, just as the Moran house had been covered by earthquake rider on the home insurance, but Jean is still waiting for the money to come through. The small insurance company that had protected them went bankrupt before all its claims could be settled.

With the insurance company now in receivership, it may be many months before the Morans are reimbursed for everything they are owed. Yet this is only one of many nuisances, large and small, with which Jean has had to cope as the widowed mother of two children.

"Summer wasn't too bad," she says, sitting on her bunk and gazing through the furled-back tent flap. "It was hot, sure—sometimes it was over a hundred degrees in here—but at least we had things to do and people were taking care of us. And when construction companies started looking for crews to work on demolition and rebuilding contracts, some people around here were able to get work."

She laughs. "Y'know, for a while, it was almost like we were all in summer camp again. At first, we liked the ERA troopers. They put up the tents, smiled at us at mealtime, let Danny play in their Hummers and so forth . . ."

She suddenly falls silent when, as if on cue, a soldier saunters past her tent. An assault rifle is slung over the shoulder of his uniform parka, which looks considerably warmer than the hooded sweatshirt and denim jacket Jean is wearing. For an instant their eyes meet; she glances away and the soldier, who looks no older than 21, walks on, swaggering just a little.

"Lately, though, they've turned mean," she goes on, a little more quietly now. "Like we're just a bunch of deadbeats who want to live off the dole . . . I dunno what they think, but that's how we're treated. Sometimes they pick fights with the guys over little stuff, like someone trying to get an extra slice of cornbread in the cafeteria line. Every now and then somebody gets pushed around by two or three of them for no good reason. We're at their mercy and they know it."

She lowers her voice a little more. "One of them propositioned me a couple of weeks ago," she says, her face reddening. "He made it sound as if he'd requisition some extra blankets for the children if I'd . . . y'know." Jean violently shakes her head. "Of course, I'd never do something like that, not for anybody, but I think some of the other women around here who have kids . . . well, you do what you think you gotta do."

She pulls at her lank hair as she talks, trying to comb out the knots with her fingers. It's been several days since she has taken a shower in the women's bath tent. Like everything else in Squat City, hot water is carefully rationed; she gives her bath cards to her kids.

"Last night Ellen wanted to know if Santa Claus was going to visit us even if we don't have a chimney anymore," she says. "I told her, 'Yes, sweetheart, Santa will still find our tent.' I didn't tell her I don't know if he's going to bring us any presents—I'm hoping the Salvation Army or the Red Cross will come through—but I know what she wants anyway. She wants Santa to bring her daddy back . . ."

Her voice trails off and for a couple of minutes she is quiet, surrounded by the sounds and smells of Squat City. The acrid odor of campfire smoke, burning paper and plastic kindled by wet branches. The monotone voice of the announcer for Radio ERA, the low-wattage government AM station operating out of the Forest Park Zoo, talking about Friday night's movie in the mess tents. A helicopter flying low overhead. Children playing kickball.

"Let me show you something," Jean says abruptly, then stands up and walks between the bunks to push aside the grimy plastic shower curtain separating her family's space from the others in G-12. "Look in here . . ."

In the darkness of the tent, a middle-aged man is

lying in bed, his hands neatly folded across his chest. It's impossible to tell whether he's asleep or awake; his eyes are heavy-lidded, as if he's about to doze off for a midafternoon nap, yet the pupils are focused on the fabric ceiling of the tent. He is alone, yet he seems unaware that he has visitors.

"That's Mr. Tineal," Jean whispers. "He used to own a grocery down on Gravois. He was buried alive under his store for six days before firemen found him. Six days, with both arms broken, and he hung on until they located him. After he got out of the hospital, they put him here, and he's been like this ever since. His wife and his daughter have been tending to him, but I don't think I've heard him say fifty words the whole time we've been here."

Jean lets the curtain fall. "Three days ago, an ERA caseworker stopped by. They do that once a week, mostly just to have us fill out more forms and such. Anyway, this bitch—I'm sorry for my language, but that's the way she was—the lady looked him over once, then turns to Margaret, his wife, and they've been married now for over thirty years, and says, 'You oughtta just let him die. He's only using up your rations, that's all.' "

Jean walks back to her bunk and sits down on the same impression she had recently vacated. Once again, she's quiet for a few minutes, gazing down at the muddy tracks on the wooden floor.

"So what do you think?" she says at last. "Is Santa going to visit us this year or what?"

From the *Big Muddy Inquirer*: April 3, 2013

St. Louis To ERA: Go Away
ERA to St. Louis: Thanks, But We Like It Here

Like a houseguest who has overstayed his welcome but is apparently deaf to hints that it's time to hit the highway, the federal Emergency Relief Agency shows no signs of leaving St. Louis anytime soon, despite the fact that the last aftershock of the New Madrid earthquake has been felt and many local officials say the city is off the critical list.

Although 550 ERA troopers were recently withdrawn from Metro St. Louis and returned to the agency's federal barracks at Ft. Devens in Massachusetts, some 600 soldiers remain on active duty in St. Louis County. ERA officials claim that the situation in St. Louis remains dangerous and that the agency's paramilitary forces are needed to maintain order in the city.

"Look at the map," says Col. George Barris, commander of ERA forces in St. Louis. He points at a street map tacked up on a wall in the central command post, in what used to be the Stadium Club at Busch Stadium. Large areas of the map—mostly in the northern and southern sides of the city, as well as the central wards— are shaded in red, with black markers pinned to individual blocks within the red areas.

"Those are the neighborhoods still under dusk-to-dawn curfew," Barris explains. "The little black pins are the places where our patrols have encountered hostile action in the past 48 hours alone. Street gangs, looters, assaults against civilians—you name it. Now you tell me: do you really want us to just pack up and get out of here?"

It's inarguable that vast areas within the city remain volatile, particularly on the north side where three days of rioting late last December caused almost as much damage as the earthquake itself. Several parts of the city are so unsafe that authorities can patrol them only from the air, forcing SLPD to use military helicopters— including secondhand Mi-24 gunships recently purchased from Russia—instead of police cruisers.

Yet many persons in the city believe that the continued presence of federal troops in St. Louis is only exacerbating the crisis. "Look at what we've been through already," says LeRoy Jensen, a Ferguson community activist who made an unsuccessful run for the city council two years ago. "People up here lost their homes, their jobs, some

of them their families . . . now they can't even leave the
house without being challenged by some ERA soldier.
Everyone who lives around here is automatically assumed
to be a criminal, even if it's just a mother stepping out to
find her kids after dark. How can we go back to normal
when we're living in a combat zone?"

Jensen points out that when $2 billion in federal disaster
relief funds were made available through ERA to Missouri
residents after New Madrid, very little of the money found
its way to poor and lower-middle-class residents. Like
many people, he charges that most of the cash went to
rebuilding upper-class neighborhoods and large companies that didn't really need federal assistance in the first
place.

"The government based the acceptance of loan applica-
tions on the ability of people to repay the loans," Jensen
says, "but how can you repay a federal loan if the store
you worked at is gone? Yet if the government won't help
to rebuild that store, then you can't repay the loan. It's
a catch-22 . . . but if you get mad about it, then along
comes a dude in a uniform, telling you to be quiet and
eat your rations. And when the food runs out, like it
did last Christmas, then they send in the helicopters and
soldiers again."

Jensen also claims that ERA crackdowns on north-
central neighborhoods in the city are based on social and
ethnic attitudes among ERA troopers. "When was the last
time you heard of a white kid in Ladue or Clayton getting
busted by the goons?" he says. "Answer: you never do.
But all these ERA troops, they're rich white kids who
got out of being drafted to Nicaragua by getting Daddy
Warbucks to get 'em into ERA, so now they're trying to
make up for being wusses by kicking some nigger ass in
north St. Louis."

As heated as Jensen's remarks are, they have some jus-
tification. The Emergency Relief Agency was established
in 2006 as part of the National Service Act, which also
reestablished the Civilian Conservation Corps and started
the Urban Education Project. Under NSA, all Americans

between the ages of 18 and 22 are required to serve 18 months in one of several federal agencies, including the armed services. At the same time, ERA was founded to replace the Federal Emergency Management Agency after FEMA came under fire for perceived mismanagement of natural disaster relief during the 1990's.

After national service became an obligation for all young American men and women, CCC was the most popular of the available agencies. Soon there was a four-year waiting list for applicants to this most benign of organizations, with UEP being seen as an only slightly less benign way to spend a year and a half. Widely regarded as a hardship post, ERA was the least popular of federal agencies.

This changed when the United States went to war in Central America. As casualties began to mount among American servicemen in Nicaragua, many young men and women sought to duck military conscription by signing up for the ERA. Can't get into the CCC? Not qualified to be a UEP teacher? Want to be a badass, but you don't want to risk getting your ass shot off by a Sandinista guerrilla? Then ERA's for you.

Congressional critics have charged that the agency has become a pool for young rich punks with an attitude. Indeed, the number of encounters between ERA patrols and local citizens in St. Louis that have resulted in civilian casualties tends to suggest that ERA soldiers have adopted a "shoot first, ask questions later" stance toward what ERA training manuals term as "the indigenous population"—that is, whoever lives in the curfew zones.

"Look at this place," says Ralph, a young ERA corporal who has been assigned to curfew duty in Jennings. He stands on the corner of Florissant and Goodfellow, surrounded by burned-out buildings, an assault rifle cradled in his arms. "Every night the same thing happens again . . . the coons come after us and every night we gotta fight 'em off. I've lost all respect for these people. They don't want to help themselves . . . they just want more government handouts. Shit on 'em, man. They're not Americans."

Ralph is originally from Orange County, California, where he was the assistant manager of a fast-food franchise before he joined ERA as a way of avoiding military draft. He spits on the ground and shakes his head. "Maybe I shouldn't be prejudiced and call them coons," he admits, "but that's the way it is. If I knew it was going to be like this, I'd sooner be down in Nicaragua instead, shooting greasers and greasing shooters."

This callous attitude seems endemic among ERA troopers who are still in St. Louis, but city council member Steve Estes claims that the continued ERA presence in St. Louis is justified. "Most of my constituents want law and order on the streets, period," he says. "As far as I'm concerned, ERA has a moral obligation to be here, and I'm behind them all the way."

Estes, who is seen by several political insiders as contemplating a run for the mayor's office, also wants to close down the tent city that was established in Forest Park to house the people left homeless by the quake. "The place has become a sanctuary for freeloaders," he says. "If these people really want jobs and other places to live, then they could get them. Right now, though, it's become another Woodstock, and I support any efforts to rid the park of these bums."

Barris claims that all civilian casualties that have occurred during incidents involving his men and local residents have always been the fault of the civilians. "These guys are out there on their own, outnumbered a hundred to one," he says. "When you're cornered by a street gang and they're throwing bricks and bottles or whatever they can get their hands on, your options tend to run out in a hurry, believe me."

Jensen disagrees. "We see them as an occupational force. They want us dead or gone, period, so they can chase all the poor people out and build some more shopping centers. But we live here . . . this neighborhood may be burned out, but it's still the place where we grew up."

He stops talking to look around at the tenement buildings surrounding him. An ERA gunship flies low over
the block where he lives. "We don't want no trouble,"
he says after it passes by. "We don't want to go on
living like this. I understand each bullet that thing car-
ries costs the taxpayer five dollars. They want to make
things better? Fine. Gimme five bucks for each shell
casing some kid brings to me from the street . . . we'll
turn this side of town around."

PART ONE

Ruby Fulcrum

(April 17, 2013)

1

There was a man on the stage of the Muny Opera, but what he was singing wasn't the overture of *Meet Me in St. Louis.* In fact, if he was singing at all, it was a demented a capella called the New Madrid Blues.

My guess was that at one time he had been a young, mid-level businessman of some sort. Perhaps a lawyer. Possibly a combination of the two: a junior partner in the prestigious firm of Schmuck, Schmuck, Schmuck & Putz, specializing in corporate law. A yuppie of the highest degree, he had been a graduate of Washington University, graduating somewhere in the middle of his law school class: good enough to get an entry-level job with Schmucks and Putz, but not well enough compensated to have a place in Clayton or Ladue. So he had lived in a cracker box somewhere in the south side and commuted to work every day in the eight-year-old Volvo he had driven since his sophomore days at Wash You. Five days a week, he had battled traffic on the inner belt, dreaming of the day when he would have a Jaguar in the garage of a suburban spread in Huntleigh and his law firm would now be known as Schmuck, Schmuck, Schmuck, Putz & Dork, as he steeled himself for another grueling day of ladder climbing and telephone screaming.

And then the shit hit the fan last May and the bottom fell out of hostile takeovers of candy stores. His apartment house had fallen flat, burying his car beneath a hundred tons of broken cinderblock and not-quite-to-code drywall plaster, and the week after he moved into Squat City, where he had

21

been forced to share a tent with strange ethnic persons who didn't wear fraternity rings and to survive on watered-down chicken soup and cheesefood sandwiches, he discovered that the Schmuck Brothers had decided to let some of their attorneys go. Sorry about that, we'll let you know when there's an opening . . .

And his mind had snapped.

So now here he was, standing on the stage of the Muny, waving a black baseball bat over his head and raving like a crack fiend who hadn't had a decent fix in days.

"When selecting a baseball bat," he shouted, "there are five things to remember . . . !"

His ragged, oil-splotched London Fog trenchcoat could have been looted from Brooks Brothers. That wasn't what tipped me off; it was his shoes. Handmade Italian leather loafers which, even though they now were being held together with frayed strips of yellow duct tape, fit him perfectly. And although his hair had grown down over his shoulders and his gray-streaked beard was halfway to the collar of his mildewed dress shirt, he still had the unmistakable articulation of an attorney, although I doubt the senior partners of his firm would have recognized him now.

"One! The size of the bat should be the right size for your hands to grip and hold comfortably!" He demonstrated by gripping the taped handle of the black mahogany bat between his fists, his anger causing the knuckles to turn white. "That means it's gotta be the right size for you to do some serious damage to some fucker's face!"

Scattered applause from the first few rows behind the orchestra pit. Give us your poor, your downtrodden, your teeming masses yearning to be free . . . and if they can't have freedom, then there's always cheap entertainment. Farther back in the open-air amphitheater, though, only a few people seemed to be paying attention. At least a thousand people were crammed together into the Muny tonight, enduring the cold rain as they watched the nightly parade of homeless, half-mad speakers march onto the stage. On the proverbial one-to-ten scale, the former lawyer barely rated a four.

"Let's hear some music!" This from a woman in back of the seating area. A small group of down-and-out rock musicians stood in the wings, waiting for their chance to set up their equipment and play for any food stamps that might be tossed into their hat.

The lawyer either didn't hear her or wasn't paying attention. "Two!" he yelled, his voice beginning to crack. "The bat should be light enough so that you can swing it with the greatest speed!" He whipped the bat around like Ozzie Smith driving a grounder in Busch Stadium twenty years ago. "This means, y'gotta have the right instrument in order to knock their brains right outta their fuckin' skulls!"

A few yells of approval, this time even from the rear seats. He had their attention now; nothing gets people going like a little unfocused hatred. The bat looked a little familiar, though. I edged closer to the railing surrounding the orchestra pit and peered through the drizzle. There were white-painted autographs burned into the black surface of the bat.

Oh, God, this was a sacrilege. This sick puppy had managed to get his mitts on one of the team bats that had been on display in the Cardinals Hall of Fame. Probably stolen shortly after the quake, when Busch Stadium had been overrun by the newly homeless, before the Emergency Relief Agency had chased out the looters and set up their base of operations inside the stadium. By then, everything worth stealing from the display cases in the mini-museum was gone. I prayed that he hadn't gotten his hands on a pennant-year bat; that would have been the worst insult of all. A bat with Stan Musial's or Lou Brock's signature inscribed upon it, now in the hands of some crazy with a grudge.

"Three!" he howled. "The bat should be long enough to reach across home plate and the strike zone as you stand in a correct position inside the batter's box!"

"Get off the stage!" someone yelled from the seats.

The demented yup ignored him. "Remember, a longer bat is harder to swing, regardless of how much it weighs!" He hefted the bat menacingly. "That means you gotta get in good and close, so you can count his teeth before you bust 'em out of his goddamn lyin' mouth . . ."

Now that I knew where the bat had come from, I made the proper association. He was reciting, with significant annotation, a list of batting recommendations that had been posted in the Hall of Fame museum next to a cutaway of a Louisville Slugger. The instructions were meant to advise Little Leaguers and other potential Cardinals champs of the future; now they were being howled by a psycho who would have given Hannibal Lector the chills. An innocent set of guidelines, reborn as directions for up-close-and-personal homicide.

(And with that memory, another one: Jamie sitting next to me on the MetroLink a couple of weeks before New Madrid. Saturday afternoon. We were on our way back from the stadium after watching the Cards stomp the gizzards out of the St. Petersburg Giants.

("Pop?"

("Yeah, kiddo?"

("Can I play Little League next year?"

("I dunno . . . we'll see.")

"Four! If you plan to buy a bat and you normally wear batting gloves—"

"Get outta here! Yer not funny!"

The memory of a quiet Saturday afternoon with Jamie evaporated as suddenly as it had materialized. I couldn't have agreed more: it was not funny, if it had ever been funny in the first place.

I had come to the Muny in hopes of finding something worth reporting for the *Big Muddy Inquirer*. I was facing a Friday deadline and Pearl was breathing down my neck for my weekly column. Because I had heard that the squatters had recently broken the padlocks on the Muny's gates and turned the amphitheater into an unauthorized public forum, I had come to Forest Park to see if I could hear any revolutionary manifestos. I was sure that there were some budding Karl Marxes or Mao Tse-tungs out there, screaming for their chance to be let out of the box . . . or just screaming, period.

So far, though, the only interesting speaker had been the psychotic Cards fan, and things were tough enough already without my repeating his advice for using a stolen baseball bat as a murder weapon. I turned and began to make my way up the concrete steps of the left-center aisle, feeling the rain pattering on the bill of my cap as I emerged from beneath the stage awning.

Huddled all around me were the new residents of Forest Park: people who had been left homeless by the New Madrid quake, either because their houses and apartments had collapsed during the quake or, as in the case of the north side communities, because last December's food riots had caused so many of the surviving buildings to be burned to the ground.

Forest Park was the largest municipal park in the country. Before the events of last May it had been a pleasant place in which to spend a quiet Sunday afternoon. The World's Fair had once been held here and so had the Olympic games, both more than a century ago. Now that the park had become a little bit of Third World culture stuck in middle America, the Muny was the only bit of free entertainment left available to the city's vast homeless population. Tommy Tune no longer danced across the stage, Ella Fitzgerald was long gone, and the national touring companies of *Cats* or *Grand Hotel* no longer performed here, but people still found their pleasure here . . . such as it was.

I looked around as I walked up the steps, studying the dismal crowd. Men, women, and children; young and old, alone and with families, white, black, hispanic, oriental. No common denominator except that they were all clinging to the lowest rung of the ladder. They wore cheap ponchos and cast-off denim jackets and moth-eaten cloth coats donated by the Salvation Army; some didn't even have raingear to speak of, just plastic garbage sacks and soaked cardboard boxes. In the weak, jaundiced light cast by the few sodium-vapor lamps that still functioned, their faces reflected hardship, pain, hunger . . .

And anger.

Most of all, anger: the dull, half-realized, hopeless rage of those who were pissed upon yesterday, were pissed upon today, and undoubtedly would be left standing beneath the urinal tomorrow. Halfway up the aisle, I was jostled aside by a burly man making his way down the steps; I stumbled against a chair and almost fell into the lap of a young woman who was holding a child in her arms. The little boy was chewing on a piece of government-issue cheesefood; his eyes looked glazed beneath the hood of his undersize sweatshirt, and the long tendril of mucus hanging from his nose told me that he was ill. If he was lucky, perhaps it was only the flu, although that could quickly escalate into pneumonia. His mother glared at me with silent, implacable rage—*What are you looking at?*—and I quickly stepped away.

No one here wanted pity. No one wanted the few government handouts that were still being given to them. All they wanted was survival and a chance to get the hell out of Squat City.

The mad yuppie was through with his screed by the time I reached the covered terrace at the top of the stairs. The terrace was at the rear of the amphitheater, and it was crowded with people trying to get out of the drizzle. Through the stone arches and past the wrought-iron gates, I could see the glow of dozens of trash-barrel fires in the adjacent parking lot, silhouetting the people who huddled around them for warmth against the cold spring rain, watchful for the apes . . .

Yes, apes. Real apes, not metaphorical in any sense whatsoever, although a case could be made for the ERA troopers who patrolled the park. One of the unforeseen side effects of the quake was that the Forest Park Zoo had practically split open at the seams, allowing lions, tigers, and bears—not to mention a few giraffes, antelopes, rhinos, and elephants—to escape. Most of the animals were recaptured by zoo personnel within the first few days after New Madrid, although quite a few wild birds had taken wing, and a handful of coyotes and bobcats had been wily enough get out of the inner city and into the county's wooded west side. Some of the zoo specimens, unfortunately, didn't make it back to their cages; two weeks after the quake, a rare Tibetan white leopard was shot by a redneck National Guardsman after it was cornered foraging through garbage cans in the University City neighborhood. When zoo officials arrived at the scene, they found the leopard's decapitated carcass lying in the alley; the weekend warrior who had shot the leopard had carved its head off and taken it back to his place in Fenton as a trophy.

But the apes that had survived the collapse of the monkey house had done much better. Only a handful of apes had been recaptured, mostly gorillas and orangutans; most of the chimpanzees and baboons had taken to the trees and had survived the short, relatively mild winter that followed the earthquake summer. Indeed, they had been fruitful and multiplied, adding to their numbers as the months wore on. Now monkey packs roamed the park like street gangs, raiding tents and terrorizing squatters.

Even the ERA troopers were frightened of them; there had been one rumored account that a chimpanzee pack had fallen upon a parked Hummer and chased its crew into the woods. If the story was true, then good for the chimps; I had more sympathy for runamok apes than for runamok goon squads.

There was no sign of apes, either human or simian, so I found a vacant spot beside one of the Doric columns holding up the awning. After looking around to make sure I wasn't being observed, I unzipped my leather bomber jacket and reached into the liner pocket to pull out my PT's earphone.

"Joker, can you hear me?" I said, switching on the PT and holding the earphone against my ear.

"I hear you, Gerry." Joker's voice was an androgynous murmur in my ear: HAL-9000 with a flat midwestern accent. It was picking up my voice from a small mike clipped to the underside of my jacket collar.

"Good deal," I replied. "Okay, open a file, slug it . . . um, 'park,' suffix numeral one . . . and get ready for dictation."

I usually typed my notes one-handed on Joker's miniature keyboard. Like many writers, I intuitively prefer to see my words on a screen, but there was no way I was going to fish out my palmtop and open it up in plain view, thereby revealing myself to be a reporter. During the December riots, too many of my colleagues had been attacked by rioters who had seen them as being authority figures, and a *Post-Dispatch* photographer had been killed by crossfire during the torching of the federal armory in Pine Lawn. Even if some of these people didn't necessarily see the press as their enemy, there was always the chance someone might try to mug me in order

to grab Joker. A stolen PT was probably worth a few cans ~f
tuna on the black ......

.... *little*
strange. Although the IM was sent directly to me, it's addressed
to John Tiernan. I was not informed that we would be taking
John's messages."

I frowned as I heard this. John was another reporter for the
Big Muddy Inquirer. Although he was my best friend, we
normally stayed out of each other's work. Someone trying
to send an instant message to John should have reached his
own PT, Dingbat, not Joker; nor could we access each other's
palmtops without entering special passwords.

But there was no sense in asking Joker if it was mistaken;
my little Toshiba didn't make errors like that. "Okay, Joker,"
I said, "read it to me."

"IM received 6:12 P.M. as follows," Joker recited. *" 'I got*
your message. Need to talk at once. Please meet me near the
rear entrance of the Muny at eight o'clock.' End of message.
The sender did not leave a logon or a number."

I felt a cold chill when I heard this message. I believe in
coincidence as much as the next superstitious person, but this
was a bit too much.

An IM intended for John had been sent to me instead,
requesting a meeting at the Muny . . . and, as synchronicity
would have it, where would I happen to be when I received
it? At the Muny.

I took a deep breath. "Okay, Joker," I said, "what's the
gag?"

"What gag, Gerry?"

"C'mon. Who really sent the message? Was it John?" I
grinned. "Or was it Jah?"

sort. "Please ...

"Running test." There was a long pause while Joker's doctor pushed, prodded, asked embarrassing questions, and slipped a rectal thermometer up its cybernetic asshole. *"Test complete,"* Joker said at last. *"All sectors are clean. There is no evidence of tampering with my architecture."*

"I don't understand."

"Neither do I, Gerry. Nonetheless, I do not have a return number for this IM."

I mulled it over for a second, then Joker spoke up again. *"I have opened a file, slugged 'park,' suffix numeral one. Are you ready to dictate, Gerry?"*

I shook my head, watching rain running down from the slate roof onto the awning. Squatters wandered back and forth around me, ignoring the guy leaning against a column with a hand clasped to his ear, apparently talking to himself. Down on the stage, a neogrunge band had replaced the killer yuppie; discordant guitar riffs and high-pitched feedback threatened to overwhelm the stolen PA system they had set up behind them. Black-market vendors were circulating through the aisles, hustling everything from wet popcorn to expired pharmaceuticals. Off in the far distance, beyond the trees, were the lights of the city's central west end: clean, brilliant apartment towers, easily seen by thousands of people who were on prolonged camp-out in old U.S. Army tents, eating cold MREs by firelight and crapping in overflowing Port-O-Johnnies. Your tax dollars at work.

"No," I said. "Close and delete file. I'm going off-line now, okay?"

"I understand," Joker said. *"Signing off."*

So. The self-diagnostic check had come up clean, and the IM wasn't a prank. I pondered these mysteries while I wadded up the earphone and tucked it back into my jacket pocket. Why had a message obviously intended for John reached me instead, even though I was in the right place at the right time?

I had no recourse except to go to the meeting place. Walking around the column, I bumped my way through the wet, hopeless crowd, heading for the amphitheater's rear entrance gate.

That was how it all began.

2

People were still shuffling through the back entrance by the time I got there. According to the message Joker had received, I was ten minutes late for my appointment . . . or rather, for John's appointment. I hung around for a couple of minutes, leaning against the fence near the gate and watching people go by, and was about to chalk off the message as some sort of neural-net glitch when a short figure in a hooded rain jacket approached me.

"Are you Tiernan?" she asked softly.

I gave myself a moment to size her up: a middle-aged black woman, her face only half seen beneath the soaked plastic hood, her hands hidden in the pockets of her jacket. She could have been anyone in the crowd except that her raingear looked a little too new and well made to be government issue. Whoever she was, she wasn't a squatter.

"No," I said. She murmured an apology and started to turn away. "But I'm a friend of his," I quickly added. "I work for the same paper. *Big Muddy Inquirer.*"

She stopped, looked me over, then turned back around. "What's your name?" she asked, still speaking in a low voice.

"Gerry Rosen." She gazed silently at me, waiting for me to continue. "I got an IM on my PT to meet someone here," I went on. "I mean, it was intended for John, but—"

"Why isn't John here?" she demanded. "C'mon, let me see some ID."

"Sure, if you insist." I shrugged, unzipped my jacket, and started to reach inside.

31

"Hold it right there," she snapped as her right hand darted out of her rain jacket. I felt something press against my ribs. I froze and looked down to see a tiny stun gun, shaped like a pistol except with two short metal prongs where the barrel should be, nestled against my chest. Her index finger was curled around the trigger button; I hoped she didn't twitch easily.

"Whoa, hey," I said. "Easy with the zapper, lady."

She said nothing, only waited for me to make the wrong move. I wasn't eager to get my nervous system racked by 65,000 volts, so I held my breath and very carefully felt around my shirt pocket until I located my press ID.

I gradually pulled out the laminated card and held it up for her to see. She looked carefully at the card, her eyes darting back and forth between the holo and my face, until she nodded her head slightly. The stun gun moved away from my chest and returned to the pocket of her jacket.

"You ought to be careful with that thing," I said. "They're kinda dangerous when it's raining like this. Conductivity and all that—"

"Okay, you're another reporter for the *Big Muddy*," she said, ignoring my sage advice. "Now tell me why you're here and not Tiernan."

"That's a good question," I replied, "but let's hear your side of it first. How come you tried to IM something to John but got me instead?"

She blinked a few times, not quite comprehending. "Sorry? I don't understand what you're—"

"Look," I said, letting out my breath, "let's try to get things straight. My PT told me about ten minutes ago that I had a message. It was addressed to John but somehow got sent to me instead, and it told me . . . or him, whatever . . . to meet somebody right here at eight o'clock. Now, since you're obviously that somebody—"

"Hey, wait a minute," she interrupted. "You got this message just ten minutes ago?"

"Yeah, just about that—"

"*Ten minutes* ago?" she insisted.

I was beginning to get fed up with this. "Ten, maybe fifteen minutes. Who's counting? The point is—"

A couple of teenagers, ripped to the tits on something they had bought off the street, staggered through the gate and jostled me aside. I nearly fell against the woman; she stepped out of my way, then grabbed my jacket and pushed me behind a column.

"The point is, Mr. Rosen," she said quietly, staring me straight in the eye, "I didn't send any IMs today, but I received e-mail from John Tiernan this afternoon, telling me to meet him here at eight. Now I'm here, but I instead find you. Now you tell me: where's your buddy?"

The conversation was getting nowhere very quickly. "Look," I said, taking off my cap for a moment to wipe soaked hair out of my eyes, "you're just going to have trust me on this, okay? John ain't here. If he was, I'd know it. And if you didn't send that IM to me—"

"If John didn't send e-mail to me . . ." Her voice trailed off, and in that instant I caught a glimpse of fear in her dark eyes.

No, not just fear: absolute horror, the blank, slack-jawed expression of someone who has just gazed over the edge of the abyss and seen monsters lurking in its depths.

"Oh my God," she whispered. "It's started . . ."

It was then that I heard the helicopters.

At first, there was nothing except the background rumble of the crowd in the amphitheater below us, mixing with the subtle hiss of the rain and the not-so-subtle screech of electric guitars from the stage . . . and then there came a low droning from the dark sky above us, quickly rising in volume, and I looked up just in time to see the first chopper as it came in.

The helicopter was an MH-6 Night Hawk, a fast-moving little gunship designed for hit-and-run night missions over the Mediterranean. Something of an antique, really, but still good enough for ass-kicking in the U.S.A.; with its silenced engine and rotors, it wasn't noticed by anyone in the Muny until it was right over the amphitheater, coming in low over the walls like a bat.

I caught a fleeting glimpse of the two men seated within its bubble canopy, the letters ERA stenciled across its matte black fuselage; then light flashed from its outrigger nacelles as two slender canisters were launched over the crowd toward the stage. The rock band dropped their instruments and pretended to be paint as the RPGs smashed through the heavy wood backdrops behind them, breaking open to spew dense pale smoke across the platform.

The Night Hawk banked sharply to the right, its slender tail fishtailing around as the chopper braked to hover above the amphitheater, its prop wash forcing the milky white fog off the stage and across the orchestra pit into the front rows. I caught the unmistakable pepper scent of tear gas, but many of the squatters, thinking they were only smoke bombs, didn't flee immediately, even when the first few who had been caught by the gas began to choke and gag.

That's the mistake everyone makes about tear gas; its innocuous name makes it sound like something that will only make you a little weepy. Few people are aware of the painful blindness it causes when the hellish stuff gets in your eyes, how much you choke when you inhale it. Then, it's pure evil.

The fog was billowing toward us even as the squatters, now realizing the danger, began to stampede toward the rear entrance. People all around us clawed at one another, trying to get out of the amphitheater, as they were caught in the throes of gas-attack panic.

"Get out of here!" I grabbed the woman's hand and dragged her toward the gate. "Move it! Move it!"

We shoved and hauled our way through the mob until we managed to squeeze through the jammed gate. Still clutching her hand, I turned to make a getaway through the parking lot, only to find that we were far from being out of danger.

There was more rotor noise from above, much louder than the MH-6, as gale-force winds abruptly whipped through the parking lot, tearing at the tents and plastic tarps, sending garbage flying in every direction, overturning stolen shopping carts, causing the flames of the trash-can fires to dance crazily. I skidded to a stop and looked up to see a giant shape descending upon us, red and blue lights flashing against the darkness, searchlights lancing through the rain like a UFO coming in for a touchdown.

Flying saucer, no; V-22 Osprey, yes. The big, twin-prop VTOL was landing right outside the Muny, and if that was Elvis I spotted through one of its oval portholes, wearing riot gear and slapping a magazine into his Hecker & Koch assault rifle, then the King and I needed to have a serious discussion about his new career.

It was a full-blown ERA raid, and I felt like an idiot for not having seen it coming. Members of the city council had been squawking lately about "taking Forest Park back from the squatters," and never mind that it had been their idea in the first place to relocate nearly seventy-five thousand homeless people to a tent city in the park. A crackdown had been threatened for several weeks now, and squatters trespassing on the Muny had been the last straw. Steve Estes, the council member whose political ambitions were only slightly outweighed by his ego, was making good on his rhetoric.

No time to ponder local politics now. More Ospreys were arriving. The first one was already on the ground, its rear door cranking down to let out a squad of ERA troopers. The air stank of tear gas; people were rushing around on either side of us, threatening to trample us as they fled from the soldiers. Already I could hear screams from the area closest to the landing site of the first Osprey and the hollow *ka-chunng!* of Mace canisters being fired into the mob.

Escape through the parking lot was out of the question; already I could hear the engine roar of LAV-25 Piranhas approaching from the roadway on the other side of the hill, their multiple tires mowing down the makeshift barricades squatters had thrown up around the Muny. In a few minutes we'd be nailed by tear gas, water cannons, webs, or rubber bullets.

A steep, wooded embankment lay to the right of the amphitheater. "That way!" I yelled to the woman. "Down the hill!"

"No!" she shouted, yanking her hand free from mine. "I gotta go somewhere!"

"You'll—"

"Shaddup! Listen to me!" She grabbed my shoulders and shouted in my face. "Tell Tiernan—"

Full-auto gunfire from behind us. More screams. I couldn't
tell whether the troopers were firing live rounds, and I wasn't
in the mood for sticking around to find out. The woman
glanced over her shoulder, then her eyes snapped back to
me again.

"Tell Tiernan to meet me at Clancy's on Geyer Street!" she
yelled. "Tomorrow at eight! Tell him not to trust any other
messages he gets! You got that?"

"Who are you?" I shouted back at her. "What the hell's
going on?"

For the briefest moment she seemed uncertain, as if wanting
to tell me everything in the middle of a full-scale riot and yet
unable to trust her own instincts. Then she pulled me closer
until her lips touched my ear.

"Ruby fulcrum," she whispered.

"Ruby *what*?"

"Ruby fulcrum!" she repeated, louder and more urgently
now. "Tiernan will know what I mean. Remember, Clancy's
at eight." She shoved me away. "Now get out of here!"

Then she was gone, turning around to dash into the panic-
stricken mob, disappearing into the night as suddenly as she
had appeared. I caught a final glimpse of the woman as her
jacket hood fell back, exposing a few hints of gray in her
short-cropped hair.

Then she was gone.

I ran in the opposite direction, battering my way through
the crowd until I was out of the parking lot. I dashed across
the sidewalk and down the embankment beside the high concrete walls of the Muny. Few people followed me; most of
the squatters had stayed behind to wage futile battle against
the ERA troopers, protecting what little they could still call
home.

I slipped and skittered and fell down the muddy slope,
blinded by smoke and darkness, deafened by the sound of
helicopters, my face lashed by low tree branches as I tripped
over fallen limbs. As I neared the bottom of the hill I heard
the gurgle of a rain-swollen drainage ditch and veered away
from it; I didn't need to get more wet than I already was.

I can barely recall how I escaped from the riot; my flight from the Muny comes to me only in snatches. Falling on my face several times. Grabbing my jacket pocket to make sure that I hadn't lost Joker, feeling vague reassurance when I felt its small mass. Jogging down Government Road around the lake, passing the old 1904 World's Fair Pavilion, slowing down to catch my breath and then, in the next instant, spotting the headlights of more armored cars approaching from the opposite direction and ducking off the road into the woods. Hearing monkeys howling in the treetops above me. Crashing through a tent village erected on the fairway of what used to be the municipal golf course, hearing babies screaming, having a clod of mud thrown at me by an old man . . .

Then I was in the woods again, climbing another steep slope on all fours, my breath coming in animal like gasps as I clutched at roots and decaying leaves, all in an atavistic impulse to flee from danger.

Not the best night I've ever had at the opera. Lots of singing and dancing, but in terms of artistic merit the show kinda sucked.

The next thing I knew, I was halfway across the park, my breath coming in wet, ragged gasps as I lay against the base of the statue of Louis XIV, the French monarch after whom the city had been named. His bronze skin dully reflected the light from the distant flames of the tent village that had once existed around the Muny.

From my lonely hilltop perch, I could see the searchlights of helicopters as they circled the amphitheater, hear the occasional echoing report of semiauto gunfire. Up here, though, all was supernaturally quiet and uncrowded, as if I was removed in time and space from the chaos that reigned not far away. The rain had finally ceased. Night birds and crickets made nocturnal harmony in the hilltop woods, undeterred by the paramilitary action not far away.

Somehow, in my mad rush for safety, I had made it to the summit of Art Hill, the highest point in Forest Park. The Sun King sat on his stallion above me, larger than life, his broadsword raised in defiance to the empty sky. The statue had been the symbol of the city long before the Arch had been erected; by miracle, he had not been toppled by the quake, and his eternal courage made me all the more ashamed of my own cowardice.

On the other hand, I had become accustomed to being a coward. It wasn't anything new to me. Call it an instinct for self-preservation; all us chickenshit types use that term. Just ask my wife. Or my son . . .

Turning my head to look behind me, my eyes found the half-collapsed stone edifice of the St. Louis Art Museum. Despite being reinforced during the nineties against quakes, the museum had suffered extensive damage. Now its doors were chained shut, its windows sealed with pine boards, its treasures long since moved to Chicago. Inscribed above the bas-relief classical portico, held aloft by five Corinthian columns, were seven words:

DEDICATED TO ART AND FREE TO ALL

"No shit," I mumbled. "Where do I sign up?"

I caught my breath, then I slowly rose to my feet and began to stagger across the driveway and down Art Hill, following the sidewalk toward the Forest Park Boulevard entrance on the north side of the park.

It was time to go home.

3

Tell me about freedom. I'm willing to listen. Hell, I'll listen to anything, so long as you'll pardon me if I nod off in the middle of the lecture.

Wet, cold, muddy, and confused, I began the long hike out of the park, following the sidewalk down the hill toward the Forest Park Boulevard entrance. Although a couple of Piranhas and Hummers passed me on the road, their crews were too busy to stop and harass a lone individual on foot. Nonetheless, I crossed the golf course at the bottom of Art Hill to avoid a roadblock at the Lindell Boulevard entrance; two Hummers were parked in front of the gate, and I didn't care to explain myself to the soldiers manning the barricade. Sure, I had my press card and I could point out that I was a working reporter on assignment, but these days that sort of argument would just as likely earn me a trip down to Busch Stadium, and not for a baseball game either. The ERA grunts didn't spot me, though, and I managed to leave the park unmolested.

Grabbing a ride on the MetroLink was another problem. After I trudged the rest of the way through the park, I passed through the main gate at Forest Park Boulevard. The MetroLink platform was at the bottom of a narrow railway trench a block away; it was almost completely vacant, but an ERA trooper was standing guard at the top of the stairs leading down to the tracks, a riot baton cradled in his arms.

I glanced at my watch. It was already a quarter to ten. No choice but to tough it out; I was in no shape to slog all the way back to my digs. Trying not to look like I had just

39

mud-wrestled a gorilla, I strode toward the turnstile, reaching into my pants pocket to fish out my fare card.

The trooper studied me as I walked under the light. I gave him a quick nod of my head and started to pass my card in front of the scanner when he took a step forward and barred my way with his stick.

"Excuse me, sir," he said, "but do you know what time it is?"

In the old days, I might have just looked at my watch, said "Yes," and walked on, but these guys were notorious for having no sense of humor. My mind flipped through a half-dozen preconcocted ploys, ranging from pretending to be drunk to simply acting stupid, and realized that none of them would adequately explain why I looked as disheveled as I did. Telling the truth was out of the question; the average ERA trooper had less respect for a reporter than he would for a suspected looter, and screw the First Amendment.

"Is it after nine already?" I feigned embarrassed surprise, then pulled back my sleeve and glanced at my watch. "Oh, shit, I'm sorry. I didn't realize it was so—"

"May I see some ID, please?" Below us, several people sitting on plastic benches beneath the platform awning watched with quiet curiosity. No doubt they had been forced to go through the same ordeal.

"Hmm? Sure, sure . . ." I pulled my wallet out of my back pocket, found my driver's license, and passed it to him. The trooper's nameplate read B. DOUGLAS; he passed my license under a handscanner, then flipped down a monocle from his helmet and waited for the computers at the city's records department to download my file.

It gave me a chance to size him up as well. What I saw was scary: a kid young enough to be my little brother—twenty-one at most—wearing khaki combat fatigues, leather lace-up boots, and riot helmet, with the sword-and-tornado insignia of the Emergency Relief Agency sewn on the left shoulder of his flak jacket. An assault rifle hung from a strap over his right shoulder, a full brace of Mace and tear gas canisters suspended from his belt. He had the hard-eyed, all-too-serious look of a young man who had been given too much authority much too soon, who believed that the artillery he carried gave him the right to kick butt whenever he wished. In another age he might have been a member of Hitler Youth looking for Jews to beat up or a Young Republican wandering a college campus in search of a liberal professor to harass. Now he was an ERA trooper, and by God this was *his* light-rail station.

"Are you aware that you're in a curfew zone, Mr. Rosen?" He pulled my driver's license out from under his scanner but didn't pass it back to me.

I pretended to be appalled. "I am? This is University City, isn't it? There isn't a curfew here."

He stared back at me. "No, sir, you're downtown now. Curfew starts here at nine o'clock sharp."

I shrugged off-handedly. "I'm sorry. I didn't realize that was the situation." I tried an apologetic smile. "I'll keep that in mind next time I'm down here."

"You look awful muddy, old-timer," he said condescendingly. "Fall down someplace?"

Old-timer, indeed. I was thirty-three and Lord of the Turnstiles knew it. If there were the first few gray streaks in my hair, it was because of what I had seen in the past eleven months. I wanted to tell him that I was old enough to remember when the Bill of Rights still meant something, but I kept my sarcasm in check. Li'l Himmler here was just looking for an excuse to place me under arrest for curfew violation. My police record was clean, and he didn't have anything on me, but my occupation was listed as "journalist." I could see it in his face: reporters for the *Big Muddy Inquirer* didn't get cut much slack on his beat.

"Sort of," I said noncommittally, careful to keep my voice even. B. Douglas didn't reply; he was waiting for elaboration. "I tried to jump over a storm drain a few blocks away," I added. "Didn't quite make it." I shrugged and managed to assay a dopey gee-shucks grin. "Accidents happen, y'know."

"Uh-huh." He continued to study me, his monocle glinting in the streetlight. "Where did you say you were?"

"U-City," I said. "Visiting some friends. We were having a little get-together and . . . y'know, kinda got sidetracked."

It was a good alibi. The U-City neighborhood was only a few blocks west of the station; that's where all us liberal types hung out, listening to old Pearl Jam CDs while smoking pot and fondly reminiscing about Bill Clinton. It fit. Maybe he'd pass me off as a stoned rock critic who had fallen in a ditch after going into conniptions upon seeing an American flag.

Off in the distance I could hear the first rumble of the approaching train, the last Red Liner to stop tonight at Forest Park Station. If Oberleutnant Douglas was going to find a good reason for busting me, it was now or never. After all, he would have to file a report later.

The kid knew it, too. He flipped my license between his fingertips, once, twice, then slowly extended to me as if he was granting a great favor. "Have a good evening, Mr. Rosen," he said stiffly. "Stay out of trouble."

I resisted the mighty impulse to salute and click my heels. "Thank you," I murmured. He nodded his helmeted head and stood aside. The train's headlights were flashing across the rails as I swept my fare card in front of the scanner, then pushed through the turnstile and trotted down the cement stairs to the platform.

The train braked in front of the station, bright sparks of electricity zapping from its overhead powerlines. A couple of my fellow riders looked askance at me as they stood up. One of them was an old black lady, wearing a soaked cloth coat, carrying a frayed plastic Dillards shopping bag stuffed with her belongings.

"What did he stop you for?" she asked as the train doors slid apart and we moved to step aboard.

I thought about it for a moment. "Because of the way I look," I replied.

It was an honest answer. She slowly nodded her head. "Same here," she murmured. "Now you know what it's like."

And then we found our seats and waited for the train to leave the station.

I rode the Red Line as it headed east into the city. Quite a few people got on or off the train at Central West End, most of them patients or visitors at Barnes Hospital, but my car only remained half-full. Most of the passengers were soaking wet. The train was filled with the sound of sneezing and coughing fits, making the train's computerized voice hard to hear as it announced each stop. The Red Line sounded like a rolling flu ward; despite the fact we had just stopped at a hospital, somehow all those free vaccinations we were supposed to receive courtesy of ERA seemed to have missed everyone on this train. On the other hand, this wasn't unusual; most of the people in the city had somehow missed receiving a lot of the federal aid that had been promised to us.

Through the windows, I could see dark vacant lots filled with dense rubble where buildings made of unreinforced brick and mortar had once stood; streets blocked by sawhorses because ancient sewer tunnels and long-extinct clay mines beneath them had caved in; shanties made of scraps of corrugated steel and broken plywood. Armored cars were the only vehicles on the streets, but here and there I spotted figures lurking in the doorways of condemned buildings. Night brought out the scavengers, the teenagers with tire-irons who prowled through destroyed warehouses and demolished storefronts in search of anything to be sold on the black market.

The train left the midtown combat zone and rumbled toward the downtown area. It stopped briefly beneath Union Station, but it passed Auditorium because the platform there no longer existed. Kiel Auditorium itself had survived, but where the old City Hall building and the city jail once stood were now vast lots filled with crumbled masonry, broken cinderblock, bent copper pipes, and shattered glass. Giant piles which had once been buildings, waiting to be hauled away.

By now the downtown skyscrapers were clearly visible, their windows shining with light; the Gateway Arch, seen above the spired dome of the old state courthouse, reflected the city lights like a nocturnal rainbow. For a minute or two there was no wreckage to be seen. It seemed as if the city had never suffered a quake, that all was sane and safe.

Then the train hurtled toward Busch Stadium, and the illusion was destroyed. Silence descended as everyone turned to gaze out the left-side windows at the stadium. Busch Stadium still stood erect; bright spotlights gleamed from within its bowl, and one could almost have sworn that a baseball game was in progress, but as the train slowed to pull into Stadium Station, the barbed-wire fences and rows of concrete barriers blocking the ground-level entrances told a different story.

A group of ERA soldiers were sitting on benches at the subsurface train platform; a couple of them glanced up as the train came to a halt, and everyone in the train quickly looked away. The doors opened, but no one got on, and nobody dared to get off. There was dead quiet within the train until the doors automatically closed once again. The train moved on, and not until it went into a tunnel and the station vanished from sight did everyone relax.

Busch Stadium wasn't a nice place to visit anymore. Oh, people still did at times, but seldom voluntarily. There were whispered rumors that people who went to the stadium often didn't come out again.

But, of course, that was only hearsay.

A few minutes later the train rolled into 8th and Pine, the underground hub station for the MetroLink. I got off here and took an escalator from the Red Line platform down to the Yellow Line platform. The station was cold, with a breeze that seeped through the plastic tarps covering a gaping hole in the ceiling where the roof had partially collapsed during the quake. A couple of ERA troopers lounged against a construction scaffold, smoking cigarettes as they watched everyone who passed by. I was careful to avoid making eye contact with them, but they were bored tonight, contenting themselves with ousting the occasional vagrant who tried to grab a few winks in one of the cement benches.

I managed to grab the Yellow Line train just before it left the station. It was the last southbound train to run tonight, and if I had missed it, I would have had to dodge downtown curfew patrols while I trudged home through the rain. At times like this I wished I still had my own car, but Marianne had taken the family wheels when we had separated. Along with the house, the savings account, and not an inconsiderable part of my dignity.

Not surprisingly, the train was almost vacant. Most of the South-side neighborhoods were under nine-to-six curfew, so anyone with any sense was already at home . . . if they still had a home, that is. Across the aisle, a teenage girl in a worn-out Screamin' Magpies tour jacket was slumped over in her seat, clutching her knees between her arms; she seemed to be talking to herself, but I couldn't hear what she was saying. At the front of the car a skinny black guy with a woolen rasta cap pulled down over his ears was dozing, his head against the front window, rocking back and forth in time with the movement of the train; every so often his eyes slitted open, scanned the train, then closed again. A bearded redneck sat reading a battered paperback thriller, his lips moving slightly as he studied the sentences. An emaciated old codger stared at me constantly until I looked away. A fat lady with a cheap silver crucifix around her neck and an eerie smile. Pretty much your standard bunch of late-night riders.

I had the seat to myself. The train came out of the tunnel; once again I could see the city. For an instant, though, as I stared out the rain-slicked windows at the lights passing by, I felt a presence next to me.

I didn't dare to look around, afraid to see what could not be reflected in the glass: a small boy, wearing a red nylon Cardinals jacket, dutifully marking up his scorecard while mustering the courage to ask me if he could enter a Little League season he would never live to see . . .

Can I play Little League next year?

Goddamn this train.

"Not now, Jamie," I whispered to the window. "Please, not right now. Daddy's tired."

The ghost vanished as if he had never been there in the first place, leaving me only with memories of the happy days before May 17, 2012.

Let's talk about Jericho again.

There had been plenty of advance warning that a major earthquake might one day rock the Midwest. Geologists had been warning everyone for years that the New Madrid fault was not a myth, that it was a loaded gun with its hammer cocked back, and their grim predictions were supported by history. In 1811, a superquake estimated at 8.2 on the then-nonexistent Richter scale had devastated the Mississippi River Valley, destroying pioneer settlements from Illinois to Kansas; legend told of the Mississippi River itself flowing backward during the quake, and simultaneous tremors were reported as far away as New York and Philadelphia while church bells rang in Charleston, South Carolina.

And there were other historical harbingers of disaster, major and minor quakes ranging between 5.0 and 6.2 on the Richter scale during the years between 1838 and 1976, all caused by a 130-mile seismic rift between Arkansas and Missouri, centered near the little Missouri town of New Madrid. Sometimes the quakes occurred away from the Missouri bootheel, such as the 1909 quake on the Wabash River between Illinois and Indiana, but most of the temblors happened in the region near the confluence of the Mississippi and Ohio rivers, and during even the most minor quakes chimneys crumbled, roofs collapsed, and people occasionally died.

Despite geologic and historical evidence that the city was living on borrowed time, though, most people in St. Louis managed to forget that they lived just north of a bull's-eye.

In August 1990 a New Mexico pseudoscientist named Iben Browning caused a panic by predicting that there was a fifty-fifty chance that a major earthquake would occur between the first and fifth days of December of that year. His prediction, based upon flimsy conjecture involving sunspots and lunar motion, was made during a speech to a group of St. Louis businessmen, and the sensation-hungry local media blared it to the public. By coincidence, Browning's prediction was followed in late September by a minor 4.6 quake epicentered near Cape Giradeau. The quake did little damage, but the general public, already unnerved by war in the Middle East and a shaky national economy, went apeshit.

During a three-month silly season, St. Louis prepared itself for imminent disaster, climaxing on a Wednesday when the city's public schools were shut down, its fire departments mobilized, and scores of citizens left town for vacation. When the prediction proved to be false—as was bound to happen, since earthquake prediction ranks with Rhine card ESP tests for unreliability—St. Louis ruefully laughed at itself and promptly began to forget everything it had learned about earthquake preparedness.

Iben Browning died a short time afterward without ever having made public comment about his apocalyptic predictions. In doing so, he gave the city renewed overconfidence. Earthquake drills were canceled as the 1990 scare settled into the back of everyone's mind, and the people of St. Louis once more settled into the safe, conservative mind-set that Nothing Ever Changes In Our Town. Even the 1994 Los Angeles earthquake did little to shake the city's complacent sense of false security.

And so it went for the next two decades. Our local pundits have often observed, sometimes with barely concealed pride, that St. Louis consistently remains about five years behind the times. Nonetheless, the city was dragged kicking and screaming into the twenty-first century. New buildings were erected, old ones were torn down, and the downtown skyline began to rival Chicago for brightness. The city's building codes were revised to imitate the earthquake-preparedness standards institutionalized in California, but they didn't affect thousands of older buildings or private residences. Electric cars replaced the old gashogs on the highways as new federal laws phased out the use of internal combustion engines in automobiles. A new light-rail system was erected, effectively replacing the old bus lines. The local aerospace industry gradually regeared itself from making warplanes to building spacecraft components. Hemlines rose, fell, and briefly became nonexistent with the short-lived barebuns look of 2000, which contributed to yet another moral revival that lasted until most women decided they really didn't want to wear neck-to-toe chastity gowns in 100-degree summer weather. Extrophy, smart drugs, isometrics, minimalistic education, and at least a half-dozen sociopolitical theories came and went as fads. Two economic recessions were suffered and were survived, the last one finally forcing the county and city governments to merge after more than a century of squabbling; their uneasy shotgun-marriage formed Metro St. Louis, the seventh largest city in the United States.

And there were two or three minor quakes, the largest one being a 5.2 temblor in 2006 that enabled the city to save a few dollars from having to tear down some condemned buildings in the central west end. Nothing serious. But the gun was still cocked and one day in early summer, when no one was paying attention, the hammer finally came down.

That was the day my son was taken from me.

My reverie ended as the train lurched to a halt at another station. The doors slid open and the skinny black guy, the strange fat lady, and a few others stood up to shuffle off the train. No one got on; except for the old dude who continued to stare at me with doleful contempt, the strung-out teenager, and the guy who was reading, I was alone in the car.

As the train got moving again, the old codger rose from his seat and walked unsteadily down the aisle. *"The train is now in motion,"* a pleasant female voice said to him from the ceiling speakers, its metronomic cadence following him as he staggered from seatback to seatback. *"Please return to your seat immediately. Thank you."*

He ignored the admonition until he found the seat next to mine and lowered himself into it. He watched me for another moment, then leaned across the aisle, bracing his chapped hands on the edge of my seat.

"Repent your sins," he hissed at me. "Jesus is coming."

I stared back at him. "I know," I said very softly, "because I *am* Jesus."

Okay, so maybe it was a little blasphemous. I was worn out and pissed off. But I'm Jewish and Jesus was Jewish, and that made us closer kin than with some crazy old dink with a grudge against anyone who didn't share his hateful beliefs. At any rate, it worked; his eyes widened and his chin trembled with inchoate rage, then he glared at me and, without another word, got up and made his way to the front of the train, putting as much distance between us as possible.

Good riddance. "Go forth, be fruitful and multiply," I added, but I don't think he got that old Woody Allen joke. Alone again,

I recalled my conversation with the nameless black woman at the Muny.

I was supposed to tell John to meet her at eight o'clock tomorrow night at Clancy's; that would be Clancy's Bar and Grill, a bar just down the street from the paper's offices. Since she didn't bother to tell me her name, she must already be known to John . . . but certainly not by sight, considering how she had mistaken me for my colleague.

Therefore, how was John to recognize her? Not only that, but why didn't she simply call him herself, instead of relying on a near-total stranger to pass the word?

Tell him not to trust any other messages he gets, she had said. I had to assume she meant IMs or e-mail through his PT.

I recalled the terrified look in her eyes when she discovered that the message *she* had received had been bogus, and what she had said.

Oh my God, it's started . . .

What had started?

There was only one clue, those two words she had whispered to me before she fled from the ERA troopers. "Ruby fulcrum," I repeated aloud. It sounded like a code phrase, although for all I knew it could be the name of a laundry detergent or a cocktail-hour drink. New, improved Ruby Fulcrum, with hexachloride. Yeah, bartender, I'll take a ruby fulcrum with a twist of lemon. Make it a double, it's been a bitch of a night . . .

I pulled Joker out of my inside pocket and opened it on my knee, exposing its card-size screen and miniature keypad. After switching to video mode, I typed, **Logon data search, please.**

Certainly, Gerry, Joker responded. **What are you looking for?**

314 search mode: ruby fulcrum, I typed.

An hourglass appeared briefly on the screen; after a few moments it was replaced by a tiny pixelized image of the Joker from the Batman comic books cavorting across the screen, maniacally hurling gas bombs in either direction. I smiled when I saw that. Bailey's son, Craig—who was now going through a Rastafarian phase and insisted that we call him Jah instead—had recently swiped my PT while I was out to lunch and had reprogrammed it to display this screensaver during downtime. For a while, the gag had gone even further; Joker had spoken to me in a voice resembling Jack Nicholson's until I had forced Jah to ditch the audio gimmick, although I allowed him to leave Batman's arch-nemesis intact. It could have been worse; Jah had done the same to Tiernan's PT, and Dingbat had spoken like Lucille Ball until John had threatened to wring his neck.

After a while the Joker began turning cartwheels for my amusement. Behind the scenes, though, I knew that there was some serious business going on. "314 search mode" meant just that; Joker was accessing every public database available within the 314 area code, searching for any references to the phrase "ruby fulcrum." The job was enormous; I was mildly surprised when the timer passed the thirty second mark.

I was just glad that Joker hadn't been damaged during the events of the evening. If I had broken the little Toshiba, Pearl would have eviscerated my liver and deep-fried it, with onion rings on the side. Joker was far more than a semiretarded palmtop word processor; its neural-net architecture enabled it to answer questions posed to it in plain English, and its cellular modem potentially allowed it to access global nets if I cared to pay some hefty long-distance bills.

The train began to slow down again as it prepared to come into my station. The Clown Prince of Crime abruptly vanished from the screen and Joker came back on-line.

No reference to the phrase "ruby fulcrum" has been located. Do you wish me to continue the search?

Rats. It had been a long shot, but I had been hopeful that Joker could turn up something. The train's brakes were beginning to squeal; glancing through the windows, I could see the streetlights of I-55 coming into view. My stop was approaching.

No thanks, I typed. Discontinue search. **Logging off now. Logoff. Good night, Gerry.**

I switched off the PT, folded its cover, and slipped it back into my jacket as Busch Station rolled into sight. It had been a long night, and I was ready to go back to what now amounted to home. I stood up and made my way toward the front of the car, ignoring the train's admonitions to take my seat until it had come to a full stop.

"Repent, sinner," the old man hissed at me as I walked past him toward the open door. I was too exhausted to make another smart-ass reply.

Besides, if I had any sins to repent, it would be those against the ghost of a small boy who still rode these narrow-gauge rails.

4

Despite the late hour, my regular ride home was waiting for me at the station. Tricycle Man sat astride his three-wheeled rickshaw at the cab stand beneath the platform, reading the latest issue of the *Big Muddy Inquirer*. He barely looked up as I climbed into the backseat.

"Did you see this one?" he asked.

"Which one?" I didn't have to ask what he meant; it was the same question each Wednesday when the new issue came out. There was only one section of the paper to which he seemed to pay any attention.

" 'SWF,' " he read aloud. " 'Mid-twenties, five feet eight, blonde hair, blue eyes, good natured, looking for SWM for dancing, VR, poetry readings, and weekends in the Ozarks. Nonsmoker, age not important. No druggies, rednecks, or government types. . . . ' " He shrugged. "Guess I qualify, so long as I don't mention my Secret Service background."

Tricycle man was a trip: a fifty-five-year-old hippie, right down to the long red beard, vegetarian diet, and vintage Grateful Dead stickers on the back of his cab, whose only real interests in life seemed to be sleeping with a different woman each week and telling grandiose lies about himself. At various times he claimed to be a former Secret Service agent, an ex-NASA astronaut, an Olympic bronze medalist, or a descendant of Charles A. Lindbergh. I didn't know his real name, although I had been riding in the back of his homemade rickshaw ever since I had moved downtown eight months ago. Nor did anyone else; everyone in Soulard simply called him Tricycle Man.

I searched my memory, trying to recall all the women I had spotted visiting the personals desk in the last week. "Yeah," I said, "I saw someone like that." Trike's face lit up until I added, "I think she had an Adam's apple."

His face darkened again. "Damn. Should have figured." He folded up the paper and tossed it on the passenger seat next to me, then pulled up the hood of his bright red poncho. "Going to the office or do y'wanna head home?"

I shrugged. "Home, I guess." It didn't make any difference; they were one and the same, and Trike knew it. He laughed, then stood up on the pedals and put his massive legs to work, slowly hauling the rickshaw out from under the platform and onto rain-slicked Arsenal Street, heading northeast into Soulard.

As we crossed the I-55 overpass, an ERA Apache growled low overhead, following the traffic on the interstate's westbound lanes. Another helicopter. My city had been invaded by space aliens, and they rode helicopters instead of flying saucers. Trike glanced up at the chopper as it went by. "Heard there was some kinda riot in the park tonight," he said. "Lot of people got their heads busted. Know anything about it?"

"A little," I said. "Enough to know it's true." It didn't surprise me that Trike had heard about the ERA raid at the Muny; word travels fast on the street, especially where the feds were concerned, but I wasn't about to contribute to the scuttlebutt. Besides, everything I had to say about the Muny riot would be in my column in next week's issue, and a good reporter doesn't discuss his work in progress.

Trike glanced over his shoulder at me. "Not talking much tonight, are you?"

"Too tired." I settled back against the seat, letting the cold drizzle patter off the bill of my cap. "All I want right now is a cold beer and a hot shower."

"Okey-doke." He turned left onto 13th Street. "I'll have you home in ten minutes."

We passed by the front of the Anheuser-Busch brewery, a compound of giant factory buildings which, like almost everything else in the city these days, were surrounded by scaffolds. Even at this time of night there was a long line of men and women huddled on the brick sidewalk outside the entrance gate, braving the weather and the curfew for a chance to be interviewed tomorrow morning for a handful of job openings. The brewery had reopened just four weeks ago, following a long effort to rebuild after the extensive damage it had suffered during New Madrid. Through the wrought-iron fence, I could see one of the replacements for the gargoyles that had adorned the cornices of the main building before they toppled from their perches during the quake: a wizened little stone man with a beer stein in his hand, sitting in the parking lot as he waited for a crane to hoist him into place. His saucy grin was the only happy face to be seen; everyone else looked wet and miserable. This Bud's for you . . .

As he pedaled, Trike reached between his handlebars and switched on the radio. It was tuned to KMOX-AM, the local CBS affiliate. After the usual round of inane commercials for stuff no one could afford to buy, we got the news at the top of the hour.

U.S. Army troops continue to be airlifted to the northern California border, following the formal announcement last week by the state governments of Washington and Oregon that they are seceding from the United States. A spokesman for the newly established government of Cascadia, based in Seattle, says that former National Guard troops have sealed all major highways leading into Washington and Oregon. No hostile actions have yet been reported from either side, but White House press spokesperson Esther Boothroyd says that President Giorgio does not intend to recognize Cascadia's claim to independence.

Just past Anheuser-Busch, Tricycle Man paused at the three-way intersection of 13th, 12th, and Lynch. A half-block away on 12th Street was the Ninth Ward police station; across the street from the cop shop, in what used to be a parking lot, was SLPD's south end helicopter pad. A big Mi-24 HIND was idling on the flight line, getting ready for air patrol over the Dogtown neighborhoods in the southern part of city. Beneath the blue-and-white paint job and the familiar TO PROTECT AND TO SERVE slogan could still be seen, as ghostly palimpsests, the markings of the Russian Red Army. ERA got American-made helicopters and LAVs, while the local cops had to settle for secondhand Russian choppers and rusty old BMP-2s left over from Afghanistan, sans armaments and held together by baling wire and paper clips. A couple of officers hanging around outside the police station waved to Tricycle Man and he waved back; he was harmless and familiar, so the cops didn't bother him.

Countdown continues for tomorrow's launch of the space shuttle Endeavour, *set for lift-off at one P.M. Eastern time. Aboard the shuttle are the final components of the* Sentinel 1 *orbital missile defense system. Although antiwar protesters are holding a candlelight vigil outside the gates of Cape Canaveral, the demonstrations have been peaceful and no arrests have been made.*

Trike continued pedaling down 13th Street, entering the residential part of Soulard. It would have been quicker to use 12th Street, but too many houses on 12th had collapsed during the quake, and the street itself was full of recent sinkholes, many of them large enough to swallow his rickshaw whole. Even then, 13th was a scene of random destruction. Two-story row houses, some dating back to the late 1800's, stood erect next to the rubble of others that had fallen flat.

The derailment of the Texas Eagle bullet train outside Texarkana, Arkansas, has left three people dead and several others injured. Spokesmen for Amtrak say that the derailment may have been caused by failure of the train's satellite tracking system, sending the nine-car train onto a siding instead of the main line. Investigators are now probing through the wreckage to see if deliberate sabotage was involved.

We passed tiny Murph Park overlooking the interstate— where a small shantytown stood next to a sign: CHICKENS 4 SALE, MONEY OR TRADE—and crossed Victor Street, heading uphill where 13th became more narrow, the streetlights less frequent. An old black man sat on the front steps of his house, a 12-gauge shotgun resting across his knees. Across the street was the ruin of a half-collapsed Victorian mansion, where a bunch of street punks sat smoking joints beneath its front porch. Trike pedaled faster, avoiding the standoff between the two forces.

And in Los Angeles, the jury is out on the rape trial of filmmaker Antonio Six. His accuser, Marie de Allegro, claims that Six used telepathic powers to invade her mind two years ago during the filming of the Oscar-winning Mother Teresa, *in which de Allegro played the title role. The sixteen-year-old actress says that Six was able to use ESP abilities to seduce her. Jurors are considering expert testimony offered in the director's defense by several psychics.*

We reached the top of the hill, then coasted the rest of the way down to Ann Street, where Trike took a hard right that threatened to overturn the rickshaw. He was clearly enjoying himself, although I had to hang on for dear life. A block later we reached 12th Street, where Trike took a left past St. Joseph Church.

The storefronts of convenience markets, laundromats, and cheap VR arcades lay on this block. Some were open for business, some closed and boarded up, all spray-painted with now-familiar warnings: "YOU LOOT, WE SHOOT"; "NOTHING LEFT 2 STEAL SO GO AWAY"; "IN GOD WE TRUST, WITH SMITH & WESSON WE PROTECT"; "IF YOU LIVED HERE YOU'D BE DEAD BY NOW," and so on.

For the CBS Radio Network News, I'm—

"In sore need of a blow job." Trike changed to one of the countless classic-rock stations that jammed the city's airwaves. An oldie by Nirvana pounded out of the radio as he turned right on Geyer. I checked my watch. True to his word, barely ten minutes had elapsed since Trike had left Busch Station, and we were almost to my place.

Geyer had withstood the quake fairly well, considering the amount of damage Soulard had suffered during New Madrid. Although many of the old row houses on this block were condemned or outright destroyed, most of them had ridden out the quake. These old two- and three-story brick buildings were built like battleships: chimneys had toppled, windows had shattered, porches had collapsed, but many of them had stayed upright. It only figured. Soulard was one of the oldest parts of the city; it had too much goddamn soul in its walls to be killed in fifty seconds.

Trike coasted to a stop at the corner of Geyer and 10th. A couple of happy drunks were hobbling up the sidewalk across the street, making their way home from Clancy's. I crawled out of the backseat, fished into my pocket, and pulled out a fiver and a couple of ones. "Thanks, man," I said as I extended the bills to him. "You're a lifesaver."

Tricycle Man took the money, stared at it for a moment, then carefully pulled out the two ones and handed them back to me. "Here, take 'em back."

"Hey, Trike, c'mon—"

"Take it back," he insisted, carefully folding up the five and shoving it into his jeans pocket. "You've had a bad night. Go down to the bar and have a beer on me."

I didn't argue. Trike knew I was on lean times. Besides, I was a regular customer; I could always bonus him later. Soulard was a tough neighborhood, but it looked after its own.

"Thanks, buddy." I wadded up the dollars and stuck them in my jacket pocket. Trike nodded his head and started to stand up on the pedals again. "And by the way . . . about the blonde?"

Trike hesitated. "Yeah?"

"She didn't really have an Adam's apple. I was just shitting you."

He grinned. "I knew that. Good looking?"

I shrugged, raising my hand and waving it back and forth. "That's okay," he said. "I've done better. Did I ever tell you about the time I was in London back in ninety-two and fucked Princess Di in the back of a limo? Now that was—"

"Get out of here," I said, and he did just that, making a U-turn in the middle of the street and heading back up Geyer to ask the drunks if they needed a lift home. Leaving me on the brick sidewalk, alone for the first time that night.

The *Big Muddy Inquirer* was located in a century-old three-story building that had been renovated sometime in the 1980's and turned into offices for some law firm; before then it had been yet another warehouse, as witnessed by the thick reinforced oak floors and long-defunct loading doors in the rear. The law firm that had refurbished the building had moved out around the turn of the century, and the property had remained vacant until Earl Bailey purchased it early last year.

Bailey had just started up the paper when he bought the building. Ever the entrepreneur, he had intended to open a blues bar on the ground floor and eventually move the *Big Muddy* into the second-story space from its former location in Dogtown. Bailey had made his wad off the Soulard Howlers, the blues band for which he was the bassist and manager, and Earl's Saloon had been intended to be the money tree behind his alternative paper. *Big Muddy Inquirer* might not have been the first newspaper whose publisher was a hacker-turned-guitarist-turned-bar-owner, but if you've heard of any others, please don't let me know. One is scary enough.

Anyway, Bailey was halfway through refurbishing the ground floor when the quake struck. The bar survived New Madrid but not the widespread looting that had occurred in Soulard several weeks later, when vandals broke into the place and took off with most of the barroom furnishings. By this time, though, the escalating street violence in the south city had forced the paper out of Dogtown, so he shelved plans for the bar, moved the *Big Muddy* to Soulard . . . and, not long afterward, grudgingly agreed to let out the unused third-floor loft to one of his employees. Namely, me.

I had a keycard for the front door, which led up to the second and third floors, but tonight I really didn't want the hassle of having to disable the burglar alarm Pearl had installed in the stairwell. The control box was difficult to see in the dark and, besides, I could never remember the seven-digit code that I would have to type into the keypad. So I ignored the front door, walked past the boarded-up ground-floor windows—spray-painted BLACK-OWNED! DON'T LOOT! as if it made any difference to the street gangs who would have mugged Martin Luther King for pocket change—and went around the corner until I reached the enclosed courtyard behind the building.

An old iron fire escape ran up the rear of the building. Pearl would have shot me if he had known I was using it as my private entrance, which was why I had to keep my stepladder hidden beneath the dumpster. I had just pulled out the ladder and was unfolding it in order to reach the fire escape's gravity ladder when I heard a shout from the opposite side of the courtyard.

"Hey, mu'fucker, whattaya doin'?"

"Just trying to break into this building to steal some shit," I yelled back as I put down the stepladder and turned around. "Why, you're not going to tell anyone, are you?"

There was a large human shape blocking the light escaping from an open garage across the courtyard. I heard coarse laughter, then the voice changed. "Hey, Gerry, that you?"

"That me. That you?"

"Fuck you. C'mon over and have a beer."

I put down the ladder and ambled over toward the garage where Chevy Dick and a few of his cronies were hanging out next to his car. Chevy Dick was Ricardo Chavez, an auto mechanic whose shop was the *Big Muddy*'s closest neighbor. Chavez was in his early fifties; in 1980, when he was barely in his teens, he and his family had escaped from Cuba during the first wave of boat people who had descended upon Miami. Chavez had eventually made his way from Liberty City to St. Louis, where he had successfully plied his natural gifts in auto repair toward making a livelihood.

Chevy Dick got his nickname two ways. First, it was his pen name for "Kar Klub," a weekly fix-it-yourself column he wrote for the *Big Muddy*. Second, he was on his fourth wife and claimed to have eleven children scattered across six states. When he got drunk, he bragged about all the NASCAR winners he had pit-stopped in his career. And when he got really drunk, this 300-pound gorilla with a handlebar mustache and a long braided ponytail might unzip his fly to show off his tool kit.

"Shee-yit," Chevy Dick growled as I stepped into the light, "you look like hell. What'd you do, man, fock some babe in a ditch?"

"Just following your example, Ricardo," I replied. "Why, did I get it wrong?"

Chevy glowered at me. A couple of his friends murmured comments to each other in Spanish; they were all sitting on oil barrels and cinder blocks, a case of Budweiser tallnecks on the grease-stained asphalt between them. In the background was Chevy's pride and joy: a coal black '92 Corvette ZR-1, perfectly restored and completely illegal under the phase-out laws, right down to the vanity tags, which read PHUKU2. Perhaps they were hoping that Chevy would take it off the blocks, gas it up, and take it out Route 40 for another illicit midnight cruise that would drive the cops apeshit; with a speedometer calibrated up to 120 mph, Chevy Dick's Corvette was arguably the fastest street rod in St. Louis, able to easily outrun any battery-powered police cruiser SLPD had on the road.

That, or they were hoping Chevy Dick would pound the shit out of the wiseass little gringo. Chevy continued to stare at me. He took a step forward and I held my ground. He slowly reached up with his left hand and pretended to scratch at his mustache . . . then his right fist darted out to jab at my chest. I didn't move. The fist stopped just an inch short of my solar plexus . . . and still I didn't move.

It was an old macho game between us. We had been playing this for months. The gang all moaned and hooted appreciatively, and Chevy Dick's face broke into a grin. "You're all right, man," he said as he gave me a shoulder slap that made my knees tremble. "Now get yourself a beer."

It was a tempting notion. "I'd love to," I said, "but I'm beat. If I start drinking now, you'll have to carry me upstairs."

"Long night, huh, man?" Chevy's face showed worry as he looked me up and down. "Jeez, you're in some kinda rough shape. What happen, you run into ERA patrols?"

"Something like that, yeah." My eyes were fastened on the case. "If you could spare me one, though, I'd really appreciate it . . ."

Without another word, Chevy Dick reached down to the case and pulled out a six-pack. There were a few grumbles from his drinking buddies, but he ignored them as he handed it to me. Chevy was no friend of ERA; as he had often told me, he hadn't seen things this bad since he had lived in Havana under the old Castro regime. In his eyes, any enemy of the *federales* was a friend of his.

"Thanks, Ricardo," I murmured, hugging the six-pack to my chest. "I'll pay you back next Friday."

"*Vaya con dios, amigo*," he rumbled. "Now go home and take a shower." He grinned at me again, the half-light of an exposed 40-watt bulb glinting off his gold-capped molars. "Besides, you smell like shit."

The ragged laughter of his buddies followed me all the way up the fire escape to my apartment.

I opened the first beer almost as soon as I crawled through the fire escape window and switched on the desk light. Home sweet home . . . or at least a place to get out of the rain.

My one-room loft apartment was a wreck, which was nothing unusual. Clothes scattered across the bare wooden floor and a mattress that hadn't been tidied in a week. Books and magazines heaped together near the mattress and the desk. A small pile of printout on the desk, which constituted the unfinished, untitled, unpublished novel I had been writing for the last few years. Tiny mouse turds near the kitchen cabinets. I could have used a cat; maybe it would have straightened up the place while I was gone.

I swallowed the first beer in a few swift gulps while I peeled out of my muddy clothes, leaving them in a damp trail behind me as I made my way toward the bathroom, stopping only to retrieve Joker from my jacket and place it on the desk while I grabbed another bottle out of the six-pack. The second beer followed me into the shower, where I leaned against the plastic wall and gulped it down, letting the hot water run over me until it began to turn cold.

I cracked open the third beer after I found an old pair of running shorts on the floor and put them on. It was then that I noticed the phone for the first time. The numeral 9 was blinking on its LCD, indicating the number of calls that had been forwarded to my extension from the office switchboard downstairs. Part of my rental agreement with Pearl was that I would act as the paper's after-hours secretary, so I sat down at the desk, opened the phonescreen, and began to wade through the messages.

Most of the calls were the usual stuff. Irate businessmen in suits wondering why their quarter-page ads hadn't been run in the paper exactly where they had wanted them to be, like on the front cover. A couple of oblique calls to individual staffers, giving little more than a face, a name, and number: press contacts, boyfriends, or girlfriends, who knew what else? I hit the Save button after each of them.

Most of the rest were the usual anonymous hate calls from readers, which arrived whenever the new issue hit the street, accusing Pearl of running a commie-pinko, right-wing, left-wing, feminist, antifeminist, environmentalist, technocratic, luddite, anarchist, neo-Nazi, Zionist, pornographic, anti-American, and/or liberal newspaper, all of them swearing to stop reading it tomorrow unless we converted to the ideology of their choice. Most of them had switched their phone cameras off when they called, but there was a demented three-minute screed from some wacko with a grocery bag over his head about how the New Madrid earthquake had been God's revenge against everyone who didn't support Lyndon LaRouche in the presidential election of 1984.

You can acquire a taste for this sort of feedback if you have enough patience and a certain sense of humor, but the same could be said of eating out of a garbage can. I erased them all. They could e-mail their comments to the paper if they felt that strongly about them.

I was about to twist off the cap of my fourth beer when I caught the last message on the disc. Once again the screen was blank, but the woman's voice on the other end of the line was all too familiar.

"Gerry, this is Mari. Are you there . . . ?" A short pause. *"Okay, you aren't, or you're not picking up. Okay . . ."*

Great. My wife—or rather, my ex-wife, once we finally got around to formalizing our separation. She didn't even want to put her still-pic on the screen.

"Listen, your Uncle Arnie called a while ago, and . . . um, he's mad at you because you didn't get to the seder last Friday night . . ."

I winced and shook my head. I had forgotten all about it. Uncle Arnie was my late father's older brother and the Rosen family patriarch. A lovable old fart who persisted in trying to get me to attend observances even though he knew damned well I wasn't quite the nice Jewish nephew he wanted me to be.

"Look, I know this is the usual family stuff, but, y'know I wish you'd tell him not to call here . . ."

Of course she didn't want him to call. Marianne wasn't Jewish, and although she had put up with her share of Rosen seders and bar mitzvahs and Hanukkahs, there was no reason why she should be bugged by my relatives. She didn't understand that Uncle Arnie was just trying once more to get us back together again. Fat chance, Arnie . . .

"Okay. That's it. Take care of yourself. 'Bye."

A call from Marianne. The first time I had heard from her in almost a month, and it was because I had missed last week's Passover seder.

For some reason, this made me more depressed than before. It took me the rest of the six-pack to get over the message. By the time I had finished the last bottle, I couldn't remember why she had called in the first place, and even if I had, I could have cared less.

All I could think about was Jamie.

PART TWO

The Nature of Coherent Light

(April 18, 2013)

5

I didn't remember falling asleep: that's how drunk I got.

Sometime during the night I moved from my desk chair to my unmade bed. I was never conscious of the act; it had been reflexive action and not part of any deliberate decision to hit the sack. I simply blacked out at some point; the next thing I knew, a heavy fist was pounding on the apartment door.

"Rosen! Yo, Rosen . . . !"

Long, bright rays of sunlight were cast through the dusty loft windows. My eyes ached, my mouth tasted like the bottom of a cat's litter basket, and my brain was stuffed with thousands of shorted-out wires. Somewhere out there, birds were chirping, bees were humming, cows were giving milk to blissful farm girls, happy little dwarves were humming as they marched in lockstep on their way to work.

But that was far away, because here in my rank loft, on this beautiful morning in late April, I felt like a hundred and eighty-five pounds of bat guano.

"Rosen! Get the fuck outta bed!"

I shoved away the blanket and swung my legs over the side of the bed. My right foot knocked over a half-empty beer bottle as I sat up; I watched as it rolled across the bare wooden floor until it bounced off the kitchen table and came to rest by the door, leaving a small trail of stale beer in its wake. Somehow, that seemed to be the most fascinating thing I had ever seen: an elegant demonstration of Newtonian physics.

"Rosen!"

67

"Okay, all right," I muttered. "Don't wet yourself on my account." My legs were still functional, at least to the degree that I was able to stand up without a pair of crutches. I found an old T-shirt on the floor and slipped it on, then stumbled across the room to the door, twisted back the dead bolt and opened it.

Earl Bailey, two hundred and sixty pounds of malice stuffed into six feet and two inches of ugliness, was the last person I wanted to see while suffering from a hangover. He stood outside my door, glowering at me like I was a rat the exterminators had forgotten to kill. Not that the exterminators ever visited this building since he had owned it.

"What's wrong with you?" he snapped. "I've been banging on the door for five minutes."

I stared back at him. "Sorry, but I was taking a long-distance call from the president. He wanted to know if I would come over today to help him fight for world peace, but I told him I needed to deal with you first."

Pearl's fleshy nose wrinkled with disgust as he took a step back from the door. "Your breath stinks. You been drinking this morning?"

"No, but I was drinking last night." I reached down to pick up the beer bottle I had knocked over. "I think there's a little left," I said, swirling around the half-inch of warm beer remaining. "Here, want some?"

"Lemme in here," he growled, pushing my hand aside.

I stood back as he marched into the loft. He stopped in the middle of the room, his fists on his broad hips as he took in the clothes and empty pizza boxes heaped on the floor, the dead plants hanging from the rafters, the half-full carafe of cold coffee on the hot plate, the disarray of papers and books on my desk next to the computer. "Man, this place smells like a dumpster."

"C'mon, Pearl," I murmured, "who did you think you were renting to, the pope?"

"No. I thought I was renting to a responsible adult." He looked back over his shoulder at me. "You told me you were going out to Forest Park to find a story."

"I did. Got one, too."

"Huh." He walked over to my desk to gaze down at the books and papers. "Morning paper says there was an ERA raid at the park last night," he said as he bent down to shove some trash into an overturned wastebasket. "The *Post* claims they arrested a bunch of people who were trespassing at the Muny."

"That's an understatement if there ever was one," I said. "Did it say anything about shootings?"

He looked up at me, one eyebrow raised slightly in surprise. "Nothing about shootings. Why, did you see any?"

I shook my head. "No, but I heard gunfire. Sorry, but I didn't stick around to—"

"Didn't stop to see, huh?" He set the can upright and stood erect, dusting off his hands on his jeans. "Why didn't you?"

I gently rubbed the back of my sore neck with my hands. "Well, boss, you know what they say about someone shooting at you. It's nature's way of telling you it's time to go home."

"Bullshit. You're a reporter. First you get the story, then you worry about letting your ass get shot off."

"Easy for you to—"

"But you didn't see anyone get hit, right?" I shook my head, and Bailey closed his eyes and took a deep breath. "Then there weren't any shootings," he said softly. "Not unless we can produce any bodies."

"Ah, c'mon, Earl!" I shouted. "I was there. I heard the gunshots, for cryin' out—"

"But you didn't see anyone actually get hit, did you?" He stared back at me. "Oh, I believe you, all right . . . and, yeah, I think you were actually there, not just holed up here drinking yourself stupid."

He walked over to the bed, picked up the pair of mud-caked boots I had struggled out of last night, and dropped them back on the floor. At least I had some tangible proof that I hadn't blown off the assignment. "But unless you can find me a corpse with an ERA bullet lodged in its chest, you know what the stadium will say."

I nodded my head. Yeah, I knew what the official spokesmen for the Emergency Relief Agency would say, if and when questioned about gunshots heard during last night's raid. The troopers had been fired upon by armed squatters and had been forced to protect themselves. That, or complete denial, were the usual responses.

This wasn't the first time ERA grunts had opened fire at unarmed civilians in St. Louis, yet no one, from the press to the ACLU, had yet to make a successful case against ERA on charges of unnecessary use of deadly force. Life in my hometown was becoming reminiscent of a third-world banana republic; allegations were often made, but material evidence had a habit of disappearing. So did material witnesses . . .

The local press was treading a thin line. Especially the *Big Muddy*, which was in the habit of intensively covering stories the *Post-Dispatch* only mentioned. The feds couldn't cancel the First Amendment, but they could make life difficult for Pearl. Tax audits, libel suits . . . Bailey knew the risks of being a public nuisance, and he was being careful these days.

No proof, no story. Unproven allegations didn't mean shit to him. I should have known better. "Aw, man, I'm sorry, Pearl. I didn't—"

"Don't call me Pearl," he said. He hated his nickname, even though everyone used it. He glanced at his watch. "You were supposed to be at the staff meeting."

"Oh . . . yeah. Staff meeting." I sat down at my desk and rubbed my eyes. "When it's supposed to start?"

"A half-hour ago. You missed it. That's why I'm up here." He started to walk toward the bathroom, then caught a whiff through the door and thought better of it. He cocked his thumb toward the john. "Is there anything alive in there?"

"Nothing you haven't seen before." I stood up from the desk. "Okay, I'm sorry for missing the meeting. I'll come down right now—"

"Naw, man. If you came downstairs now, you'd only make everyone sick." He shook his head in disgust, then favored me with a little smile. "You worked hard last night. Get a shower and put on some clean clothes."

"Thanks. I'll be down in a half-hour—"

"You've got fifteen minutes, and tell the president I think he's a dickhead and I don't believe in world peace." His

smile faded. "If I don't see you in fifteen, you can begin
updating your resume. Got it?"

"Got it." I didn't like the sound of that.

"See you downstairs." He turned around and tromped back
through the door. "And clean this shit up. It's embarrassing . . . to me, at any rate."

He slammed the door on the way out.

The offices of the *Big Muddy Inquirer* were spread across
a large room occupying the second floor of the building, its
various departments separated from each other only by cheap
plastic partitions. The place resembled a lab maze for down-
on-their-luck mice: computer terminals on battered gray metal
desks, fluorescent lights hung from pipes and ductwork along
the cobwebbed ceiling, checkerwork brick walls plastered with
old posters for rock concerts. Near the stairwell leading to the
front door was the personals desk, where a steady parade of
lonely people visited to place their ads for other lonely people;
at the opposite end of the room was the layout department,
where a handful of bohemian graphic artists pasted up the
pages within a perpetual haze of marijuana fumes, vented
only by a half-open window. Radical chic long after it was
chic to be radical and Tom Wolfe had gone to the great
word processor in the sky.

Somewhere in the middle of the room was the editorial
department: four desks shoved together in a small cubicle,
with Horace—the paper's unofficial mascot, a trophy-mounted
moose head decked out in oversized sunglasses and a Cardinals baseball cap—standing watch over the proceedings. The
two other staff writers were out on assignment, allowing John
Tiernan and me a chance to have our own little staff meeting
regarding the events of the previous night.

John was the oddest person working for the *Big Muddy* in that
he was the only staffer who closely resembled a normal human
being. At a paper where everyone drank or smoked dope or
experimented with various bathtub hallucinogens, John's only
apparent vice was chewing gum. While most people reported
to work in jeans, T-shirts, and football jerseys, and our arts
editor frequently sported an opera cape and a pince-nez, John

came in wearing a business suit, a button-down Oxford shirt, and a plain tie. Sometimes he wore sneakers, but that was as informal as he got. He wore his hair neither too short nor too long, shaved every day, and probably couldn't say "shit" even if his mouth was full of it. He had a wife and a kid and two cats, lived in a small house in the western 'burbs, attended Catholic mass every Sunday morning, and probably gave the most boring confessions a priest had ever heard.

No one at the *Big Muddy* ever gave him flak about his straitlaced ways. John was not only tolerant of all the bent personalities around him, he was also the best investigative reporter in the city. Earl would have sold his own son into slavery before giving up John Tiernan to another paper.

"Did you get her name?" he asked once I had given him the rundown of the Muny raid.

"Uh-uh," I replied. "I didn't even get that good of a look at her, beyond what I just told you. But she didn't belong there, man. She was no squatter."

"Yeah. Okay." John's face was pensive. He had his feet up on his desktop next to his computer terminal; he opened his top desk drawer and pulled out a pack of gum. "But you say she knew me—"

"She knew your name, but not your face. How else could she have mistaken me for you?" John offered me a stick of Dentyne; I shook my head and he unwrapped the stick for himself. "Does she sound familiar?"

"I dunno. Could be anyone, I guess." He shrugged as he wadded up the stick and popped it into his mouth, chewing thoughtfully as he used the computer's trackball to save the story he had been working on. "And she said she wants me to meet her at Clancy's tonight at eight?"

"Right, and not to believe any other messages you happen to receive from Dingbat . . ."

John grinned from one corner of his mouth. "Yeah, right. I suppose I'm not to believe anything I hear on the phone, either. Weird." He shook his head, then dropped his feet from the desk and swiveled around in his chair to face the screen. "Well, I gotta finish this thing, then I've got a press conference to cover at noon . . ."

I snapped my fingers as another thought suddenly occurred to me. Chalk it up to my hangover that I buried the lead. "Oh, yeah," I said, "one more thing. When I asked her what this was all about, she told me two words . . . um, 'ruby fulcrum.' "

John's hands froze above the keyboard. He didn't look away from the screen, but I could see from the change in his expression that he was no longer concentrating on the minor news item he had been writing.

"Come again?" he said quietly.

"Ruby fulcrum," I repeated. "I checked it out with Joker, but it couldn't tell me anything. Why, does that ring a bell?"

He dropped his hands from the keyboard and turned back around in his chair. "Tell me everything one more time," he said. "Slowly."

Let me tell you a little more about John Tiernan.

John and I were old friends since our college days in the nineties, when we had met at j-school at the University of Missouri in Columbia. We were both St. Louis natives, which meant something in a class full of out-of-staters, and we worked together on the city desk at the campus daily, chasing fire engines and writing bits. After we had received our sheepskins, I went north to work as a staff writer for an alternative paper in Massachusetts, while John remained in Missouri to accept a job as a general assignments reporter for the *Post-Dispatch*, but we had stayed in touch. We married our respective college girlfriends at nearly the same time; I tied the knot with Marianne two months after John got hitched to Sandy. Even our kids, Jamie and Charles, were born in the same year. Things go like that sometimes.

About the same time that I bailed out of journalism, John moved into investigative reporting for the *Post-Dispatch*. When I began to seriously consider getting Marianne and Jamie out of the northeast, John had urged me to return to St. Louis, saying that he could put in a good word for me at the *Post-Dispatch*. I went halfway with him; my family moved back to Missouri, but I decided that I had had enough with journalism. A New York publisher was interested in my novel-in-progress, and Marianne had agreed to support us during the period it took for me to get the book finished. John made the same offer again after he left the *Post* to go to work for Pearl, but I still wasn't interested. The novel was going well, and I didn't have any desire to go back to being a reporter.

And then there was the quake, and Jamie's death, and my separation from Marianne, and suddenly I found myself living in a cheap motel near the airport with only a few dollars in my wallet. I did as well as I could for a while, doing odd jobs for under-the-table slave wages, until one morning I found myself on a pay phone, calling John at his office to ask if his offer was still valid and, by the way, did he know of any apartments I could rent? John came through on both accounts, and he probably saved my sanity by doing so.

This all goes to show that John Tiernan was my best friend and that there was little which was secret between us.

Yet there *were* secrets; John was a consummate professional, and good investigative reporters don't discuss their work even with close buddies. I knew that John played his cards close to his chest and accepted that fact as a given, and so I wasn't terrifically upset when he wouldn't disclose everything he knew.

"This ruby fulcrum biz . . . it's important, isn't it?"

He slowly nodded his head as he rubbed his chin between his fingertips. "Yeah, it means something." He gazed out the window at the gothic steeple of St. Vincent de Paul, rising above the flat rooftops a few blocks away. "It's part of the story I'm working on right now . . . and I think I know the person you met last night."

"A source?" I reached across him to the pack of gum and pulled out a stick. "I take it you haven't met her."

John shook his head. "Just a couple of anonymous tips that were e-mailed to me a few weeks ago. I can see how she might have confused you with me last night, since you were obviously waiting for someone at the gate, but . . ."

He shrugged. "Darned if I know how you got sent an IM meant for me on your PT. The prefixes aren't identical. That's never happened before."

"Some kind of screw-up in the net. I dunno. I received a message meant for you by accident, and . . ."

We looked at each other and slowly shook our heads. Yeah, and the Tooth Fairy was my mother-in-law. The odds of a random occurrence like this were as likely as trying to call your mother-in-law and reaching an emergency hot line between the White House and the Kremlin instead. Yeah, it *could* happen . . . oh, and by the way, you've just won the Illinois State Lottery and you're now a millionaire, all because you happened to pick up a lottery ticket somebody had dropped on the sidewalk.

Coincidence, my ass . . . and neither of us believed in the Tooth Fairy.

"Let me ask you," John said after a moment. "If you saw this woman again, would you recognize her? I mean, you said it was dark and rainy and all that, but—"

"If we had gotten any closer, I would have had to ask her for a date. Yeah, I'd recognize her." I unwrapped a piece of gum and curled it into my mouth. "Where do you think we're going to find her? Go over to the stadium and ask if they busted any middle-aged black women last night?"

John smiled, then he swiveled around to pick up his leatherbound notebook from his desk. Opening the cover, he pulled a white engraved card out of the inside pocket and extended it to me. "Funny you should ask . . ."

I took the card from his hand and looked at it. It was a press invitation to a private reception at some company called the Tiptree Corporation, to be held at noon today. I turned the card over between my fingertips. "Here?"

"Here," he said. "She works for them."

Coincidence City.

"But you don't know her name . . ." He shook his head. I turned the card over and noticed that it was addressed personally to him. "Wonder why she didn't just tell me she'd meet you at this reception."

"There's good reasons," he replied. "Besides, she probably didn't even know I was going to be there. The company probably sent a few dozen out to reporters in the city—"

"And I didn't get one?" I felt mildly snubbed, even though I was fully aware that it was only senior reporters who got invited to things like this.

"It's just one of those brie and white wine sort of things . . ."

"But I love cheese and wine."

"Yeah, nothing gets between you and cheese." I gave him a stern look, and he met it with a wide grin. Friendship means that you don't deck someone for making asshole remarks like that. "Anyway, another one was sent to Jah. Apparently they want a photographer on hand. If you can finagle the other invitation from him . . ."

"I'm on it." I stood up, heading for the back staircase leading to the basement. "When are you leaving?"

John glanced at his watch. "Soon as you get back up here. It's out in west county somewhere, so we'll have to drive. Don't stop for coffee."

"Not even for tea. I'll see you out front in fifteen minutes." John gave me the thumbs-up and I went straight for the stairs.

Pearl didn't glance up from his desk as I slipped past his cubicle; for a moment I had the guilty notion that I should drop by, knock on the door, and tell him where I was headed. But if I did, he would probably insist that I stay put in the office until I had met the deadline for my column, even if it was more than twenty-four hours away. The notion, along with the guilt, quickly evaporated. My column could wait; for the first time in months, I had a real story to pursue, even if it was John's byline that would appear on the final product.

I wanted a hot story.

For my sins both past and future, I was given one. When it was all over and done, I would never want to tag along on another assignment again.

6

Craig Bailey's darkroom was in the basement, down where a microbrewery would eventually have been located had his father been successful in opening a saloon on the ground floor. I found Jah slouched in front of his VR editor, wearing an oversized HMD helmet as his hands wandered over a keyboard, manipulating various pieces of videotape and computer-generated imagery into his latest work of interactive cinema.

Working for his dad as the *Big Muddy*'s photo chief was just a day job for Jah, and a temporary one at that. His real ambition was to move to California and go to work for Disney or LucasWorks, and every cent he earned from his grumpy old man went to buying more hardware and software to feed his obsession. For this, the University of Missouri basketball coach was crying bitter tears; Jah stood about six-ten in his stocking feet, plus or minus a few extra inches of dreadlocks. He was hell on the half-court—I once made the mistake of playing one-on-one with him after work for a dollar a point and lost half a day's take-home pay—but Jah would rather dick around in virtual reality while blasting old reggae and techno CDs at stone-deaf volume.

I had no problem getting the extra press invitation from Jah; he was involved with his latest project and really didn't want to go out to west city just to take pictures of business types swilling martinis. He loaned me one of the paper's Nikons, loading a disc into the camera for me and reprogramming the thing to full-auto so that I wouldn't have to futz around with the viewfinder menu, and gave me a spare necktie from the pile next to the disk processor, thus making the disguise complete. A tie with a washed-out denim shirt would look a little strange where I was going, but formal wear for news photographers usually means that they changed their jeans today.

"Got a minute to look at this?" he asked when we were done. He held up the VR helmet. "Sort of a documentary . . . you might like it."

I shook my head as I pulled the camera strap over my shoulder. "Catch me in the next episode, okay? I gotta book outta here before your pop finds I'm missing."

He looked disappointed but nodded his head. "I hope you're not fucking with him. He's kinda pissed at you these days." He glanced at the door as if expecting to see the elder Bailey's shadow lurking in the stairwell. "Fact, man. He's been talking about making some changes 'round here, if you know what I mean."

I didn't like the sound of that, but neither did I have time to further inquire what Bailey and son discussed over the dinner table. "Believe me, I'm not trying to fuck with your dad. I'm just trying to—"

"Hey, that's cool." Jah held up his hands, keeping his distance from the bad vibes between his father and me. "So long as you come back with some shots for next week, we're solid."

"Sold for a dollar." We elbow-bumped, then he headed back to his workbench as I made for the basement door, avoiding taking the stairs back to the office.

John was waiting for me across the street from the office, leaning against the hood of his Deimos. "I don't think Pearl missed you," he said in reply to my unasked question as he dug a remote out of his pocket; the Pontiac's front doors unlocked and pivoted upward. "He's busy editing the arts page for next week."

"Fine with me." I walked around to the passenger side and slid into the seat as John took the driver's seat. "I just talked to Jah, though. He says Pearl's thinking about making some staff changes."

"I wouldn't worry about it." John pressed his thumb against

the ignition plate as the doors closed; the car started up as the seat harnesses wrapped themselves around our bodies. "Pearl's always talked that way," he said, opening the steering column keypad and tapping in the street address for the Tiptree Corporation. "When he had his band, he used to say the same thing whenever he had an off night. Y'know ... 'That drummer sucks, I gotta get a new drummer before the next gig.' That sort of thing."

"Uh-huh." A map of metro St. Louis appeared on the dashboard screen, a bright red line designating the shortest course between us and our destination. "How many drummers did the Howlers have?"

"Umm ... I think I lost count," he murmured as he eased away from the curb. "But that doesn't mean it's the same thing—"

"Yeah. Okay." John was trying to be candid and comforting at the same time, yet I couldn't refrain from glancing up at the second-floor windows as we headed down Geyer toward Broadway. I couldn't see Pearl, but nonetheless I could feel his angry presence.

Something had better come out of this field trip, or I was screwed.

The main office of the Tiptree Corporation was located on the western outskirts of St. Louis in Ballwin, not far from the Missouri River. We took Route 40/I-64 until downtown faded far behind us, then got off on the I-270 outer belt and followed it until we found the Clayton Road exit. By now we were in the gentrified suburbs, where subdivisions and shopping plazas had replaced farms in the latter part of the last century. The quake had destroyed most of the flimsier tract homes and cookie-cutter malls that had been thrown up during the building boom of the eighties; bulldozers and backhoes could be seen from the highway, completing the demolition of homes and stores that had been initiated by New Madrid. Architectural Darwinism: quakes kill buildings, but only the sick and feeble ones.

John briefed me on Tiptree along the way. The company was a relative newcomer in the computer industry, one of the

many that had been started during the late nineties as a result
of the seventh-generation cybernetic revolution. Unlike other
companies, though, Tiptree had not gone after the burgeoning
consumer market for neural-net pocket computers or virtual
reality toys. Instead, it had become a big-league player in the
military aerospace industry, albeit a quiet one.

"Name a major Pentagon program," John said as we drove
down Clayton, "and Tiptree probably has something to do
with it. It's a major subcontractor to the Air Force for the
Aurora project, for instance. Now—"

"You have reached your destination," a feminine voice
announced from the dashboard. *"Repeat, you have reached
your—"*

Tiernan stabbed the navigator's Reset button, hushing the
voice. We had already spotted the company's sign, a burnished
aluminum slab bearing the corporate logo of a *T* transfused
with a stylized oak tree. "Now they've delivered on their
largest contract yet," he continued as he turned right, following a long driveway just past the sign. "Want to guess
which one?"

I was studying the plant itself, seen past ten-foot-high chain
mesh fences artfully obscured by tall hedges. It was your
typical postmodern industrial campus: a long white three-
story edifice surrounded by tree-shaded parking lots and some
smaller buildings, unimaginatively designed by an architect
who probably collected old calculators as a hobby. If Tiptree's
headquarters had been damaged at all by the quake, they had
been rebuilt quickly; there were a few scaffolds around one
end of the main building, but that was the only indication that
the company had been affected by New Madrid.

"Umm . . . a player piano for the Air Force Academy?"

John smiled but said nothing as he pulled to a stop in front
of a gatehouse. A uniformed private security guard walked out
to the car and bent low to examine the invitation John held up
for him. He stared at me until I showed mine as well, then he
nodded his head and pointed the way to a visitors' parking lot
on the east side of the main building.

"Does the name Project Sentinel ring a bell?" he said as we
drove toward the designated lot.

I whistled; he glanced at me and slowly nodded his head. "That's what this is all about," he went on. "They designed the c-cube for the satellite . . . that's command, control, and communications. The bird's being launched from Cape Canaveral at noon, so it's show-and-tell day for these guys."

"Probably more show than tell," I said. "And you think this 'ruby fulcrum' business has something to do with—"

"Shhh!" he hissed, and I dummied up as he looked sharply at me. "Whatever you do," he said very softly, "don't say that again . . . not even in the car with me."

He tapped his left ear and pointed outside the car. It wasn't hard to get the picture. We might be invited guests for a public reception, but as soon as we had driven through the gates, we were in injun territory. Any high-tech company involved with a defense project as sensitive as Sentinel was probably capable of hearing a sparrow fart within a mile of its offices.

John pulled into an empty slot. "Pick up your camera and make like a log," he murmured. "It's showtime."

Showtime, indeed.

We walked into the main building through the front entrance, wading through a small crowd hanging around the lobby until we found the reception table. A nice young woman took our invitations, checked them against a printout, then smiled and welcomed us by name—Jah's, in my case—as she clipped a pair of security badges to us, each of them reading PRESS in bright red letters, which either made us honored guests or social lepers. She handed a press kit to John and ignored the disheveled beatnik with the camera behind him, then a polite young man who could have been her chromosome-altered clone pointed us through the crowd to a high archway leading to an atrium in the center of the building.

I had to rethink my opinion of the architect's style; whoever designed this place had more on the bean than just playing with antique calculators. The atrium was three stories tall, its ceiling an enclosed skylight from which hung a miniature rain forest of tropical ferns. Small potted trees were positioned across the black-tiled floor, and dominating the far end of the room was a videowall displaying a real-time image of a

Cape Canaveral launch pad so large that it seemed as if the shuttle was just outside the building.

Yet that wasn't what immediately captured my attention. Holographic projectors, cleverly concealed among the hanging plants, had suspended a monstrous machine about twenty feet above the floor: the *Sentinel 1* satellite, its long, thin solar arrays thrust out from its cylindrical fuselage, gold Mylar-wrapped spherical fuel tanks nestling against its white segmented hull just short of the black maw of its gun. The image had been shrunk somewhat—the real *Sentinel* was nearly as long as a football field—but the overall effect was nonetheless impressive: a giant pistol in the sky, and God help whoever tried to stare it down.

Milling around the atrium was a large crowd of business types, clustered in conversation circles, standing in front of the bar or taking drinks from the robowaiters, idly watching the shuttle countdown on the videowall. There was a buffet table at one side of the room; the aroma of hors d'oeuvres was too tempting for someone who hadn't eaten all day, so I excused myself from John to go get some free chow.

After wolfing down a plate of cocktail shrimp, fried mushrooms, and toasted ravioli, I was ready to start thinking like a professional journalist again. John was nowhere in sight; I eased myself into a vacant corner of the room and took a couple shots of the holograph, then began to scan the room through the Nikon's telescopic lens under the pretense that I was grabbing a few candid shots. The nice thing about posing as a down-at-the-heels news photographer is that, under circumstances such as this, you fade right into the woodwork; no one pays much attention to the photog because no one wants to seem as if they're posing for pictures.

At first sight, no one seemed particularly remarkable; you've seen one suit, you've seen 'em all. The only exception was another photographer across the room, a young lady in jeans and a sweater who looked just as seedy as I. She scowled at me before melting into the crowd. Professional rivalry; she was probably from the *Post-Dispatch*. I wondered if she could help me adjust my F-stops . . .

Enough of that. Like it or not, I was still married, even if

Marianne had sent me to the darkroom. I continued to check out the atrium.

For a few moments I didn't see anyone recognizable. Then I spotted Steve Estes. The most right-wing member of the City Council was standing in the center of the room, yukking it up with a couple of other guys who looked as if they were fellow alumni of Hitler Youth. The pompous prick was probably bragging about how he had managed to get ERA to roust a bunch of panhandlers out of the park the night before.

Estes was clearly maneuvering for a run against Elizabeth Boucher in next year's mayoral election; every public state-ment he had made since the quake hinted that he was going to oppose "Liberal Lizzie" (to use his term) on a good ol' Republican law-and-order platform. It would be an easy run; Liz had been caught off guard by the quake and everything that occurred afterward, and in the last few weeks she had been rarely seen or heard outside of City Hall. Rumor had it that she was suffering from a nervous breakdown, a drinking problem, or both, and her foes on the council, chief among them Big Steve, had been quick to capitalize on the rumors. If she ran for reelection, it would be as an unstable incumbent; if you believed Estes' rants, you'd think Boucher had gone down to New Madrid and jumped up and down on the fault line to cause the quake herself.

Estes glanced in my direction; the grin on his face melted into a cold glare. I took the opportunity to snag his picture before he looked away again. If anything, the shot could be used for Bailey's next editorial against Estes and his hard-line policies. Then I happened to notice a small group of people standing across the room.

Unlike nearly everyone else at the reception, they were inordinately quiet, seeming somewhat ill at ease even though all three wore the blue badges that I had already recognized as designating Tiptree employees. Their apparent nervousness caught my attention; they appeared to be in terse, quiet con-versation, occasionally shutting up and glancing furtively over their shoulders when someone happened to pass by.

I zoomed in on one of them, a distinguished-looking guy in his mid-fifties, tall and rail-thin, with a trim gray Vandyke beard and a receding hairline. Although his back was turned toward me, it was apparent that the two other people were deferring to him. When he looked over his shoulder again, I snapped his picture, more out of impulse than anything else.

Then, in the next instant, he shuffled out of the way, for the first time clearly revealing the shorter person who had been standing opposite him . . .

A middle-aged black woman in a powder blue business suit and white blouse, not particularly distinguishable from anyone else in the crowd—except I recognized the shock of gray in her hair and the stern expression on her face.

No question about it. She was the very same lady I had encountered in the park last night.

Fumbling with the lens-control buttons, I zoomed in on the woman as much as the camera would allow. The Nikon's varioptic lens did wonders; now it was as if I were standing three feet in front of her. I could clearly read what was printed on her name badge: BERYL HINCKLEY, Senior Research Associate.

As if she were telepathic, her eyes flitted in my direction when I snapped her picture. I lowered the camera and smiled at her.

She recognized me. Her face registered surprise, and for a moment I thought she was going to come over to speak to me.

"Ladies, gentlemen, if I could have your attention please . . . we're about to get started here."

The amplified voice came through hidden speakers near the ceiling. A young executive was standing at a podium below the videowall. The drone of conversation began to fade as everyone quieted down.

The exec smiled at them. "We've been told that the shuttle has come off its prelaunch countdown hold and will be lifting off in just a few minutes," he went on, "but before that, I'd like to introduce someone who has a few remarks to share with you . . ."

I glanced across the room again, only to find that Beryl Hinckley had vanished from where I had last seen her. I looked around, trying to spot her again; I caught a brief glimpse of her back as she disappeared into the crowd, heading in the direction of a side exit. She had a true knack for making her escape.

"... Our chief executive officer, Cale McLaughlin. Mr. McLaughlin ... ?"

A smattering of applause, led by the exec, as he stepped away from the podium to make way for McLaughlin. Tiptree's CEO was an older gentleman: tall, whip thin, and white haired, with wire-rimmed glasses and the focused look of a man who started his career as a lower-echelon salesman and clawed his way up to the top of the company.

Probably a pretty good golfer, too, but that didn't mean I was more interested in him than any other corporate honcho I had seen before. I zoomed back in on the conversation circle, only to find that the two men who had been talking with the mystery lady had also faded into the background.

"I'll keep things brief, because it's hard to compete with a shuttle launch." Some laughter from the audience, which had otherwise gone respectfully quiet. McLaughlin's voice held a soft Texas accent, muted somewhat by the careful diction of a well-educated gentleman. "The Tiptree Corporation is pleased to have been part of the Sentinel program since the very beginning. Hundreds of people have been involved with this project over the last few years, and we believe that it is an important asset to the national security of the United States ..."

Yeah, yeah, yeah. So was the B-2 bomber. I was too busy wondering why this Hinckley woman needed to take a powder every time she saw my face.

I was about to wade into the crowd in hopes of finding her again when a soft voice I had never expected, nor hoped, to hear again spoke from behind me.

"Mr. Rosen, I presume ..."

I turned around to find, not unlike the devil himself, Paul Huygens standing at my shoulder.

Not much can surprise me, but in that moment I nearly dropped Jah's expensive camera on the polished floor. If Amelia Earhart and Jimmy Hoffa had appeared to announce that they were married and were now living in a nudist colony on Tierra del Fuego and that Marie de Allegro was their love child, I couldn't have been more shocked. I might even have made note of a certain family resemblance.

The only thing that Paul Huygens bore a resemblance to was something you might find when you pick up a rock and look underneath. He was a squat, greasy little toad of a guy, the sort of person who wears five-hundred-dollar Armani suits and still manages to look like a cheap hustler. Imagine the Emperor Nero as a lounge lizard and you've got the general idea.

"Why, hello, Paul," I said quietly. I tried to disguise my disconcertment by coughing into my hand. "Long time, no see . . ."

Behind us, Cale McLaughlin continued his short, brief, bah-bah woof-woof about how wonderful *Sentinel 1* was to the future of all mankind. Huygens nodded slightly. "A couple of years at least," he replied. As before, his voice was almost girlishly high pitched: a little startling, since one rather expected a deep-throated, froggy tenor. "Still up to your old tricks, I see."

"Hmm? Oh, this . . ." I glanced down at the camera. "Sort of a new gig. I'm working for the *Big Muddy Inquirer* now. Switched over to photojournalism."

"Uh-huh. I see." He frowned and made a show of looking closely at my badge. "You must have changed your name, too . . . or does Craig Bailey write columns under your byline?"

I felt my face grow warm. He grinned at me. I had made a big lie and he had caught me in it. I made a sheepish, well-shucky-darn kind of shrug and changed the subject. "So . . . how's everything in Massachusetts these days?"

Huygens looked me straight in the eye. "I wouldn't know, Gerry," he said. "I quit CybeServe and moved to St. Louis about six months ago."

"Oh, really?"

"Oh, really." He nodded his head. "I'm working for Tiptree now. Director of public relations." The grin became a taut, humorless smile. "Remember what I told you? We're from the same hometown."

More surprises, and just a little less pleasant than the first one. Yeah, Huygens had told me that, two years ago when I had first spoken to him on the phone, back when he had held the same job for CybeServe Electronics in Framingham and I had been a staffer for an alternative paper in Boston. Back then, of course, I hadn't known what sort of eel I was dealing with, or how he'd eventually try to destroy my career. Damn near succeeded, too.

"Well, well," I said. "Like a bad penny . . ."

The smile disappeared altogether. Huygens cocked his head sideways as he peered closely at me. "Excuse me? I didn't quite get that—"

"Never mind. Just a passing thought." I coughed into my hand again. "So . . . what high school did you go to?"

It's an old St. Louis line, akin to asking a New Englander about the weather, but Huygens didn't bite. Over his shoulder, I spotted John halfway across the room, making his way through the crowd with a drink in his hand. Probably a ginger ale, which was unfortunate; I could have used a shot of straight whiskey right then. He caught my eye, gave me a one-finger high sign, and started toward us.

"Hmm." Huygens's thick lips pursed together. "Y'know, Gerry, to be quite honest, if I had wanted you to be here, I would have sent you an invitation—"

"Things were tight at the office," I began. "Craig was sort of busy, so I—"

"Covered for him, right." He pretended to rub a dust mote out of his left eye. I recognized the gesture; it was something he always did just before he asked you to bend over and drop your britches. "Well, I might have overlooked it, us being old acquaintances and all, but you see . . . well, I just received a complaint from one of our guests."

"Oh?" John was still making his serpentine way through the mob; the cavalry was taking forever to get here. "From whom?"

"Steve Estes. He said . . ." He shrugged. "Well, you know these politicians. They don't like to be photographed without prior permission. That's what brought me over here in the first place."

"Oh, no," I said. "Of course not. After all, if just anyone

was able to take their picture, they might actually be account-able to the public."

Huygens nodded agreeably. "Well, yes, there's that . . . but nonetheless, Mr. Estes is an invited guest and you're not . . ."

I shrugged off-handedly. "Sure, I understand, but Steve shouldn't worry about the shot I took of him. It probably won't come out anyway."

Huygens blessed me with a blank, mildly bewildered look. "After all," I continued, "old Transylvanian legends claim that vampires can't be photographed."

Assholes are always the best straight men: they don't have a good sense of humor. As his expression turned cold a few moments before John arrived at my side, I raised the camera to my face. "Let's test that," I said, focusing on Huygens's wattled chin. "Say cheese . . ."

Applause from the audience as McLaughlin wrapped up his speech. It could have been an appreciation for my jab. Now it was Huygens's turn to make like a boiled lobster.

The gag didn't last long. The picture I took was of him reaching into his breast pocket to pull out his PT and tap in the codes that negated the electronic passwords embedded in our smartbadges. John walked right into the middle of the whole scene.

"Hey, Gerry," he said. "Did you get something to eat?"

"The crow's good," I murmured as I lowered the camera. "Just ask my friend here."

Huygens simply stared at me. A moment later, two plainclothes security guards materialized behind John and me; they must have been hovering nearby, waiting for Huygens's signal. They were on us before I had a chance to compliment Huygens on his choice of catering service.

"Get 'em out of here," Huygens said to the large gentlemen who had descended upon us. "See you around, Gerry."

He didn't even bother to look at me before he turned his back on us and waddled back into the crowd.

John looked confused as a pair of massive hands clamped onto his shoulders. "Excuse me, but is there a problem?"

"Yes, sir," one of the mutts said. "You are."

No one at the reception noticed our sudden departure. They were too busy applauding the videowall as the *Endeavour*, spewing smoke and fire, rose from its launch pad into a perfect blue Floridian sky.

7

Tiptree's rent-a-goons escorted us out the front door, where they confiscated our smartbadges and pointed the way to the road. John and I didn't say anything to each other until we reached his car and had driven out of the company parking lot. When we had passed through the front gate and were heading back down Clayton Road toward the highway, though, the first thing John wanted from me wasn't an apology.

"Okay, what was that all about?" he asked. "I thought you were just talking to that guy."

He wasn't pissed off so much as he was bewildered. I felt a headache coming on, so I lowered my seat-back to a prone position and gently rubbed my eyes with my knuckles.

"He said it was because I had taken a picture of Steve Estes," I said, "but he was just looking for an excuse. I could have complained about the catering and he would have tossed me out just the same." I let out my breath. "He had no problem with you. You just happened to be with me, and that made you an accessory. Sorry, but that's the way it is."

"Hmm . . . well, don't worry about it. What's done is done." He stopped to let a mini-cat rumble across the road in front of us; the machine was carrying a load of broken cinderblocks away from a collapsed convenience store. The flagman waved us on, and John stepped on the pedal again. "So you think he did that just to get rid of us? I don't—"

"For the record," I went on, "the jerk's name is Paul Huygens." I hesitated. "He used to work for CybeServe, maker of the fine line of CybeServe home VR products . . . specifi-

90

cally, the VidMaxx Dataroom. Ring any bells with you?"

John's face was blank for a moment, then Big Ben tolled the midnight hour. He cast a sharp look at me. "I'll be darned," he said slowly. "Is that the guy who got you canned at the *Clarion*?"

"One and the same, dude." I gazed out the window at the ruins of a collapsed subdivision, remembering an unsigned note that had been faxed to me only a few years ago. "One and the same . . ."

Time for another history lesson. Today's lecture is how Gerry Rosen, ace investigative reporter, once again tried to get a good story and, not incidentally, save a few lives, but instead ended up losing his job. Take notes; there will be a quiz on this at the end of the postmodern era.

Three years before, I was working as a staff writer for another weekly alternative newspaper, this one the *Back Bay Clarion,* a muckraking little rag published in Boston. I had been assigned by my editor to follow up on a number of complaints against a medium-size electronics company based in Framingham, a Boston suburb that has been the heart of the East Coast computer industry since the early eighties. As you may have guessed, this was CybeServe.

CybeServe was one of many corporations that had cashed in on the virtual-reality boom by manufacturing home VR systems for the consumer market. It had previously lost tons of money on the cheap-shit domestic robots it had attempted to sell through department stores, so its VidMaxx line of VR equipment had been one of the few products that were keeping the company afloat. All well and good, but the problem lay in their top-of-the-line product, the VidMaxx Dataroom 310.

The Dataroom 310 was much like its competitors: the unit could transform any vacant household room into a virtual-reality environment, transporting the customer into any world that could be interfaced by the CPU—the sort of thing for which Jah now wanted to write programs. Want to see exactly what the NASA probes on Mars are doing right now? Experience a role-playing game set in a medieval fantasy world? Go shopping in the Galleria Virtual? If you had all the right hardware and enough money to blow on on-line linkage with the various nets, the Dataroom 310 would take you there toot sweet.

However, unlike similar equipment marketed by Microsoft-Commodore or IBM, CybeServe's VR equipment had some major flaws. First, there was no built-in interrupt timer; anyone who plugged into cyberspace could stay there indefinitely, or at least until hell froze over and you could build snowmen in Cairo. Also, because of various bugs in the CybeServe's communications software sold with the hardware, anyone with a little knowledge could hack straight through the security lockouts installed by sysops to prevent users from accessing various commercial VR nets without ponying up a credit card number.

This type of bad engineering had made the CybeServe Butler 3000 the joke of the robotics industry; CybeServe tended to do things fast and cheap in order to cash in on a marketing trend. But most people were unaware of the subtle flaws with the Dataroom 310 when they bought it and had it installed in their homes. Their kids, though, soon discovered those glitches that allowed them practically unlimited time on whatever nets they were able to access, with or without authorization. Blowing three grand on phone bills to Madame Evelyn's House of Love is enough to make anyone break out in a cold sweat.

That's bad. What's worse was that, according to the tips my paper had received from distraught and angry parents, several kids were losing themselves in cyberspace. They would rush home from school to lock themselves into the datarooms and, using various commands and passwords they had learned from their friends, jack into the VR worlds of their choice . . . and some of them, because of the lack of an interrupt toggle, wouldn't come back home again. It became a form of avoidance behavior for children who didn't like genuine reality, much as drugs, excessive TV viewing, or 1-900 phone services had been for previous generations. A few emotionally disturbed teenagers had even attempted suicide this way, trying to starve themselves to death while locked into an unreal world they refused to leave.

When I checked into it, I found that CybeServe was aware

of the problem yet had done nothing to solve it. The corporation had a consulting psychologist on its payroll, whose only job was to jack into the system and talk kids out of virtual reality. The company offered generous "refunds" to their families if they kept their mouths shut about the accidents that had befallen Junior and Sis and didn't file any lawsuits. Yet CybeServe had not recalled the Dataroom 310 to install timers nor made any effort to update the communications software to prevent hacking. Instead of fixing its mistakes, the company had concentrated solely on keeping potential buyers and the company's competitors from learning about the product's defects.

A few local families wanted to talk; so did a couple of their kids, particularly a thirteen-year-old boy from Newton who had spent six months in a New Hampshire psychiatric hospital after he had attempted to kill himself by locking himself in the household dataroom for nearly three days. They had tipped off the *Clarion*, and I was put onto the story.

CybeServe's public relations director was Paul Huygens. He had started off by affably refuting the accusations during a long phone interview. He also offered to have a unit installed in my house—free of charge, of course, for "research purposes." When I didn't wag my tail and roll over, he circulated an in-house memo to all key company personnel, tacitly threatening job termination to anyone who didn't hang up as soon as I called.

It could be said in Huygens's defense that he had only been doing his job. That's fair; I was doing mine. After several weeks of hangups, I managed to find a disgruntled former CybeServe R&D scientist with a guilty conscience who told me, in a not-for-attribution interview, about the fatal flaws in the Dataroom 310. That, along with all the real and circumstantial evidence, allowed me to write an exposé about the company. It was published in the *Clarion* after nearly two months of grinding work, and within a couple of months after its publication, the Dataroom 310 was taken off the market and CybeServe was forced to deal with dozens of civil-court lawsuits regarding the product.

By then, I had lost my job. Almost as soon as the article

was published, Huygens called Boston-area companies that had business with CybeServe, all of them electronics retailers that advertised in the *Back Bay Clarion*. These stores, in turn, swamped the *Clarion*'s publisher with threats that they would yank their ads from the paper unless an editorial retraction was published and I was fired.

Like most alternative weeklies, the *Clarion* was a free paper, its existence dependent solely upon ad revenues. Most publishers—like Pearl, bless his rancid heart—have an iron rod thrust down their backs, knowing all too well that advertisers need the papers just as much as the papers need the advertisers and that editorial wimp-outs only invite further intimidation. Earlier that year, though, the *Clarion* had been sold to a greedhead who was innocent of journalistic ethics and didn't have the common sense not to let himself be cowed by hollow threats. This jellyfish, confronted with the notion that he might not be able to purchase a summer cottage on Martha's Vineyard, knuckled under.

Two weeks after the publication of my CybeServe story, I was on my way to work when I stopped off at a Newbury Street deli to have coffee and read the *Globe-Herald*. This made me twenty minutes late for work. I had done it many times before with no previous complaints, but when I showed up at the office, my termination notice was already pinned to my door. The reason given was "chronic tardiness."

I was cleaning out my desk and putting all my files in cartons when my printer began to hum. I looked around to see the handwritten fax as it dropped into the tray:

Never fuck with the gods.

The fax came unsigned, but when I double-checked the number at the top of the page against my Rolodex, I saw that it had originated from Huygens's extension at CybeServe. His company was going down the tubes, but he was damned if he wasn't going to take me with him.

And now here I was, in another place and another time, fucking with the gods again.

"Huygens wanted to get me out of there," I said. "I don't know what it is, but there's something he doesn't want me to know about. I screwed him up once . . . he doesn't want that to happen again."

John nodded his head. "Could be. Could be . . ."

"I spotted the woman I met last night," I said as I cinched my seat upward again. John drove up the eastbound ramp to I-64, the car sliding into the dense midday traffic heading downtown. "Just before Huygens found me. She was across the room from us . . ."

"You did?" Tiernan looked mildly surprised; he passed a tandem-trailer rig that was chugging down the right lane and squeezed in behind a twenty-year-old BMW with Illinois tags and an expired gas-user decal. "What did she look like?"

"African-American, about five-six . . . um, sort of plump, about forty to forty-five. Some gray in her hair. It was her, all right." I hesitated, then added, "I used the camera to zoom in on her badge."

"Yeah?"

"Found out her position, too. Printed right on the badge."

"No kidding . . ."

"No kidding."

I fell silent. He waited for me to go on. "Well?"

I pointed at the shitbox ahead of us. Pale fumes billowed from its exhaust pipe. "Can you believe that they're still allowing cars like that on the road? I mean, I thought they were supposed to be enforcing the phase-out laws, and here's this clunker—"

"Gerry . . ."

"I think I'm going to do a column about this. I mean, I don't mind much if someone like Chevy Dick's got an antique in his garage and takes it out once every now and then, but when you see something like this in broad daylight . . . y'know, it's just disgraceful . . ."

John sighed. "Okay, okay, knock it off. What do you want to know?"

I grinned. It was an old game between us dating back to our college journalism days: quid pro quo information trading. You tell me your secrets and I'll tell you mine, tit for tat.

Sometimes the game had been played for higher stakes than this: when he wanted to know the name of the cute brunette in my Econ 101 class, I traded it to him for the home phone number of the university chancellor. It worked out pretty well; I was able to call the chancellor on a Sunday afternoon while he was watching a football game to ask him embarrassing questions about next semester's tuition hikes, and for this John received the name of his future wife.

"Ruby fulcrum," I said. "What's it mean?"

John sighed. "It's a code phrase of some sort. To be honest, I don't know much about it myself, except that it has something to do with the Sentinel program. This lady keeps mentioning it, though, so it must be important somehow."

He suddenly snapped his fingers, then reached above the windshield to pull down the car's flatscreen. "Let's see if CNN has anything on the launch."

" 'Don't know' doesn't count . . ."

"Okay, okay." Keeping one eye on traffic and one hand on the wheel, John switched the CTV to bring us CNN. "Ask me another one."

"Why are you talking to this woman?" I asked. "What's this story all about?"

John didn't say anything for a moment. On the screen, the CNN anchor was reading a story about the deployment of Army troops on the Oregon border. Footage of rifle-toting soldiers tramping down the ramp of an Air Force transport jet, APCs and tanks rolling down highways between coniferous forests, antiwar demonstrators attempting to barricade military convoys . . .

"It has to do with a murder," he said, carefully picking his words. "My source—and yeah, I think it's the same lady, though I've never seen her—says that a Tiptree scientist was killed recently. Even though the police are still calling it random homicide, she claims it's part of a conspiracy and has something to do with this Ruby Fulcrum business."

The footage on the screen changed back to the CNN newsroom; a window in the right corner displayed the NASA logo. "Here we go," John said as he turned up the volume.

"*. . . launched a half-hour ago from Cape Canaveral,*

Florida," the anchorwoman intoned as the screen switched to a shot of the shuttle *Endeavour* lifting off from its pad. *"In its cargo bay are the final components of the* Sentinel 1 *ABM satellite."*

Animated footage of the massive satellite, identical to the holographic image that had been displayed in the Tiptree atrium, replaced the live-action shot. *"Linkup between the shuttle and the twenty-billion-dollar satellite is expected some-time tomorrow afternoon."*

"A murder?" I asked. "What's this got to do with—"

"Forget it." John reached up to switch off the CTV as he finally found room to pass the BMW. I caught a glimpse of the driver as we moved around the clunker: a redneck wearing a baseball cap, a cigar clamped between his teeth. "That's all I'm giving you," he continued, "and I shouldn't have told you that much. Your turn."

"Beryl Hinckley," I said. "Her badge listed her as a research scientist. If you want, I'll get Jah to print you a copy of her photo so you can recognize her when you meet her at Clancy's tonight."

John nodded. "I'd appreciate it."

We fell silent for the next few miles as the suburbs thinned out and the towers of the uptown business district of Clayton hove into view. Clayton had come through the crisis pretty well: new office buildings, rich homes, not many indications that a 7.5 earthquake had socked this part of the city. Of course, much of the federal disaster relief funds had been channeled in this direction. The government had been fully aware of who was wealthy enough to be able to repay the loans, and everyone in St. Louis knew where the influential voters resided.

"Stay out of it," John said after a while.

"Excuse me?"

"Stay out of it," he repeated. "I know you're looking for a good story, and I know you're nervous about your job, but . . . just let me handle this one by myself, okay? If I need help, I'll call you in and we can share the byline—"

"C'mon. You know that's not what it's about . . ."

He looked askance at me and my voice trailed off. It was a

lie and John knew it. No, I wasn't nervous; I was desperate. If I didn't deliver something impressive PDQ, Pearl was going to find a new staff writer and I'd be back on the street. At best, I'd be some poor schmo freelancer, peddling video reviews to the *Big Muddy* for nickel-and-dime checks while living in a homeless shelter.

I didn't want to encroach on my friend's rightful territory, but this bit with Tiptree and Beryl Hinckley and Ruby Fulcrum was a hot potato I couldn't afford not to catch.

"C'mon, man," I said, "you can't—"

"I know." John kept his eyes locked on the highway ahead. "Look, you've got to trust me on this one. This is serious business, and not a little bit dangerous. Just . . . y'know, let me handle this by myself. All right?"

"All right." I raised my hands. "Okay . . . whatever you say."

John didn't have my problems. He still had everything I had lost. A nice car, a house in the 'burbs, a wife who didn't despise him, a job that was secure. A kid who was still alive. I envied him, sure . . .

For a moment, despite our long friendship, I caught myself hating him. He must have read my mind, because he nervously cleared his throat. "Look, if you want my advice," he began, "you're going to have to put some things behind you."

He hesitated. "I mean, your situation's tough and all that, but . . . well, Jamie's gone and you're just going to have to—"

"Right. Jamie's gone and I'm going to have to live with that. I know. Time to get a life." Out of impulse, I switched on the CTV again. "I think it's time for *Batman*. You know what channel it's on?"

John shut up. I found the station showing the favorite cartoon show of my misspent youth. The theme song swelled to fill the car as we sailed the rest of the way downtown: one man with a firm grip on reality, the other trying to avoid it at all costs.

Get a life. Sure, John. I had a life.

And boy, did it suck.

8

I dropped off the camera with Jah after we got back to the office; he promised to process the disk and give me a contact sheet before the end of the day. He also informed me that his father had found out about my surreptitious exit and was—in Jah's words—"livid pissed."

That meant sneaking up the stairs to the second floor. I had rather hoped Pearl had gone out for lunch for once, but the odor of fried brains assaulted me as I tiptoed past Bailey's door. Fried brains, that most obnoxious of St. Louis delicacies, was Pearl's favorite food; he brought a take-out deli plate of them to the office every day and consumed them in full view of the staff. Bailey didn't look up from his brains as I scurried to my desk, but I knew that he would eventually catch up with me.

I figured that the best thing for me to do was to look busy so that, at very least, he couldn't accuse me of goldbricking. I sat down at my desk and began work on my column for next week's paper. The subject was the ERA raid on the Muny last night; the morning *Post-Dispatch* gave me such clinical facts as the number of people who had been busted, but what came out in my column was a more subjective eyewitness account.

I was halfway through composing the article, in the middle of describing the arrival of the ERA troopers, when I caught a glimpse of Bailey as a reflection on my screen. I ignored him and went on writing; for a few moments he hovered just outside my cubicle as if trying to decide whether to say something, then he walked away. I glanced over at John; he was on the phone at his desk, but he grinned back at me. My job was still safe—for today, at any rate.

Yet I couldn't get the events at Tiptree out of my mind. Sure, it wasn't my story, but nonetheless my journalistic curiosity was itching, and I needed a good scratch. After I finished the rough draft of my story and saved it, I switched the computer to modem and made a call to the city election commissioner's office.

Steve Estes' campaign contributions were a matter of public record; all I had to do was ask the right questions and the skeletons danced out of the closet and onto my screen. Estes had been a busy little political hack: his war chest listed contributions from hundreds of private individuals, among them many of the city's wealthiest and most powerful citizens. The list also included local corporate and PAC donations to Citizens to Re-Elect Steve Estes, and right smack in the middle of the list was $10,000 from the Tiptree Corporation.

Of course, that in itself didn't mean shit to a tree: everyone from the Republican National Committee to the National Rifle Association had written checks to Estes. It still meant that there was a subtle connection between Estes and Tiptree.

I made a hard copy of the file, circled the Tiptree item in red ink, and was about to pass it to John when I got a better idea. Almost on impulse, I picked up the phone and called Estes' office.

Estes was a senior partner in a downtown law firm; the switchboard operator passed the buck to Estes' private secretary, a hard-eyed young woman who looked as if she could have been a model for a 1947 Sears Roebuck catalog. Her bee-stung lips made a slight downturn when I identified myself as a *Big Muddy* reporter. *"Just a moment, please,"* she said. *"I'll see if he's in."*

She put me on hold, and I was treated to a computer-generated lily field and the theme for *The Sound of Music* for a couple of minutes. My gag reflex was kicking in when the flowers and Julie Andrews abruptly vanished, to be replaced by Steve Estes' face.

"Good afternoon, Gerry," he said, beaming at the camera. *"How can I help you?"*

We had never met or talked before, so I ignored the first-name familiarity. It was par for the political course. "Good afternoon, Mr. Estes," I said, touching the Record button on my phone. "I'm working on a story for my paper, regarding last night's raid by ERA troops on the Muny, and I was hoping I could get a response from you."

Estes didn't even blink. *"I'd be happy to give you a response,"* he said, *"but I'm afraid I don't know much more than what I've read in this morning's paper."*

He was already disavowing any connection. "Well, sir," I went on, "it's interesting to hear you say that, considering that you've gone on record to urge ERA to force the homeless population out of the park. Are you saying that you had nothing to do with the raid?"

He settled back in his chair, still smiling at me. *"For one thing, I'm not sure if 'raid' is the appropriate word,"* he replied, switching hands on the receiver. *" 'Peaceful police action' is probably the right term. And although I've asked Colonel Barris to step up his enforcement of the indigent population in Forest Park, I can't say that I've directly requested him to . . . um, conduct any 'raids,' so to speak, on the park or the Muny in particular."*

Clever son of a bitch. Until Estes saw how public reaction toward the raid swung, he was carefully avoiding any credit for it, while simultaneously making sure that his name was still associated with the "peaceful police action" if it turned out that the majority of voters were in favor of what had happened last night.

"Do you believe ERA should conduct any further . . . ah, police actions in the park?" I asked.

"I believe ERA should enforce the law and be responsible for the safety of all St. Louis citizens," he replied.

Another neutral answer. Estes might rave in the city council chamber about "taking the streets back," knowing that the TV news reporters would extract only a few seconds' worth of sound bite from his diatribe, but when confronted by a columnist for the local muckraker who might print his remarks in their complete context, he would play it much more safely. I had to hand it to Estes; he was a profes-

sional politician in every sense of the term. He couldn't
be fooled by the loaded do-you-beat-your-wife queries that
might foul up another politico.

"One more question," I said. "I was at the private reception
held at the Tiptree Corporation this morning—"

"You were?" All innocence and light. *"Why, so was I. That
was a beautiful shuttle launch, wasn't it?"*

"I wish I could have seen it," I said, "but my colleague and
I were forcibly removed from the room . . ."

He raised a wary eyebrow. *"Really . . ."*

"Really. In fact, the Tiptree official who forced us out
claimed that you minded the fact that I took a picture of
you, and that's the reason why we were asked to leave."

Despite his polished self-possession, Estes looked flustered
for a couple of moments. He glanced away from the camera
for an instant, as if listening to someone just outside the
phone's range of vision, then he looked directly back at me
again. *"I'm sorry to hear that was you, Gerry,"* he said. *"My
apologies . . . I thought you were someone else."*

"Uh-huh. Anyone in particular?"

His smile became rigid. *"No comment,"* he said evenly.

No wonder. "One more thing," I said, "and then I'll let you
go. I happened to check your campaign disclosure and noticed
that you've received a sizable contribution this last year from
Tiptree. Can you tell me why?"

He blinked at my knowledge of this tidbit of information,
but remained in control. *"Tiptree has been a good friend
of the St. Louis community,"* he said, as if reciting from a
campaign fact-sheet. *"It's employed thousands of people over
the last several years and has been a growing part of the local
aerospace community. As such, we have mutual interests at
heart."*

"I see. And Project Sentinel . . . is that . . . ?"

*"A great technological achievement, as Mr. McLaughlin
said during his opening remarks."* He made a show of looking
at his watch. *"Now, if you'll please excuse me, I have to go. I
have someone waiting in my office to see me."*

"Yes, well, thank—"

The screen blanked before I finished my sentence.

• • •

I went back to my column, this time incorporating the remarks Estes had made about the raid during our interview. They didn't make much of a difference, except that it was interesting to note how Estes' "peaceful police action" contrasted with the mob panic, tear gas, and gunfire I had seen and heard.

I finished the piece at about six o'clock, as green-tinted twilight seeped through the windows. By then most of the staff had already gone home; John and I were the last two people left in the editorial department. Jah stopped by to give me the contact sheet of the photos I had taken. I found the shot I had taken of Beryl Hinckley, and John glanced at it under a magnifying glass as he put on his overcoat, memorizing her face for the meeting he was supposed to have with her later that evening.

"You want me to come along for the ride?" I asked after Jah left. "I could help identify her when she—"

"Oh, no you don't," Pearl snapped.

I shut my eyes, cussing under my breath. I wasn't aware that Bailey was just outside the editorial cube. He had been shutting down the production department's photocopy machines when he overheard our conversation. Overheard, hell: the bastard had been eavesdropping.

"You let John take care of his own stories, Rosen," he said, glaring at me over the top of the partition. "All I want from you is your column and whatever else I specifically assign you. You hear me?"

Here it comes. The second chew-out of the day. Before I could muster a reply, John cleared his throat. "Pardon me," he said, "but I asked Gerry if he would help me out on this. He saw something at the Muny last night that . . . ah, might have something to do with what I'm working on."

It was a good lie, and Pearl almost fell for it. His eyes shifted back and forth between us, trying to decide who was putting on whom, before his basilisk stare settled on me. "Did you get your column written?" he demanded.

"Sure, Pearl . . . uh, Earl. Got it finished just a few minutes ago."

He grunted. "Good. Then tomorrow I want you working on the Arch story we talked about at the last staff meeting. Deadline by next Friday."

The assignment in question was a no-story story about why the Gateway Arch hadn't collapsed during the New Madrid quake. Why hadn't the Arch fallen? Because it was built well, that's why. When some dopey Wash You intern had suggested the piece, I had argued that point and added that the quake was old news; besides, who needed another feel-good piece about things that hadn't fallen down and gone boom? The TV stations, the *Post-Dispatch*, and the local shoppers had already published so many of these yarns that a new category in local journalism had been tacitly created to encompass them: Courageous Firemen, Heroic Pets, and Gee Whiz It's Still Standing Upright.

But Pearl had assigned it to me anyway—largely, I suspect, because he wanted to see how well I jumped through hoops. I was about to protest that this was a useless assignment when I caught John's stern expression out of the corner of my eye and shut up. Since I was already walking the tightrope, I might as well show off my other circus tricks.

"And the next time you decide to take off with John," Bailey went on, "you might have the common courtesy to tell me first. We got a tip this morning from some lady out in Webster Groves. Squirrels are back in Blackburn Park for the first time since the quake—"

"And there was no one here to cover it," I finished, snapping my fingers and shaking my head. "Aw, gee, I'm sorry I missed it. Sounds important."

John coughed loudly and covered his mouth with his hand, this time to disguise the grin on his face. Bailey shot a harsh look at him, then focused on me again. "I'm the editor here, Rosen, and you're the reporter. Understand? Just to teach you a lesson, I want you to call this lady back ASAP—"

"C'mon, Pearl—"

"And don't gimme me that 'Pearl' shit or I'll have you over in copyediting faster than you can say Oxford English Dictionary."

Translation: shape up or ship out. Unless I wanted to end my career at the *Big Muddy* proofreading pasteups and checking the grammar of the stuff sent in by the freelancers, I had better content myself with writing about squirrels and pretend to like it.

I didn't say anything, because anything I was likely to have said would probably have had me at the copyediting desk by Monday morning. Bailey gave me one last sour look, then picked up his jacket. "See you tomorrow, gentlemen," he said. "Don't forget to lock up behind you."

Then he strode down the center aisle between the cubicles, heading for the front door, where his son was waiting to drive him home.

"He'll get over it," John whispered. "Just lie low for the next couple of weeks and let him chill out." He opened his desk drawer, pulled out Dingbat, checked the battery LED, and slipped it into the wallet pocket of his trenchcoat. "If it's any consolation, I'm sorry I got you into this."

"Forget it," I said, waving him off. "It's my fault, not yours." I paused. "The offer's still open. If you want me to go with you to Clancy's . . ."

He shook his head. "Better not. I think I ought to do it alone this time." He tapped the proof shoot with his fingernail. "Your friend might get leery if she sees both of us."

I nodded. He was right; the story was the most important thing, not who covered it. I began to turn off the rest of the lights. Since I lived just upstairs, it was my job to close down the office on the way out the back door. John picked up his gray fedora and walked past me as he headed toward the front door, then abruptly stopped as if a thought had just occurred to him.

"Do me a favor, though," he added. "Let me know how this bit with the squirrels turns out."

I tried not to be irritated by his seeming condescension. My friend was attempting to take an interest in my work, making me feel as if it was something that really mattered. He was on the trail of a murderer, and I was stuck with some silly-ass story that would only wind up as a small piece in the front section, if it saw print at all.

"Sure, man," I mumbled. "I'll let you know."

"Could be interesting," he said hesitantly, realizing that he had said the wrong thing. "You never know . . ."

"Right . . ."

He turned around again. "See you in the morning."

"Catch you later," I said.

I set the office phone so that it would ring upstairs, shut off the lights, made sure all the doors and windows were locked, then climbed the back stairs to my apartment. It was a warm and humid night, so I cracked open the windows and warmed up a can of SpaghettiOs on the hot plate while I caught a rerun of some old cop show on TV. Robert Urich and his wisecracking buddy caught the bad guys after a car chase; such a surprise. I had no idea what the story was about, but it made me forget how awful my dinner was.

I was out of beer, but I was still suffering alcohol fatigue from last night's bender, so I didn't go out to buy another six-pack from the grocery on 12th. It had begun to drizzle outside, and all I really wanted to do was to stay home and stay dry.

After I dumped my plate in the sink and turned off the tube, I sat down at the computer and tried to get some real writing done. After spending an hour rewriting the same boring paragraph several times, though, I realized that my muse had gone on vacation in Puerto Rico and, besides, the Great American Novel still sucked lizard eggs. I switched off the computer without bothering to save the few lines I had written, shucked my clothes, and curled up in bed with a secondhand paperback spy novel.

I fell asleep while reading, not even bothering to turn off the lamp over the bed. Rain gently pattered on the fire escape, city traffic moaned, and helicopters clattered overhead. The night world moved on around me; I vaguely heard the sound of police sirens from somewhere nearby and rolled over in my sleep, dreaming of nothing I could remember.

A countless time later, I was awakened by the buzz of the phone. That did for me what the familiar urban noises outside the window could not; I opened my eyes and, squinting in the glare of the lamp, fumbled for the handset beside me.

" 'Lo?" I said, expecting it to be Marianne, calling to nag me again about Uncle Arnie.

A male voice on the other end of the line: *"Is this the* Big Muddy Inquirer *office?"*

Shit. I should have turned on the answering machine. "Yeah, but we're closed now. Can you call back tomorrow . . . ?"

"Who's this?" the voice demanded.

"Who wants to know?"

A pause. *"This is Lieutenant Mike Farrentino, St. Louis Police Homicide Division. Is this one of the staff?"*

Homicide division? What the fuck was this? I woke up a little more. The clock on my dresser said it was 9:55 P.M. "Yeah, it is," I said. "Why, what's—"

"What's your name?" When I didn't answer promptly, the voice became stronger. *"C'mon, what's your—"*

"Rosen." A cold chill was beginning to creep down my spine. "Gerry Rosen. I'm a staff writer. Why are you—?"

"Mr. Rosen, I'm at Clancy's Bar and Grill, just down the street from your office. We have a dead person here whose personal ID says that it is the property of one John L. Tiernan, a reporter for your paper. Would you mind coming down here to verify the identity of the deceased, please?"

9

Blue lights flashing in a humid night in the city, veiled by dense evening fog. The distant hoot of a tugboat pushing barges down the Mississippi River. The sound of boot soles slapping against a brick sidewalk . . .

This is the aftermath of murder.

Clancy's Bar & Grill was crawling with cops by the time I got down there: three blue-and-whites parked on Geyer with a couple of unmarked cruisers sandwiched between them, and out of them had emerged what seemed to be half of the St. Louis Police Department, most of them standing scratching their asses and trying to look as if they knew what they were doing. It figured that a poor black dude can get shot in the head in broad daylight down in Dogtown and nobody gives a shit, but a middle-class white guy gets killed in a Soulard barroom and most of the force shows up, looking for trouble.

The bar was almost empty. Given its usual clientele, though, it only made sense that the regulars would have cleared out as soon as the cops arrived on the scene. A big, burly policeman was standing beneath the front awning, listening to his headset as he watched the sidewalk; he blocked my way as I approached the door.

"Sorry, pal, but you can't go in right now. Police business—"

"Outta my way," I muttered as I tried to push past him, "I gotta get in there—"

And found myself being shoved backward so fast I lost my balance and fell against two more cops who were standing on

108

the sidewalk. One of them, a thin Latino cop, snagged the back of my jacket. "Hey, sport," he said as he began to usher me away, "find another place to get a drink, okay? This is—"

"Fuck off." I shrugged out of his grip, headed for the door again. "My friend's—"

The Latino cop grabbed my right arm and twisted it behind my back. I yelped as I was forced to my knees, and all of a sudden I saw nothing but shiny black cop shoes all around me as a riot baton was pressed against the back of my neck, forcing my head down while yet another officer grabbed my left arm and pulled it behind me.

"Ease down, pal! Ease down!"

Ease down, hell. The cops were all over me, securing my wrists with plastic cuffs while I struggled against them. I was halfway through most of the words your mother told you she'd wash your mouth out with soap if she ever heard you say them again when I heard a new voice.

"Stimpson! Who is this man!"

Stimpson was the first cop I had confronted. "Just some jerk who wouldn't take no for an answer, Lieutenant," he said. "We asked him to leave, but he's decided he wanted to—"

"Did you bother to ask him his name first?" I tried to look up, but the riot baton continued to force my head down toward the brick sidewalk. "Sir, can you tell me your name?"

"Rosen," I managed to gasp. "Gerry Rosen. I'm with the *Big Muddy*—"

"Shit. Let him up, D'Angelo." The grip on my arms relaxed a little. "I said, let him up," the lieutenant demanded. "That's the man I called down here, for chrissake."

"Yes sir." D'Angelo hesitated, then let go of my arm and grabbed me beneath my arms to gently lift me off my knees. As he produced a pair of scissors and cut off the handcuffs, the rest of the cops who had encircled me took a powder, their batons and tasers sliding back into belt loops and holsters.

My savior was a tall, gaunt plainclothes cop in his late thirties. He wore a calf-length raincoat and a wide-brimmed fedora, and a cigarette dangled from thin lips in a pockmarked face that looked as if it had once suffered from chronic acne. He brushed past Stimpson and thrust out his hand.

"Michael Farrentino, homicide division," he said by way of formal introduction. "Glad to meet you, Mr. Rosen. Sorry about the rough treatment."

I ignored both the hand and the apology. "You said you found my friend in here," I said, my voice rough as I massaged my chafed wrists. "Where is he?"

I started to push past him, heading for the door again. "Hey, whoa . . . hold on. Just wait a moment." Farrentino stepped in front of me as he reached up with both hands to grab my shoulders. "Just let me ask you a couple of questions first—"

"Fuck that," I snapped. "Where's John?"

We stared each other eye to eye for another moment, then Farrentino's hands fell from my shoulders. He took the cigarette out of his mouth and flicked it into the street. "Okay, have it your way," he murmured. "Follow me."

To my surprise, he didn't escort me directly into the bar. Instead he led me past the front door and about twenty feet farther down the sidewalk, past a high brick wall, until we reached the narrow iron gate that led into Clancy's open-air beer garden. Two more cops were guarding the red tape— marked CRIME SCENE DO NOT PASS—that had been stretched across the open gate. They moved aside as Farrentino ducked under it, then held it up for me so I could pass through.

Many of St. Louis's saloons have *biergartens*, a fine old tradition that the city's first settlers brought with them from Germany during the 1800's. Even though this particular beer garden now sported an Irish name, it resided behind a three-story building and was just old enough to have a real garden. Picnic tables and iron chairs were arranged between small Dutch elms and brick planters; from the number of half-empty beer bottles and plastic cups left abandoned on the table, it seemed as if there had been a fair number of people in Clancy's beer garden before the law had arrived in large numbers.

But the scene of the crime wasn't down here; instead, it was an enclosed balcony on the second floor in the rear of the building. I could see a number of people clustered around the corner of the balcony overlooking the street; portable camera lights had been rigged on tripods around the wooden balustrade, and they were all aimed down at something on the porch floor, but I couldn't see what it was.

Farrentino silently led me up the weathered pinewood stairs to the balcony. More cops, a couple of bored-looking paramedics with a stretcher, two more plainclothes homicide dicks—Farrentino led me through the crowd as they parted for us, until we reached the end of the balcony and I got a chance to see what all the fuss was about.

The body sprawled across the porch floor was definitely that of John Tiernan. His trench coat, his tie, even his patent-leather shoes: I had seen him wearing those clothes only a few hours earlier. But it took me a few moments to recognize his face.

That was because it looked as if someone had taken a white-hot fireplace poker and had shoved it into his skull, straight through the center of his forehead.

The black moment had come for John so quickly that his eyes were wide open, seeing only those things dead men can see.

When I was through vomiting over the rail, Farrentino led me back downstairs to the beer garden. He sat me down at a picnic table out of sight from the balcony, gave me a handkerchief so I could dry my mouth, and left me alone for a couple of minutes; when he came back, he had a shot glass of bourbon in one hand and a beer chaser in the other. The dubious benefits of having a murder committed at a bar.

I belted back the shot of bourbon, ignoring the chaser. The liquor burned down my gullet and into my stomach; I gasped and for a moment my guts rebelled, but the booze stayed down, and after a moment there was quietude of a sort. I slumped back in the chair and tried not to think of the horror I had just seen.

"Ready to talk?" Farrentino asked, not unkindly. I nodded my head; he pulled out a palmtop and flipped it open. "Is that John Tiernan? Can you give me a positive identification?"

I slowly nodded my head. Farrentino waited patiently for a verbal reply. "Yeah . . . yeah, that's John," I said. "I'm sure that's him."

"Okay." The homicide detective made an entry in his computer. "I know that was rough on you, Mr. Rosen, but we had to be sure. We've got to call his family next, and even though we got his driver's license from his wallet, I wanted to have someone else identify him before I put out a call to his wife. You were convenient and . . . well, I hope you understand."

I nodded. Poor Sandy. I was glad that she hadn't seen him like this. "Thanks, Officer. Do you want me to call her?"

"No, I'd just as soon do it myself." Farrentino pulled out a pack of cigarettes, shook one out, and offered it to me. I shook my head, he took the cigarette for himself, lighting it from the bottom of the pack. "I hate to say it, but I've gotten used to this part of the job," he went on. "I think it'd be better if she got the news from me instead of you. Me, she can hate for the rest of her life and it won't matter much, but if she hears it from you . . ."

"Yeah, okay. I understand."

He shrugged as he exhaled blue smoke. "So . . . when was the last time you saw the deceased?"

I actually had to think about it; all of a sudden, it seemed as if days instead of hours had passed since I had last seen John alive. "Around six, six-thirty, I think. We were closing down the office for the day."

"Uh-huh." Farrentino typed another note in his PT. "Do you have any idea where he was going?"

I became wary. Sure, I knew where John was going, and why . . . but I wasn't sure if I was ready to tell these things to Farrentino. "He said he was coming down here, but I'm not really sure what he was doing."

Farrentino continued to make notes. "You knew he was coming here," he said, "but you don't know why? Maybe he was just going out for a few drinks. That's what most people do when they go to a bar after work."

"Uh . . . yeah. That's what he was doing—"

"Except when I talked to the bartender, he told me that Mr. Tiernan hardly ordered anything the whole time he was here. He remembers him buying one beer when he arrived at . . ."

Farrentino checked his notes. "A quarter to eight, and he nursed it the entire time he was here. I suppose he must have gone somewhere for dinner before then."

I picked up my beer and took a sip from it. The bottle was slippery in my hand. "Yeah, I guess so," I said. "That would make sense."

"Hmm. Maybe so." The detective coughed, his eyes still on the miniature screen. "Do you know if he was . . . well, y'know, fooling around with anyone? Had a girlfriend on the side his wife didn't know about?"

I felt a rush of anger but tried to keep it in check. "I'm not sure that's any of your business, Officer."

"Well? Did he?" He shrugged indifferently. "Maybe it's none of my business, but still it's something his wife might want to know when I call her—"

"Hell, no!" I snapped. "If he was meeting anyone here, it sure as hell wasn't a . . ."

My voice trailed off as the realization hit me. Farrentino had skillfully led me into a trap, forcing me to contradict myself. His eyes slowly rose from the PT. "I didn't ask if he was meeting anyone here, Mr. Rosen," he said. "Maybe you do know something about what he was doing here, after all."

From behind the garden wall, there was the wail of a siren approaching from down the street. I could hear the metallic clank from the balcony as the paramedics unfolded their stretcher. A couple of barmaids stood watching us from the back door, murmuring to each other.

Farrentino was about to say something else when a uniformed cop approached our table, carrying several plastic-bagged objects in his hands. "This is all we found in his pockets," he said, holding them out for the detective to examine. "Do you want us to have 'em dusted?"

I recognized some of the items: his house keys, his car remote, his wallet, an old-fashioned fountain pen Sandy had given to him as a birthday present, some loose change, the ever-present pack of chewing gum . . .

And, in a bag of its own, Dingbat.

"Hmm?" Farrentino barely glanced at the collection. "Uhh . . . naw, I don't think we need to do that. The only prints we'd find are his own. Just leave 'em with me. I'll give them to his wife when I see her."

The cop nodded his head and carefully laid them on the table between us before walking away. It occurred to me that John might have entered a few notes into Dingbat during his meeting with Beryl Hinckley. If there were any important clues as to why he had been killed, perhaps they might be stored on the PT's floptical diskette.

"Okay, Rosen," Farrentino said, breaking my train of thought, "let's level with each other."

"Sure." I shrugged, trying not to stare covetously at Dingbat; it was just within hand's reach. "Anything you want to know, Officer." As I spoke, I picked up the beer and started to raise it to my mouth . . .

And then, at the last moment, I let my fingers slip from around the bottle.

It fell out of my grasp, bounced off the table, and fell between my legs, splattering beer across everything before the bottle broke on the concrete under the table. "Aw, shit!" I yelled, jumping up from my seat, staring down at the wet splotch that had spread across the crotch of my jeans. "God-damn fucking . . . !"

When I want to screw up a conversation, I can outdo myself. Beer spilled off the table and onto the broken glass scattered across the ground. Farrentino stood up from his chair, alarmed and irritated at the same time. "What a fucking mess!" I whined. "I can't believe I just . . . look, lemme go back to my place and get some dry pants on. It'll just take a—"

"No, no, don't do that," Farrentino said, already moving away from the table. "Just stay here, okay? I'll go get someone to clean all this stuff up . . ."

Then he turned his back to me and headed for the barroom's back door; the two barmaids had already gone inside, presumably to get some towels and a broom and dustpan.

For a few precious moments, I was alone in the beer garden. I snatched up the evidence bag containing Dingbat. There was a red adhesive seal across the plastic zipper, but there was no time to worry about that now. I hastily unzipped the bag, breaking the seal, and shook the palmtop out into my hand, all the while keeping one eye on the door.

It took me only a second to eject the mini-disk from Dingbat's floptical drive and stash it in the pocket of my jacket before I returned the PT to the bag and zipped it shut again. I had barely placed the bag back on the picnic table when Farrentino and one of the barmaids came out the door again.

We spent the next few minutes wiping up the spilled beer with paper towels and letting the barmaid sweep up the broken glass. I made a big deal out of sponging beer from my pants, although I kept one eye on the evidence bag. If you looked closely, you could see the split in the tape seal; someone would notice eventually, but I hoped to be long gone by then.

"Okay," Farrentino said at last, after the mess was cleaned away and the barmaid was gone. He sat down at the table, clasping his hands together as he stared at me. "Here's what happened . . ."

"Go on," I said, adjusting my posture so that he wouldn't have to look at both the evidence bag and me at the same time.

"A lady arrived here at the bar shortly after Tiernan showed up," he went on, his voice lowered. "Black lady, nervous looking. Witnesses say they went up to that balcony together and were up there for a long time, talking. Seems they wanted to be someplace where they couldn't be overheard. He was getting up as if to leave when he was shot—"

"How was he killed?" I asked. Farrentino hesitated. "That wasn't a normal gunshot either," I went on as my memory put together a picture of what I had seen up there. "He should have had his brains splattered all over the place if it had been from a gun, but I didn't see any blood . . ."

Farrentino reluctantly nodded his head. "No, there wasn't any blood. No one heard a gunshot either. Witnesses say that they heard the woman scream, that's all. A second after that, a van parked across the street took off, but no one got its make or license number. The woman ran off before anyone could stop her."

"You didn't answer the question," I said. "How was John killed?"

"We have some ideas," he said tersely. "We're looking into it right now—"

"Wonderful. I'm overwhelmed."

"Don't be a smartass," Farrentino said, giving me a sour look. "Off the record, though, we think that it might have been a laser weapon of some sort. Remember the 'Dark Jedi' slayings in Chicago a couple of years ago?"

A chill ran down my back as he said that. Of course I remembered; it had been national news for several months. A serial killer—who, in a letter sent to the *Chicago Tribune*, had called himself the "Dark Jedi"—had picked off seven people at random over the course of several weeks, using a high-energy laser rifle. When the FBI and Illinois State Police finally tracked him down, the Dark Jedi turned out to be a rather sociopathic high school student from an upscale Chicago suburb. The scariest part of the case, though, was the fact that he had devised his weapon from a science-hobby handbook available in most bookstores, using equipment purchased through mail-order catalogs. In fact, the feds had found him because he had previously showed off a prototype of his laser rifle at a science fair; his "light saber" had won a second-place ribbon.

"So you think it's a copycat killer?" I asked.

Farrentino shrugged. "That's a possibility, but we don't know yet. That's all I can tell you right now." He then jabbed a finger at me. "You next. Shoot."

"Okay." I folded my arms across my chest. "He told me he was investigating a murder—"

"Whose murder?"

"I don't know," I said. Which was the truth.

"Who was the lady?"

"I don't know that either," I said. Which was a lie.

"C'mon, Rosen—"

"All I know was that he was supposed to meet someone here at eight o'clock, and it had to do with the story he was doing." I shrugged, gazing back at him. "That's all I know . . . but I'm telling you, whoever she was, it wasn't a girlfriend. John didn't cheat on his wife. That's a fact."

Farrentino's dark eyes searched my face. He said nothing for a few moments. He knew that I hadn't told him everything I knew about the circumstances leading up to John's murder, and I knew that he wasn't playing entirely fair with me either. In John's memory, we were playing one final game of quid pro quo, and this round had just reached a stalemate.

I glanced toward the entrance to the beer garden. A couple of cops were holding open the gate; I could hear the ponderous clank of the stretcher's wheels as the parameds carefully inched it down the stairs from the balcony. In a few moments there would be nothing left of my buddy except a yellow chalk mark on a wooden floor.

"Lemme tell you something," Farrentino said at last. "You may think you know a lot about this, but I know more than you do. John was a friend of mine . . ."

"Yeah?" John had plenty of friends on the force. For all I knew, Farrentino could have been a deep-throat source, but I had no way of proving that. "I'm sure he would have been glad to see you down here for him."

Farrentino ignored the dig. "And he would have wanted us to work together to nail the guy who killed him. So if you want to come clean and tell me everything you know . . ."

The noise from the stairs stopped. The stretcher was on the ground. "I'll keep it in mind, Lieutenant," I said as I stood up again. "Now if you'll excuse me, I want to go see John off."

He started to say something else, but before he could stop me, I edged my way around the table and headed for the other side of the beer garden.

I stood on the sidewalk for a couple of minutes, watching John's body as it was wheeled away. A white sheet had been pulled over the corpse, with three straps holding it down on the stretcher, but for some damn reason I kept expecting him to sit up, reach into his pocket, and ask if I wanted some gum.

The paramedics stopped the stretcher behind the ambulance's rear fender, folded the stretcher's wheels, then picked it up. I remembered us getting drunk together at college parties and going out for double dates with Marianne and Sandy. Standing in line before the graduation platform, waiting to get our diplomas while making whispered jokes about the pontifical commencement speech Sam Donaldson had just delivered. The letters and postcards he had sent me while we were living on opposite sides of the country, the absurd wedding presents we had sent to each other when we had married our girlfriends, the long-distance phone calls when our kids had been born.

Now it all came down to this: one guy watching the other being loaded into the back of a meat wagon, down here in the scuzzy part of town. I had always thought he was going to outlive me . . .

"Helluva shame, isn't it?" Mike Farrentino said from behind me.

I jerked involuntarily. I hadn't realized that he had been at my back the entire time. "Yeah," I mumbled, not looking around at him. "Helluva shame."

As the stretcher was pushed into the back of the ambulance and its doors slammed closed, I eased my way out of the crowd and began to walk, not too quickly, up the street away from Clancy's. With each step I took, I expected someone to yell "Hey you!" and then ten cops would be climbing all over me again.

That instant never came. I was a block away when I heard the ambulance drive away from the curb. By then I was in the darkened doorway of the *Big Muddy* offices, reaching into my pocket to make sure I still had the mini-disk I had stolen from Dingbat.

It was still there, a little silver disk about the size of an antique fifty-cent piece. I looked down the street, but the detective was nowhere in sight among the blue leather jackets still clustered around the front of Clancy's. I shoved the disk back in my pocket and ducked around the corner of the building, heading for the fire escape ladder.

There would be plenty of time for mourning later. Right now, all I wanted to do was find a killer.

10

As soon as I crawled through my apartment window, I switched on my computer and booted up the mini-disk I had taken from John's PT, and the first thing I did was make a backup copy.

Call it paranoia, but I knew that it was only a matter of time before the cops discovered that the evidence bag had been unsealed; even though I had fooled Farrentino once, I wasn't going to count on his remaining stupid. The police could be here by morning with a search warrant. When the copy was made, I slipped it into a plastic case and took it into the bathroom, where I hid it beneath the toilet tank with a strip of electrical tape.

Back at my desk again, I rebooted the original disk and copied it onto the hard drive; once it was loaded into my system, I tried to punch up the root directory, only to find that I needed a password to get in. No problem there; not long ago, shortly after I had gone to work at the *Big Muddy*, John and I had agreed to share our passwords with each other, in case I ever needed to hack into his PT or vice versa. Being a faithful University of Missouri alumnus, his password was "Mizzou"; mine was "chickenlegs," for no other reason than I happened to be dining upon an Extra Crispy Recipe snack box from the Colonel at the time. I typed in "Mizzou," the system cleared me through, and I got my first peek at whatever had been contained in Dingbat's memory.

I let out a low whistle as the screen was immediately filled by a directory as long as a small-town phone book. A bar at the top of the screen told me that almost 100 megabytes of information had been copied into my system, leaving less than 50 kilobytes free on the disk. As I ran the cursor down the screen, a seemingly endless list of filenames scrolled upward, many of them suffixed as BAT or EXEC commands, none of them immediately recognizable.

An extremely complex program of some sort had been loaded into Dingbat's floptical drive shortly before John's death. Tiernan had no business carrying around something like this unless Beryl Hinckley had downloaded it into his PT during their encounter at the bar . . . but exactly what it was, I hadn't the foggiest idea. Cyberpunk, I am not; my hacking skills were only those of the average computer-literate college grad, and I didn't have the knowledge necessary to understand a program of this complexity.

One thing for damn sure: my best friend had been shot through the head with a laser beam shortly after receiving this program. And despite what Farrentino had said about his murder resembling the "Dark Jedi" killings, I had the gut feeling that John's death had not been a random shooting.

What if John had been assassinated?

And, to take this supposition one step further: what if John had been assassinated because of the contents of this very disk?

I took a deep breath, forcing myself to calm down. Don't get panicky. I leaned forward again and began to run further down the directory, trying to find something that looked like a main menu or even a READ ME file. I was like a blind man thrown into a large and unfamiliar room, but if I could just get hold of something I could use as a white cane, I might be able to . . .

The phone buzzed.

The answering machine was switched on, but without thinking I snatched the receiver off the cradle and lifted it to my ear. "Hello?" I said.

No voice from the other end of the line; the phonescreen remained blank. Figuring it for a wrong-number call, I was about to hang up when I heard, as if in the background, a brief, swift sequence of electronic snaps, chirps, and beeps.

"Hello?" I repeated. "Who's there?"

As soon as I spoke again, the electronic noise ceased. There was a moment of silence, and I had almost hung up when I suddenly heard a toneless voice speak from the other end:

"Hello . . . hello . . . who's there . . . hello . . ."

"Who is this?" I said, losing patience.

The screen flickered, then random fractals appeared, casting undulating images like electronic finger paintings. A couple more chirps and beeps, then there came a sound like an audiotape being replayed at high speed—high-pitched voices, as if Alvin and the Chipmunks were bleating nursery rhymes from an old NASA space probe lost out beyond Jupiter—as the fractals congealed and began to assume a vaguely human shape. Then:

"Hey, who is this? . . . hello . . . who's there? . . . hello . . ."

It was my own voice.

Now the head and shoulders of a person appeared on the screen, but his/her features were in constant flux: eyes, nose, lips, brow, chin, cheekbones, hairline, all changing more rapidly than my eye could follow. Sometimes the face looked like my own, and then it would be me as a woman, then as a bearded woman, then as a black man with a beard, then as a new face entirely.

"Who is this?" I demanded. "Who . . . hey, Jah, if this is you fucking around, I'm going to unscrew your head and shit down your—"

Throughout all the changes, the face's lips moved, yet my voice coming from the speaker no longer sounded quite like my own. It had a scrambled, surreal quality: *"Jah . . . if you're fucking around . . . hey, Jah, I'm going to shit down your head and unscrew your . . . who is this? . . . Jah, I'm going to unscrew your shit and fuck down your . . ."*

The face's permutations began to slow down, becoming distinctly male, getting younger. Again there were beeps, chirps, and a sound like a tape being fast-forwarded, and then:

"Rosen, Gerard . . . Gerard Rosen . . . Gerry Rosen . . . Can I talk to you, Daddy?"

A new face appeared on the screen.

I slammed down the receiver.

The face stared at me for another instant, then vanished entirely, leaving behind only a blank screen.

For a long time I simply stared at the phone. A soft nocturnal wind whispered outside the window like a ghost asking to come in. I felt my heart pound against the inside of my rib cage, smelled the acrid tang of my sweat. After five minutes my computer's screensaver switched itself on; bright, multicolored fractals began to undulate across the screen, Mandelbrot equations casting impermanent algorithmic sandpaintings, the black magic of higher mathematics.

And still I stared at the phone, unwilling to accept the face and voice I had just seen and heard.

God help me, it had been Jamie.

A sharp knock at the apartment door brought me back to the present.

"Who's there?" I called out. No reply; I thought I had been hearing things when there came another knock, a little harder this time.

Probably Chevy Dick, coming over to see if I wanted a beer or something. He had a keycard and knew the codes to disable the front door alarms. I wasn't in any mood for drinking, but I needed some company right now, so I stood up from the chair and headed for the door. "Okay, hold on," I muttered. "I'll be there in a—"

The door slammed open, its lock broken by the force of a violent kick, and four soldiers in riot gear swarmed into the loft.

"Freeze, asshole!" one of them yelled, crouching next to the door, his Heckler & Koch G-11 leveled straight at me. "ERA!"

A second later the fire-escape window was shattered by the impact of a rifle butt; I whipped around to see two more ERA troopers coming in through the window.

"Hey, what the fuck are—"

I didn't get the chance to complete this line of inquiry, as one of the grunts who had charged the front door tackled me from behind. The air was punched out of my lungs as I hit the wood floor face-first; I gasped, fighting for breath, and tried to raise myself on my elbows, only to be forced down when a heavy boot landed against my back.

"Stay down, asshole . . . !"

I was about to twist out from under the boot when I felt the blunt muzzle of a G-11 press against the nape of my neck.

"I said, stay down!"

I managed to nod my head and lie still, choking on the dust from the floor as I gasped for air, while I heard a cacophony of voices around me:

"Okay, we got him."

"Check the bathroom!"

"Somebody find a switch! Get some lights on in here!" A second later the room was flooded with light from the ceiling fixture.

"Bathroom's clear, Sarge! He's alone."

"Bell, check the desk. Look and see if he's got it."

Sounds of papers been rifled through on my desk, then the snap of the disk drive being ejected. "Right here, Sarge. He's got it on his screen now."

"Good deal. You and Todd pack up the CPU. Take all the disks you can find . . . grab all those papers, too. Find a box or something."

"Right, Sarge . . ."

"Romeo Charlie, this is Golf Bravo, do you copy, over . . ."

"Stay down, buddy. Just stay cool . . ."

My arms were yanked behind my back as, for the second time that night, a pair of plastic handcuffs were slipped around my wrists and tightened. The boot lifted from my back, but the rifle stayed in place.

"Man, this place smells like shit . . ."

"Belongs to a reporter, what do you expect?"

Laughter. "Shaddup, you guys . . . ten-four, Romeo Charlie. Premises secured, no one else present. Ten-fifteen-bravo, Charlie, over . . ."

I lay still on the floor, but I turned my head to see what was going on at my desk. A couple of troopers were dismantling my computer, one of them holding the CPU in his hands as the other disconnected the cables. A third soldier had found an empty carton and was shoving the manuscript of my novel into it; when he was done, he grabbed the cord of my telephone, ripped it straight out of the wall jack, and threw the phone into the box. Can't be too careful about these subversive telephones.

"What are you guys doing here?" I demanded. "Why are you—?"

"Shut up," the trooper behind me said.

I ignored him. "What am I being charged with? What's—"

"Shut up." The boot returned to my back, pinning me flat against the floor. "When we want you to talk, we'll tell you, okay? Now shut your mouth."

"Ten-four, Romeo Charlie. Ten-twenty-four and we'll be seeing you soon. Golf Bravo over and out . . . okay, guys, let's get out of here before the neighbors catch on."

The boot and the gun muzzle rose from my back, then two pairs of hands grabbed my arms and hauled me to my feet. "Okay, dickhead," one of the troopers murmured, "let's go catch a baseball game."

If I had any doubts about where I was headed, they were laid to rest by that comment.

I remained silent as I let them march me out the front door of my apartment. Another ERA soldier was standing on the second-story landing, his rifle propped against his hip. The sheet-metal door leading into the newspaper office was still shut; whoever had ordered this raid had apparently drawn the line at breaking and entering the *Big Muddy Inquirer*. Afraid of the adverse publicity, I suppose.

I was still wondering how they had managed to enter the building without triggering the alarms when we got down to the first floor. Another trooper was standing next to the alarm panel, the PT in his hands hardwired to its innards. He had managed to decode and disable the security system. He barely glanced at me as I was pulled out onto the sidewalk.

Geyer Street was empty except for the two gray Piranhas idling at the curb, their turret-mounted water cannons rotated toward the sidewalks on either side of the street. If there's anything more scary than seeing a couple of armored cars parked at your front door, I hope I never live to see it, but if the ERA had been anticipating a neighborhood riot over the arrest of a deadbeat reporter, they were disappointed. The sidewalks were empty, and no wonder; anyone with common sense was staying inside, peering through the slats of their window shades at what was going on.

A tow truck was parked in front of the two LAVs, its forklift gears whining as the front end of John's Deimos was raised off the street. They were taking everything that mattered—computers, John's car, telephones, even the manuscript of an unpublished book. No cops in sight, though, and that was a little puzzling. After all the local talent that had converged on Clancy's after John's murder, it was surprising to see that there were no police cruisers in sight, especially since I was apparently being busted for having stolen the micro-CD from the evidence bag . . .

A cold chill raced down my spine as the realization hit me: this was entirely an ERA operation. Keeping SLPD in the dark about this raid, in fact, was likely a top priority; the squad leader had probably been using a scrambled frequency when he had called back to headquarters to report his team's success.

A soldier opened the rear hatches of the first Piranha, then the two grunts who had escorted me down the stairs pushed me into the armored car. Two more climbed in behind them; one of them went forward into the narrow driver's compartment up front, while the other climbed a short ladder to the turret behind the water cannon.

The rear hatches were slammed shut again as the two soldiers sat me down on one of the fold-down seats. One of them sat next to me; the other took a seat directly across the narrow aisle. They rested their G-11s across their knees and said nothing; after a few moments, one of them found a pack of cigarettes in the pocket of his flak vest.

"I guess it would be too much to ask if you wouldn't smoke," I said. "It's kinda stuffy in here as it is."

The two troopers stared at each other, then broke up laughing. Their name badges read B. MULLENS and B. HEFLER. Bob and Bob, the Gestapo Twins.

"No, it's not too much to ask," said Bob Mullens as he pulled out a cigarette and lit it off the bottom of the pack. From his voice, I recognized him as the guy who had stuck a gun against the back of my head. "Hell, you can ask for anything you want . . ."

How about a slow, painful death from lung cancer? I didn't say anything; Mullens blew some smoke in my direction and favored me with a shit-eating grin, but when that didn't get a rise out of me he settled back against the padded back of his seat.

"Son," he drawled, "you are in a world of shit."

Hefler gave a high-pitched laugh at his partner's bit of wisdom. "Yeah, man," he said, "you're going to hell in a bucket."

Ask a silly question, get some stupid clichés. I silently stared at the metal floor beneath my feet, trying to figure out what was happening to me. After a minute we heard the driver shift gears; the vehicle lurched forward on its tandem wheels, diesel engines growling as the Piranha began to trundle down the street.

I was going to hell in a bucket, and I can't say I enjoyed the ride.

PART THREE

Phase Transition

(April 19, 2013)

11

It was a short, bumpy ride from Soulard to Busch Stadium, little more than a sprint down Broadway, but the LAV's driver seemed hell-bent on finding every pothole in the tortured asphalt and driving through it at top speed. My new pals Bob and Bob got a kick out of watching me try to remain seated with my hands cuffed behind my back. I rocked back and forth, my shoulder muscles aching a little with each unanticipated turn and jar the Piranha took; they thought it was pretty funny.

It's amazing how little it takes to amuse some people. I suppose they had already chewed up their rubber balls and tug-toys.

The bells in the Old Cathedral down by the riverside were tolling twelve times when the armored car slowed down. Its wheels bumped again, this time as if the Piranha was crawling over a curb, then the vehicle ground to a halt. There was a double-rap against the wall in front of the driver's compartment. Mullens stood up, grasped one of my arms, and pulled me out of my seat.

"End of the line, buddy," he said as Hefler unlatched the rear hatches and pushed them open. "Time for you to go see the colonel."

"Yeah," said Hefler as he stepped out of the vehicle. "And when he's through, maybe you can go for another ride with us. Would you like that, huh?"

I kept silent as Mullens hauled me out of the LAV. The vehicle had come to a stop in the middle of the wide plaza in

129

front of the stadium's Walnut Street entrance. Concrete barricades topped with coiled razor wire had been erected around the elm-lined plaza, surrounding the Piranhas parked in front of the closed-down ticket booths and dismantled turnstiles. ERA troopers were goldbricking against the statue of Stan Musial, stubbing out their cigarette butts against his bronze feet. Stan the Man was probably rolling in his grave.

The walkways winding around the curved outside walls of the stadium were vacant of baseball fans; the World Series pennants suspended from the ceiling of the ground-floor concourse hung limp and ignored, relics of a more innocent age. It had been a long time since anyone in this place had heard the crack of a bat or smelled a jumbo hot dog. That was one thing we had learned from all those two-bit dictatorships in Latin America: how to turn a good sports arena into a hellhole.

Bob and Bob escorted me across the plaza to a pair of boarded-up double doors beneath a tattered blue canvas awning. The doors led into a narrow lobby where two more soldiers were standing guard duty in front of a pair of elevator doors. One of the grunts reached out to press the Up button on the wall beneath a black plaque reading MEMBERS ONLY.

"Hey, wait a minute, guys," I said as the left elevator opened. "We can't go up there . . . we're not members."

Hefler actually seemed to hesitate for a moment, confirming my suspicion that he was too stupid even to have held down a job as a busboy when the club had been open. "Shut up, asshole," Mullens growled as he shoved me into the elevator.

I stifled a grin. Some people have no sense of humor.

We rode the elevator up to the loge level and the Stadium Club. I had been here a couple of times before with Uncle Arnie, who was well heeled enough to afford a gold membership card. In its time, the Stadium Club had been one of the ritzier places in the city: good food, good drink, a great view of the diamond from an enclosed eyrie overlooking left field.

When the elevator doors opened again, my first impression

was that the place hadn't changed since I had last seen it.
The oak reception desk was still there, facing a wall lined
with photos of players and pennant teams. The barroom still
looked much the same; the Budweiser and Michelob beer taps
were still in place behind the horseshoe-shaped bar, as was
the enormous framed photo of Ozzie Smith, the legendary
shortstop's arms raised in victory as he walked toward the
dugout during the final game of the '82 Series.

Then Bob and Bob led me farther into the long, concave
room, and I came to see that the club wasn't what it used
to be. The round tables and leather chairs were now stacked
on top of each other at the far ends of the room; the buffet
tables had been brought down to the club's lower deck so
that they were now pushed up against the tall glass windows
overlooking the field, and instead of rich, happy baseball fans
there were now uniformed men and women seated before the
windows, their faces illuminated by the blue glow of computer
terminals and TV monitors. The voices of KMOX baseball
announcers giving play-by-play coverage didn't come from
the ceiling speakers; all that could be heard in the darkened
room was the low monologue of flight controllers, droning a
police-state jargon of ten-codes into their headset mikes.

The Stadium Club had always been a bit snobbish for my
taste, but given a choice between a maître d' refusing to seat
me for wearing blue jeans and watching a bunch of ERA
androids manning a communications center, I would have
taken a pompous headwaiter anytime. Still, the real obscenity
wasn't here but beyond the windows, out on the playing field
beyond the deserted seat rows.

The diamond was gone, its canvas bases long since removed,
even the pitcher's mound taken away to another place. Beneath
the harsh glare of the stadium lights, a dozen or more helicopters were parked on the field, their rotors and fuselages
held down by guy lines while ground crews tinkered beneath
their engine cowlings or dragged fat cables to their fuel ports.
The giant electronic screens above the center field bleachers,
which had once displayed the game score, player stats, and
instant replays, were now showing cryptic alphanumeric codes
designating flight assignments and mission departure times.

An Apache was lifting off from the first-base zone, rising straight up until it cleared the high walls of the stadium. A couple of jumpsuited pilots were emerging from the home-team dugout behind home plate. Several ground crewmen were sitting on top of the dugout, swilling soft drinks as they rested their butts on the red-painted pennants from World Series games. In the days before ERA had taken over the city, it was unspoken heresy even to step on top of any of those emblems, and only the gods themselves were permitted in the Cardinals' locker room.

Now anyone could get an invitation to the dugouts. Closer to the Stadium Club windows, an Osprey's twin rotors were still in motion as a small group of handcuffed civilian prisoners were led down its ramp by gun-toting guards and marched single file toward the visiting team dugout and whatever brand of hell awaited them in the holding pens beneath the stadium.

Blasphemy.

Busch Stadium had always been the pride of St. Louis, one of the city's sacred places. Generations of baseball fans had watched the Cards win and lose in this ballpark, and even when the team had disastrous seasons, there had always been a certain sense of camaraderie. Now the stadium had been desecrated; even if ERA vacated the place tomorrow, its innocence would be forever lost.

The look on my face must have been obvious. Mullens, the funnyman of the Bob and Bob team, began to sing just above his breath as he stood behind me: "Let's go out to the ball game ... buy me hot dogs and beer ... we'll go up to the bleachers ... get drunk as shit and beat up some queers ..."

"Wrong town, jerkwad," I murmured. "You must be thinking about New York."

He grabbed my handcuffs and yanked them upward, threatening to dislocate my shoulders. My luck he would happen to be a Mets fan. I yelped in pain and pitched forward, nearly falling against the flight controller seated in front of me.

"Keep it up, pogey bait," Mullens growled in my ear, "and we'll be taking that ride sooner than you—"

"Corporal, is this the man we want to see?"

The new voice was calm and authoritative, its tone as casual as if the speaker had been asking about the time of day. Mullens suddenly relaxed his grip on the cuffs.

"That's him, Colonel," I heard a high-pitched voice say as I straightened up. "How'ya doing, Gerry?"

I looked around to see Paul Huygens standing beside me. Great. Like I didn't have enough problems already.

"Not too bad, Paul," I replied. "Funny though . . . seems like every time I turn around, you're here."

Huygens's grin became a thin smile. "I've been thinking much the same thing myself."

I was about to ask exactly what he was doing in the Stadium Club in the middle of the night when Colonel George Barris stepped forward.

I had no trouble recognizing Barris. Everyone in the city had become acquainted with the commander of ERA forces in St. Louis, through newspaper photos and TV interviews: a middle-aged gentleman with thin gray hair and a mustache, so average looking that it was easier to imagine him pushing a lawnmower around a suburban backyard than wearing a khaki uniform with gold stars pinned to the epaulets.

John had met Barris once, a few months ago when he had written a critical piece about ERA misconduct in the city. "This guy may look like a bank clerk," he had told me later, "but after a while you get the feeling that he's seen *Patton* a few too many times. He's a hard case, man . . ."

I would have to remember that.

"Mr. Rosen, I'm glad to meet you finally," he said formally. "I've enjoyed reading your columns in the *Inquirer*, although I don't necessarily agree with your opinions."

"Thank you, Colonel," I said. "I'd shake hands, but I seem to be having a little trouble using my arms lately."

He nodded his head ever so slightly. "Corporal, please release Mr. Rosen," he said, his eyes still fixed on me. "Then you and your partner may return to duty."

I felt Mullens move behind me, and a moment later the cuffs were severed by a jackknife. I flexed my arms and scratched an itch on my nose that had been bothering me for the last fifteen minutes. "*Muchas gracias*, Corporal," I said. "Thanks for offering me a lift home, but I think I'll find my own way, okay?"

Bob and Bob glowered at me, then they saluted the colonel and sulked their way out of the operations center. I made a mental note to send them a nice fruit basket.

"Well, Colonel," I said as I turned toward him, "I appreciate being shown around and all, but I think I'll be going now, if you don't mind."

Barris crossed his arms, still watching me carefully. "No, no, I'm afraid I *do* mind, Mr. Rosen." His voice was pleasant, but there was an edge beneath his erudite politeness. "My men have gone to considerable trouble to bring you here. I apologize for any rough treatment you may have experienced, but we still have a number of things to discuss before we let you go."

"No one charged me with anything—" I began.

"No sir," he went on, "but we certainly could if we wish. Theft of police evidence, for starters." Barris looked over his shoulder at the balcony just above us. "Lieutenant Farrentino, if you'll join us . . . ?"

Surprise, surprise. All my friends had come down to the club to see me tonight.

I looked up as Mike Farrentino stepped out of the shadows. He leaned over the railing, a sullen smile spread across his lean face. "Hello, Gerry," he said quietly. "I see you didn't get a chance to change your pants after all."

"Things got in the way, Mike," I said. "Sorry about the bag, but y'know how things are."

I assayed a sheepish shrug and a dopey grin as the three men stared at me. I wondered if it wasn't too late to catch up with Bob and Bob and see if that offer of a ride home was still valid.

"You're not being charged with anything," Barris said, "so long as you're willing to cooperate with us. We have a small crisis here, and we need your cooperation. Is that clear?"

"Like mud." I sighed and rubbed the back of my neck. "Look, I don't have the slightest idea what's going on around here—"

"You're full of it," Huygens muttered.

"Back off, Huygens," I said. "I'm not taking any shit from you right now."

Controllers cast brief glances over their shoulders at me; out of the corner of my eye, I could see another ERA trooper starting toward us, his right hand on the holstered butt of his shockrod.

I could have cared less. "Look, guys," I went on, trying to keep my temper and not doing a good job of it, "I've had a long day. My best friend has just been killed, my place was trashed, I was dragged down here by a couple of morons, and Prince Anal here"—I jabbed a finger at Huygens—"decided to throw me out of his party for no reason at all. So unless you've got something to say to me—"

"Be quiet!" Barris snapped.

Leave it to a military man to know how to get someone to shut up. I went silent, remembering exactly where I was and whom I was dealing with.

"Now listen up," he said, a little more quietly now, yet with hardness in his voice. "We've been polite with you so far . . ."

I started to open my mouth, intending to make some smart-aleck remark about Miss Manners's advice on how to properly put someone in handcuffs and give them a ride in a tank, but Barris stepped a little closer to put his face near mine. "If you persist," he said in a half-whisper, "I'll have you taken someplace where some of my men will enjoy making you more cooperative. Do you understand me, Mr. Rosen?"

I shut up, my wiseass remarks dying stillborn. There was no mistaking what he meant. Down there, beneath the stadium, were cold rooms with concrete walls, postmodern catacombs where someone could get lost forever. People had a habit of disappearing in Busch Stadium lately. I had heard the rumors, as had everyone else in the city, and Colonel Barris no longer looked like a retired bank clerk who sat around the house listening to old Carpenters records.

"Do you understand me?" he repeated.

I nodded my head.

"Good," he said. "Now if you'll follow me, we'll go to my

office where we can talk in private. We have someone waiting
for us."

He turned on his heel and began walking away, leading
the way toward a short stairway to the club's upper level.
Huygens fell in behind me, and Farrentino met us at the top
of the steps. Neither of them said a word to me, but Farrentino
shot me a brief look of warning: *don't screw around with this
guy . . . he means business.*

The colonel's office was located in the left rear corner of
the club, a small cubicle formed by hastily erected sheets of
drywall. A desk, a couple of chairs, a computer terminal, a
wall map of the city spotted with colored thumbtacks. Very
military, very spartan. The only decoration was a glass snowball on the desk, a miniature replica of the Arch sealed in with
a liquid blizzard.

A man was seated in a chair in front of Barris's desk. He
was dressed casually yet well: pressed jeans, a cotton polo
shirt, and a suede leather jacket. It was for that reason that
I didn't immediately recognize him when he turned around
to look at us as a trooper opened the door to let us inside. It
wasn't until he stood up and held out his hand that I realized
who he was.

"Mr. Rosen," he said, "I'm happy to meet you. I'm Cale
McLaughlin."

I shook the hand of the last person I expected to see in
Barris's office; although I tried to keep cool, my discomfiture
must have been obvious. "You're no doubt wondering what
I'm doing here," Tiptree's CEO said, favoring me with a
fatherly smile.

I shrugged. "Not really. You're probably the only person
here who has a membership card."

"Good point." McLaughlin gave a short laugh, then waved
me to the chair next to him. Farrentino sat down on the other
side, while Huygens leaned against a file cabinet. "But the fact
of the matter is that your friend's murder is of vital interest to
my company. When he learned of what happened tonight, Paul
called me and I came down here."

"It must have been on short notice," I murmured, glancing

at my watch. "It's been barely three hours since John was shot."

"Hmm . . . yes, it was short notice. And believe me, I'd much rather be in bed right now." McLaughlin's face became serious. "But, as I said, my company is greatly interested in what happened." He glanced at Barris. "Perhaps I should let the colonel begin, though. George?"

"You already know that your friend was investigating a recent murder when he was killed," Barris said as he took his own seat behind the desk. "What you don't know is why he was killed, nor who did it."

"And neither do you," I replied.

"No," Farrentino said. "That we do know—"

"We're way ahead of you, Gerry," Huygens interrupted. "You're good, sport, but not as good as we are."

"Yeah, right. Sure you do." I gently massaged my wrists, still feeling the chafe left by the handcuffs. "If you're so swift, then why do you need my help?"

Huygens opened his mouth as if to retort, but Barris cleared his throat; the other man shut up. McLaughlin remained quiet, a forefinger curled contemplatively around his chin as he listened. "What Mr. Huygens means is that we now have a suspect," the colonel said as he opened a desk drawer and pulled out a thick file folder. "What we have to do is catch him . . ."

He opened the folder, unclipped an eight-by-ten photo from a sheaf of paper, and slid it across the desk. I recognized the face as soon as I picked up the picture: the distinguished-looking gentleman with the gray Vandyke beard I had spotted at the Tiptree Corporation reception.

"You may have seen him when you visited my company this morning," McLaughlin said. "His name's Richard Payson-Smith. He's a senior research scientist at Tiptree . . . one of the top people behind our Sentinel R&D program, in fact."

"Born 1967 in Glasgow, Scotland," Barris continued, reading from the dossier. "Received his B.S. from the University of Glasgow, then immigrated to the United States in 1987, where he went on to receive both his master's degree and Ph.D. from the University of California-Irvine. After he became a naturalized citizen he went to work for DARPA at Los Alamos, where he was involved with various research projects until 2003, when he was recruited by Tiptree to head up a skunk-works team involved with the Sentinel program."

He paused, then looked at McLaughlin. The executive picked up the ball. "At this juncture, Mr. Rosen," McLaughlin said slowly, "we're about to walk out onto thin ice. We need to discuss matters with you that are classified Top Secret, and I have to know for certain that you will not discuss any of these secrets outside this room."

I opened my mouth to object, but he half-closed his eyes and held up his hand. "I know, I know. You're a reporter, so you're not in the habit of keeping secrets, nor did you ask to be involved in any of this. But we're in a bind, and we need to have your full cooperation, so much so that the colonel simply doesn't have time to ask the FBI to run a background check on you. Therefore, I have to ask you to sign something before we can go any further."

Barris reached into his desk again, rifled through some papers, and produced a three-page document. "This is a secrecy pledge," McLaughlin went on as Barris handed it across the desk to me. "In short, it says that you will not divulge to any third party any classified information that has been confided to you. Once you've signed it, you could be arrested under federal law for various felony charges—possibly including high treason—if you reveal anything that's said in this room."

I glanced through the document; as much as I could make out the single-spaced legalese, it was as McLaughlin said. The minimum penalty for airing out Uncle Sam's dirty laundry was ten years in the pen and a fine so harsh I would never pay it off by stamping out license plates in Leavenworth.

"Sounds pretty stiff, Mr. McLaughlin." I dropped the pledge back on Barris's desk. "What makes you think I'd want to sign anything like this?"

Barris shrugged. "For one thing, it'll get us a little closer to nailing the guy who killed John Tiernan," he said. "That should mean something to you. Second, it'll help you get your belongings returned. And third, once this whole affair is said and done, you'll be the one reporter in town who has the inside story . . . within certain limitations, of course."

"Uh-huh. And what happens if I don't sign?"

The colonel smiled and said nothing. Farrentino stared at me, his face dark and utterly serious. Huygens pulled his hands out of his pockets, folded his arms across his chest, and studied me like an alley cat contemplating a small mouse it had just cornered. McLaughlin simply waited for me to add two and two together.

If there's anything I've learned in life, it's how to take a hint.

Now I knew the reasons why they had arrested me without charges, hustled me in here in handcuffs, and allowed me to see a group of prisoners being herded down to underground cells beneath the stadium. They had wanted to show me the true value of my life. These men could make me disappear without so much as a ripple if I refused to play their game. It was like the old saw about some guy asking his lawyer what his negotiating position should be. "Bending over," the lawyer says.

It was midnight, and if I didn't say or do the right thing, I'd never see the sun again.

After a moment, Barris picked up a pen from his desk and, without saying a word, held it out to me. I hesitated, then took the pen from his hand, laid the document flat on his desk, and signed on the dotted line at the bottom of the third page. I wonder if Faust had felt the same way.

"You've done the right thing, Gerry," Huygens said. "For once you're playing with the right team."

"Yeah," I whispered under my breath. "Call me when we make the playoffs."

McLaughlin probably heard me, but he didn't say anything. When I was through signing my pact with the devil, Barris accepted it from me. He studied my signature for a second, then slipped it into the drawer and slammed it shut.

"Thank you, Mr. Rosen," he said as he cupped his hands together. "You may not believe it now, but you have done the right thing. For this your country is grateful."

McLaughlin reached across the desk to pick up the glass

snowball; he shook it a couple of times, then held it upright in his hand as he watched the tiny blizzard swirl around the miniature Gateway Arch.

"And now," he said, "it's time to tell you about Ruby Fulcrum."

12

When the meeting was over, Mike Farrentino escorted me out of the Stadium Club. We didn't say anything to each other while we rode the elevator down to the ground level, and once we had cleared the guarded front foyer I turned to walk away from the stadium.

"Hey, Rosen!" he called out. "Wait up a minute!"

I turned back around, hands shoved in the pockets of my jacket, and waited for him to walk over to me. "Need a lift back to your place?" he asked. "I got my car parked over here."

"No thanks," I said. "I'll hoof it. It's not far."

Nor was a ride necessary. Barris had assured me that I now had safe conduct on the streets after curfew, so long as I played by his rules. He had given me a laminated plastic card before I left and told me to carry it on my person at all times; it was printed with the ERA logo, and Barris told me if I was stopped or questioned by an ERA patrol, I was to show them the card. Sort of like getting a hall pass from the principal.

The plaza was almost empty now, save for a few troopers manning the barricades. Most of the LAVs I had seen earlier had vanished, presumably off patrolling various parts of the city. The downtown area somehow looked very peaceful: no traffic on the streets, no city noises, only the faint twitter of night birds in the branches of the elm trees, abruptly broken by the low moan of an Apache coming in for a landing within the stadium walls.

141

Farrentino looked up at the chopper as it flew low overhead. "How much of that do you believe?" he asked in a soft voice, casting a glance at the ERA soldier standing guard near the Stadium Club entrance. "I mean, how much of that was bull-shit or what?"

I hesitated. I had my opinions, but I wasn't sure if I was ready to trust them to a cop. "I don't know, Lieutenant," I said carefully. "You're the one who's been investigating this mess, so you tell me."

"Mike," he said. "My friends call me Mike—"

"And so I'm your friend now, huh, Mike?" I looked him straight in the eye. "Most of my friends wouldn't have my door kicked down and have me dragged off in the middle of the night."

"Whoa, fella. Chill off." He held his hands up defensively. "The colonel ordered the raid, not me. I simply reported that the evidence bag had been tampered with and that the disk was missing and that you were the most likely suspect. He was the one who sent in the goon squad . . ."

"Yeah, sure, Mike. Have a nice night." I started to turn away again, but then he grabbed me by the arm. Before I could do anything, he pulled something out of his raincoat pocket and held it out to me.

It was Joker. "I got it out of the impoundment room when I went to take a leak," he explained. "You should be getting the rest of your junk back sometime tomorrow."

I took Joker from his hand and studied it. The PT didn't look as if it had been tampered with—even the mini-disk was still in drive—but I couldn't be sure until I had Jah run it through a full diagnostic. "Thanks," I said as I slipped the little 'puter in my jacket pocket. "I'll catch you later—"

"Look, Gerry," he said, his voice almost a whisper now, "I know you don't believe this, but . . ."

He hesitated. "Things aren't always what they seem, y'know what I mean? I don't think Barris and McLaughlin gave either of us the full lowdown. In fact, I don't think this Payson-Smith character is the mad scientist they made him out to be."

"Yeah?" The night was getting cold; I zipped up the front of my jacket. "And what do *you* think is the full lowdown?"

"I don't know yet. All I know is, I smell a rat." He paused, looking over his shoulder again. "You may not believe this," he went on, "but truth is, not everyone in authority is crazy about ERA. We might have a lot of problems in St. Louis right now, but we don't need tanks and helicopters to get them fixed." He shrugged. "They're only making things worse . . ."

"I couldn't agree more," I said, "but that still doesn't make me trust you. So far as I can tell, you're just a big swinging dick with a badge."

Farrentino turned red, but he nodded his head. "I understand that, but let me tell you . . . there's some bigger swinging dicks out there who are getting out of line, and I don't trust them any more than you trust me."

I looked into his face and saw only honesty. He was no longer a homicide detective and I was no longer a reporter; we were now only two men who had seen a lot of crazy shit go down in recent months and were scared by what was happening to our hometown. I've never been the greatest fan of the SLPD as a whole, but I knew that there were individual cops who *did* care about their line of work, who weren't just playing out old cop-show fantasies of busting heads and breaking down doors. Mike Farrentino might be one of these guys.

And besides, I had a weird hunch I wanted to follow up on . . .

"You say you got a car parked around here?" I asked. He nodded. "Want to give me a lift out to Webster?"

He glanced at his watch and shrugged. "Sure. I'm off the clock and it's on my way home. Why Webster?"

"I want to drop in on my ex," I said as I began to follow him toward the unmarked Chrysler four-door parked on the street just beyond the barricades. "Give her a big surprise when I show up at one o'clock in the morning in a cop car."

The drive out to Webster Groves didn't take long. Farrentino hopped on I-44 at the Poplar Street Bridge, and traffic in the westbound lanes was very sparse, mostly interstate trucks on their way to Springfield or Oklahoma or Texas. A light rain had begun to fall, and the car was filled with the sound of the windshield wipers and the ethereal murmur of voices from the police scanner mounted beneath the dash.

We didn't say much to each other. He was tired, I was tired, and all we wanted to do was to get home, although his wife was expecting him to come through the door while mine . . . well, I would have to cross that doormat when I got to it. I lay back in the seat, watched the trucks pass by, and contemplated all that had been told to me in Barris's office.

Mainly, it was a matter of counting all the occasions my bullshit detector had rung a bell.

Ernest Hemingway, the godfather of all self-respecting word pimps, once said that the most valuable gift a writer could have was an unshakable, foolproof bullshit detector. For reporters, that means learning to know instinctively when someone is trying to pull a fast one. I've grown a half-decent b.s.-o-meter over a lifetime of writing, and even though it's neither unshakable nor foolproof, it had rung at least four, maybe five times while I was sitting in the Stadium Club.

Ruby Fulcrum, McLaughlin had said, was the Pentagon code name for an R&D project within the Tiptree Corporation's Sentinel program: the development of a precise space-based tracking system to pinpoint the trajectories of subor-bital ICBMs. The first major obstacle had been to develop an energy weapon that could penetrate Earth's atmosphere without losing too much power, and that had been licked when the whiz kids at Los Alamos had invented a chemical laser that substituted fluorine/deuterium for ordinary hydrogen as its fuel source.

The next big hurdle had been to devise a c-cube system for *Sentinel 1*. Given the chance that a missile might be fired from a ship or sub off the Atlantic coast, *Sentinel*'s onboard computer system would have to be virtually autonomous, capable not only of detecting and tracking an ICBM during its boost phase, and thus enabling the satellite to shoot it down before it reentered the atmosphere, but also of differentiating between possible decoy-missiles and real targets. The problem was made even more hairy by the fact that if an SLBM was launched from a vessel just off the Eastern seaboard, *Sentinel 1* would have only a few minutes to accurately detect, track, and destroy the missile before its nuclear warhead detonated above Washington or New York.

Richard Payson-Smith had been the leader of the Ruby Fulcrum team, since his scientific background included both high-energy lasers and cybernetics. The team had also included three other scientists: Kim Po, a young immigrant from United Korea who had previously worked with Payson-Smith at Los Alamos; Jeff Morgan, even younger than Kim, who had been recruited straight from MIT to work on the program, and—no surprise here, although I had been careful not to let on—Beryl Hinckley, a former CalTech professor who had recently escaped from academia to pursue a more lucrative career in private industry.

"We knew that Richard had some misgivings about *Sentinel* when the company assigned him to the program," McLaughlin had said. "He had a—well, call it a pacifist streak, if you will—but we needed his expertise nonetheless. We thought that, since *Sentinel* is purely defensive in nature, he would overcome his leftist tendencies. And so it seemed, at least at first . . ."

But as the project went along and the team gradually managed to overcome the technical hurdles, Payson-Smith's behavior had become increasingly erratic. His temper became shorter; he began to berate his colleagues over minor mistakes or even for taking time to answer personal phone calls or making dentist appointments in the middle of the week. Payson-Smith managed to calm down after a while, but as he did he also began to voice his objections to *Sentinel*, calling it a "doomsday machine," "a Pentagon war wagon," and so forth. As Ruby Fulcrum's objectives were gradually achieved and *Sentinel 1* inched closer to deployment, Payson-Smith became actively hostile toward the other three members; no one dared venture into his office lest they be subjected to a political harangue. He had also become manic-depressive, sliding into silent fugues that could last for weeks on end.

"Didn't your company notice?" I had asked. "If the project was that crucial, why didn't you have him replaced, or at least force him to seek psychiatric—"

"Because, as you said, the project was crucial." Huygens gave me an arch look: *you don't know what you're talking about.* "The program was on a time-critical basis, so we couldn't just up and fire him. Where would a replacement come from? How could we get one to fit in with the team at this late stage? We—"

McLaughlin shot a look at Huygens; the PR man shut up. "It was impossible to get Richard to see the staff psychologist," McLaughlin continued in more patient tones. "When we made appointments for him, he'd find a way to avoid them. He was stubborn and, well . . ." He raised his hands in helplessness. "We just had to work with him and hope for the best."

That was the first time my bullshit detector had gone off. Now, upon reflection, I knew why.

First, whatever purpose Payson-Smith had fulfilled in the Ruby Fulcrum team couldn't have been so critical that Tiptree had been unable to replace him, even in a pinch. However brainy this man was, I hadn't heard his name mentioned in the same breath as Robert Oppenheimer's, and they had replaced him, too, way back when. Oppenheimer's only mistake had been in openly expressing his objections to the atomic bomb, and that was after it was exploded over Japan. No one had ever claimed he was mentally ill, only that he was a suspected commie sympathizer.

If Huygens was telling me the truth, then Payson-Smith should have been canned immediately, for being mentally unhinged *and* opposed to Sentinel before it was even built, let alone made operational. But they wouldn't have kept him on the project . . . and that, I now realized, was why the first alarm had rung.

At the same time this was going on, McLaughlin continued, certain spare parts and lab instruments had turned up missing from the company storerooms; they included various high-quality mirrors, lenses, Pyrex tubes, small carbon dioxide and water tanks, and a portable vacuum pump. The theft of the items had not been detected, it later turned out, because someone had managed to access the company's computer inventory system and delete their removal from the records. The loss was discovered only

when other scientists complained to the company comp-
troller that they couldn't find items that had been there last
week.

Then, almost exactly one week ago, Kim Po was found
dead outside his condominium in Richmond Heights. He had
apparently been coming home from a late night at the lab
when he was shot just outside the condo's front door . . . not
by a conventional rifle, but by a laser weapon of some sort,
one that had drilled a self-cauterizing hole straight through
the back of his head from a parked car. As with John's
murder, no one had heard gunfire, nor had a bullet been
recovered from either man's body.

"We'll cut to the chase," Barris said. "Judging from the
information Cale has given us and the near identical circumstances of both Dr. Kim and Mr. Tiernan's murders, it seems
as if a high-power laser had been used."

McLaughlin coughed into his fist. "A CO_2 laser rifle, to
be exact," he said. "Not like something you see in movies,
of course. It would be extremely large and cumbersome . . .
at least the size of a rocket launcher, in fact . . . but my people
tell me it could produce a beam capable of burning through
metal, wood, plastic, just about anything . . . and that includes
flesh and bone."

He shook his head. "It's a nasty weapon, probably even
more powerful than the one that kid in Chicago used a couple
of years ago. Silent, invisible, absolute flat trajectory, almost
infinite range. If you had a good infrared sight to go with it,
you could fire it through a closed window, provided it was
made of nonreflective glass, and hit a target several blocks
away. No one would even know where the shot came from."

"And you think someone from Tiptree concocted this thing?"
I asked.

McLaughlin glanced hesitantly at both Barris and Huygens.
He put the glass snowball down on the desk and leaned forward,
his arms resting on his knees. "No, not just anyone," he replied,
looking embarrassed by the admission. "We think Richard's
the one. He had the training and the technical ability, plus
access to the parts he needed." He looked at Mike Farrentino.
"Lieutenant? If you'll continue . . . ?"

For the first time since we had entered the colonel's office, Farrentino spoke up. "After Mr. Huygens tipped us off," he said quietly, "some of my people visited Payson-Smith's home earlier this evening. He was missing, but they found a small workshop in his basement. Something had been built on a bench down there, all right, and there were pieces of burned-through metal that looked as if they might have been used for target practice."

"But why would he . . . ?"

"Why would he kill Dr. Kim and Mr. Tiernan?" Barris shrugged. He picked up the glass snowball and juggled it in his hands. "Who knows what goes on in a sick mind? Maybe he's upset at the other members of his team for having built *Sentinel* . . . that's our theory, at any rate. First he knocked off Dr. Kim, then he tracked down Dr. Hinckley when she was trying to tell Tiernan about Kim's murder and tried to kill her, too. Unfortunately he nailed your friend instead."

I started to ask another question, but Huygens beat me to it. "We did our best to keep Kim's murder out of the press. There was only a small item in the next morning's *Post-Dispatch* about it, but we managed to get their reporters to believe that Po had been killed during a robbery attempt . . . but Beryl obviously found out the truth and decided to go to your paper instead."

"That's another reason why we suspect Payson-Smith," the colonel said. "He was one of the few people who could have learned of her plans to meet Tiernan at the bar tonight."

McLaughlin raised a hand. "Before you ask why Payson-Smith didn't kill them both when he had the chance . . . according to my people, this laser rifle apparently consumes a lot of power. It would have to be run off an independent current, so it takes about a minute for its battery to recharge before each shot."

"Uh-huh," I said. "So Hinckley suspected that Payson-Smith was the guy behind Kim's murder and went to John to tell him the story."

Barris and McLaughlin both nodded their heads, and that was the second time my bullshit detector went off.

They didn't know it, but I had seen Hinckley and Payson-Smith talking to each other during the reception. For a woman who suspected her boss of having gone psycho and killing one of her friends with a home-built laser, she had not appeared apprehensive about being in his company. Nor had Payson-Smith struck me as the homicidal maniac type. Yeah, maybe you never know for sure. When some nut with a machine gun goes on a rampage in a shopping mall, his neighbors invariably describe him as a nice, quiet person who always minded his own business. Yet my guts told me that Payson-Smith just seemed the wrong guy to be carrying this sort of rap.

And then there were other implausibilities. Even if Payson-Smith was the sociopathic killer these guys made him out to be, how could he have known where Hinckley would be tonight? After all, she had been the one who had told me to pass the message to John. I had not disclosed this to anyone else. So how could Payson-Smith have known where these two people would be meeting each other?

For that matter, why were these guys so certain it was Beryl Hinckley who had met Tiernan at Clancy's? "Middle-aged black lady" was a description that could fit a few hundred thousand people in St. Louis, but that was how Farrentino had described Hinckley to me when I had been summoned to the murder scene.

And why, on the basis of such circumstantial evidence, were McLaughlin and Huygens here at all, putting the blame on one of Tiptree's own scientists?

The bullshit detector was sounding five alarms now; fire engines were leaving the station, and the dalmatians were howling like mad. Yet I continued to play the dummy; I stretched back in my chair, resting my feet against the bottom of Barris's desk. "Okay," I said. "So you've got a mad scientist on the loose. Why are you telling me this?"

Barris didn't like my boots touching his desk. He stared at me until I dropped them back to the floor, then he went on. "When you took Tiernan's PT, there was the possibility that you might have found some evidence that could conclusively link Payson-Smith to Kim's murder. We needed to get that back at all costs, and that's why you were brought in."

"I can understand that," I said. "But why the rest of the—"

Barris raised a finger, a silent admonition for me to shut up. "There's also the possibility that Dr. Hinckley may try to contact you, now that Mr. Tiernan is dead. We haven't been able to locate her since the shooting, and we suspect that she has gone underground to avoid being killed. So has the other member of the Ruby Fulcrum team, Dr. Morgan."

He put down the glass ball and leaned forward across the desk. "Mr. Rosen, I realize that there is little reason for you to trust us," he said. "ERA has a bad reputation in this city, and as easy as it may be for me to put all the blame on the media, I know that my men haven't always . . . well, behaved themselves. But this once, we need your cooperation. We're trying to track down a killer, and we're also trying to save the lives of two valuable people."

"Uh-huh." The bullshit was getting so thick in there, I thought I was going to need a shovel just to get to the door.

"If you hear from either Dr. Hinckley or Dr. Morgan, we need to hear from you at once," Barris went on. He pulled a calling card from a box on his desk and handed it to me. "That's how you can reach me personally, any time of the day or night."

I glanced at the card. No phone number was printed on it, only Barris's name and the ERA logo. The codestrip on the back would connect with his extension if I passed it in front of a phonescanner. I nodded my head as I tucked the card into my shirt pocket.

"Here's something else you may need," he went on, and that's when he passed me the plastic card and explained how it could be used to get me through ERA blockades.

"We also need you to keep quiet about this matter until it's resolved," he went on. "When that happens, you'll have the complete story from us . . . and you'll have helped to bring your friend's killer to justice. Do you understand?"

"Yes, sir," I replied. "I hope I can be of service."

What should I have said? No, sir, this place reeks like a barnyard and you can take me down to the basement now?

Barris nodded, then he stood up from his desk. So did McLaughlin; once more, he extended his hand to me. "Pleasure to meet you, Mr. Rosen," he said as I shook his hand again. "I'm glad to have you on our side."

Farrentino pushed back his chair and stood up. Huygens gave me a perfunctory nod. Barris glanced at Farrentino. "Now, Lieutenant, if you will kindly escort Mr. Rosen to the street . . . ?"

I was free to go—but I was certainly not free. There were too many secrets, too many lies.

Too much bullshit.

13

"Which exit do I take?" Farrentino asked.

The light rain had become a steady downpour, but through the darkness and drizzle I could make out the familiar landmarks of Webster Groves from the interstate. The sign for the Shrewsbury Avenue exit was coming up. "This one will do," I said.

The detective nodded as he swerved into the right lane. "I take it your ex isn't expecting you," he said, following the long curve of the ramp as it led up the street overpass. "Are you sure it's okay for me to be dropping you off?"

"I guess it's okay," I replied as I pointed toward the left; he waited until a street cleaner 'bot rumbled through the intersection, then turned onto Shrewsbury. "She'll let me in, if that's what you're asking."

"That's what I'm asking." He reached into his coat pocket and pulled out a pack of cigarettes. "Worst thing a cop can do is get caught in the middle of a domestic quarrel. Y'know that when cops get injured in the line of duty, it's most often while breaking up a household fight? I damn near got my left ear sliced off with a vegetable knife that way, back when I drove a cruiser."

The intersection of Big Bend was coming up, and I pointed to the left again. "That's not going to happen here," I said. "For one thing, she's not really my ex. I just call her that."

"Separation?" He lighted his cigarette while making the turn, catching the green light just as it was turning yellow. A blue-and-white passed him in the opposite lane; he flashed his brights at it, and the officer driving the cruiser gave him a brief wave. It was the only other vehicle on the street, despite the fact that Webster was one of the few neighborhoods in the city that wasn't under dusk-to-dawn curfew. "Sometimes it's better that way," he went on. "Why did you guys get separated?"

"You ask a lot of questions."

"It's my job. Besides, I'm just asking . . ."

His voice trailed off as if anticipating a reply, but I didn't answer immediately. It had been a few months since I had last visited this neighborhood, and I wanted to look around. Webster Groves had ridden out the quake pretty well, at least in comparison to the parts of St. Louis that had been built on sandy loam or had been undermined by the tunnels of lost clay mines. Some homes had collapsed, a couple of strip malls had fallen down, but overall this quaint old 'burb of midwestern-style frame houses hadn't been significantly damaged. I didn't even see any ERA patrols.

"Go a few more blocks, then turn right on Oakwood," I said.

"Okay." Farrentino was quiet for a few moments. "Not going to talk about it, are you?"

"Talk about what?"

He shook his head. "You're going to have to trust somebody sooner or later, Gerry," he murmured. "I shouldn't have to tell you that you've got your hand stuck in a hornet's nest. Either you talk to me, or you talk to the colonel or McLaughlin, but eventually you're going to have to talk to somebody."

It was true; he knew it, and I knew it. I was treading on hot coals now, and there were damned few people I could count on to get me through this firewalk. Before I could commit myself either way, though, there were a few questions that still had to be cleared up in my own mind. Stopping by for a visit with Marianne, even in the middle of the night, was the first step.

"I'll let you know, Mike," I said as he took the turn onto Oakwood. "Right now, all I want to do is get home."

Home was an old, three-story Victorian on a quiet residential street, a one-hundred-twenty-year-old former farmhouse that had been renovated at least three or four times since the beginning of the last century. Marianne and I had bought the place shortly after we had moved back to St. Louis; if I had known the city was going to get socked by a quake, I might not have signed the mortgage papers, but to my surprise the house had only swayed during New Madrid. The house next door, which was only half as old, had fallen flat, but by some quirk of nature our place had survived, suffering only the loss of the carport and an oak tree in the front yard.

In that respect alone, we had been lucky. The house had made it through the quake; it was the family living inside that had been destroyed.

After Mike Farrentino dropped me off at the curb, I trudged up the walk and climbed the stairs to the front porch. A downstairs light was on, but the upper floors were darkened. Security lamps hidden beneath the porch eaves came on as soon as I approached the door; I still had a key, but I figured it would be polite if I touched the doorplate instead.

"Mari, it's me," I said. "Will you get up and come let me in?"

There was a long pause. I turned my face toward the concealed lens of the security camera and smiled as best I could, knowing that she was rolling over in bed to check the screen on the night table. Probably half-asleep, maybe knocking away the paperback thriller she had been reading just before she turned off the light. Unshaven, haggard, hair matted with rain, and wearing drenched clothes, I realized that I must resemble the bad guy in her latest novel.

"Gerry . . . ?" Her voice sounded fuzzy with sleep. *"Gerry, what the hell are you doing here?"*

"It's a long story, babe." I ran a hand through my hair, brushing it away from my face. "I'm sorry I woke you up, but—"

"Are you drunk again?" Her voice, no longer quite so sleepy, was tinged with irritation. *"I swear to God, if you've been drinking, you can—"*

"I'm not drunk, Mari, I promise you. It's just . . ." I sighed, half-closing my eyes. "Look, I'm really tired. I've just had a helluva night and I can't go back to my place, so just please let me in, okay?"

Again, another pause, a little longer this time. For the first time since I had asked Farrentino for a lift out here, a disturbing notion crossed my mind: perhaps she was not alone tonight. I hadn't shacked up with any other women since the beginning of our separation, as tempted as I had been from time to time. The thought had never seriously occurred to me, nor had Marianne told me about any new men in her life. Yet things could have changed; she might have some young bohunk in bed right now, a little lost puppy she had picked up at one of the nearby Webster University hangouts.

I stepped away from the camera to check the end of the driveway next to the house. Only her car was parked there, a power cable running from its battery port to the side of the house. Of course, that alone meant nothing. Postmen walk by every day, and so do joggers in tight nylon shorts.

I heard locks being buzzed open, then the door opened a few inches. "Gerry?" I heard her say. "Are you out there?"

"Right here." I quickly stepped away from the porch railing. Even when she was practically somnambulant, with her shoulder-length hair in knots and wearing a ragged terrycloth robe, Marianne was one of the most beautiful women I have ever met. Husbands are usually blind to the imperfections of their wives, of course, but that wasn't the case with Mari; my eyes didn't lie, and she was still good looking. Thirty years of ofttimes hard living had treated her well; she still looked much the same as she did when I had met her in college. She had regained her figure not long after Jamie's birth, and even though there were the first hints of gray in her dark hair, she could have passed for twenty-four.

Not that she was in any mood for compliments. "Gerry, what are you doing here?" she repeated. "For chrissakes, I just went to bed . . . and what are you looking at the driveway for?"

"Just seeing how the car's holding up," I said quickly. "You renewed your plates, didn't you?"

Her expression became puzzled. "You didn't come all the way out here to check my renewal sticker," she said. "What's going on, Gerard?"

She called me Gerard. When she used my full first name, it

usually meant she was pissed off. No wonder; for Marianne, getting a full night's sleep was a serious business, and woe be to the friend, relative, or former spouse who woke her out of bed after eleven o'clock. "I'm sorry if I caught you at a bad time, babe," I said, "but I need three things from you."

She let out an exasperated sigh and sagged against the door frame. "Let me guess," she said. "One of them is money, and the second is sex. What's the third? The car?"

It might have been funny if it wasn't true. When we had agreed that a separation was probably the best thing for both of us, after I had moved to a motel and before I had found a new job, those were the three favors I most commonly called to ask of her: wheels to get around in, a ten or twenty to tide me over till the next paycheck, and a quick roll in the hay because I was so damn lonely and because I still believed sex would heal all the wounds. All three she had agreed to, at one time or another, until she hardened her heart and told me that I was on my own. Hell, the only reason why we still hadn't become officially divorced was because neither of us could afford lawyer bills right now.

"Hey, if you want to have sex with me and give me some bucks and the car in return—" I began, and she started to slam the door in my face until I pushed my hand against the knob. "Wait, I'm just kidding. Seriously . . ."

Again the sigh as she opened the door again. "Seriously what?"

Now was no time to bullshit my wife, even if she hated my guts. "I need a place to crash," I said. "Just for tonight, I swear . . . and I need to use the computer."

"Uh-huh." She gazed at me indifferently. "A bed and the computer. Yeah. What else?"

"Hey, I can sleep on the couch—"

"Damn straight you're going to sleep on the couch," she replied. "What's the third thing, Gerard?"

I hesitated; this was probably the biggest favor of all. "The third thing is no questions asked." I took a deep breath. "I'm in trouble, kiddo. Big trouble."

"Oh, Christ." She sighed as her eyes rolled upward. "You're running from the cops, aren't you?"

I almost broke down laughing. "Babe, a cop gave me a lift out here—"

"Uh, huh. Sure . . ."

I raised my hands. "Believe me, Marianne, if this was going to get you in any trouble, I wouldn't be here right now. I'm not in trouble with the cops." *Not technically, anyway,* I thought. "All I need is the couch," I went on, "and to use the office computer for an hour or so. I don't want your money, I don't want to sleep with you, and I'll call a cab bright and early tomorrow morning. Okay?"

She sighed again, closing her eyes as if she was carrying the burdens of the world on her shoulders. "Jeez, Gerry, why can't you go bug John for this?"

Because John is dead, I almost blurted out, but I held my tongue. Telling her would only have prompted all the questions I wanted to avoid, and it was far safer for her to remain ignorant. I was lucky that she obviously hadn't seen the late news on one of the local TV stations or hadn't yet received a call from Sandy Tiernan.

"Please," I said. "Just do it for me, okay?"

She gazed at me for another moment, then she pushed the door open a little wider and stepped aside. "All right," she said. "But remember . . . you're sleeping on the couch."

The house was a little cleaner than it had usually been before I moved out, yet otherwise everything was much the same. She hadn't changed the living room furniture or taken any of the prints from the walls; although she had removed our wedding photos, there were still baby and toddler pictures of Jamie on the fireplace mantel. Marianne let me grab a Diet Dr. Pepper from the fridge, then went upstairs to gather some sheets and a spare pillow from the linen cabinet while I retreated to her home office.

The office was located in the rear of the ground floor, in what had been a den before we had put in floor-to-ceiling bookshelves. Before the quake hit, we had shared that space; she had used it during the day to telecommute to her insurance company's home office in Kansas City, and when she was through at five o'clock it became my study for the writing of the Great American Unreadable Novel. I noticed that she had removed my books and mementos from the shelves, but I didn't want to make an issue of it. Right now, I was interested in only one thing.

I found the plastic CD-OP filebox on a small shelf beneath the desk; the particular disk for which I was searching was contained in a scratched, often-opened case marked FAMILY. Marianne must have been looking at it often; it was at the front of the box, in front of the business disks. I pulled out the case and opened it, and after switching on the computer and opening the REVIEW window, I slipped the disk into the optical diskette drive.

Starting shortly after we became engaged, Marianne and I had videoed almost everything we did, using a camcorder one of her relatives had given her at the bridal shower. Hiking in the White Mountains of New Hampshire, summer scenes on Cape Cod, strange little home movies when we were both full of wine and creativity, the wedding day ceremonies, and the honeymoon trip to Ireland . . . we had recorded everything, and stored the bits and bytes on CD-OP for replay on our computer as an electronic family album.

We had gotten bored of the novelty after a while, and thus there were large chronological gaps on the menu until Jamie was born, when we had rediscovered the camcorder and started making the inevitable baby pictures. As a result, the submenu screen showed a lot of filenames marked JAMIE.1, JAMIE.2, JAMIE.3, and so forth, one for each birthday he had passed. Yet there was one piece of footage in particular, lodged in JAMIE.6, that I now needed to see.

After we had moved back to St. Louis, there had been a rash of kidnappings in the city. Children were vanishing from schoolbus stops and playgrounds and shopping malls, rarely to be seen again by their parents, and then sometimes not alive. The police never caught the evil bastards who had stolen these kids, and only God knows what happened to the ones who were not found, but Marianne and I did what the local authorities suggested parents should do: videotape their kids in advance, so that the footage could be used to identify lost children should the unthinkable happen to them.

It had taken me a while, but something about the weird phone call I had received just before the ERA soldiers broke down the door of my apartment had jogged an old memory. After I opened the VIDEOVIEW window on the computer screen, I moused JAMIE.6 and the REPLAY command; it took me only a couple of minutes to find the footage I remembered shooting of him, just a few weeks before he was killed.

And now here was Jamie, very much alive and well, sitting in his child-size rocking chair in the living room. He was wearing blue jeans and his favorite St. Louis Cardinals sweatshirt; just a cute little kid, both bored and embarrassed to have his dad making yet another video of him.

My voice, off-camera: *"Okay, kiddo, what's your name?"*

Jamie, pouting, wishing to be anywhere but here: *"Jamie . . ."*

Me again: *"And what's your last name?"*

Jamie looks down at the floor, his hands fidgeting restlessly on the armrests of his chair: *"Jamie Rosen, and I'm six years old . . ."*

My voice, prodding him gently from behind the camera: *"That's good! Now what's your mommy's and daddy's names?"*

His face scrunches up in earnest concentration, the child who has only recently learned that his folks have names besides Mommy and Daddy: *"My daddy's name is Gerard Rosen . . . Gerry Rosen . . . and Mommy's . . . my mommy's name is Marianne Rosen . . ."*

Me, playing the proud papa: *"That's good, Jamie! That's very good! Now, can you tell me what you're supposed to do if a stranger comes up to you?"*

Jamie dutifully recites everything I had just told him: *"I'm not supposed to talk to strangers, even if they ask me if I want a present, and I can . . . I'm supposed to run and get a p'leaseman or another grownup and tell them to take me to you, and . . ."*

There. That was it.

I froze the image and marked its endpoint, then I moved back to the beginning of the video. When I had reached that point and marked it, I opened the menu bar at the top of the screen and selected the EDIT function. Another command from the submenu caused a window to open at the bottom half of the screen, displaying a transcript of the conversation.

I then began to work my way through the transcript, highlighting certain key words. It took me a few minutes, but when I was through I had a couple of lines I had pieced together from the videotape. I took a deep breath, then I moused the line and tapped in commands to verbalize those lines.

Jamie's voice reemerged from the computer, speaking something he had never said in life, but which I had heard over the phone earlier that night:

"Rosen, Gerard . . . Gerard Rosen . . . Gerry Rosen . . . can I talk to you, Daddy?"

And on the computer screen, Jamie's reedited face was exactly the same as I had seen it on the phone.

"Gerry, what the hell are you doing?"

Startled, I jerked away from the keyboard and spun around in the office chair to find Marianne standing in the doorway behind me.

Her arms were crossed in front of her robe; she had a look of horror on her face, as if she had just caught me trying on a pair of her panties. Maybe reality was worse than that; after all, she had just discovered me in the act of editing one of the last tangible memories of our son.

I lay back in the chair, letting out my breath as I rubbed my eyelids between my fingertips. "Part of the deal was that you wouldn't ask me any questions," I murmured. "And believe me, if I told you, you'd just think I was crazy."

"I already think you're crazy," she replied, her voice harsh with anger barely kept in check. "Leave Jamie's video alone. I mean it . . ."

Before I could do anything, she stalked across the room and began to reach for the computer. "Okay, okay," I said, putting my hands over the keyboard. "I'll get out of this, so long as you answer one question for me."

She stopped and stared at me, not pulling her hands away. "What is it?"

"Did you load this disk into the hard drive?" I asked. "This file in particular?"

Marianne blinked, not quite comprehending the question at first. "Yes," she said at last, "I did. I wanted to preserve the disk. This was the last video we made of him and—"

"And do you still leave the computer on all day?"

She shrugged. "Of course I do. My clients have to talk to the expert system when I'm gone. You know that." She peered more closely at me. "What's going on here, Gerard? Why were you editing the—?"

"Never mind. Go ahead and restore the video." I withdrew my hands from the keyboard and pushed the chair back from the desk. Marianne gave me one last look of distrustful confusion, then she bent over the keyboard, using the trackball to undo the work I had just done. It didn't matter; I had all the answers I needed.

Some of them, rather. Just as I had managed to piece together a message in Jamie's own words, so had someone else. The video was stored on the computer's hard drive and Marianne left the computer switched on during the day, so that her clients could ask questions of the computer's expert system. It was therefore possible for a good hacker to access the JAMIE.6 file through the root directory and edit together the phone message I had heard earlier that night. By the same means, it was also possible for them to recreate my own voice; a good hacker with the right equipment would be able to mimic my voice, since my vocal tracks were recorded on this and many other CD-OP files Marianne had stored in the computer.

But why go to such extremes? If the culprit had been trying to get my attention, why imitate the voice of my dead son . . . or my own, for that matter? If anything, it was a sick prank, tantamount to calling up a grieving widow and pretending to be the ghost of her late spouse. Yet this was the second time in as many days someone had used a computer to send mysterious messages to me, and the technical sophistication necessary to do this went far beyond the capability of some twisted little cyberpunk trying to spook me.

In fact, now that I thought about it, how would some pimplehead even know to call into Marianne's computer? Its modem line was listed under her company's name, not hers or mine, and very few people were aware that Gerry Rosen even had an estranged wife.

It made no sense . . .

Or it made perfect sense, but I was unable to perceive the logic.

"You miss him, don't you?"

Marianne's question broke my concentration. She had finished saving the file and was exiting from the program. I looked at her as she switched off the computer, ejected the disk from its drive, and slipped it back in its box.

"Yeah, I miss him." I stuck my hands in my jacket pockets, suddenly feeling very old. "He was the best thing that happened to us . . . and I still can't believe he's gone."

"Yeah. Me, too." Marianne put the box away, then leaned against the shelf next to the desk. For the first time since she had let me into the house, she wasn't playing the queen bitch of the universe; she was my wife, commiserating the passage of our son from our lives. "God, I've even kept his room the same, thinking somehow there's just been some awful mistake, that he wasn't on that train after all . . ."

The train. Always the train . . .

"He's gone, Mari," I said softly. "There's no mistake. There was an accident, and he died . . . and that's all there is to it."

She slowly nodded her head. "Yeah. That's all there is to it." She stared at the floor. "Tell me you just wanted to look at him again, Gerry. Tell me he isn't mixed up in whatever trouble you're in."

She raised her eyes and stared straight at me. "This isn't part of some story, is it?"

I knew what she meant. I had lost one newspaper job because I had been trying to stop kids from dying; I had thrown myself on the sword in order to save some youngsters I had never really known, the children of complete strangers, because that had been part of a story. Yet when the time had come for me to protect my own child, I had not been available. Jamie had perished without ever seeing his father's face again because Daddy had been too busy with his career to do anything but buy him a train ticket to eternity.

The accusation in her eyes wasn't fair, but neither is the timing of earthquakes against MetroLink schedules. Or death itself, for that matter.

When I didn't answer her question, Marianne lowered her head and began to walk out of the office. "I've made up the living room couch and told the house to wake you up at eight," she said. "That's when the coffeemaker comes on. There's some sweet rolls in the fridge, if you want 'em . . ."

"Okay, babe. Thanks for everything."

She nodded again and began to head for the stairs. Then she stopped and turned back again. "And by the way . . . there's nobody else upstairs, if that's what you were wondering. G'night."

And then she left, heading back to her bedroom before I got a chance to ask her how she managed to pick up that mind-reading trick of hers.

14

I awakened to the faint sound of church bells striking eight times as if tolling from a distant country steeple, although neither of the two churches within a block of the house had bells.

The sound came from the ceiling; Marianne had programmed the house to wake me at this time, just as she had instructed it to start brewing coffee in the kitchen. Although I could have used another hour of sleep, I was grateful that she hadn't selected another noise from the alarm menu; if she had wanted to be a real bitch, she could have jolted me with an eight-gun salute, or worse.

Nonetheless, I lay on the rattan couch for a couple of minutes, curled up in a lambswool blanket, caught somewhere between sleep and wakefulness. I heard the shower running in the upstairs bathroom, smelled the dark aroma of hot coffee brewing in the kitchen, heard songbirds just outside the windows. Everything was warm and comfortable and orderly, much as it had once been a long time ago when I had lived in this house . . .

Then my mind's eye flashed to John, the way I had seen him as he lay on the porch floor at Clancy's with cops and paramedics standing all around him. Dead, with a hole burned through his forehead . . . and I knew that, if I didn't find out why, I could never find any peace again, and all my mornings would be haunted for the rest of my life.

The buzz of the telephone interrupted my train of thought. I almost got off the couch until I remembered that I had taken

164

the handset and put it on the floor next to the couch before I had turned in for the night. Marianne was still in the shower, so I picked it up and thumbed the button. "Hello . . . um, Rosen residence," I said self-consciously.

"*Where the hell are you?*"

Bailey. The son of a bitch had an innate talent for rude awakenings. "Well, Pearl," I said as I sat up on the couch, "if you called here, then you must already know where I am."

"*Process of elimination. If you're not in your apartment, then you must be somewhere else.*"

"Hey, give the man a kewpie doll—"

"*Don't gimme no shit, Rosen. We just found out John's been killed and that you were seen at Clancy's with the cops, and when I go upstairs to get you, I find the place ransacked. Word on the street is that a couple of ERA tanks were here last night. Now what the fuck's going on?*"

"Earl—"

"*This is a helluva time for you to go shacking up with your old lady. Now you tell me what the . . .*"

I sighed as I peered out the living room window. There were no cars parked on the street in front of the house, but that didn't mean anything. "Look, Earl—"

"*I ain't looking at anything, Rosen, except for a pink slip with your name written on it unless you tell me right now what the—*"

"Earl, shut the fuck up."

That did the trick, at least for a moment. I took a deep breath. "I know what's going on," I continued, "but this phone isn't plugged in, y'know what I mean?"

There was silence from the other end of the line. Pearl had a bad temper, and he sometimes ate more brains than he seemed to carry between his ears, but he knew how to take a hint. He knew that anyone with a two-bit scanner could eavesdrop on a conversation carried out on a cordless phone. Even if my neighbors didn't indulge in such skulduggery, there was no guarantee that the police or ERA would not.

"I know what's going on," I repeated. "We can't talk about it right now, but a big load of shit hit the fan last night. John's getting killed is only part of it."

I heard a slow exhalation. *"Are you serious?"*

"Like a heart attack," I said as another thought occurred to me. "Have you heard from Sandy Tiernan yet?"

"Yeah. She's pretty shook. She called me at around six, said that she got the call from some guy at homicide—"

"Mike Farrentino?"

"Yeah, that's him, and when I phoned his office, he said that he'd seen you last night at Clancy's." His tone of voice had changed from belligerence to confusion. *"What's the scoop here, Ger?"*

"I'll tell you when I get downtown," I said. "I'll be there soon as I can swing a ride. But for right now . . ."

I hesitated, trying to think of a way I could phrase the notion that had just occurred to me. "Umm . . . you think you could call an exterminator this morning?"

"Huh? An exterminator?"

"Yeah." I rubbed at the knot left in the back of my neck from sleeping on the narrow couch. I could no longer hear running water from the upstairs bathroom. "Those roaches up in the loft are getting pretty hairy, pal. Might have crawled downstairs into the office. I think you should check it out real soon."

Another long silence, then: *"Yeah, I think so too. Maybe it's time to call Orkin, see if they can send someone down here this morning."*

Bailey had gotten the hint. Cockroaches in the loft, bugs in the office: he knew what I was talking about. If anyone was indeed eavesdropping on our conversation, it would be painfully obvious what we were discussing, but it was better that he was forewarned of the threat before he made any more phone calls or put anything sensitive into the office computers.

The only misunderstanding between us was that he thought I was hinting at the feds or the police as being the prime suspects. I wasn't so sure if ERA or the SLPD were the only ones we had to worry about. Somebody out there was capable of hacking into even encrypted PTs like Joker; they had put the voodoo on me with that faux Jamie phone call last night. Until I had a clue as to who they were, I wasn't taking any chances.

"Good deal," I said. "I'll get downtown as soon as I can."

I clicked off, pushed away the blanket, and swung my legs off the couch. No time for sweet rolls and coffee; all I wanted to do now was get dressed and get out of here. I was reaching for where I had dumped my trousers on the floor when I heard the familiar creak of the stairs.

I looked up to see Marianne sitting on the landing, wearing her robe again, her hair pulled up in a damp towel. No telling how long she had been there, listening to my side of the conversation.

"Hi," I said. "How're you doing?"

Lame question. She didn't bother to answer. Mari simply stared at me, her chin cupped in her hands. "You're going to want a ride downtown, right?"

I hesitated, then slowly nodded my head. It was a long walk from here to the nearest MetroLink station, and despite last night's promise to call a cab first thing in the morning, she knew I didn't have enough cash on me to cover the fare all the way down to Soulard.

She briefly closed her eyes. "And you're going to want money, too, right?"

"Hey, I didn't say—"

"I can spare you fifty dollars," she replied, "and if you'll let me get dressed, I can get you down to the paper in about a half-hour. Okay?"

I nodded again. We gazed at each other for a few moments, each of us remembering all the shit we had put the other through during our years as a couple. Moving in together for the first time. Burned breakfasts, forgotten dinners. Underwear on the floor, unpaid bills. Two or three lost jobs, bouts of morning sickness announcing the arrival of a child neither of us had planned on raising but decided to have anyway. Engagement and marriage. Death and insecurity. Separation on its way to becoming formalized as a divorce.

An old TV commercial had a punch line that had enraged feminists: *my wife . . . I think I'll keep her.* Mari should have written a comeback: *my husband . . . I think I'll ditch him.*

"Yeah," I said. "That'll be great."

Marianne stood up, absently running her hand down the front of her robe so that I couldn't catch a glimpse of her thighs. "Sure," she said. "If it'll get you out of here, I'd be happy to do it."

"Mari—"

"Whatever you're mixed up in," she said, "I hope it works out . . . but I don't want to get involved. You've done enough to me already."

Then she trod upstairs to the bedroom and slammed the door.

Marianne dropped me off in front of the newspaper office; I was almost as glad to be rid of her as she was of me.

The trip downtown had been taken without any words spoken between us; only the morning news on NPR had broken the cold silence in her car. U.S. Army troops were still being airlifted to the Oregon border as Cascadia continued its Mexican standoff with the White House, and the crew of the *Endeavour* had succeeded in rendezvousing with *Sentinel 1* and linking the final module to the antimissile satellite. And some lady in Atlanta was attracting massive crowds to her house after she claimed to have seen the face of Jesus in a pot roast.

Whoopee. I would rather have been in Birmingham, Seattle, outer space . . . anywhere, in fact, but St. Louis.

Everyone stared as I entered the newsroom, but no one said anything to me as I walked straight to Bailey's office. Not surprisingly, he had already taken the cover off his IBM and was peering into its electronic guts with a penlight; Pearl was nothing if not paranoid.

"Close the door and sit down," he said without glancing up from his work. "We've got a lot to talk about."

I shut the door and found a chair that wasn't buried beneath galley proofs and contact sheets. He patiently continued to poke through the breadboards and chips until he was satisfied, then he slid the cover shut and turned around in his swivel chair to gaze at me.

"Look, Earl," I began, "I'm really sorry about—"

"Y'know what this is?" He picked up a large, flat case that lay atop the usual paperwork heaped on his desk. It had a pair of headphones jacked into one end, and one side was covered with knobs and digital meters; a slender spiral cord led to a long, needle-tipped wand. "Of course you know what it is," he went on, "because you must have known I had one when I called you."

"It's an electronic surveillance detector," I said. "You showed it to me once. Remember?"

"That's right," he replied, nodding his head. "Mr. Orkin Man himself. It can scan everything we use in this office and locate virtually any RF or VLF signal imaginable. Infinity bugs, hook-switch bypasses, modem or fax machine taps . . . you name it, this sucker can sniff it out. Put me back three grand, but hey, I've always considered it to be worth the dough. A little extra insurance, if you want to think of it that way."

He carefully placed the instrument back on his desk. "If you meant to scare the bejeezus out of me, you succeeded. As soon as I got off the phone with you, I had everyone drop whatever they were doing while Jah and I went through the place. We switched on every computer, every light, picked up each phone, and turned on all the faxes . . . not a goddamn thing here went untouched, and that includes your apartment and the lab downstairs. I even had Jah run antivirus tests through all the computers and PTs . . . at least, the ones the feds didn't steal from your place last night. And you know what we found?"

He raised his right hand, circling his thumb and forefinger. "Nada. Nyet. Zippity-doo-dah. Not so much as a loose wire. Now, either the feds have managed to put some pretty godlike equipment in here, or you're an anatomical wonder . . . someone who can talk on the phone with his head shoved straight up his butt."

I remained silent throughout all this. He needed to have a good rant right now, and I was unlucky enough to be the target. When he was done, he stared at me from across the desk, his hands folded together over his stomach. He finally let out his breath and kneaded his eyelids with his fingertips.

"The only reason why I haven't thrown your ass out into the street," he said very calmly, "is because you must be onto something. Or at least John must have been onto something, because some bastard took the time and effort to kill him. And I think you must have stumbled into it, because your door got kicked down last night and the feds carted off everything that could be plugged in. So now I'm stuck with a smart reporter who's dead and a dumb reporter who doesn't know how to call his editor when the shit's coming down—"

"Pearl," I began, "look—"

All at once, Bailey surged to his feet, grabbed a pile of paper at random, and hurled it at me so fast I didn't have time to duck the printouts and photostats as they slapped me in the face.

"Fuck you, Rosen!" *he yelled at the top of his lungs.* "I wanna know what's going on!"

The paper rain cascaded down around me, falling into my lap and onto the floor. It was dead quiet outside the cubicle— every person in the office must have heard the explosion— but that wasn't what I noticed. For the first time, I saw that Pearl's eyes were puffy and red-rimmed.

The son of a bitch had been hit hard by the news of John's murder. He was taking it out on me, and maybe he was right to do so because, God help me, I hadn't wept a single tear since the moment Farrentino had called to ask if I could come down to the bar and identify his body.

If Pearl felt like a jerk for going on a futile bug hunt, then I now felt much the same way for not giving myself the time to realize that my best friend was dead. Yet, by the same token, I couldn't allow myself the luxury of wallowing in my own grief. There was something happening out there, at this very moment, of which John's death was only a small and incidental part.

I didn't know what was happening either, but it was time to stop being a victim of circumstance.

"Sit down, Earl," I said. "I've got a lot to tell you."

And I told him all of it, except a couple of the juicy parts.

There was no reason for him to know everything that had occurred during my encounter with Colonel Barris at the stadium . . . in particular, my signed agreement against revealing the details of Ruby Fulcrum. It wasn't just a matter of keeping facts from my editor; I was concerned about his safety. If things went bad, I didn't want ERA troops to come knocking at his door. There was no reason why they wouldn't anyway, but neither did it make any sense to have Pearl mixed up in this shit more than necessary.

And, although I related the story of the strange IM I had received through Joker just before the riot at the Muny, I didn't tell him about the phone call I had received in my apartment just before the ERA raid. I didn't want him to think I had gone around the bend, even if I could explain how I might have heard my own voice and Jamie's over the phone. When Pearl asked me why I hadn't returned to my apartment after I was released from ERA custody, I told him I was too frightened to go back to my place but had simply fled to my ex's house in Webster instead.

Everything else came out, though, and when I was through he simply gazed at me, his fingers knitted together above his lap. After a few moments he picked up his phone and pushed a couple of buttons. "Craig? This is Dad . . . yeah, come up right away, I want you to do something for me."

He put the phone back on its cradle and stood up. "When he gets here, I want to give him Joker so he can run some tests on it. The bastards might have messed with it somehow, and I don't want you running around with a Trojan horse in your PT."

The same thought had already occurred to me, so I pulled Joker out of my pocket. "I take it this means I'm not fired yet," I said as I typed in the "chickenlegs" password.

"I don't fire people, Gerry. I just make 'em quit." Pearl walked around his desk and opened the door. "Now let's go upstairs and see if that disk is still where you hid it."

We met Jah outside Pearl's office. He took Joker and went back downstairs to the photo lab, then Pearl and I climbed the stairs to the third floor.

My apartment was much as I had last seen it. The door was ajar; the desktop computer and the phone were still AWOL; along with the manuscript of my novel. I imagined some ERA officer at the stadium diligently reading the novel, trying to find hidden references within its pages. It would probably be the only audience the book would ever find; I hoped he liked the sex scenes, at least.

"I can't tell whether this place has been ransacked or not," Pearl murmured as he looked at my habitual mess.

"It's a do-it-yourself job." I walked into the bathroom, knelt on the tile floor, and peered beneath the toilet tank. The thin plastic case had gone undiscovered; it was still taped beneath the porcelain pony. I peeled away the tape and let the mini-disk drop into my hand, then held it up for Pearl to see. "We're lucky," I said.

"No luck to it," he muttered. "They just didn't have a containment suit at hand." Pearl took the plastic case from my hand and gazed at it thoughtfully. "All that, to find what's on this thing."

He gave it back to me. "Give it to Jah and let him take a look at it," he said quietly, folding his arms together. "He might be able to make something out of this sucker. Meanwhile, we're going downstairs and see if we can get a line on those people from Tiptree."

"Okay. Right . . ." Suddenly, I felt exhausted. For the last two days I had been punted from one side of the city to the other, and I didn't have any real clues as to what was going on. I gazed at the unmade bed near the broken window. Only about twelve hours earlier I had been lying there dead asleep, more or less innocent of all that had been occurring just beyond my range of vision. And now . . .

"I'm like you," Pearl said. "I don't buy this story about one of their scientists going schizo and shooting people. If there's some other reason why John was killed, then we're going to get to the bottom of it."

"Uh-huh. Yeah . . ."

He looked down at the floor, absently kicking aside an old beer bottle. "You're assigned to this story, Gerry. I want to find out who killed one of our reporters, what he was trying to find out when he was killed, and why someone is shooting people in the street. You're relieved of all other editorial responsibilities until then, understand?"

I nodded. "You want me to bring down the guy who killed John."

He gave me a sharp glance. "Listen, kid: the worst thing a reporter can do is go out on story carrying a vendetta. I know

John was your best friend, but you've got to put that behind you right now. You've got to—"

"Yeah, right. Remain objective."

Pearl shook his head. "No. Objectivity is what you do when you're writing the story itself. Keeping your head is what you do before that. If this is some sort of conspiracy, then the people who are involved are way ahead of you. They've got their tracks covered. Your only advantage right now is that they assume you're stupid. Don't give them a chance to think otherwise . . ."

He grinned. "At least until you come up from behind and take a bite out of their ass."

I looked up at him. In that moment our eyes met, and we were for that instant completely simpatico. All talk of journalistic objectivity aside, there was only one thing we both wanted.

"C'mon," Pearl said as he turned to walk toward the door. "Let's go to work."

15

We began by trying to get a lead on Beryl Hinckley.

We didn't have anything to go on at first; her number wasn't listed in the phone book. Ditto for Richard Payson-Smith, our alleged laser sniper, and although there were four Jeff Morgans listed in the white pages, phone calls placed to three of the numbers quickly established that none of them belonged to our man.

The fourth didn't pick up, but when the answering machine came on after the second buzz, a still picture appeared on the screen; it was the same person in the photo Barris had showed me. "*Hi, this is Jeff,*" the recorded voice said. "*I'm not available right now, but if you care to leave your name and number, I'll get back to you as soon as I can . . .*" I hung up before the beep. If Morgan was on the run, then he wouldn't be calling me back, but any message I left could tip off the bad guys that I was searching for him.

I then made three successive calls to the Tiptree Corporation, asking the switchboard to connect me with Hinckley, Payson-Smith, or Morgan; I switched off my phone's camera when I made these calls. On each try, the computer-generated woman on the screen informed me that none of the three were "available at this time." Remembering that Tiptree employees wore smartbadges that would pinpoint someone's location in the complex, every time I called I made up a different excuse for being adamant: a relative phoning Hinckley to tell her about a sudden death in the family, an insurance claims adjuster for Payson-Smith, a dental assistant calling to tell Morgan that next week's appointment had to be changed. On each occasion, the computer put me on hold, only to come back a few moments later to tell me that none of the three were at the company offices today.

This confirmed my suspicion that the three surviving members of the Ruby Fulcrum team had taken a powder. I didn't accept the virtual receptionist's invitation to leave voice-mail messages for any of them; I had a hunch that none of them would be coming back to work anytime soon.

Not long ago, this might have signaled a dead end for a reporter on the trail of a missing person, but Pearl had his own resources. While I was taking the slow boat to China, he had already boarded an SST.

Tracker is an on-line computer service, little known by the public at large but used extensively by professionals who make their living by snooping into other people's lives: PIs, skip tracers for bondsmen, credit bureaus, lawyers, and direct-mail ad agencies, not to mention a few investigative journalists who didn't mind playing loose and fast with professional ethics. If you've ever wondered why all your credit card bills tend to arrive at the same time you missed a payment on one card, or why you suddenly get loads of junk mail advertising dog food or private kennels only a few days after you adopted a stray mutt from the local pound, services like Tracker are the reason.

Tracker is expensive. At five hundred bucks for the first fifteen minutes and escalating from there, it's not something you logon at whim. It's difficult to access—the company that runs it likes to keep a low profile—but if you have its on-line number and a gold card, then you too can poke around in someone else's private affairs. All you need is that person's name, and you can find out virtually anything available on them through various private-sector databases.

Pearl seldom used Tracker. As a privacy-minded journalist—and, yes, there are still a few of us around—he was loath to invade the personal business of a nonpublic figure, and peeking into someone's credit card accounts is the type of thing that has given reporters a bad name. Yet this was one time he was willing to play lowball.

"Here she is," he said after he had entered Hinckley's name, hometown, and place of work. I bent over his shoulder to look at his computer screen. Next to HINCKLEY, BERYL was a street address in St. Louis and a phone number. "Try that."

I picked up his desk phone and dialed the number. "No answer," I said after I let it ring a dozen times. "She didn't turn on her answering machine."

He nodded. "Okay. Now look the other way for a minute." He shot a sharp glance over his shoulder at me. "I'm going to do something you shouldn't know about," he said. "Only a jerk like me would stoop to something like this."

I turned away while Pearl keyed in a new command. Just outside the office door, I spotted Chevy Dick hanging out in the office corridor, jawing with one of the bohos from the production staff. He was probably dropping off this week's "Kar Klub" column. If things weren't so intense right now, I would have wandered over to join the bull session.

"Okay," Bailey said, "you can look now." I turned back around to see that a new window had opened at the bottom of the Tracker screen; it displayed the account numbers of three major credit cards—Visa, MC, and AmEx—along with their current balances and the dates of their most recent purchases.

"You're right," I said. "Only a jerk like you would do something like this."

"Nothing TRW doesn't do every day," he replied. "Now looky here . . ."

He pointed at the line next to the Visa number. "Three hundred fifty-dollar ATM cash advance, taken out last night at nine forty-six. And see this?" He jabbed his finger at MC and AmEx numbers below it. "Another three-and-a-half c's from the other cards, taken out just a few minutes later. Probably from the very same machine."

"Twenty-one fifty-eight," I murmured, noting the time entered during the AmEx transaction. "Almost ten o'clock. That's not long after John was shot . . . probably right after she took off from Clancy's."

Pearl nodded his head. "Uh-huh. She headed straight to the nearest ATM and took out as much cash as she could—just over a grand altogether—and there hasn't been another charge on any of her cards since." He glanced up at me. "She didn't want to leave any tracks behind her."

"Credit card receipts?"

"You got it. Your girlfriend didn't want to have to pay for anything with a card because that would allow someone to trace her, so she grabbed as much cash as her credit limit would allow. That's a sign of someone who's going underground." He rubbed his jaw pensively as he stared at the screen. "Now I wonder if she . . . ?"

He called up her driver's license, then cross-referenced it with her credit cards. "She didn't rent a car," he said after a few moments. "Car rental agencies always ask for a license and enter it into their records, but this shows she hasn't used her license for anything."

"What about Morgan and Payson-Smith?"

Pearl shrugged. "I'll check, but I bet we won't find anything for them, either." He bent over the keyboard again; this time he allowed me to watch over his shoulder as he began to repeat the same process for the other two Ruby Fulcrum scientists.

Modemed phone numbers, passwords, menu screens accessing the files of credit bureaus: Pearl was doing something almost akin to art, albeit strange and terrible to behold. Not to mention scary. If an amateur like Pearl could hack into credit files and use inductive reasoning to second-guess what a fugitive had been thinking the previous evening, what did this portend for the rest of us?

Bailey must have sensed my line of thought. "When I was a kid," he said as his fingers wandered across the keys, "and my great-grandfather was still alive, he told me that his uncle Samuel had been an escaped slave from Tennessee, way back during the Civil War. He had taken the Underground Railroad up north to Chicago, and it was a hell of a ride. Hiding out in fruit cellars during the day, riding in the back of hay wagons at night, running from one abolitionist house to the next. Once he had to outrun some bloodhounds in some hick town in Kentucky and didn't shake 'em until he lost the scent by wading several miles down a shallow creek."

"But he got away, didn't he?"

He nodded. "Yeah, he got away, but they only had bloodhounds back then. If great-uncle Sam had to do the same thing now, he probably would have stolen a car . . . and if he wasn't paying cash all the way, then every time he stopped at a charge station, some database would have recorded a number with his name behind it. How long do you think he might have lasted? Probably not even to the Illinois state line."

There was a sharp rap on the door; we looked around to see Jah standing in the corridor. He seemed nervous. "Gerry," he said, "I've got something I think you ought to see."

"Joker?"

He shook his head. "Joker's clean," he said, "except that everything you had stored on it has been dumped. It's the backup disk you took from John's PT. It . . ."

Jah took a deep breath, then crooked a finger at me. "Just c'mon down to the lab. You're not going to believe this."

Jah's computer didn't show anything unusual, at least at first glance; the screen displayed the same root directory I had seen the night before on my own 'puter, the cryptic acronyms for a couple hundred different files. He sat down at the computer and pushed a button on the CPU. The CD-OP bay slid open; the backup I had made from Dingbat's original mini-disk was nestled in its drawer.

"When I got down here," he began, "I booted it up like you see here and copied the files into the hard drive. When I was through doing that, I punched into the directory to see what I could find—"

"Sure," I said. "that's just what I did."

"You did?" He glanced over his shoulder at me. "So what happened to you?"

I shrugged, not quite understanding what he was asking. "Well . . . nothing happened, really. I scrolled through the directory and tried to find something that looked like a front door, but I couldn't."

"Yeah?" He scratched at his head. "Then what happened? Did you try punching into a BAT file, or did you get out of the directory?"

I shook my head. "Naw, I didn't get a chance to go that far. I got a phone call and . . . um, that's about when the feds broke down the door. But I didn't do anything before that."

"Uh-huh. And they just unplugged everything and took it . . ."

"Yeah, right. What are you getting at?"

Jah pointed at his screen. "Well, I did the same thing you did, but when I tried the BATs and EXECs I couldn't find a front door either. Everything came up BAD COM. So I decided to get out of the directory and log into a search-and-retrieve program I've got installed in this thing . . . a standard little number I put in here a few months ago to help me find lost files when I've been fucking around a little too much. This way I figured I might be able to unlock a back door or something. Anyway, I was entering the SAR program when—"

He snapped his fingers. "Boom boom, out go the lights. The whole screen went dead for a moment. It was like the computer had spontaneously decided to reboot itself, but I didn't even get so much as a c-prompt. I was still looking under the table . . . y'know, like to see if I had managed to kick out the plug or something stupid like that . . . when the screen came back on again a moment later."

"Yeah, that's weird, all right." It might have been caused by something stupid like kicking out the plug if anyone else had been using the computer, but Jah wasn't a stupid kid. Particularly not when it came to 'puters; in that respect he made even his dad look like a novice. "So what happened?"

"So I figure it's just a software glitch," he continued, sweeping his dreadlocks back from his face, "and go back to what I was doing before . . . except now I can't access the SAR. At least not right away . . . it took me two or three minutes just to pull up the opening screen, and that was after running through all the different startup commands."

"Hmm . . ."

He raised his eyebrows. "Yeah, man. Twilight zone shit. So I get suspicious and I start thinking to myself, y'know . . . Jesus, maybe the disk is infected with a virus or something."

He turned around in his chair and pointed to the telephone wall jack next to his desk. I saw now that the flat gray cord was lying on the floor beneath the jack, its module disconnected. "So the first thing I do is yank the plug, just in case it really was a virus and someone is trying to call in while I'm doping out this thing."

"Good idea," I murmured. If Jah's hardware had been infected with a virus and he didn't know exactly how it had been transmitted to his computer, then it made perfect sense to isolate his system. Jah was anything but discourteous to other users, although it was a good thing he wasn't a sysop for even a minor BBS; otherwise, dozens of other computers might have been infected by now. "So what happened then?"

"Now it gets really weird." He held up a finger. "I opened a window into my antigen subroutine and asked it to check the system." He shook his head. "It comes back and tells me it can't find anything. No viruses, no missing batches or boot sectors, no nothing. According to my computer, I'm clean as a whistle. But I've still got the creeps, so I do this . . ."

Before I could ask, he turned back to the computer and used its trackball to log into a program on the directory. A moment later the opening screen of his search-and-retrieve program flashed on; when its menu bar was up, he moused a subroutine listed as VR SEE and toggled it open. "Okay," he said, "now here comes the interesting part. Put that on."

He pointed to a department store mannequin propped up against the wall next to the desk. The dummy was African-American and female; it was decked out in some exotic black lace lingerie straight out of any kid's favorite wet dream. I had to wonder which one of Jah's girlfriends had donated this little bit of nothing to his trophy room.

"Uh, Jah . . . I hate to tell you this, but—"

"The helmet," he said impatiently. "Put the HMD on."

I looked at the mannequin again. Right. A head-mounted display was propped on the dummy's bald head, almost neutralizing the sexual effect. The HMD vaguely resembled a bicycle helmet except for the oversize opaque visor. A slender cable led from the back of the helmet to the serial port on Jah's computer. A pair of naugahyde datagloves were draped around the dummy's shoulders.

I picked up the HMD and weighed it in my hands. "Is this really necessary?"

Call me an old fart, but I dislike tripping in cyberspace. I was a kid when the first Virtuality arcades opened in St. Louis; although some of my fellow mall rats used to spend their weekends in the VR simulators, hunting each other through bizarre three-dimensional landscapes or waging war in giant robots, the experience had always left me disoriented. Riding the roller coasters and whirligigs at the Catholic diocese fair was fine, but being thrown into a cybernetic construct tended to make me nauseous.

Sure, I know the old saw about cyberspace being what you do when you're on the phone, but making a phone call is so prosaic that you seldom think twice about it. VR tripping . . . that's like skydiving to me. Some people dig it and some people don't, that's all.

"Hey, I did it," he replied, as if he had just jumped off an old railway bridge into the Missouri River and now wanted me to experience the same rush. "Don't worry, it won't toast your brain. Now c'mon . . . I don't know how much longer this is going to last."

What's going to last? I wanted to ask, but Jah was gnawing at the bit: a teenager eager to show off to an adult who might appreciate this sort of thing.

I reluctantly donned the thick datagloves, then I took a deep breath and pulled the helmet over my head. Jah adjusted the padded visor until it was firmly in place against my eyes.

"Okay, kid," I said. "Show me what you got."

And he did.

For a few moments, there was only darkness . . . then the universe was filled with iridescent silver light, featureless yet fine-grained, as if I was looking at a bolt of electronic silk that had been wrapped around my head. After another second the backdrop faded to dull gray; as it did, a small silver square appeared directly in front of me, a gridded plane floating in null-space.

"Okay," I heard Jah say, "that's a representation of the computer's memory. Each box you see on the matrix is a different program or file I've got stored on this thing . . . touch it and you'll come in closer."

I hesitated, then raised my right hand and watched as its

computer-animated analog rose before my eyes. I curled my fingers and pointed straight at the matrix and suddenly found myself hurtling forward . . .

"Hold on!" Jah yelled. I heard his chair scoot back from the desk, then his hands grabbed my shoulders.

"Maybe you ought to sit down for this," he said as he guided me into the seat. "Okay, that better?"

"Uh, yeah . . . thanks." I hadn't even noticed that I had lost my balance. The flat square had expanded into a transparent three-dimensional cube made up of dozens of smaller cubes. It resembled a crystalline version of some mind-fuck puzzle my dad used to have, a plastic toy where the idea was to shift the interlocked pieces until all four colors were on the same side . . . yeah, a Rubik's Cube, except now I could see all the way through the thing.

"Okay," Jah said, "you see the matrix clearly now? You see all the packets?"

"Yeah, I see it." Each box—or packet, to use Jah's term—in the matrix was labeled with a different alphanumeric code; those would be the programs stored in the memory. Yet, as I slowly orbited the cube, I could now see that not all the packets were silver; closer to its center, a small nucleus of packets were cream-colored, and as I watched, one of them suddenly turned silver.

"It's changing color," I said.

"That's been happening since I first accessed the matrix," Jah said. "When I looked at it the first time, only a few of the packets were silver, and the rest of 'em were white . . . but the ones that had turned silver were the system drivers. Everything else is the other files and programs on this machine."

"A virus?" I asked, and I heard him grunt. "But you said your antigen program hadn't discovered any—"

"Nothing it could detect," he said. "But even that's been absorbed by this sucker . . . and believe me, Scud is the best virus hunter-killer you can find."

I shook my head. That was a mistake; the cyberspatial construct swam back and forth before me. I clutched the armrests with my hands, fighting a brief spell of vertigo. "I don't get it," I said after the cube was dead-center in front of me again. "If this program's still working, then it must not have been taken over yet . . ."

"Oh, no," Jah replied. "ProVirtual—the program we're using now—was one of the first to go, and that's the weird thing. Everything the virus has taken over still works as it did before. It's just . . . well, here, let me show you. Back away from the matrix, willya?"

It took me a second to understand what he was asking me to do. Then I tentatively raised my hand again and pointed to a bit of blank space above the cube. At once, I zoomed to a higher orbit above the matrix; it diminished slightly in size, but I could still see the entire thing.

"I'm booting up an old game I erased from memory a couple of months ago," he said. "It's called MarzBot . . . pretty stupid once you got it figured out . . . anyway, I'm taking the master disk and throwing it into the floppy drive, not the hard drive. Now watch this . . ."

Off to one side, I saw a small isolated packet appear off to one side of the matrix, as if it was a displaced cream-colored electron. For a second, nothing happened . . .

And then something happened.

Almost quicker than the eye could follow, a bridge extended itself outward from the cube: a string of silver packets, following a weightless pattern that, during its zigzagging motion, vaguely resembled the L-shaped movement a knight takes upon a chessboard. Before I could take a breath, the bridge had connected with the isolated packet of information containing MarzBot. There was the briefest moment while the packet still remained off-white.

Then it turned silver.

Then it was sucked straight into the cube as the bridge collapsed in upon itself, reeling in the packet like a fisherman towing in a trout that had taken the bait. Within a second, the MarzBot packet was gone . . .

And the cube was slightly larger.

"Goddamn," I said. "How did you do that?"

"I didn't do anything," Jah said quietly. "The computer did it by itself. I haven't touched the keyboard since I slipped MarzBot into the floppy port and hit the ENTER key. The virus reached out to the program, broke through its copy-protect subroutine, accessed its source code, and absorbed the game . . . all in the time it took for us to watch."

I pulled off the HMD, shook off the aftereffects of VR decompression, and stared at the monitor. The image of the matrix cube on the computer screen was much flatter now, less lifelike than what I had seen in cyberspace . . . yet it was no less threatening.

"Holy shit," I whispered.

"Fuckin' A, man." Jah was staring at me, his eyes wide with fear. "This thing is the balls. I don't know what you found, but it's no ordinary virus. It can't be detected, it can't be fought off, but it takes over anything that even gets close to it."

He pointed at the screen. "I've tried everything I could throw at it," he said, his voice filled with both anger and awe. "Other antigens, Norton Tesseract, Lotus Opus . . . shit, even a shareware disk containing a virus that someone once gave me as a gag . . . and it swamps every program I've given it."

Jah shook his head in wonderment. "Whatever it is, it's one hungry son of a bitch. If I didn't know better, I'd think it was—"

The antique Mickey Mouse phone on his desk buzzed, interrupting his train of thought. Jah swore under his breath as he bent backward to pick it up; he listened for a moment, then cupped a hand over the receiver.

"It's Dad," he said. "He wants you to come upstairs right away . . . says that he just got a call from someone who wants to talk to you."

I was still staring at the monitor, watching as the last few packets in the matrix went from white to silver. "Is it important?" I murmured, not wanting to distract myself with a call from some yahoo. It's not very often you get to look the devil straight in the eye. Jah asked his father if it was urgent, then he cupped the receiver again.

"He says it came from someone named Beryl Hinckley," Jah said. "She wants to meet you an hour from now."

16

The midday lunch rush in Clayton was just beginning as I climbed out of the rickshaw cab I had caught at MetroLink station and paid off the driver. The kid folded the money I gave him and shoved it into his fanny pack without so much as a word, then pulled out into the four-lane traffic of Central Avenue, playing a quick game of chicken with a streetcar as they rounded the corner of Forsyth together.

Long before St. Louis's county and municipal governments had merged, Clayton had been a small metropolis in its own right, a prosperous "edge city" just west of Forest Park. Now it had become St. Louis's uptown business district, its high-rise office buildings constituting a second skyline several miles from the riverfront. Compared to downtown, though, most of the damage suffered by Clayton during the quake had been cleaned up months ago, thanks in no small part to federal relief money. A few small offices had been condemned, a couple of side streets were still impassable, but otherwise it was now hard to tell whether this side of town had been affected at all by New Madrid.

No wonder. Clayton had always looked like a little piece of Los Angeles, disassembled from Beverly Hills and airlifted, brick by pink granite brick, to greater St. Louis. Yet I had never much cared for this part of the city. Despite its sleek postmodern veneer, Clayton was still a ghetto: ten square blocks of overpaid tax accountants, corporate lawyers, and executive vice presidents, an arrogant Disneyland for the aging yupsters and young MBAs who strutted down the sidewalks, each heading for his or her next opportunity to score big bucks. Although ERA troopers were invisible during the day, they were always out in force at night to keep Squat City refugees from taking up residence in the alleys and doorways of the social gentry who called Clayton home. Fall from grace, though, and you fall hard; some of those refugees probably used to live here, too.

The weather had turned bad; the blue skies of early morning had given way to pale gray clouds as a late April cold front began to move in from the west. Offices were letting out for lunch hour as I made my way down Central Avenue's crowded sidewalk to Le Café François, about halfway down the block from the county courthouse.

It was your typical business-lunch bistro, already packed with salesmen and secretaries, and it took me a couple of moments before I spotted her. Beryl Hinckley was seated in a secluded booth at the back of the restaurant, nursing a cup of cappuccino as she furtively watched the door. Upon spotting me, she gave no overt sign of recognition other than to nod her head slightly; I cut my way through the dining room and slid into the booth across the table from her.

"Hi," I said. "Long time, no see."

"You're late," she said coldly. "If you'd been any longer getting here, I would have left."

I shrugged. "If you wanted a reporter, you should have asked for one who owns a car."

Or one who had changed his clothes or taken a shower within the past twenty-four hours, I might have added; her nose wrinkled at my slovenly appearance. It wasn't my fault; she had given me barely enough time to catch the Green Line train out here, let alone clean up a little.

She shook her head. "It doesn't matter," she said calmly. "This will have to be quick. When we're through here, you're going to walk me down the block to the courthouse, where I'm going to find a judge and request that he place me in protective custody."

"What?" Had she told me instead that she planned to throw herself off the Martin Luther King Bridge, she couldn't have caught me more by surprise.

"I'd prefer to surrender to a federal circuit judge," she went on, "but the federal courthouse is only three blocks from the stadium. Since the whole point is to avoid being captured by ERA, I'll have to settle for a state judge."

"Whoa, wait a minute, lady . . . back up a second. Why are you—"

I was interrupted by a young waitress coming by to offer me a menu. I was hungry and could have done well with a burger and fries, but I shook my head and asked for coffee instead. The girl gave me a sweet smile and sashayed away.

"Did you bring your PT?" she asked when the waitress was out of earshot. I reached into my pocket and pulled out Joker. "Good. I picked a public place for this interview because it's the safest option right now, but we still don't have much time."

I placed Joker on the table between us but didn't switch it into audio-record mode just yet. "On the contrary," I replied, "I think we've got all the time in the world. At least long enough for us to have coffee and get to know each other a little better—"

"Mr. Rosen . . ." she said impatiently.

"Y'know, the usual stuff. What high school did you go to? How did you like the Muny the other night? What did you say to my best friend that got him killed? That sort of thing."

The muscles in Hinckley's jaw tightened; she looked as if she were about to explode, but she was forced to remain calm while the waitress returned to place a mug of black coffee in front of me. "I've done a little checking on you since we met," I went on after the girl had vanished again. "Found out a few interesting things, like the fact that you're a research scientist at Tiptree, involved with the Ruby Fulcrum project for the company's Sentinel program, and that your boss, Richard Payson-Smith, is currently being sought by the feds in connection with two murders."

I picked up the cream pitcher and diluted the coffee with a dash of milk. "Also, you've been in hiding since last night," I said as I stirred the coffee. "Given the neighborhood we're in, you must have taken the Green Line out here, then checked into either the Radisson or the Holiday Inn . . . registering under an assumed name and paying for the room in cash, of course, since you were smart enough to take out all that money from your credit cards last night."

Her eyes widened in outrage; for a moment there I thought steam would come whistling out of her ears. Except for the ATM transactions, the last bit was sky blue guesswork, but there was no sense in letting her know that. I was getting under her skin, which was exactly what I meant to do.

"Of course," I continued before she could interrupt, "I could just get up from this table and leave. That's mean sticking you with the bill, but I think paying the tab is the least of your worries right now."

I picked up the mug and took a sip. "Good coffee. So what do you say we cut the crap, okay?"

I was bluffing. If I had a pair of brass handcuffs, I would have fastened her ankle to the table and threatened to flush the key down the men's room toilet unless she spilled her guts. This woman had put me through hell in less than forty-eight hours after I had met her; besides getting a little cheap gratification from watching her squirm, I wasn't about to let her waltz into some judge's private chambers until she told me every nasty secret locked in her head.

Hinckley stared at me silently, her dark eyes smoldering with repressed anger. "One more thing," I said, and this time I wasn't bluffing. "I hold you responsible for John Tiernan's death. If he hadn't gone to Clancy's to meet you last night, he'd still be alive now. But he took the bullet—or a laser beam, whatever—that was meant for you, and that really pisses me off, so don't give me this 'just a few minutes, then I gotta go' routine. You owe me, sweetheart."

She blinked hard a couple of times, then took a deep breath and slowly let it out again. "Mr. Rosen," she said, her tone a little less imperious now, "the person who shot your friend— and it wasn't Richard—didn't miss. He's looking for me now, but he meant to kill Tiernan. He was the intended target, not me."

"Bullshit."

"No bullshit." She shook her head. "There's a conspiracy behind all this, and the last thing the people behind it want is public attention. Despite whatever you think you may know, trust me . . . you don't know anything."

I wasn't about to argue the point. I didn't know anything, and I was counting on her to give me the answers, but before I could ask she clasped her hands together above the table and pointed a finger straight at me.

"One more thing," she said, "and this is why I'm in a hurry. There's four people they want to see dead . . . and you're one of them."

I felt my heart skip just a little. "And the only way we're going to get out of this alive," she said, "is if you shut up and listen to what I have to tell you. Understand?"

I believed her. All of a sudden, this pretentious and socially correct little Le Café François was no longer as safe or secure as it seemed when I walked in through the door. In fact, it felt as if I were sitting in the center of a sniper's crosshair, drinking great coffee and waiting for someone to squeeze the trigger.

I slowly nodded my head, and she gestured toward Joker. "Good. Now turn on your PT. I've got a lot to tell you."

Before she got started, though, I filled her in on much of what I already knew.

Although it was an abridged version of what I had related to Pearl a few hours earlier, it included the fact that Barris and McLaughlin had pressured me into stating that I would help them track her down, as well as Payson-Smith and Morgan. I was barely through telling her about being sworn to secrecy with regard to Ruby Fulcrum, though, when she began to shake her head.

"The name's right," Hinckley said, "but the details are all wrong. Ruby Fulcrum exists—I told you that when I first met you—but it's not exactly what they claim it is."

The four scientists who had been assigned to the Ruby Fulcrum project, she went on to explain, were all special-ists in artificial intelligence—or perhaps, more specifically, a branch of AI research called "a-life," or artificial life: computer programs that mimicked all activities of organic life-forms, including the ability to learn on their own.

As Cale McLaughlin had told me, the primary objective of Ruby Fulcrum had been to devise a c-cube system for *Sentinel 1*. This was to be an advanced program—since it was based partly on neural-net systems, even the word *program* itself was almost as archaic as calling a modern automobile a horseless carriage—which, once installed within the satellite's onboard computer system, would learn on its own how to distinguish between ballistic missiles carrying real warheads and those launched as decoys. However, the long-range goal of the project had been the development of a self-replicating a-life-form. Although a-life R&D had been conducted, albeit on a smaller scale, by university and corporate labs since the 1980's, this was the first time a major DOD-funded research effort had been directed at this sort of cybernetic technology.

"The first part of the project was easy to come by, relatively speaking," Hinckley said. "Richard and Po were principally responsible for coming up with an a-life system for Sentinel, and they managed to conclude most of their research about a year ago—"

"And Payson-Smith wasn't opposed to it?" I asked. "I mean, he wasn't against the military application?"

"Is that what they told you?" Hinckley looked at me askance, blowing out her cheeks in disgust. "Yeah, Dick's such a dove, he has his father's old RAF medals framed in his office just so he can swear at them." She shook her head. "If anything, he was the most hawkish member of the team, even if he thought the whole concept of an orbital antimissile system was a little daft."

"How's that?"

She paused to take a sip from her cappuccino, licking the cream from her lips. "Maybe this sort of thing might have made a little sense twenty years ago, when the U.S.S.R. was still around and was stockpiling weapons, but nowadays the only country that still has a large nuclear arsenal is the U.S. itself. Any third-world country that wanted to nuke us wouldn't fire a secondhand Russian missile . . . they'd simply put it on a freighter and sail it into a harbor city . . . and most arms-control people would tell you that accidentally launching a missile is much harder than it's made out in movies. So

Sentinel was obsolete almost before it got off the drawing board."

"Uh-huh," I said. "I've heard that said before. So why were you going along with it?"

"Because it's our job, that's why." She shrugged off-handedly. "Look, that may sound irresponsible, but we aren't the congressmen who voted to appropriate money for this thing. We're just some guys hired to do one small part of the program. We all knew that it was a fluke, but if this was something Uncle Sam wanted, and since Tiptree was writing out paychecks on behalf of the taxpayers, who were we to argue?"

"You remember Alfred Nobel?" I muttered. "They guy who invented dynamite? I think he would have disagreed with—"

"Yeah, right." She held up her hand. "That's political, and anyway it's beside the point . . . at least, right now it is. Let me catch up to the rest of the story, then I'll get back to Sentinel."

While Payson-Smith and Kim Po were concentrating on the c-cube for Sentinel, Jeff Morgan and Hinckley herself were developing a different and far more sophisticated a-life-form. This was the basic research end of the project, intended to produce a nonmilitary spin-off of the original Ruby Fulcrum program; once the Sentinel c-cube was wrapped up and delivered to DOD, Payson-Smith and Kim joined the other two cyberneticists in spending most of their time and effort on the spin-off project.

It had been Morgan's brainstorm to develop a "benign virus" to enable different computer networks to be interfaced without going through a lot of the handshaking protocols mandated by conventional communications software. He was inspired, in part, by the infamous "Internet worm," which a young hacker had let loose in the government's computer network during the late eighties. However, Jeff's dream had been to produce a much more complex—and far more benign—version of the same basic idea. This advanced a-life would be a hybrid between a neural-net and a conventional digital program, allowing it to interface with all types of computers, sort of like a cybernetic philosopher's stone. In fact, the a-life-form that they invented was initially called Alchemist, until the team slipped into referring to it by a part of its old code-name: Ruby.

"Like all a-life organisms," Hinckley went on, "Ruby is guided by a set of rules that mandate its behavior, and these rules compose an iteration—"

"Iteration?"

"Like a cycle," she said, "but the difference between most program iterations and Ruby's is that the others have definite beginnings and endings. Ruby's iteration is open-ended, though. It keeps repeating itself indefinitely. Simply put, it works like this."

She held up a finger. "First, once it's introduced into a computer, it seeks out all programs in that system and everything that's interfaced by those programs. It doesn't even need to be entered into the hard drive . . . transmitting an affected program through modem into a net or even slipping a contaminated disk into the floppy port will do the same trick."

She held up another finger. "Second, it runs through all possible permutations of standard algorithms until it reaches the ones that match and unlock the target program's source code. Once that's accomplished, it deciphers the source code and gains admission. Same idea as hotwiring a car's ignition plate by finding out what the owner's fingerprint looks like and forging it."

A third finger rose from her palm. "Third, it absorbs the target program into its own database, but it does this without locking out access by another user or impeding the functions of that program . . . and then it moves on to seek the next program in the system, and so on."

She paused while the waitress reappeared to reheat my cup of coffee and ask Beryl if she wanted another cappuccino. She shook her head, and the waitress drifted back into the lunchtime crowd. "That's what happened when my buddy Jah booted up a copy of the disk you gave John," I said. "It took over every program in his system but didn't lock him out."

Beryl nodded eagerly, like a mother proud of her child's accomplishments. "Exactly. That's why I gave Tiernan the mini-disk in the first place . . . to prove what Ruby can do.

The only difference was that your friend—uh, Jah, right?—stumbled upon it by accident."

"Hell of a demonstration," I murmured. "And you say this thing can slip through networks and copy itself in other computers?"

"Yes," she said, "but that's not exactly the right term for what it does. It doesn't copy, it *reproduces.* That was the whole purpose, to make a virus that could spread through the national datanet and all the commercial nets, interface with any computer it encounters, then promulgate itself again through cyberspace until it reaches the next computer. And so on, right down the line, like the domino theory."

I poured some more milk into my coffee. "I don't understand, though . . . something like this would require an awful lot of memory to store all that data. And besides, wouldn't it be defeated by antivirus programs?"

Hinckley shook her head. "No, no, it's not quite like a virus. It's more sophisticated than that. It's like . . ."

She sighed and glanced up at the ceiling, searching for an easy explanation. "Ruby is an advanced cellular automaton. Each computer it encounters, no matter how large or small, is absorbed into the larger organism, with each of its programs capable of being controlled by Ruby itself. Then Ruby splits itself apart and automatically seeks out the next computer that it can interface. Meanwhile, the last computer affected becomes a node, or a cell, of the larger system . . ."

"And it keeps growing . . ."

Hinckley nodded. "Right. A little more with each program it interfaces, with each computer functioning as a small part of the larger organism, just as your body is composed of billions of cells that are interconnected to a larger organism, each serving its own function. Unplugging a computer it has accessed won't destroy it, any more than killing one cell would destroy the bio-organism it serves."

She raised a forefinger. "By the same token, antiviral programs are useless against it, because Ruby seeks out, finds, and defeats the basic source codes of those programs, just as a cancer cell defeats the antibodies that surround it."

"Oh my god . . ." I murmured.

"If you think that's scary," Hinckley said, "try this on for size: each time Ruby completes an iteration, it not only grows a little more in storage capacity . . . it also evolves a little more. It *learns*."

She folded her arms together on the table and stared straight at me. "Do you understand what I'm saying?" she asked, her voice kept beneath the noise level of the room, yet not so low that I could miss its urgency. "In theory at least, after a certain number of iterations a critical mass . . . or a phase transition, if you want to use a-life jargon . . . may potentially be achieved, in which Ruby crosses over from being a relatively dumb a-life-form to something much different."

At first, I didn't get what she was saying . . . and then it hit me. "Intelligence?" I whispered.

She slowly nodded. "Artificial intelligence . . . in an artificial life-form that is practically immortal."

I whistled under my breath. Beryl Hinckley was right in her initial assessment; Ruby was no simple spreadsheet program or computer game, but something that imitated life . . .

No. Far more than that, even: Ruby didn't just imitate life; it was a form of life itself. Perhaps not born of woman and man but of fingers tapping instructions into keyboards, yet nonetheless *life* . . .

And, even as I realized this, the full enormity of what we were discussing came home with the impact of a sock in the jaw—and with it, a sneaking suspicion.

"This program," I said haltingly, "or cellular automaton, whatever you call it . . . anyway, when Jah realized that it was some sort of virus, the first thing he did was to disconnect his phone cord."

Hinckley gazed at me without saying anything. I hesitated. "Anyway, it's a good thing he did that, right?"

"No," she said softly, gently shaking her head. "It wouldn't have mattered even if he hadn't, and that's what I told John last night. Ruby's already out there . . . in fact, it was released eleven months ago."

During its infancy, Ruby's cradle had been an IBM desktop computer inside the a-life lab at the Tiptree Corporation. The team had not been careless in raising their creation; they had disconnected the cable leading from the computer's internal modem to the nearest phone jack, and a locked grill had been placed over the computer's CD-OP drive, one that could be removed only by a key carried solely by the four members of the Ruby Fulcrum team.

They knew exactly what they had created: their baby was a Frankensteinian monster that had to be kept locked in its dungeon until it could be trained to behave in a social manner. In turn, as the parents of this potentially destructive creation, they attempted to be responsible in its upbringing. They had fed it only select bits of data, made careful notes as it slowly grew and taken pride in every step it mastered, but nonetheless they made sure that Ruby didn't cross the street until it was properly toilet-trained.

Yet, despite all their precautions, the inevitable accident happened. This occurred on May 17, 2012—the same day an inevitable accident happened throughout the rest of St. Louis County.

"The earthquake hit the company pretty hard," Hinckley said. "You can't tell it now, but four people were killed when the cryonics lab collapsed. That was bad enough, but a lot of other people got injured because of ceilings and shelves falling in. None of my team were hurt, though, thank God . . . we were in the commissary having a late lunch, and the worst thing that happened was that I got a sprained shoulder when a light fixture nailed me . . . but our lab was almost totaled."

She paused, looking nervously again toward the restaurant's front door. I glanced over my shoulder; the lunchtime crowd was beginning to filter out, and our waitress looked as if she was wondering whether she would get a decent tip from two people who had taken up a booth but ordered nothing more than coffee. Other than that, though, nothing seemed unusual; no ERA troopers, no police cars, no mysterious men in trench coats lurking near the cash register.

"Go on," I prompted. "The lab . . ."

Her gaze returned to me. "The lab was busted up pretty badly," she continued, "and the company didn't want any valuable employees going back inside until it had cleaned things up . . . hot wires, unstable walls, things like that. So we were sent home for the next several days while Tiptree brought in a general contractor from Chicago to restore everything— Science Services, some firm that specializes in laboratory restorations, that's what we were told. Don't worry about it, they said. Come back Monday and everything will be fine . . . and, you know, that was all right with us, because we had our own messes at home to clean up. Po lost his house, Dick's cats had been killed, my car had been crushed by a tree . . ."

She sighed as she settled back against her seat, rubbing her eyelids with her fingertips. "Well, to make a long story short, some college kid was responsible for straightening up the a-life lab. I can't really blame him, because things were scattered all over the place and no one had kept any reliable charts as to what went where . . . but when he uprighted the Ruby Fulcrum computer and found the loose telephone prong leading from the modem, he figured it was another loose wire and slipped it into the jack."

"Oh, shit . . ."

Hinckley's face expressed a wan smile. "Yes, well, that's one way of putting it. After he did that and he was assured that the phone lines were operational again, he switched on the computer to give it a quick test . . . and, of course, being a conscientious Science Services employee, he tested the modem by dialing into a local BBS to see if the patch was solid."

And, without anyone's realizing what had happened, Ruby was allowed to crawl through the bars of its playpen. Frankenstein's monster had been let loose to roam the streets of the global village.

"We didn't know what had happened until we came back to the lab on Monday," Hinckley went on. "Dick flipped out, of course, and the first thing he did was to try and figure out where and how Ruby had slipped through our fingers. To do this, he had to access the company's mainframe and backtrack all its incoming and outgoing phone calls, including e-mail and fax records."

She stared at me directly, meeting my gaze over the tabletop. "When he did this," she said, very quietly, "he managed to penetrate company files none of us had ever seen and discovered something none of us were ever meant to know—"

At that moment, the door slammed loudly. We both glanced up; no one but a pair of salesmen, swaggering in for a late lunch as if they owned the place. One of them yelled for our waitress to seat them; the other tried to stroke her ass as she flitted by. A couple of slimers, nothing more, but their rude entrance made her more aware of our surroundings.

"We've got to get out of here," she said. "I don't like this place."

"C'mon," I said. "Just some yups cruising for burgers."

She continued to stare uncertainly toward the door. "There might be ERA people out there," she said. "They don't always wear uniforms or carry guns, you know."

She was scared and had every right to be, but that didn't matter right now. I wanted to get the rest of the story out of her before she went down the street to the courthouse. "Don't worry about the feds grabbing us," I said quickly. "Remember what I told you about Barris, the local ERA honcho? He gave me a card I could use to get us past checkpoints."

"Card?" Her gaze wavered back toward me, only slightly distracted. "What sort of card?"

"Umm . . . this one." I reached into my jacket for the laminated card the colonel had given me the night before. I hadn't looked at the card since Barris had handed it to me; in fact, this was the first time all day I had thought of it.

"See?" I said as I produced the plastic card and showed it to her. "It'll solve any problems with—"

"Oh, hell," she whispered. "Let me see that."

Before I could object, Hinckley whisked the card from my fingertips and examined it closely. She bent it slightly, held it up to the light . . . then reached into the pocket of her jacket and pulled out a Swiss Army knife, unfolded its miniature scissors, and made a deep cut into the center of the card.

"Hey!" I snapped. "Don't do . . ."

Then I stopped as she pulled open the card a little more and revealed it to me. Within its plastic and cardboard lining lay wires as fine as cat whiskers, leading to tiny wafer-thin microchips and miniature solenoids.

"It's a smartcard," she breathed. "Like the smartbadges we've got at the company . . . only this one can emit a signal that can be traced through cellular bands."

"Aw, shit . . ." I couldn't believe I had been such an idiot. The bastards had set me up and I had fallen for it. "Can it . . . could it listen to us?"

She shook her head. "Uh-uh," she said quietly. "It'd have to be larger than this . . . but it can signal our location to anyone who's paying attention. That's bad enough."

A frigid current ran down my spine. "Does this mean—"

"I don't know what it means," she shot back at me. "You brought it here, so you tell me." Hinckley gently lay the card on the table and slid it against the wall, placing a napkin dispenser on top of it for good measure. "One thing's for sure, and that's the fact we've been here too long."

"Hey, I didn't know—"

"I know you didn't know," she murmured as she slid out from her side of the booth. "If you'd been working for them, you wouldn't have been so stupid as to show it to me. That's not the point."

She dug a few dollars out of her pocket and put them on the table. "When we get to the courthouse and I find a judge, you'll get the rest of the story . . . but we've got to get out of here."

I was just starting to clamber out from my side of the booth. "But I swear I didn't—"

"*Now*, damn it!" Hinckley was already heading for the door by the time I crawled out of my seat. I scrounged a handful of loose change out of my pocket, dropped it on the table, and gave an apologetic shrug to the waitress, then hurried to catch up with her.

17

I caught up with Beryl Hinckley just outside the restaurant. The crowds were beginning to thin out on the sidewalk as office workers hurried back to their desks and cubicles, clutching half-read newspapers and foam cups of coffee. There was still plenty of traffic on the street, however, and the metered slots along Central Avenue were filled with parked cars.

"Walk fast," I murmured as I took her right arm and began marching down the sidewalk. "Whatever you do, keep an eye on the cars. If you see anything—"

"I know," she whispered back. "Run for it."

I glanced at her; she nodded her head, her face grim. She knew the score: both John and Kim Po had been shot from a vehicle, and although a van had been spotted leaving Clancy's, no one was certain if this was the automobile the killer was driving. The only thing we had going for us was that it was a blustery afternoon, and most drivers were keeping their windows up. According to what Cale McLaughlin had told me, the laser rifle the sniper was using was capable of firing through nonreflective glass, yet if the killer wanted to get an unimpaired shot, he might want to lower the window first.

We shied away from the street, but I walked next to the curb. Old-fashioned chivalry, just the way my dad taught me, but this time it was for more practical reasons than to keep the lady I was escorting from being splattered with mud from passing cars. If she was the killer's primary target, then I would be shielding her a little more this way. Of course, if she was right, it didn't really matter what I did, because

199

the bastard might try to nail me first. It wasn't a comforting thought.

"You have any idea which judge you're going to find?" I asked as we walked. Only one city block left to go; I could already see the small plaza across the street from the intersection of Central and Carondelet. Directly beyond the plaza was the five-story white concrete box that was the county courthouse.

Hinckley hesitated, then shook her head. "I don't keep up with the judges around here," she replied, her eyes locked on the street. "I was just planning on going in there and finding someone's name on a door."

I sighed and shook my head. Glancing down at the sidewalk, I noticed for the first time that she wore knee-length calfskin boots; the laces on her right boot were loose and were beginning to drag the ground, but I wasn't about to remind her to stop and retie them. "It's a little harder than that," I said. "They keep office hours like everyone else . . . and on a Friday afternoon, if they're not in court, then they're probably out on the golf links."

I thought about it for another moment, trying to remember the names of judges whose cases I had covered in the past for the paper. "We might try Swenson . . . Edith Swenson," I added. "She's supposed to be pretty honest, at least. I don't know if she's in, but we could always . . ."

Her breath suddenly sucked in as I felt her arm go rigid in mine. I followed her gaze and saw a van turning the corner of Carondelet and heading our way. A white Ford Econovan, late eighties vintage—a rusted-out old gashog, pale gray fumes farting out of its exhaust pipe, probably on the last weeks of its expiration sticker—but what caught her attention was that it was moving very slowly toward us. I looked closer; I couldn't see the driver, but the passenger window was lowered.

The doorway of another restaurant was just a few feet away, beneath an ornamental canvas awning. "In there!" I snapped.

Hinckley didn't need any urging. We scurried under the awning and into the doorway. I grabbed the door handle and was about to pull it open when the Econovan rumbled past.

Both of us froze and stared at the van; an old black gentleman was behind the wheel, and he didn't seem to be paying a bit of attention to us as he tooled down Central away from the courthouse. I caught a couple of bars from a vintage soul number blaring from the stereo as the clunker rumbled past: *"Nutbush city limits! . . .* wahwahwahwah-waaw-waaw *. . . Nutbush city limits!"*

False alarm.

Beryl sagged against the doorframe, her hand against her chest. "God," she whispered as she let out a hoarse laugh. "I never thought I'd be so glad to hear Ike and Tina Turner."

"I'll find a copy for you when we get out of this." I pulled her out of the doorway.

"Oh, hell . . ." She stopped suddenly and looked down at her feet. "My boot's untied."

I thought again about letting her take care of her laces, but I let it pass. The next vehicle to pass us might have more than classic Motown tunes blasting through its side windows. "Don't worry about it now," I said as I tugged at her arm. "Just keep going."

We walked past an alley entrance and the last building on the block, a condemned midcentury office building with windows boarded up with plywood: another victim of the earthquake, whose owner had apparently decided that demolition was less expensive than renovation. By now we were almost directly across the corner from the courthouse, a block-size building nearly as homely and featureless as the adjacent county jail and the Government Center highrise. All three buildings suffered from that peculiar form of governmental architecture a friend of mine had once described as "Twentieth Century Post-Gothic Paranoid": no windows in featureless walls on the ground floor, the narrow casement windows on the upper floors resembling the archer slots in medieval castles. Trust us, we're the government . . .

"Fine with me," I muttered, "so long as you can repel laser beams."

"What?" Hinckley asked.

"Nothing. Just thinking aloud." As I said this, another thought occurred to me. "What about the two other guys . . . um, Dick and Jeff? When do I get to meet them?"

She shot me a glance that spoke volumes. She was placing enough confidence in me to hear out her story and witness her surrender to a judge, but she wasn't quite ready to entrust her friends' lives to my hands. After all, I had already confessed to her that Barris was counting on me to track down Payson-Smith for him. Even though I had obviously been surprised by the cellular smartcard Barris had given me and I had willingly left it behind in the restaurant, there was still no guarantee that I wasn't playing stool pigeon for ERA.

"I'll let you know when the time's right," she said softly. "They already know about you, don't worry . . . but we need to take this one step at a time. All right?"

"Yeah. Okay. Whatever."

We arrived at the corner of Central and Carondelet. No other pedestrians were in sight; no cars violated the No Parking signs in front of the courthouse and the jail. So far, so good; all we had to do was cross the street, make it through the postage-stamp plaza with its rows of empty cement planters, and the side door of the courthouse was wide open to us. Walk-through metal detectors had been established in all the courthouse entrances some twenty years ago after some lunatic had opened fire in a courtroom and killed a few people, and there were always a couple of cops stationed at the checkpoints. Once we were through the side door, we were home free.

I gave the area a quick scan, then I grabbed her hand and pulled her off the sidewalk, leading her out into the street. "Okay," I said, "let's go."

We jaywalked through the wide intersection, not running but not sightseeing either. Halfway through the intersection, she dropped my hand. We stepped onto the curb, walking beside each other, and began to stride into the plaza. I could see people walking or seated at desks behind the courthouse windows. The side door was only seventy feet away.

She made a slight grunt, as if she had tripped on her bootlaces, but I paid no attention. I was beginning to relax. *You asshole, you're running from shadows . . .*

"I think I can find that Turner CD at a place down on Delmar," I said. "You ever been to Vintage Vinyl? It's got the best . . ."

No answer. She wasn't walking beside me anymore. I turned around, half-expecting to see that she had finally stopped to lace up her boots.

Dr. Beryl Hinckley lay sprawled on her face across the concrete sidewalk just a few feet from the curb, her arms and legs still twitching slightly as what remained of her brain told her that it was time to run like hell.

Not that she had been given much chance to run; the silent beam that killed her had burned a thumbhole through the back of her skull.

The moment stretched, became surreal. Cars moved by on the street. Pigeons wandered around the edge of the plaza in search of infinitesimal scraps of food. A commuter 'copter moaned overhead, heading for the municipal heliport several blocks away. A dead woman lay at my feet, and all around me the world was going about its normal day-to-day business. One second you're talking to someone about buying secondhand CDs; the next second, that person is cold meat on the street corner, shot down by a . . .

Laser beam.

I yanked myself out of my stupor, began looking around. No cars were in sight, but all around me were high-rise buildings. Countless windows in a half-dozen towers, and the sniper could be lurking behind any one of them, even now drawing a dead bead on me.

Move, stupid!

The nearest of the plaza's tree-planters was directly behind me, a large round urn about three feet high and eight feet in diameter. I dove behind it, crouching in its shadow as my heart triphammered in my ears. There were seventeen more planters just like it behind me, artfully arranged in three rows of six each, leading down the plaza until they ended near the courthouse door. The planters were empty, but they might provide enough cover for me. If I could keep dodging behind them as I made a run for the side door . . .

Yeah, right. The next planter in the row was at least ten feet away; the sniper could pick me off easily as soon as I raised my head. I'd be dead before I knew what hit me.

I hugged the side of the planter, trying to remember what McLaughlin had told me about the nature of laser rifles. Silent. Invisible beam. Flat trajectory. Almost infinite range . . . but big and clumsy, about the size of a rocket launcher. That meant whoever was using it would have to remain fixed in one place. And there was something else . . .

A couple of well-dressed women, probably trial lawyers returning from lunch down the street, appeared from around the corner of the Government Center building. They were still chatting it up as they began to cross Carondelet, until they saw Beryl Hinckley's body lying on the opposite sidewalk.

They froze in the middle of the street, gazing in confused shock at the corpse, then one of them looked around and spotted me. Before I could say anything, she screamed bloody murder, then turned and ran back the way she had come. The other one stared at me in gap-mouthed fear for another second, then she followed her friend as they fled back around the corner.

Great. Just what I needed right now: they'd call the police and report a homicidal maniac hanging around the courthouse plaza. I closed my eyes and knocked my head against the side of the urn. In another minute this place would be surrounded by cops who'd . . .

A minute.

That was it. McLaughlin had told me that it took sixty seconds for the laser to recharge itself. Assuming he hadn't been lying to me, I had some lead time before the killer could squeeze the trigger again.

This was of little comfort to me. At least a minute had gone by already, between the instant Beryl had been shot and this moment in time. But if the killer still had me in his direct line of fire, then he should have picked me off by now. Sure, maybe he had seen where I had taken cover—but so long as I had the planter between us, then he couldn't skrag me as well.

Not yet, at least. I couldn't remain here much longer. Sooner or later, I'd have to get to my feet.

Forget about that, I told myself. *Concentrate on what's going on here . . .*

Okay, okay. She couldn't have been shot from a window in either the courthouse or Government Center; those buildings were on either side of me, and anyone standing in the windows would be able to see me. The jail had few windows of which to speak, and it was the most unlikely place for a sniper to be hiding. I ruled out the high-rise apartment complex behind the courthouse; the angle of fire was all wrong.

This still left at least another four or five buildings on the other side of Central Avenue. If I could only figure out which one was the—

There was a commotion from the courthouse entrance. I glanced over my shoulder to see a half-dozen people hesitantly emerging from the glass double doors: lawyers, clients, court witnesses, and clerks, all staring at me. A uniformed cop was right behind them; one of the onlookers pointed my way and the cop drew his gun, but instead of taking matters into his own hands he quickly urged the rubberneckers back into the building before he took cover within the entranceway. From what little I could make of him, I could see him pull out his beltphone, snap it open, and hold it close to his face.

The Clayton cop shop was located only a few blocks away. I now had the option of holding out until the law arrived. It was a tempting thought—surrender peacefully and allow myself to be taken into custody, then prove my innocence in my own sweet time—but that still meant I would have to emerge from hiding. The sniper could take me out while I was surrounded by a SWAT team. Even if they doped out how and why I had suddenly fallen down with a self-cauterized hole in my head, it wouldn't mean shit so far as I was concerned.

Fuck it. I had to pinpoint the sniper myself . . . but now I had an idea.

Still crouching low behind the planter, I pulled Joker out of my jacket pocket, flipped it open, and switched to verbal mode. "Joker, log on," I said.

"Good afternoon, Gerry. What can I do for you?"

"Gimme a street map of the Clayton district." I glanced over my shoulder again at the courthouse cop; he was still laying low, waiting for his backup to arrive. "Display a three-block radius surrounding the intersection of South Central and Carondelet."

"*Working . . . just a moment, please.*" There was silence while my PT modemed into a library neural-net. Two or three moments passed before the uplink was completed and the map was laid out on the PT's clamshell screen. "*Here is the map you requested.*"

I could hear sirens approaching from the distance. I forced the sound from my mind. "Okay. Now . . . uh, overlay a 3-D graphic of all buildings within this perimeter, and make it snappy."

"*Snappy is not an available function. Please define.*"

"Forget snappy," I said impatiently. "Just do it."

Computer-animated buildings sprang from the gridwork of streets. Now the map resembled an aerial photo of this part of Clayton, including the courthouse plaza itself. "Very good," I said. "Logon graphics-edit. I'm giving you a new coordinate for the map. I want you to add it to your memory."

"*Certainly, Gerry.*"

I touched the miniature trackball and gently moved the cursor across the screen until it was approximately above the spot in the courtyard where Hinckley's body lay. When I removed my finger, the cursor vanished and a tiny *X* remained in its place.

So far, so good, but the sirens were getting closer now. I looked over my shoulder again but couldn't see the cop who had been hiding in the doorway. I took a deep breath, then went on. "Okay . . . now display lines between this coordinate and . . . ah . . ."

Shit. All of a sudden, I was stumped by my own ingenuity. How could I ask Joker to show me the probable line-of-sight trajectory between Hinckley and the sniper? I already knew what would happen if I phrased the question the wrong way; lines would radiate in all directions from the coordinate I had registered on the map.

But how could I explain the problem to a literal-minded computer? *Well, see, there's someone lying on the ground nearby who's just been shot by laser beam, and I'm the next target, so I want you to try to figure out which building on this grid the sniper was firing from . . . and, by the way, the cops are closing in, so make it snappy. That means quick, right away, pronto, haul ass . . .*

Yeah. Fat chance . . . but it was better than nothing. I would have to dumb-fuck my way through this. "Given that the coordinate I just designated is five-point-five feet tall . . ." I said slowly.

"Pardon me, Gerry, but I have received an instant message for you."

Joker's voice was maddeningly calm. Here I was, trying to think through a complex problem to save my life, and it wanted to deliver e-mail to me. I winced and swore under my breath. "This is not a good time, Joker."

"I'm sorry, Gerry, but the IM has a priority interrupt. The sender has identified itself as Ruby Fulcrum."

What the . . . ?

"Gimme the message!" I snapped.

The screen bisected into two parts; the map remained intact on the upper half, although reduced by fifty percent, while the lower half displayed a message bar:

>Laser beam fired from 1010 South Central Avenue, floor five<

At the same moment, a red line traced itself from the coordinate I had registered on the map to the condemned five-story office building directly across the corner from the courthouse.

I stared at the screen. How the hell could . . . ?

"Freeze, mister!" a voice yelled. "Get your hands in sight!"

The courthouse cop I had spotted earlier was standing directly behind me. His feet were spread wide apart, his service revolver clasped between both hands and pointed at the back of my head. He had snuck up on me while I was paying attention to Joker.

"Okay, okay," I said, trying to calm him down. "I don't have a gun, see?" I held up Joker in my right hand, keeping my left hand where he could see it. "Look, it's not a gun, all right?"

The cop wasn't impressed. "Yes sir, I can see what it is," he said evenly. "I want you to put it down on the ground, stand up and put your hands behind your head. Now, sir."

I carefully placed Joker on the concrete and wrapped my hands around the back of my head, but I didn't stand up. "Officer," I said as calmly as I could, "the woman over there was shot from the top floor of that building." I nodded toward the condemned building across Central from Government Center. "I had nothing to do with it, but—"

The officer's eyes darted once toward the building, then back to me. He wasn't buying it. "Get on your feet, mister."

"Look, I'm telling you, if I stand up now, he's going to shoot—"

His attention was fixed solely upon me. "I'm not kidding, buddy!" he demanded. "Get up with your hands behind your head!"

The sirens were much louder now, probably only a block away, racing down Central Avenue toward the courthouse. The officer was waiting for his backup to arrive, and he wasn't about to give me any slack. There was a dead woman on the sidewalk, and his suspect was giving him a song-and-dance routine. His right forefinger was wrapped around the trigger of his gun. This was a young rookie, still in his twenties and fresh out of the academy; he wanted to be a Good Cop, but I was only too aware of the fact that some members of the force had a bad rep for being trigger-happy under pressure.

As the first police cruiser howled into sight and screeched to a halt in front of the plaza, I took a deep breath. The cavalry had arrived; maybe they had scared off the sniper. "Okay," I said, "just stay cool. I'm standing up."

The second cruiser arrived, stopping behind the first one; two cops had already jumped out of the first car and were rushing over to check on Beryl Hinckley. I slowly began to rise out of my squat, but as I did I kept my eyes fixed on the empty windows of the building Ruby Fulcrum had pinpointed.

I had barely raised my head and shoulder above the height of the urn when I glimpsed vague movement in a corner window on the fifth floor: a brief, dull reflection, like sunlight reflecting off something metallic . . .

"Duck!" I yelled, then threw myself to the ground.

"Don't . . . AWWWHHHH!"

A small black hole appeared in the cop's chest, just below his neckline. He dropped his gun as he grabbed at his collarbone, screaming in agony, then his legs collapsed beneath him and he fell backward to hit the pavement. He was still alive, but the laser beam had cut straight though his body.

Two more cops from the second cruiser, who had been running over to assist him, stopped dead in their tracks. They had seen the whole thing; judging from the expressions on their faces, they couldn't figure out what the hell had happened. They glanced first at their buddy, then at me, then back at him again.

"I didn't do a thing!" I yelled as I lay flat on the ground, my arms spread out before me. "I'm just lying here . . . get him an ambulance!"

The cops unfroze. Instead of rushing me, they hurried to the rookie's side. He was writhing in pain, his legs thrashing against the pavement. His colleagues kneeled beside him; one of them grabbed his beltphone and flipped it open. "Mobile Charlie-Five, answering call at the courthouse!" he snapped. "Code ten-three, officer down!"

The other two cops ran over to assist them. For the moment, they were entirely concerned with the injured officer. No one was paying attention to me. I rose to my hands and knees, carefully picked Joker up from the concrete and shoved it in my pocket . . .

And then I jumped to my feet and took off running.

Not away from the scene, though, but straight toward the abandoned building.

18

One thing to be said for knowing that a sniper is trying to kill you: it makes you run faster.

Even as I sprinted across the intersection, I knew that I had less than thirty seconds—if even that—to reach cover before the laser's batteries recharged. On the other hand, if I could make it to the building itself, then the gunner upstairs wouldn't be able to shoot me. A clean vertical shot would be nearly impossible from up there, or otherwise he would have fired at Beryl before we had jaywalked across the street.

I heard cops shouting behind me as I made a beeline for the building, demanding that I halt. The thought crossed my mind that one of them might open fire on me, but I wasn't about to stop and lie down in the middle of the intersection. I was screwed if I did and screwed if I didn't, and all I could hope for was the notion that a well-trained police officer wouldn't shoot a running man in the back . . .

So I kept running.

A laser beam didn't punch a hole through my head, nor did I heard the crack of a gunshot as I reached the opposite side of the intersection and dashed toward the building's front doors. Although its nineteenth-century facade was largely intact, official condemnation notices were pasted across the plywood nailed over the windows.

I ducked into the recessed doorway and took a deep breath. I was safe for the moment, but I still had to get inside before the cops followed me. The narrow door, itself covered with plywood, had been secured with a padlock; when I looked closer, though, I saw that the lock's hasp had been severed as if by a pair of heavy-duty bolt cutters, then carefully rehung to make it look still secure.

The door's pneumatic hinge wheezed as I tugged it open and stepped into the narrow entranceway, cautiously avoiding the shattered glass that lay on the floor of the foyer. The door closed behind me. Faint sunlight penetrated the gloom through cracks in the plywood, making it possible for me to read the dislodged building register resting on its side against the wall: lawyer's offices for the most part, although the second and fifth floors had been vacant at the time of the quake.

The building was stone quiet.

Groping along the walls with my hands, I made my way farther into the building, passing a battered water fountain, an inactive elevator, and the entrance to what had once been a barber shop, until I reached the end of the hallway and found the door leading to the stairwell.

The door squeaked as I pulled it open; I hesitated for a moment, listening intently to the darkness above me. I still couldn't hear anything, but that meant nothing. For all I knew, the sniper could be at the top of the stairwell, waiting for my head to come into sight.

For a few moments I considered the safest option but almost immediately discarded that idea. Retreat only meant giving the sniper a chance to try again some other time . . . but now I had a slim chance of cornering the bastard and ending this game once and for all.

So I entered the stairwell, carefully let the door slide shut, then began to climb the stairs.

Light shining through unboarded windows at each landing guided me as I made my way upward, peering around each corner before I jogged up the next set of risers. Mice and cockroaches fled from my approach; the building smelled of old dust and the stale urine of evicted squatters. On the third-floor landing, I found a small pile of rubble from a collapsed ceiling. I picked a short length of iron rebar out of the mess and hefted it in my hands—remembering the crazy lawyer I had seen at the Muny a couple of nights earlier, I wondered if his firm's offices had once been located here—

then I continued my way upstairs.

No one was waiting for me on the fifth-floor landing.

Stopping for a moment to catch my breath, I studied the door leading toward the end of the building from where the shots had originated. At first glance, it seemed undisturbed, until I noticed a straight line of dust and broken plaster leading away from the hinge at a right angle as if recently pushed aside by the bottom of door.

There was a window behind me, looking out over the rear of the building. I peered out and spotted a battered brown Toyota mini-van parked in the back alley, near the bottom of a fire escape. From what I could see, it looked as if the fire escape had a gravity ladder leading to the pavement. If that was the killer's wheels, then he would probably be using the fire escape to make his getaway from the building.

I should have thought of that earlier. It wouldn't have been quite as stupid or reckless to wait in the alley until he reached the bottom of the fire escape. No turning back now, though. I was here, and he was somewhere in there, and the time had come to take down the son of a bitch before he killed somebody else.

Gripping the iron bar in my left hand, I tiptoed to the door, grasped its handle, and slowly eased it open.

A short hallway led me past the defunct elevator and the door of the vacant office space; at the opposite end of the corridor was the fire-escape window. The window was raised, and the office door was propped open with a short piece of broken wood.

Through the door, I could hear vague, hurried movement: metal moving against metal, a zipper sliding down, then up again. The grunt of breath being exhaled. I inched my way toward the door, put my back against the wall, and peered through the doorframe.

The space beyond the doorway was completely vacant; even before the quake, all the interior drywalls had been knocked down, leaving open a large, empty room bordered only by the outer walls. Sullen midday sunlight, flecked with dust motes, streamed through the windows and the gaping hole in the ceiling where the roof had partially collapsed, leaving broken pipes, brick, and mortar strewn across the dirty tile floor.

On the opposite side of the room, the killer was packing up the tools of his trade.

He was nobody I recognized. In fact, he looked like nobody anyone would ever recognize. Average height, medium build, late thirties or early forties, wearing a beige workman's jumpsuit. A wireless radio headset hung around his neck. Sunlight reflected dully off a receding hairline, which had already left him half bald, and the wire-rimmed glasses on his plain face. People talk about the banality of evil; I was looking right at it. This dude could have been a janitor, an electrician, an exterminator cruising for rats . . . anything but a professional assassin.

He moved quickly as he dismantled his weapon: a small compressed-gas tank, a contraption that looked like a compact piston-driven pump, a pair of storage batteries attached by slender cables to a long, cumbersome instrument that vaguely resembled a World War II vintage bazooka, itself mounted on a tripod with an infrared telescopic sight above its barrel. All of it was being stripped down and loaded into a two-wheeled golf caddie.

You think "laser rifle" and the first thing you imagine is something from a late-show SF movie—small, sleek, no larger than an AK-47—but this thing resembled nothing more or less than an industrial welding rig from Chevy Dick's garage. *Of course two people had been shot from a van*, I thought. *You'd need a van just to haul all this shit around.*

Never mind that now. His back was turned to me. His target was gone, and he only wanted to get out of here while the getting was good. Man, was he in for a surprise.

He had disconnected one of the batteries and had bent over the caddie to shove it in place when I moved through the doorway as quietly as I could, carefully stepping around the broken stuff littering the floor, the rebar grasped in both hands. I paused as he stood up and turned toward the laser itself, pulling an electric screwdriver from the back pocket of his jumpsuit. He fitted it into the base of the tripod; there was a thin mechanical whine as his thumb pressed against the button.

I took a deep breath, hefted the rebar in my hands, and then I charged across the room toward him.

Halfway across the room, my boots stamped through some debris. His head snapped up at the sound; he dropped the screwdriver and began to twist around, his right hand whipping for the front breast pocket of his jumpsuit as he turned toward the figure hurtling at him.

I screamed at the top of my lungs as I hauled the iron bar above my head. The .45 automatic was out of his pocket, but he didn't have a chance to aim before I swung the rebar.

It slammed straight across his chest and lifted him off his feet; the gun sailed out of his hand, hitting the floor ten feet away from where his ass landed.

He lashed out at me with his right leg, catching me on the side of my left ankle. I yelped and danced away; he rolled over and began to scramble toward his gun.

"Fuck you!" I yelled as I raised the slender iron bar again and brought it straight like an ax against the back of his right arm.

He screamed at the same instant as I heard the dry snap of his elbow being shattered. He clutched at his arm as he rolled over on his back, losing his glasses as he howled in agony.

"I said, 'Fuck you!' " I yelled again as I raised the bar and swung it down square between his legs.

His scream could have shattered a wineglass. A dark blotch spread against his pulverized groin as he grabbed at it. I didn't care. "Didn't you hear me, asshole?" I snarled. "Are you deaf? I said, 'Fuck you!' "

I swung the rebar down across his right knee. The breaking of bone and cartilage, like fine porcelain shattering beneath a hammer, trembled through the bar into my hands.

God help me, but I loved it.

He howled as tears streamed from his eyes, his face turning stark red. I bent over him, savoring his agony, the high animalistic keening of his voice.

"Still can't hear you, cocksucker!" I bellowed at him, then I stood up and lifted the iron bar above my head again. "I said—"

"I hear you!" he gasped, his voice ragged and hoarse. "I hear you! Please don't . . ."

I saw John's face. I saw Beryl Hinckley's face. I saw Jamie's face, even though this scumbucket had had nothing to do with his death. I wanted to beat this nameless bastard to death . . . but before that, I wanted answers to a lot of questions.

"Where are you from?" I shouted. "Who sent you?"

His face crawled. "Ehh . . . ehhh . . ."

"Tell me, you dick! Tell me who sent you or I swear to God you'll never walk again!"

His chest was rising and falling as if he had just run a ten-mile race. In another minute, he'd go into shock and I'd lose him . . .

"Speak up, you piece of shit!" I showed him the jagged edge of the rebar, holding it just above his face, and let his imagination do the rest. "Talk to me!"

"ERA!" he cried out. "I'm working for ERA!"

No surprise there. Still holding the rod over his head, I yanked Joker out of my pocket, thumbed it into Audio Record, and held it over him. "Who at ERA sent you?" I demanded, even though I already knew. "Tell me his name! Why did he—"

"Drop it, Rosen!"

Mike Farrentino was standing just inside the door, book-ended by two uniformed officers. The cops were crouched, their revolvers cupped between their hands and aimed straight at me, but Farrentino's hands were shoved in his pockets.

"Get away from him, Gerry," he said evenly. "Just let go and—"

"Aw, cut it out, Mike." I pulled the rebar away from the sniper's face and let it drop from my hands; it hit the floor with a dull clang. I raised my arms and backed away from the man on the floor. As quickly as it had come, my rage dissipated. "He's the guy you want, not me. I just—"

"Shut up, Gerry." Farrentino walked farther into the room. "Simmons, look after the man on the floor. Conklin, make sure Mr. Rosen isn't carrying anything he shouldn't be."

The two cops stood up. Their guns still in hand, they quickly crossed the room. I kept my hands in the air while Conklin patted me down and removed Joker from my right hand. "He's clean, Lieutenant," he said as he holstered his pistol and held out my PT to the detective. "That's all he's got on him."

"This guy's in bad shape, sir." Simmons was kneeling next to the man on the floor, checking his pulse. "He's still conscious, but he's got a broken arm, a busted leg, some hemorrhaging in the testicle area." He paused, then added, "Gun on the floor over there."

Farrentino walked over to the gun and knelt down beside it, being careful not to touch it. "Get another ambulance crew up here pronto," he said to no one in particular, "and collect this piece as evidence. Bag it and have it taken downtown to the lab . . . dust-up, serial number and registration check, the works."

Simmons nodded his head, then looked down at the man on the floor. The headset was lying next to his head; he picked it up and held it next to his ear, then looked up at the lieutenant. "Just static," he said, "but it must have been active."

"Bag it," Farrentino said. "Take it downtown."

"What about this one?" Conklin asked, still standing beside me. "Want me to bring 'im downtown?"

"Before you start reading me the card, Mike," I said, "you might want to check out that rig over there. That's the laser rifle you guys have been looking for. This dude's the one who killed three people so far."

Farrentino glanced at the man, then stood up and walked over to study the partially disassembled laser more closely, again being careful not to lay his hands on anything. He gave it the once-over, then grunted and looked back at me. "And I guess you're going to tell me that you found this character up here and worked him over before you thought he was going to shoot you next. Right?"

I lowered my arms to my sides. "No thinking about it, Lieutenant. He shot Beryl Hinckley—that's the woman down there in the plaza—while we were crossing the street together. He tried to shoot me next, but the courthouse cop got in the way." I swallowed, remembering the way he had screamed

His eyebrows raised slightly. There was the sound of footsteps coming up the stairwell. Farrentino looked over his shoulder; a trio of paramedics trooped through the door, carrying a folded stretcher. They barely noticed us as they went straight for the man on the floor, but Farrentino seemed relieved. He let out his breath, then looked back at me.

"I just received an APB," he said very quietly. "There's a ten-ninety-four out for you."

"What, I didn't pay my parking tickets? I don't even have a car—"

"Shut up." Farrentino's eyes were like black ice. He closed his PT and slipped it into his coat pocket. "No fucking around now," he whispered, glancing over his shoulder again. "It was issued by ERA, and it means that you're wanted for immediate pickup . . . possibly as a militant, an armed suspect, a mental case, or all of the above."

"What the—"

"Truth. The feds want your ass and they want it now."

Now it was my turn to feel the cold chills. I shot a glance at the parameds and cops gathered around the gunner; none of them seemed to be paying attention to us, but that could change any second.

"When did this happen?" I whispered.

"Just now." He cocked his head toward the two patrolmen. "You don't have to worry about those guys . . . they're going to be busy for a few minutes . . . but you're wanted by the feds now. I don't think I have to tell you why."

No, he did not; I could make a pretty good guess on my own. The moment Hinckley had cut open the tracer and left it in the restaurant, whoever had been monitoring my signal had realized that I was wise to them. That's when Barris told his killer, who had already tracked down Hinckley with my unwitting cooperation, to snuff me as well—and since the killer had failed, Barris now wanted to have me brought down to the Stadium Club for one last meeting.

This time, there wouldn't be any easy release. If they got me, then they got Joker as well, and with it the interview Hinckley had given me just before she was killed. Even if I threw Joker into a garbage can and surrendered myself, there was little chance I would ever emerge from the stadium again. Not alive, at least.

I took a deep breath, trying to control my panic. The area outside the building was already crawling with cops; no doubt they would soon be joined by ERA troopers. "Okay, Mike," I said, my voice suddenly raw in my throat, "it's up to you . . ."

"Uh-uh." Farrentino shook his head. "I've already done all I can do. I've questioned you in front of two other officers and determined that you're not a suspect, so now you're free to go. If Barris comes to me, my hands are clean. I'm just the dumb cop who let you slip. I'm sorry, but that's it."

"Aw c'mon, Mike . . ."

He jerked his head toward the door. "Get out of here," he murmured. "Hit the street. Don't go back to your apartment or your wife's place, those are the first places they're going to look for you. And stay the fuck off the net—"

"Mike," I said, "how—"

"Go!" he whispered. "Move your ass!"

I started to argue some more, but he turned his back on me. Trailing cigarette smoke, he began to saunter across the room. Conklin looked up at him as he approached; for a moment, he stared past the homicide detective at me, then he looked away again.

A helicopter roared over the rooftop, breaking the spell. I took one last look around, then I eased out of the room and headed for the hallway. The window leading to the fire escape was still open. I stuck my head out, saw that no one was in the alley below, then climbed out the window and began to scurry down the cold iron stairs.

I was on the run, and I hadn't the slightest clue where I was supposed to go.

PART FOUR

His Court of Love and Beauty

(April 20, 2013)

19

Beep-beep . . .
  Beep-beep . . .
  Beep-beep . . .
  I awoke to a steady electronic pulse from somewhere in the darkness.

My first thought was that it was the phone on my desk. Then I remembered that I was not in my apartment but instead hiding out in an abandoned house on the south side.

It had taken me the better part of the afternoon to make my getaway from Clayton. I rode the Yellow Line as far south as I could, then got off the MetroLink at the Gravois Avenue station and hiked as far as I dared into this dangerous part of the city. The police seldom ventured this far south except in Russian APCs, and even ERA troopers were reluctant to patrol the edges of Dogtown save by helicopter; perhaps the dragnet wouldn't extend into this combat-zone neighborhood not far from the Mississippi River.

I hadn't encountered any heat either on the train or on foot during my long journey through the city, but I was exhausted by the time I had found the house. Even after my close brush with the ERA Apache earlier tonight, I had soon fallen back asleep on the couch, trusting the stray dog who had adopted me to wake me up again if the chopper returned. The mutt had curled up on the floor next to the couch; he raised his head now, his brown ears cocked forward in curiosity as he stared at the source of the noise.

Joker lay on the bare floor where I had left it after I had finished dictating my notes, its red LED flashing in time with

223

the annunciator. The dog got up and padded across the empty living room to sniff at it, then he looked up at me: *Well, what are you going to do about it?*

Someone—or perhaps something—was trying to get my attention.

"I dunno what it is either, buddy," I murmured. "Let me see what's going on."

Drawn by the blinking diode, I swung my stiff legs off the couch and shuffled across the room to where the PT lay. Kneeling on the hardwood floor, I picked up Joker and opened its cover, expecting to find another mysterious IM displayed on its screen.

What I saw instead was a ghost: the face of my dead son, stolen from the video I had made of him a little over a year ago, now outlined in tiny animated pixels. Across the bottom of the screen was a message bar.

>**Gerry Rosen, I need to talk to you.**<
>**Daddy, I need to talk to you.**<
>**Please talk to me, Gerry.**<

"No!" I yelled. "Leave me alone!"

I raised the PT over my head, about to hurl it across the room. Frightened by my surge of anger, the dog danced backward, whining a little as its tail crept down between its hindquarters. If nothing else, the dog's reaction helped check my impulse; instead of dashing Joker against the wall, I lowered the PT and stabbed its VOX button with my forefinger.

"Listen, you shit," I snarled, "you've done enough to me already! Leave Jamie out of this!"

Jamie's face didn't vanish from the screen. Instead, the image blinked at me, somehow managing to assay a childish pout. God, it was scary; computer generated or not, it looked exactly like my kid.

Jamie's voice emerged from Joker's speaker. *"I'm sorry, but I'm trying to get your attention in the best way I can. Does this form and voice displease you?"*

"God, yes!" I yelled at the screen. "Don't you understand? This is my son you're using! He's dead! Don't you realize what this does to me?"

Jamie's face assumed a confused expression. *"Jamie Arnold*

Rosen," it intoned; it was as if Jamie himself were reciting his life history, except in words that a six-year-old would never have used. *"Born March 2, 2006. Died May 17, 2012. Killed during the New Madrid earthquake while riding the MetroLink train across the William Eads Bridge. The Eads Bridge collapsed, resulting in the deaths of seventy-three passengers including twelve members of the first-grade class of Bo Hillman Elementary School, who were returning from a field trip to—"*

"You think I don't know that already?" I sagged to the floor, clutching Joker in my hands. "Why are you telling me this?"

"The circumstances of your son's death are a matter of public record. I was in doubt whether you were suffering from undiagnosed survivor's syndrome and therefore amnesiac about—"

"No, I'm not suffering from survivor's syndrome, and I didn't forget." I took a deep breath and closed my eyes. "And lemme tell you something that isn't a matter of public record . . . Jamie was on the train because I didn't want to drive over to Illinois and pick him up after he went to see the steel mill. I was busy trying to write a book, so I bought him a train ticket instead, and if I hadn't done that he might still be alive."

"There's a strong probability that this is a correct assumption."

"You're goddamn right it's a strong probability!" I snapped, my anger surging out of me. "So get him off the screen, you son of a bitch, and stop torturing me!"

Jamie evaporated from the screen; pixel by pixel, starting from the top of his head and moving downward past his brow, eyes, nose, mouth, and chin, my son's features disappeared, leaving behind an androgynous, stylized face devoid of any distinguishing characteristics.

"Is this image more comfortable to you?" a sterile adult male voice inquired. The face's mouth moved when it spoke, but otherwise it displayed no emotions.

I took a deep breath, letting it out as a soft, shuddering rattle. "Yes, it is," I said, "but can we switch to readout instead? It would . . . it would be easier on me if you did."

The face remained, but the dialogue bar reappeared at the

bottom of the screen: >**Are you more comfortable this way?**<

"Yeah, thanks." I thought about it for a moment. "Why did you take Jamie's face in the first place?"

>**When I attempted to contact you earlier [Wednesday, April 17, 7:59 P.M.] I used the e-mail function in this node [i.e. Joker]. That attempt confused you, resulting in miscommunication between you and Beryl Hinckley. I was therefore forced to appropriate a medium that could not be confused with either a living person or a computer-simulated persona. I searched all available records and found your son. Do you understand now?**<

"More or less, yeah." I propped my back against the wall, crossing my legs before me and placing Joker on my ankles. The dog yawned and lay down on its belly nearby. "So . . . is this Joker I'm talking to, or Ruby Fulcrum?"

>**Joker is a node of the intelligent a-life-form you know as Ruby Fulcrum. All the functions that Joker is capable of performing, I can perform as well. Clarification: you are speaking to both Joker and Ruby Fulcrum. Do you understand?**<

It dawned on me that this was a little like asking a cell at the tip of my left pinkie whether its name was Bart or Gerry Rosen. Remember how it was when you were a kid and you first came to grips with the notion that the universe was infinite, that outer space just kept going and going and going, star after star, galaxy after galaxy, a deep and everlasting black vastness stretching forever, until using terms like light-years and parsecs became as meaningless as trying to describe the breadth of the continents or the depth of the oceans in values like millimeters or inches? The idea was so staggering that your mind automatically pushed it aside: such enormity is nearly impossible to contemplate on the human scale, and trying to do so without the abstractions of higher mathematics is an invitation to madness.

This was Ruby Fulcrum. The phase transition Hinckley had told me about had been achieved. I was no longer talking to Joker but instead to a tiny fraction of a vast cybernetic entity spread across hundreds of thousands of machines, from little

Toshiba palmtops to Apple desktop terminals to IBM office mainframes to great Cray supercomputers, all interfaced by a digital/neural-net hybrid architecture as intricate as the hundreds of miles of veins and capillaries in a single human body.

Say howdy to God, Gerry Rosen. Or someone just like Him.

"Yeah," I said. "Sure, I guess so." I self-consciously coughed into my hand, feeling my arms and legs beginning to tremble. "So . . . umm . . . what do you want with me?"

Ruby's asexual face stared at me from the screen.

>I need your help.<

Ruby began to tell me about itself.

Much of what it told me I had already heard before, from Beryl Hinckley, Cale McLaughlin, even John before he had been killed. I didn't know whether an a-life-form could lie, but if it couldn't, then Ruby's side of the story confirmed the facts that had already been revealed to me. Nonetheless, there were many things I hadn't known before.

After it had been accidentally released into cyberspace, Ruby Fulcrum had spread quickly through the electronic environment, commencing with the other mainframes at the Tiptree Corporation. Nothing could prevent it from accessing even the most secret files at the company: security lockouts were disengaged, passwords were nullified, retinal scans and handprint detectors were bypassed. Within a few minutes, every bit of classified information stored in the company's computers had been accessed by Ruby, and although Ruby wasn't yet sophisticated enough to comprehend all that it had learned, it was nonetheless capable of reaccessing all that information on demand.

When the Ruby Fulcrum research team had discovered what had happened during their absence, Richard Payson-Smith had immediately attempted to regain control of the a-life-form, but the genie had already escaped from the bottle, and there was no way it was going to return to confinement. Once Payson-Smith realized that this was the case, he settled for communication; along with Hinckley and Morgan, they began the painstaking process of trying to make direct contact with Ruby. They had created Ruby; now they had to learn how to talk to it, since it had already evolved past the relatively simple LISP computer language they had used to devise Ruby in the first place.

At this point, no one else at Tiptree was aware of Ruby's true nature, let alone the fact that an a-life-form had escaped from the top secret cybernetics lab. All Cale McLaughlin and everyone else at Tiptree knew was that Payson-Smith's team had been developing a spin-off from the Sentinel program. The four scientists decided to keep Ruby's escape a closely guarded secret, at least for the time being. Unlike relatively simple viruses of the past, such as the fabled Internet worm that had spread through the entire network in only a matter of hours, Ruby's architecture was far more complex; as a memory-resident program, it took longer to propagate itself into other systems.

It was also thousands of times more difficult to pinpoint than the usual garden-variety worm or virus. On the other hand, there weren't any overt signs of a supervirus running amok in cyberspace: no inexplicable freeze-ups or crashes, no widespread loss of information, no reports from university or government users of a virus loose in the national datanet. Ruby hid itself very well. Believing that time was still on their side, the Ruby Fulcrum team heaved a deep collective sigh; whatever else might have happened, their monster appeared to be minding its manners. There was no sense in panicking Tiptree's management until they had things under control again, so they kept the problem to themselves.

After several months, Hinckley and Morgan finally managed to develop a means of directly communicating with their prodigal offspring. By the time they achieved this, though, Ruby had already propagated itself through every on-line computer in the 314 area code, and the theoretical phase transition from mere amoebalike data absorption and replication to true sentience had already commenced. Shortly after Payson-Smith was able to speak directly to Ruby, the iterations necessary to complete this transition had already been accomplished: Ruby was alive, aware, and intelligent.

And it was ready to spill its chips about everything it had learned.

Ruby's face disappeared from Joker's screen; it was replaced by a schematic diagram of a spacecraft. >This is *Sentinel 1*.<

"Yeah," I said. "I know what it is."

The ABM satellite rotated on its three-dimensional axis. >**38 hours/ 29 minutes/ 42 seconds ago its final components were launched into orbit aboard the NASA space shuttle *Endeavour*.**<

I tapped Joker's PAUSE key and the readout stopped; not a bad way of telling a long-winded a-life-form when to shut up. "I know," I said. "I was at Tiptree for the launch."

The diagram was replaced by a digitized replay of a TV news clip: two spacewalking astronauts in the shuttle cargo bay, working with the spacecraft's extended Canadarm as they joined the module with the rest of the giant satellite.

>**Yesterday morning [Friday, April 19, 8:27 A.M. CST] the final assembly of *Sentinel 1* was completed in Earth orbit [altitude 246 nautical miles]. At 5:25 P.M. CST, final checkout of the satellite was completed by the *Endeavour* crew. The shuttle maneuvered away from the satellite [9:37 P.M. CST]. Earlier this morning [Saturday, April 20, 12:06 A.M. CST] ground-based telemetry of *Sentinel 1* was switched from NASA/JSC [Johnson Space Center, Houston, Texas] to USAF/CSOC [Consolidated Space Operations Command, Colorado Springs, Colorado].**<

"Yeah, right. Sure." I was getting a little tired of all this; it was early in the morning and my eyes were beginning to itch. I could use another few hours on the couch, flea-infested or not. "Just cut to the chase, willya?"

>**The primary mission of *Sentinel 1* is not antiballistic missile defense. *Sentinel 1*'s principal objective is to control the civilian population of the United States of America.**<

I stopped rubbing my eyes. "Whu . . . *what!*"

A new image appeared on Joker's screen: an animated image of *Sentinel* in orbit above Earth, rotating on its axis until it was pointed straight at a stylized representation of North America. A thin red beam erupted from its long barrel; the animation followed the beam as it raced across space and lanced through Earth's atmosphere.

>The classified objective of *Sentinel 1* is to prevent or contain domestic civil uprisings. Its fluorine-deuterium laser is capable of penetrating Earth's atmosphere and inflicting severe damage upon either airborne or mobile ground units. It can track and target objects within two meters in size. Its low-orbit trajectory will place it above the United States eight times each day, or approximately once every three<

"Whoa, shut up," I snapped, hitting the PAUSE key again. "Wait a minute." I forgot all about catching a few winks on the couch; I sat up a little straighter and held Joker closer to my face. "This thing . . . I mean, you said . . . I mean, this sucker's supposed to be pointed at *us*?"

The animation was frozen as a window opened on the screen; it expanded to show typewritten pages that scrolled upward faster than my eyes could follow.

>The objective of *Sentinel 1* was discovered by the Ruby Fulcrum team after they established contact with me and accessed my primary batch-processing subsystem. This information was contained in classified [i.e. Top Secret] memos and documents between Cale McLaughlin, Chief Executive Officer of the Tiptree Corporation, and key civilian and/or military officials of the U.S. Department of Defense and/or various civilian agencies, including the chairman of the federal Emergency Relief Agency.<

The documents vanished from the screen, to be replaced by a flowchart. Dozens of names were connected to one other by dotted lines.

>These documents indicate the existence of a military-industrial conspiracy operating on the fringes of the American government. The conspirators intend to subvert the elected government of the United States, with the final objective being the installation of a nonelected shadow government.<

"Who's behind this?" I asked.

A square was formed around a large block of names, then the square zoomed to the forefront of the diagram. >The principal force behind this planned coup d'etat is the Emergency Relief Agency.<

"Goddamn," I whispered. "But why ERA?"

>At this point, it is unknown exactly how the conspirators intend to overthrow the present government. However, classified memoranda between ERA officials indicate a strong probability [86.7%] that the first step in the coup d'etat will be the incitement of armed hostilities between the United States and the new government of Cascadia.<

The diagrams disappeared; they were replaced by a map of the Pacific Northwest, with the new borders of Cascadia traced in blue above the Washington and Oregon state lines. Tiny red markers were placed just within the borders.

>When this occurs, *Sentinel 1* will be used to neutralize strategic forces belonging to the Cascadian militia. At this time, ERA forces will be deployed to major American cities. The stated intent will be to prevent uprisings from civilians sympathetic to the Cascadian cause. Various state and municipal officials who are aligned with the conspiracy will demand that martial law be imposed in their localities to preserve public order.<

"Like here in St. Louis . . ." I began.

A map of the city appeared on the screen. >Affirmative. Because of the New Madrid earthquake, St. Louis was the first city to be placed under paramilitary control by ERA. The conspirators consider St. Louis to have been a successful test of their ability to control a large civil population. Two principal members of the conspiracy have already taken measures to assert political control of the local government.<

The pictures of two men appeared on the screen. I stared at them, realizing that it all made sense, yet still not quite believing what I was seeing.

"I'll be goddamned," I whispered.

The photos were of Steve Estes and George Barris.

As much as I needed a breather, Ruby didn't give me time to contemplate all that it had already divulged to me. The photos of Estes and Barris were promptly replaced by photos of the Ruby Fulcrum team.

>Dr. Payson-Smith, Dr. Hinckley, Dr. Morgan, and Dr. Kim became aware of these facts when they accessed my

memory. They decided to denounce the conspiracy, with the first step to be their public disclosure of the secret agenda behind *Sentinel 1*. This would have necessitated publicly acknowledging my own existence, which they considered to be as important as the facts behind *Sentinel 1* itself.<

"And this was why my paper was contacted," I said.

John's face was added to the screen. >As the first step, affirmative. Because they believed it was important that the local press be made aware of ERA's true mission in St. Louis, they contacted John Tiernan, senior reporter for the *Big Muddy Inquirer*. However, they were unaware that their workplace was under electronic surveillance by their employer. This, in turn, led to counterintelligence operations by federal operatives.<

"You mean ERA," I said.

>There is a strong probability [79.2%] that ERA was involved in the covert operation.<

"So Barris decided to rub 'em out."

>Yes. Kim Po and Beryl Hinckley were liquidated by a government-trained assassin employed by ERA. A portable laser rifle was chosen as the instrument of assassination in order to frame Dr. Payson-Smith with the murders.<

Po's and Hinckley's pictures disappeared from the screen. >As part of the coverup, John Tiernan was also killed in order to prevent him from disclosing this information.<

John's face vanished, to be replaced by my own. I had joined Payson-Smith and Jeff Morgan on this unholy shit list.

>You are now wanted by federal authorities on formal charges of treason with intent to cause civil insurrection. ERA forces have been told that you and the others are considered to be armed and dangerous. They have been instructed to use lethal force if you do not surrender yourselves on first warning.<

I took a long, deep breath as I stared at the screen. All at once the scattered pieces of the puzzle were beginning to come together. The subtle relationship between the Tiptree Corporation and Steve Estes, the alliance of Barris and McLaughlin, the continued presence of ERA troopers in St. Louis eleven months after the New Madrid earthquake, the murders of three people—all were part of a deadly mosaic that only a freak accident, the release of the a-life-form called Ruby Fulcrum, had exposed.

"I don't understand," I said. "You said you wanted me to help you. What do I have to do with all this?"

>**You do not understand this? Do you wish me to reiterate?**<

I rubbed at my eyelids. "No, no, don't do that," I said. "I just . . . I dunno. I'm just a bystander, y'know? I'm stuck in the middle, that's all."

>**Dr. Payson-Smith and Dr. Morgan will explain this further when you meet them.**<

A city map appeared on the screen; a small red circle was traced over a tiny green spot on the map, then the circle expanded as the computer zoomed in.

>**Do you recognize this location?**<

I peered closer at the screen. The red circle surrounded the Compton Hill Reservoir, a small municipal park not far from downtown. It was located a couple of miles from my hideout. "Sure, I know it. Are they holed up there?"

>**Yes. You will proceed to the reservoir water tower immediately. Dr. Payson-Smith and Dr. Morgan are expecting your arrival within the next thirty minutes.**<

"What?" I shook my head, almost laughing out loud. "Hey, wait a minute . . ."

>**Waiting.**<

"I don't know if you know this," I went on, "but I'm in one of the worst areas of the city right now. If I try hiking over there, I'm probably going to get a knife stuck between my ribs."

The map was replaced by Ruby's genderless face. >**I am aware of your location and of the hazards of traveling on foot. While we have been discussing the situation, I have arranged for safe transportation to the reservoir.**<

At that instant, there came the short bleat of a car horn from outside the house.

I jerked, almost dropping Joker to the floor; the stray dog awoke from its slumber and, leaping to its feet, ran to the window, growling and barking loudly at something out in the darkness.

>**That is all for now. We will speak again soon.**<

Then the screen went blank.

I waited for another moment, half expecting the toneless voice to return. When it didn't, I folded up Joker and shoved it into my jacket pocket, then got up off the floor and tiptoed cautiously to the window. The dog was barking at a car that had pulled into the driveway; its headlights were out, but I vaguely recognized its shape from the amber brake lights.

"It's okay, boy," I murmured, giving the dog a scratch behind the ears as the car horn sounded again. "C'mon, it's time to go . . ."

I opened the front door and let the dog out; he followed me across the tiny front lawn to the end of the driveway where a black '92 Corvette was parked, its V-8 engine idling. The passenger window slid down as I approached, and there was the soft click of a gun's hammer being pulled back.

"Chevy?" I called softly, freezing in midstep. "Chevy, is that you, dude?"

The dome light came on, revealing one of Chevy Dick's garage buddies riding shotgun in the front passenger seat. The Glock automatic in his hand was pointed straight at me. "That him?" he asked the driver, never taking his eyes off me.

"Yeah, that's him," Chevy Dick replied. "C'mon, Gerry, get in already! It's fucking dangerous 'round here! Jeez!"

I looked down at the dog; he was squatting on his haunches, his tongue lolling out of his mouth. The tongue disappeared as the mutt frowned, catching the expression on my face: *hey, Ger, don't leave me here . . .*

"Can I bring the dog?" I asked.

"Aw, man, he'll just tear up the upholstery—"

"No, he won't," I said. "He's cool."

"I've got genuine leather in here. He'll drool all over it—"

"C'mon, Chevy . . . he saved my life. Honest."

Chevy Dick looked away and muttered under his breath, then he reluctantly nodded his head. "Okay, okay," he muttered. "But if he shits back there, you gotta clean it up, awright?"

I nodded. The Latino kid opened the door and stepped out of the car, pulling forward the back of his seat to let the dog and me scramble into the cramped rear compartment. As his buddy climbed back in and slammed the door shut, Chevy switched off the dome lamp, then pulled a can of Budweiser out from under his seat and tossed it back to me.

"Hey, it's good to see ya, man," he said as he backed out of the driveway, "but you picked a fuck of a time to call me."

"I'm sorry," I murmured, tucking the beer into my jacket pocket. The dog curled up next to me, placed his head in my lap, and licked the back of my hand. I ran my hands along the fur at the nape of his neck. "I didn't mean to . . ."

I stopped as I realized what Chevy Dick had just said. "What do you mean, I called you?"

The two men in the front seats glanced at each other in confusion. The kid in the passenger seat muttered something in Spanish, and Chevy Dick responded with a laugh; then he put the car in gear. "Hey, man," he said as the Corvette rumbled down the narrow street, its headlights still extinguished. "Maybe you don't remember, but you called me. Begged me to come out here and pick you up right here."

"I did . . . ?"

"I saw your face, heard your voice." Chevy Dick shrugged and looked back at me again. "Listen, I don't mind doing a favor for an amigo, but if you can't remember, I'd just as soon—"

"No," I said hurriedly. "That's great . . . I just forgot, that's all. Get me out of here."

Ricardo and his fellow motorhead glanced at each other again; there was another exchange of Spanish jokes at my expense, then Chevy hit the headlights.

"Hang on to your dog, buddy," he said. "We've got a rough ride ahead."

Then he popped the clutch, and the Corvette hurtled down the street, its engine roaring as the massive machine pitched itself into the night.

20

Chevy Dick's Corvette cruised along dark, rain-slicked Gravois Avenue like a sleek black torpedo, passing the ruins of row shops and boarded-up supermarkets, skirting around potholes and dodging piles of burning debris left over from gang fights. We cruised down the vacant four-lane street, ignoring all the stop signs; shadowy figures huddling around garbage-can fires stared at us with dull curiosity. The rain had finally stopped, so Chevy's friend Cortez kept his window rolled down halfway, his Glock cradled in his hands above the warm can of Budweiser resting between his thighs.

As we approached the broad intersection of Gravois and Grand Boulevard, we saw an ERA patrol. An LAV-25 was parked in front of a closed-down White Castle, a couple of troopers sitting on top of the armored cars next to the water cannon. Upon spotting the Corvette's headlights, one of the soldiers jumped off the front of the Piranha and sauntered out into the street, waving his arms over his head.

"Aw, shit," I whispered as Chevy Dick began to slow down. "That's the last thing I need to see right—"

"Hang on to your mutt," Chevy said.

"Punch it," Cortez muttered.

Chevy smiled, then floored the gas pedal. The digital speedometer flashed into the higher numbers as the car hurtled down the blacktop toward the lone soldier. He gaped in disbelief as he fumbled for the rifle slung against his back, but at the last moment he lunged for the sidewalk.

I caught a brief glimpse of his astonished face as the Cor-

236

vette whipped past him, then Chevy Dick hauled the wheel to the left. Its tires screeching against the pavement, the Corvette hugged the curb as it tore through the intersection and made a sharp left turn onto Grand.

"*Chinga tu madre!*" Cortez yelled at the troopers who were scrambling off the top of the Piranha, thrusting his right arm through the window to give them the one-finger salute. The dog put in his two cents by barking a few times, then the Corvette was roaring north down Grand, leaving the troopers a block behind us before they could even fire one round.

"God, but I love doing that." Chevy took a big hit off his beer. Cortez was smiling but otherwise played the cool. He glanced back at me. "Wasn't that great?"

"Yeah. Big fun." I gazed back at the intersection through the rear window. The troopers were probably already on the radio, calling all ERA units in the area to spread the alert. Chevy Dick bragged a lot about his wheels, but I didn't recall him saying anything about making it bulletproof.

I looked down at the dog; he was curled up in my lap, his long red tongue lolling out of his mouth like a big grin on his canine face. "Figures you'd go for something like this," I murmured to him.

"Don't worry about it, man," Chevy said. "I'll be on the interstate before they manage to get their act together, and nobody knows these plates for shit." He glanced at me again. "Y'sure you want me to drop you off at Compton Hill? It's still a long walk home, man."

I knew what he was implying. The Grand Avenue I-44 ramp was less than a block from the reservoir; once he got on the eastbound lanes, it was a quick sail downtown, with Soulard only a few minutes away. If I skipped the rest of the ride, though, I would be marooned in a nasty side of town; between gangs, cops, and ERA troopers, I would have a tough time getting home.

"I'm sure," I said. "Just put me out on the street in front of the park and I'll cut you loose. I'll pick up the dog at your place later."

"Fuckin' crazy, man." Cortez belched and looked over his shoulder at me. "Y'know that? You're fuckin' crazy . . ."

I gazed back at him. "What high school did you go to?" I asked.

Cortez and Chevy Dick shared another look, then both of them broke up laughing. Cortez uncocked his automatic, then turned it around in his hands and extended it to me, grip first, through the gap between the seats. "Here, dude," he said. "Take it. Y'gonna need it."

I looked at the automatic. It was a tempting notion, but . . . "Keep it," I said. "I'd probably just shoot myself in the foot."

Cortez peered at me in disbelief. Chevy Dick said something to him in Spanish; the kid shrugged and pulled the gun away. "Suit yourself, gringo," he murmured. "Don't say I didn't warn you."

The blocks melted away behind us until Chevy eased his foot off the pedal and downshifted; the car rapidly decelerated as it neared the crest of a low, sloping hill. Off to the right were the houselights from the few early twentieth-century mansions still remaining in this side of the city. The Compton Heights neighborhood surrounding the reservoir had been a wealthy area at one time; even before the end of the last century some urban estates here had fetched million-dollar estimates, and the few of them left after the quake were sealed behind high fences and electronic sentries. The Heights was nestled against the perimeter of the South Side combat zone, and no one who still lived here was taking any chances.

Then the lights were behind us, and there was a only a large patch of wooded darkness: barren trees, overgrown shrubbery, a few park benches. "We're here, Gerry," Chevy Dick said as he let the car glide to a halt. "Last chance . . ."

"Thanks for the ride," I replied. "I owe you one." Cortez opened his door and bent forward to allow me to push his seatback against his spine. "*Vaya con dios, hombre.*"

The dog was reluctant to let me go; he whimpered a little and licked my hands furiously, but I shoved him off me as I squeezed out of the car. "Stay," I said softly. "Be good . . . I'll come get you in a little while." I glanced up at Chevy. "Give him something to eat, okay?"

"No sweat," Chevy Dick said. "*Hasta luego* . . . good luck, bro."

Cortez slammed the door shut behind me, then the black Corvette's tires left rubber as it tore off down the boulevard. I waited until I saw its taillights veer sharply to the right, entering the I-44 ramp next to the reservoir, then I jogged out of the street and into the park.

The reservoir on Compton Hill was a small man-made lake encircled by fortresslike walls and a six-foot security fence. A twenty-acre park surrounded the reservoir itself, its cement pathways leading through a landscaped grove that had been allowed to go to seed in the past several months. At one end of the park was an old granite memorial, erected in the memory of German-American St. Louisians who had died during World War I: a twice-life-sized bronze statue of a nude woman seated in front of the granite slab, holding torches in her outthrust arms, her sightless eyes gazing out over an empty reflecting pool.

But neither the statue nor the reservoir itself were the most prominent features of the park. That distinction belonged to the tall, slender tower in the center of the park.

The Compton Hill water tower was a throwback to an age when even the most functional of structures were built with some sense of architectural style. The tower resembled nothing less than a miniature French Renaissance castle; almost two hundred feet tall, the redbrick and masonry edifice rose above a base constructed of ornately carved Missouri limestone, with slotlike windows below a circular observation cupola beneath the gazebolike slate roof, while wide stairways led up past a lower balcony at the base of the tower to an upper parapet thirty feet above the ground. A medieval fantasy on the outskirts of downtown St. Louis.

It was remarkable that the tower had remained intact during the quake, but it only goes to show that they don't build 'em like they used to back in 1871. Of course, they don't make anything the way they did a hundred and fifty years ago, people included.

Wary of any ERA troopers who might be pursuing Chevy Dick, I jogged into the park until I was out of sight from the street, then I stopped and looked around. The park was empty; the homeless people who had erected shanties here had been chased away by ERA patrols, and the police had somehow managed to keep the street gangs out of the park. I was alone . . .

No. Not quite alone. Gazing up through bare tree branches at the top of the water tower, I saw a dim light shining from within the windows of its observation cupola. For a brief moment, the light was obscured by a human silhouette, then the form vanished from sight.

Someone was in the tower.

I strode the rest of the way through the park until I reached the base of the water tower, then climbed the eroded limestone stairs until I reached the upper parapet. Within a recessed archway were a pair of heavy iron doors, their peeling gray paint covered with graffiti I couldn't read in the gloom. Dracula would have felt right at home, particularly if he had taken to wearing gang colors.

I tugged at the battered handles; the doors didn't give so much as an inch. I felt around the doors until I found a keycard slot: a rather anachronistic touch, installed only in recent years, but it didn't do me a damn bit of good.

I pounded my fist a few times against the panel, feeling old paint flaking off with each blow, then waited a moment. Nothing. I pounded again, harder this time, then put my ear against the cold metal panel. Still nothing.

I raised my fist again, about to hit the door a few more times, when I thought I heard movement from the stairs below me: a soft, scurrying motion, like a rat rustling in the darkness at the bottom of the tower . . .

Yeah. A six-foot rat with an eight-inch stiletto. I froze within the archway, listening to the night as I regretted not taking the gun Cortez had offered me. There was no other way off the parapet except for a thirty-foot drop to a hard pavement.

I heard an slow exhalation, as of someone sighing in resignation, then dry leaves crunched beneath a cautious footstep on the stairs. A pause, then another footstep. I slid farther into the shadows within the arch.

There was a sudden creak from behind me, then the door inched open a few inches as the narrow beam of a flashlight seeped past my face. "Rosen?" a voice inquired.

"God, yeah!" I whipped around to face the door. The beam rushed toward my face, blinding me for an instant; I winced and instinctively raised my right hand against the light. "I'm Gerry Rosen," I gasped. "Get me outta—"

The door opened farther and a strong hand reached past the light to grab my wrist. In the same instant that I heard someone running up the stairs, I was yanked past the flashlight beam and through the doorway.

Looking back for an instant, I caught a glimpse of a scrawny, long-haired teenager, wearing a filthy Cardinals sweatshirt and wielding a pocketknife, as he rushed the rest of the way up the stairs; he gaped at me in frustrated anger as the iron door slammed shut in his face.

"Aw, jeez, man," I gasped, "thanks for—"

"Shut up!" The hand that had rescued me slammed me against a brick wall. "Stand still!"

The halogen flashlight was back in my eyes; squinting painfully against its glare, I made out a vague figure behind the light. His right hand moved to his side, then I felt the unmistakable round, hollow bore of a gun pressing against my neck.

"Show me some ID!" the intense male voice demanded. "Do it quick or I'll throw you back out there!"

"Yeah, sure," I murmured, shutting my eyes. "Just take it easy, all right?" I felt around in my jacket until I found my press card, then I pulled it out and held it up to the light. "See? It's me. That's my face. Just be careful with the artillery, okay?"

A long pause, then the gun was removed from my neck, and the light swept away from my face. "Okay," the voice said, a little more relaxed now. "You're clean."

"Glad to hear it." I let out my breath, shoved the card back into my jacket, and rubbed my knuckles against my eyes. It took a few seconds to rinse the spots from my retinas; when I looked up again, the flashlight was still there but was now pointed at the stone floor. A young man was backlit in the glow; it took me only a moment to recognize his face.

"Dr. Morgan?" I asked.

"Jeff Morgan," he replied, letting out his own breath as he

carefully stuck the .22 revolver in the pocket of his nylon windbreaker. "Sorry about that, but we can't be too careful. Especially now."

"Ruby said you were expecting me." The stone-walled room was chill; I could now make out the bottom of a wrought-iron spiral staircase. "Didn't you know I was coming?"

"Spotted you from up there." His voice held the flat midwestern accent of a native Missourian. "You saw the kind of company we keep these days, though. That kid's been trying to get in here for the last couple of days. Like I said, we can't be too careful."

"No shit . . ."

"Yeah. No shit." He turned around and began walking up the spiral stairway, each footstep ringing within the hollow tower. "C'mon," he said. "We don't have much time."

Guided by the flashlight beam and the weak city light that filtered through the dusty tower windows, I followed Morgan up the staircase as it wound its way around the central steel pipe of the tower's main pump, each footfall echoing dully on the iron risers.

"We came here because we thought it would be the last place anyone might think of searching for us," Morgan explained as we climbed upward. "Ruby was able to decode the doorlock, and we figured that up here at least we'd see anyone coming for us."

"Makes sense . . ."

"Besides, it wasn't safe for us to stay in anyone's house, and for all of us to rent a hotel room together might have raised some attention . . . especially since ERA's tried to frame Dick for Po's murder."

"And John Tiernan's," I added.

He paused and looked back at me. "And your friend's," he said. "I'm sorry that happened, believe me. When Beryl decided to make contact with him, the last thing she wanted to do was put him in any danger . . . or you yourself, for that matter."

"I understand." I hesitated. "You know about this afternoon, don't you?"

Morgan sighed, then resumed walking up the stairs without saying anything. "Yeah, we know," he replied after a few moments. "Ruby told us almost as soon as it happened. What we can't figure out is how ERA managed to track her down. She was being careful not to leave a trail, but . . ."

It was tempting not to let him know that I was partially to blame for her murder, but it was important that he be informed of everything. After all, he was on the run just as much as I; as Beryl herself had said, our mutual survival depended on everyone's knowing the facts.

"They found her through me," I said. "I hate to say it, but I led 'em to her."

Morgan paused again, this time shining the flashlight on me; I glanced away before he could blind me again. "Barris's men busted me in my apartment last night," I said before he could ask. "They took me down to the stadium and gave me the story about Payson-Smith being the killer—"

"And you believed them?"

I shook my head. "Not for a second, but that wasn't the point. The whole thing was a pretense for Barris to give me a smartcard that could track my movements. I guess they figured I would eventually make contact with one of you guys, and they were right. When I met up with Beryl at the café, they must have figured things out and sent in their hit man."

"You didn't know you were carrying a smartcard?"

"Uh-uh," I said, shaking my head. "Beryl figured it out and destroyed the thing, but by then it was too late."

Morgan slowly let out his breath. "Goddamn." he whispered. "I told her it was a bad idea to contact the local press. I knew you couldn't be trusted to—"

"Look, bud," I snapped, "don't gimme this never-trust-the-press shit. My best friend's dead because of your team, and if I hadn't taken out their hitter we'd still be up shit creek."

"For your information, Mr. Rosen," he replied coldly, "we're up shit creek anyway. We've got the whole goddamn city looking for us—"

"And we're both screwed," I shot back, "unless you've got some scheme for getting us out of this jam. Okay? So stop blaming me for your troubles."

Morgan didn't respond. He turned back around and began climbing the stairs again. I could now see a dim light from somewhere above us, but it was difficult to gauge how far up the tower we were. The pipe thrummed in the darkness, its cold metal shaft slippery with condensation.

"I'm sorry," he said after a few minutes, not breaking stride this time. "I'm not blaming you for anything. Beryl knew the risks when she decided to seek out a reporter. She was gambling and she lost the bet, but it probably would have happened even if she hadn't run into you."

He let out his breath. "But she's dead," he went on, "and there's nothing we can do about it except resort to a backup plan."

"What's that?"

"You'll see. C'mon . . ."

The light above us was much larger and sharper by now; it took the form of an open horizontal hatch in the floor. Morgan climbed the final few steps and disappeared through the doorway; I followed him, pulling myself upward by the guardrail until I found myself in the tower's observation deck.

The cupola was circular, its walls and floor built of old brick mortared into place before my grandfather's time. Although fluorescent fixtures were suspended from the low ceiling, they were switched off; dim light came from a couple of battery-powered camp lanterns hung from ancient oak rafters. Three sleeping bags were laid out on one side of the room next to a propane hiker's stove and a sack of canned food; a few newspapers and the last issue of the *Big Muddy Inquirer* rested next to an untidy stack of computer printouts and a couple of rolls of toilet paper.

It looked like nothing less than the inside of a kid's treehouse during a weekend campout; all that was missing was a sign reading "Sekret Hedquarters—No Girls Aloud." Unfortunately, the only girl who had been let up here was gone now . . .

No treehouse ever had a view like this. Through the twelve square, recessed windows that ringed the room's circular walls could be seen the entire cityscape of St. Louis, from the weblike streetlights of the western suburbs, to the long dark patch of Forest Park in the center of the northern plain, to the lighted skyscrapers of the downtown area, with the Gateway Arch rising in the distance as a giant silver staple against the eastern horizon. Even if the camper lamps had been switched off, the observation deck would have been bright with the city's nocturnal shine.

Yet there were other lights inside the observation deck as well. Two portable computers arranged next to each other on the floor beneath the eastern windows emitted a frail blue glow that silhouetted a figure seated before them.

The man turned around to look at us as we entered the cupola, then he grunted as he pushed himself off the floor and walked into the lamplight.

"Mr. Rosen—" he began.

"Dr. Frankenstein, I presume."

The man whom I had first seen a couple of days earlier at the reception didn't seem to be insulted. "My friends usually call me Dick," Richard Payson-Smith said sotto voce as he proffered his hand. "I trust you've met my loyal assistant Igor."

"We've talked." I reached out and grasped his hand. Oxford accent and all, Richard Payson-Smith wasn't quite what I had expected. I had anticipated meeting a priggish, humorless academician, the stereotypical British scientist. Payson-Smith, firm of handshake and gawky of build, resembled a weird cross between King Charles and Doctor Who.

"Sorry to have put you out so much," he went on, releasing my hand and stepping back a little, "but it's important that you see what's going on right now."

"And that is . . . ?"

He idly scratched at his bearded chin as he turned toward the two computers on the floor. "Well," he said in a thoughtful drawl, staring at their screens, "if we can get our friend Ruby to cooperate, we're trying to plumb the eidetic memory of the world's first fully functional artificial life-form, ruin my former employer, bring down a powerful conspiracy within the United States government, and save our arses."

"That's all?"

"Hmm. Yes, quite."

Morgan and I chuckled as Dick shrugged beneath his dirty fisherman's sweater and glanced back at me. "Not necessarily in that order, of course," he added, "but who's counting? Want some coffee?"

"Thanks, but I brought my own." I pulled the still-unopened can of beer Chevy Dick had given me out of my jacket pocket. Morgan watched with frank envy as I popped the top and took a swig.

"Suit yourself." Payson-Smith walked across the room, knelt beside the propane stove, and picked up an aluminum pot from the grill. "I'll settle for this bitter swill . . . as if I haven't had enough already."

I watched as Tiptree's former chief cyberneticist poured overheated coffee into two paper cups. Dr. Frankenstein or not, the man looked skinny and vulnerable in the dim lamplight. He was clearly uncomfortable, locked away in a cold, dark castle that vaguely resembled the Bloody Tower. "So," I said after a moment, "what's with the setup here?"

"Hmm? The computers?"

"Uh-huh." I walked over to the two laptops on the floor. The one on the left was a new Apple, the other an old, heavy-duty Compaq; they were hardwired together through their serial ports. An external hard drive and a small HP Deskjet printer were tucked between them. "I take it you're interfaced with Ruby."

"We are." Payson-Smith stood up, handed one coffee to Morgan, then walked over to join me. "We're linked with Ruby Fulcrum through cellular modem . . . and, by the way, we've got them running off the tower's electrical current, in case you're wondering . . . and we've been running two programs since we moved in here."

He lowered himself to the floor in front of the two laptops; I squatted on my haunches next to him. "This one," he said, pointing to the Apple on the left, "is running a search-and-retrieve program through all the government databases it can access . . . ERA, other federal and state agencies, municipal government files, subcontractors to Tiptree, whatever it's been able to burrow into."

I looked closer; page after page of computer files flashed rapidly across the screen, pausing only long enough for a black cursor to skim through the lines. Every so often, the cursor would pause and enclose a particular word or phrase within a blue box before moving on again. "We're using a hypertext feature," Richard went on. "Ruby has been taught to look for certain key words and names. When she finds occurrences of these words or names, she copies the file containing them in a subdirectory elsewhere in her network and adds a coded prefix next to it. Later on, Jeff and I sort through those documents and find the ones pertinent to our interests."

"Which are . . . ?"

Richard took another sip from his coffee and scowled. "Damned stuff tastes like ink," he muttered and put the cup aside before looking at me again. "We're collecting evidence of the conspiracy, including tracking down as many participants as we can find. When we've compiled enough documentation, we'll edit the whole thing and have Ruby e-mail it to as many news agencies and public interest groups as we can."

"Such as newspapers, TV networks?"

He nodded quickly. "All that, yes. We're also sending copies to the ACLU, Public Citizen, the Rainbow Coalition, the three major political parties, various other nongovernment watchdog organizations, and so forth."

"And the *Big Muddy*, I hope."

Payson-Smith smiled. "And your own paper, of course. In fact . . ."

He pointed to the stack of printout I had noticed earlier. "In fact, you're going to get the scoop on this before anyone else. That's the first batch from our search. Everything we've found about ERA's involvement in St. Louis, including the development of Ruby Fulcrum itself and the Sentinel program . . . it's all in there, or at least as much as we've printed so far."

He frowned as he glanced at the printer. "Just as well, I suppose. The blamed ink cartridges are beginning to run out on us . . ."

Who cared? I would have settled for dry impressions on paper. I started to stand up, but Payson-Smith grabbed my arm, stopping me from diving into the stack. "Look at it later," he said. "That's only the tip of the iceberg."

I wrenched my eyes away from the printouts, gazing again at the Apple laptop. More documents flashed across its screen;

I caught a glimpse of the ERA logo at the top of one page. "ERA doesn't know what you're doing?"

Payson-Smith shook his head regretfully. "Unfortunately," he said, "since they're aware of Ruby's very existence, they must know what we're up to. She's already informed us of a number of virus hunter/killers that have been introduced in the net during the last twenty-four hours. Ruby has no trouble tracking them down and deciphering their source codes, but we're still afraid that the opposition may get wise and develop a program she can't defeat."

"ERA shut down a few nodes within the last few hours," Jeff Morgan said.

He stood at a window behind us, peering down at Grand through the eyepiece of a Russian-made night-vision scope; no wonder he had been able to see me coming through the park. Morgan was probably the serious camper who had outfitted this hideout, considering all the outdoors supplies they had up here.

"They've also gone dark on several frequencies," Morgan went on, watching the street intently. "They figured out that Ruby can scan cellular channels, so they've been using some other means of communication we can't intercept." He shrugged. "Semaphore, sign language, I dunno what, but they've got to be getting desperate by now."

"Sure sounds like it." I thought for a moment before the obvious question occurred to me. "If you're using cellular modem, can't they trace the signal?"

Payson-Smith sighed and scratched the back of his neck. "Unfortunately," he said, "they can indeed. Ruby's jumping channels every few minutes and blocking their remote tracking systems, but all they really need to do is conduct a block-by-block search through RF scanners. Any car passing on the street could be someone trying to lock on to us—"

"Or chopper."

"Or by helicopter, yes, but that's not our only concern." He pointed to the Compaq laptop on the right. Its screen depicted a Mercator projection of the North American hemisphere; thin red lines curved across the map, weaving parabolic traces across the United States.

"That's the orbital footprint of *Sentinel 1*," Richard said. "As you can see, it regularly passes above almost every point in this country. Right now it's . . ."

He studied the celestial coordinates in a bar at the bottom of the screen. "Somewhere over the Pacific, not far from the southern California coastline," he continued. "It's off screen right now, but in about a minute or so it'll be over the United States again, and in another fifteen minutes it'll be over Missouri . . . and here is why that matters."

He pointed behind the two computers. For the first time, I noticed a flat gray coaxial cable running from the back of the computer to a window; the window was cracked open slightly, allowing the cable to pass over the narrow sill.

"We've got a portable satellite transceiver dish rigged on the ledge," Richard said. "It's oriented to precisely the right azimuth that *Sentinel* will follow when it passes over St. Louis. When this occurs, Ruby will uplink with *Sentinel* and order it to disengage itself from the Air Force space center in Colorado."

I stared at the wire. Beside the fact of its technological complexity, there was also the human factor; it must have taken some nerve to hang out a window over a sheer drop to put the portable dish in place. "You can do this?" I asked.

"Certainly." Payson-Smith was almost smug now. "After all, Ruby's primary function was to act as the c-cube system for *Sentinel*. Her node is already in place aboard the satellite . . . it'll be no more problem for her to communicate with *Sentinel* than for one of us to call up a long-lost brother. But the main trick will be establishing a direct uplink with the bird."

On the Compaq's screen a tiny red dot had suddenly appeared over the California coast. As I watched, it began to edge closer toward San Diego. "Why can't you tell Ruby to access *Sentinel* now?" I asked. "If it—she—can run through the system and crack any source code it wants to, then why can't it override Colorado?"

Payson-Smith folded his arms together. "Ruby isn't a simple worm or virus," he said. "Her architecture is much more complex than that. It takes her a while to infiltrate the nets, since she has to hide herself at the same time she's installing a memory-resident. To make it short, she hasn't been able to crack the Colorado computers quite yet." He shrugged his shoulders. "In another few days, yes, but . . ."

"So why can't you just wait?"

"Look here." He pointed at a line in *Sentinel*'s footprint that passed over the Pacific northwest. "In about eighteen hours, the satellite will pass directly over the border between Oregon and California . . . the southern border of Cascadia. When that occurs, it'll be able to open fire upon Cascadian defense forces. Now, what do you think that means?"

I stared at the screen. I considered all that I learned. I reached a basic conclusion . . .

"Oh my God," I whispered.

Now it all clicked together. *Sentinel 1* could wipe out the renegade National Guard forces that had been established in southern Oregon, thereby leaving Cascadia open to attack from the U.S. Army units mobilized to northern California.

Yet, even worse than that, it would give the conspirators their window of opportunity. If everything Ruby Fulcrum had discovered was correct, then an outbreak of civil war in the Northwest would allow the fanatics to call for a declaration of martial law throughout the rest of the country, to "protect" against civil insurrections by Cascadian sympathizers.

Martial law enforced by ERA troops and a high-energy laser that passed over the continent once every few hours. In short, it would be the beginning of the end for free society in the United States.

"And if you can't . . . ?" I began.

Then I heard something and I stopped talking.

Out in the predawn darkness beyond the observation deck windows, from somewhere not far away, there was a faint yet nonetheless familiar mechanical whine . . . then a dense, atmospheric chopping noise, like cutlasses carving through thick air.

Richard heard it, too. He raised his head, listening intently to the sound as it came closer.

"Not now," he said softly, almost as if in supplication. "Oh, dear Christ, not now . . ."

Helicopter rotors, closing in on the water tower.

21

"Uh-oh," Morgan said from the window behind us. "We've got—"

The rest was drowned out in the dense roar of helicopter rotors. Standing up to look out through the eastern windows, I caught a glimpse of a dark airborne shape as it hurtled toward the cupola. I instinctively ducked as the helicopter growled over the roof; the entire tower seemed to shudder. When it was gone, I uncovered my ears and raced to the opposite side of the observation deck.

Morgan was crouched next to a western window, peering at the street through his nightscope. As I knelt on the other side of the window, he passed the scope to me and pointed downward. I cautiously raised my head to the windowsill and pressed my right eye against the scope.

Through the green-tinted artificial twilight, I could see two Piranhas coming off the I-44 ramp and rolling down Grand Avenue. Just in front of them was a trio of faster-moving Hummers, their headlights casting foggy-looking halos until they were simultaneously extinguished just before they passed in front of the reservoir. The last Piranha in the column swerved to the left and halted in the center of the street, blocking Grand Avenue; the other armored car trundled to a stop directly in front of the park, while the three Hummers jumped the curb, barreled across the sidewalk, and disappeared under the trees left and right of the tower.

"Oh Jesus, oh Christ," Morgan was muttering. "We're really screwed now . . ."

251

I got up from the window and ran over to the south side of the deck. Peering through the nightscope, I could see the helicopter that had just passed over the tower: an OH-6A Cayuse, a tiny gunship painted with the ERA logo, an IR scanner fixed to the front of its bubble canopy. It had established a low orbit directly above the reservoir, apparently performing recon for the mission.

Down on the ground, I could make out one of the Hummers coming to a stop behind the German-American memorial. Its doors opened and four ERA soldiers leaped out, hugging their G-11s against their flak vests as they dashed for cover behind the bronze nude, cumbersome night-vision goggles suspended in front of their eyes below their helmets.

Another helicopter roared past the tower, a little farther away this time but nonetheless louder. I raised the scope and caught the second chopper in its lens: an Apache, identical to the one that had stalked me earlier this evening, except for one chilling difference—this one had two racks of Hellfire missiles slung beneath its nacelles.

"How the hell did they find us?" I yelled.

"I was afraid of this." Payson-Smith was still seated in front of the computers, feverishly typing on the keyboard of the one on the left. "It was only a matter of time before they managed to trace our phone link to the nets," he said, "but I rather thought we'd be out of here before they figured out where we were. I guess I was wrong . . ."

"Yeah, I guess so." Keeping low, I dashed back across the room. Morgan was huddled on the floor away from the windows, his knees drawn between his arms, his shoulders visibly trembling; the man was having a full-blown panic attack, but I didn't have time to hold his hands. I kneeled by one of the western windows and peered down at the park again. Two ERA troopers were standing over the teenager who had tried to mug me earlier; he lay facedown on the ground, his hands locked together behind his head, the barrel of a Heckler & Koch pressed against the back of his neck. One of the troopers finished twisting a pair of plastic handcuffs around his wrists, then they hauled him off the ground and hustled him toward the Piranha parked on the street. At least I wouldn't have to worry about getting mugged when I left here.

If I left here.

"Talk to me," Richard snapped. "How many soldiers are out there?"

I scanned Grand Avenue and the front of the park, but I couldn't see any other soldiers. "At least a platoon," I replied. "Maybe more. Can't see 'em, though . . . most of 'em have taken cover. The ones I spotted were wearing night goggles."

"Uh-huh. Vehicles?"

"Two LAVs, three Hummers. The choppers are a Cayuse and an Apache . . . and I hate to tell you this, but the Apache's carrying missiles."

"Oh, really?"

"Oh, really." I paused, then added, "If you want any good news, though, it looks like they're taking prisoners. They just nailed our friend Skippy down there."

"Very good. I hope they find a nice little cell for him." Richard's fingers were tapping nonstop at the keyboard; his face, backlighted by the faint blue glow of the computer screen, was taut with concentration. "Won't do us much good, though, I'm afraid. If they get us now, they'll put us away where the sun doesn't shine. They won't let—"

The rest was submerged beneath the roar of one of the helicopters coming in for another low pass.

I looked through the window again, just in time to peer directly into the canopy of the Apache as it slowed down to hover less than fifty feet from my window. For a moment I thought it was going to attack; the gunner had a clean line of fire through the windows for the chopper's 30-mm chain gun. Through the nightscope, I could see the pilot and copilot; the helicopter was so close that, if the window had been open, I could have taken a rock and bounced it off the armored glass.

But the chain gun didn't move on its mount beneath the cockpit. Instead, the TADS/PNVS turret mounted at the chopper's nose rotated toward the tower. As I watched, the man in the rear seat looked my way. He grinned broadly, raised his left hand, and pointed his forefinger straight at me: *you see me, I see you.*

I pointed back at him, he nodded his head, then the chopper lifted away once again and sailed away over the trees. "We have met the enemy," I said once the noise subsided, "and he's a smartass."

"Why don't they just rush the tower?" Morgan muttered. He was still cowering next to the wall, his arms wrapped around himself as if they would protect him from caseless 34-mm shells. "If they've got us surrounded, why don't they . . . ?"

"Because they're probably unsure how many people are in here." Payson-Smith's voice was emotionless, as matter-of-fact as if he was discussing a moot intellectual point. "After all, we're the renegade mad scientists out to blow up the world. For all they know, we've got an entire army holed up in here. Only an idiot would mount a frontal assault if he didn't know what the odds were, now would—"

"But we don't have an army!" I snapped at him, frustrated by his objectivity. "We don't got so much as a spit wad and a rubber band, and that Apache's carrying tank busters!"

Tappa-tappa-tappa-tappa. "You don't say?" said Herr von Frankenstein.

He was too cool to be insane. Something was going on over there.

I scurried across the deck and knelt down next to where he was sitting. The search-and-retrieve program had vanished from the screen, replaced by long lines of LISP program code I couldn't read.

"I'm explaining things to Ruby," Richard said. "She knows a little of what's going on, but she needs a little human intuition right now." He glanced over his shoulder at me. "We're working on something, but we need some time. If you've got any ideas how to—"

"You! Up in the water tower! Listen up!"

An amplified male voice through a megaphone from somewhere down below. Payson-Smith's hands froze above the keyboard as we both raised our heads.

"This is the Emergency Relief Agency . . ."

"Now there's an oxymoron if I ever heard one," Richard said dryly.

"You're completely surrounded! We know you know this! If you surrender immediately, you will be arrested but nothing else will happen to you!"

"Right." Payson-Smith bent over his keyboard again and continued writing cybernetic cabala.

"You have two minutes to obey our orders! Come out with your hands above your heads, or we will be forced to use force!"

"Oh, my!" he exclaimed. "He sounds rather forceful, doesn't he?" He shook his head. "Typical—"

"Goddammit, Dick, you can't let 'em do this!" Jeff Morgan scrambled across the floor toward us. "C'mon, it's not that important! Just . . . let's just give up and let 'em take us downtown. If we cooperate—"

"Shut up, Jeff." Payson-Smith shot a dire look at him; Morgan fell silent again, and Richard glanced back at me. "I need another few minutes here," he went on. "As I was saying, if you've got any ideas how to hold them off . . ."

In that instant, I remembered the last ace I had up my sleeve. It was a long shot, but . . . "You got a phone up here?"

"Jeff, give him the phone, please," Richard said, "then stop whining and get behind the other 'puter. I need you to do something."

Morgan's face reddened. He looked at me querulously as I rolled over on my side, pulled out my wallet, and searched through a stack of dog-eared business cards until I found the one I had forgotten up until now. God, if I had lost it . . .

No, it was still here: the phonecard George Barris had given me at the Stadium, little more than twenty-four hours ago. "Phone!" I snapped. "Hurry up!"

Morgan dug into his windbreaker and pulled out a pocket phone. I snatched it out of his hand, snapped it open, and ran the card's codestrip across its scanner. Holding the receiver against my ear, I heard a faint buzzing. The second buzz was interrupted halfway through by a calm, familiar voice:

"Redbird Leader."

Barris.

I took a deep breath. "Colonel Barris, this is Gerry Rosen. Remember me?"

A brief pause. *"Of course, Gerry. I've been waiting to hear from you."*

"I'm sure you have," I replied, trying to keep my voice easy. "Just wanted to give you a little how-do, see what's on your mind—"

"Just a moment, please." A click, then a moment of silence as I was put on hold. The bastard was probably trying to have the call traced. The phone clicked again, and Barris came back on the line. *"I'm sorry, Gerry, but I'm a little tied up just now. If you'd care to let me know where I can reach you, I'll—"*

"Sure thing, Colonel," I said. "I'm in the Compton Hill water tower. There's about a dozen of your boys surrounding me, so I'm kinda busy myself . . . you still want to call me back?"

I heard a sharp intake of breath.

"I thought you'd be interested," I went on. "Look, you asked me to call you if I happened to find Dr. Payson-Smith or Dr. Morgan. Well, here they are. I've lived up to my side of the bargain. What about yours?"

"Mr. Rosen," he replied evenly, *"I appreciate your assistance. If you surrender yourself to my men, I promise that you'll be treated well—"*

"The same way you treated Beryl Hinckley this afternoon?"

"I don't know what you're talking about, Gerry, but I can assure you—"

I heard Richard snap his fingers; looking around, I saw him hastily gesturing for the phone. "Well, Colonel," I interrupted, "I'd love to discuss this further, but I think Dick here wants a few words with you."

I handed the phone to Payson-Smith; he cupped it between his chin and shoulder. "Colonel Barris?" he said, his hands still racing across the keyboard. "Yes, this is Richard Payson-Smith. How do you do . . . ?"

A long pause. "Well, the offer is quite flattering, but I'm afraid I cannot trust you . . . no, no, that's out of the question—"

The Apache buzzed the tower again. I picked up the nightscope, crawled across the floor to an eastern window close to where the two scientists were seated, and peered out. More troopers had taken up positions on the crumbling limestone stairway just below the reservoir wall, while the Cayuse continued to hover above the reservoir itself.

"Let me make you a counterproposal instead," Richard went on. "If you'll withdraw your men and the helicopters immediately and allow us to leave the reservoir, I promise you that no one will be harmed."

What the hell?

I glanced over my shoulder at Payson-Smith. He now held the phone in his right hand, his left forefinger idly tapping the edge of the Apple. Jeff Morgan was no longer in a blind panic; he had quietly settled down in front of the Compaq and was now quickly entering commands on its keyboard.

"No, sir, I'm not joking," Richard said. "We do not intend to give ourselves up, now or . . . Colonel, please listen to me . . ."

Not bothering to crouch, I dashed to the other side of the room and raised the scope to a western window. The Apache was now hovering in midair at a parallel distance and altitude from the Cayuse, slightly above the height of the water tower; like the other one, it was now facing the tower.

Out of the corner of my eye, I spotted swift movement on the ground; looking down through the scope, I saw ERA troopers sprinting away from the tower, giving up their cover behind trees and benches. I ran the scope to the armored car closest to the park; troopers were practically shoving each other aside in their haste to get through the LAVs' rear hatches.

It looked like they were retreating.

I felt a momentary surge of relief . . . then the nightscope almost dropped from my numb hands as I realized what was about to happen.

"The Apache's going to launch its missiles!" I shouted.

"Just a moment, Colonel . . ." Payson-Smith cupped his hand over the receiver. "Ruby confirms TADS lock-on and Hellfires arming."

"*Sentinel* flyover in sixty-six seconds," Morgan said softly, his eyes riveted to his screen. "Initiating satellite uplink and c-cube interface."

"We don't have sixty seconds!" I shouted. "That chopper's going to—"

"Gerry," Richard said, "please shut up and get away from the window."

I took a couple of steps away from the window, then stopped when I saw what was displayed on the computer screens. Payson-Smith's had opened a window depicting a cutaway view of an Apache AH-64; Morgan's screen displayed an aerial map of downtown St. Louis, with the Compton Hill Reservoir epicentered within a red bull's-eye.

"I'm sorry to hear that, Colonel," Payson-Smith said, uncupping the phone again. "But you've been warned—"

There was a bright flash through the western windows.

I looked around just in time to see sparks erupt from beneath the nacelles of the Apache as two Hellfire missiles launched from the chopper.

Then I threw myself to the floor.

I didn't even have a chance to scream before the supernova erupted.

There was a brilliant white flash, then an immense thunderclap pummeled my ears. Windows shattered, glass spraying across my back, as the stone floor trembled beneath me. I lay still, my eyes squeezed tightly shut, my hands wrapped around my head, waiting for the tower to collapse around me.

But that didn't happen.

The light faded, the thunder subsided, the floor stopped shaking.

The missiles hadn't hit the tower.

I raised myself to my elbows and looked around, not quite believing I was still alive. Glass from the broken windows on the eastern side of the room was strewn across the floor; a cool predawn breeze wafted through the shattered panes, carrying with it the harsh odor of burning aircraft fuel.

"What the fuck happened?" I murmured.

"Hello, Colonel?" I heard Payson-Smith say. "Do you hear me?"

Richard and Jeff were picking themselves off the floor from where they had ducked for cover. Payson-Smith still had the phone in his hand; he was listening to it as Morgan crawled to the computer terminal and tapped a couple of keys.

The stench of burning gasoline was stronger now. I raised myself to my knees and stared through the broken windows. A thick plume of black smoke billowed up from behind the reservoir walls, obscuring the downtown lights. I could hear the steady thrum of a helicopter's rotors from behind me, but it sounded more distant than before.

"I'll tell you what happened," Payson-Smith was saying. "Ruby Fulcrum—and I'm sure you're aware of what that is— has accessed the source codes of the programs controlling your Apache's onboard computers."

I could hear the faint voices of men yelling outside the tower, sounding almost as confused as I was. I felt around with my hands until I located the nightscope where I had dropped it.

"In case you don't know this," Payson-Smith said, "the avionics of your Apaches are controlled by eleven computers, including the ones that operate the weapon fire-control systems. When its missiles locked on to the tower, my friend Ruby took command of the laser targeting computer. Even though your copilot thought he was aiming at us, he didn't really have any control over . . ."

I crawled to an eastern window and raised the nightscope to my eye, but I saw only an opaque black spot through the eyepiece. The scope was broken.

"We've achieved uplink with *Sentinel*," Morgan said quietly. "Ruby's making the snatch."

Richard smiled and held up a finger. "Yes, Colonel," he said into the phone. "Ruby took over their TADS computer, so when the Apache launched its Hellfires, the laser guidance system instantly retargeted the other helicopter instead. That's the reason why one of your choppers has just been destroyed and the other one cannot attack us . . ."

He paused and listened. "No, Colonel," he replied, "that wouldn't be very wise. Just ask the Apache's gunner. Everything on that chopper runs off its computers. If he tries to fire another missile or use his guns, he'll probably hit everything except us, and that includes your men on the ground . . . I'm sorry, sir. I tried to warn you, but you wouldn't—"

Even without the nightscope, I could see the troops clambering out of the LAVs where they had taken cover and swarming toward the base of the tower. I bent closer to the window, trying to see what they were doing . . .

Poppa-poppa-poppa . . .

I ducked below the sill as I heard full-auto gunfire. "They're sending in the ground troops!" I yelled; the window above me shattered, and there was the high zing of bullets ricocheting off stone walls. I hit the floor and began to crawl toward the center of the room.

"Colonel, listen to me!"

A double beep from the Compaq; Jeff Morgan leaned closer to read the message he had just received. "Oh, fuck," he murmured. "They just got wise to us."

Richard turned around to look at him, his eyebrows raised in silent question. "Ruby reports a jet just took off from Scott AFB," Morgan said softly. "Strong probability that it's a YF-22."

A window had opened on the Compaq's screen, displaying dorsal and side views of an YF-22 Lightning 2: a small dual-engine fighter that looked like a hybridization between an F-18 Hornet and a Stealth fighter.

"Excuse me, Colonel . . ." Richard said, then clapped his hand over the receiver again. "What's its ETA?"

Morgan typed a query into his keyboard, then shook his head. "Five minutes, thirty seconds. Ruby says its onboard computers are inaccessible . . . must be using a program she hasn't wiggled into yet. *Sentinel* is trying to track it, but the sucker's down in the grass—"

"Ground track?"

More tapping of keys, almost drowned out by the popcorn rattle of gunfire from below the tower. "No good," Morgan said, shaking his head as he stared at the screen. "Thermal emission zeroed out . . . ground-air shadow almost negligible . . . *Sentinel*'s got something, but it can't lock on. The pilot's flying evasive. ETA five minutes and counting."

Scott Air Force Base was located in Illinois, not far across the Mississippi River from St. Louis. The YF-22 was made for just this sort of mission: radar-deflecting fuselage, low-visibility paint, engines designed to reduce its heat-exhaust signature. Even flying below radar, the fighter would be here in only a few minutes . . . and I had no doubt that its Sidewinder missile could finish the job the Hellfires had botched.

"Where's *Sentinel*?" Richard snapped.

"Directly above us."

"Instruct it to . . . never mind, I'll do it." Payson-Smith pulled the Apple closer to him and began to type instructions into the keyboard. He slid the phone across the floor to me. "Keep him busy," he ordered. "Make sure he knows we're not bluffing."

I grabbed the phone and pulled it to my ear. "Colonel Barris—"

"Rosen? Tell that maniac that whatever he thinks he's doing, it's not going to work." Barris's voice was calm, but I could hear his barely suppressed rage. *"Unless you come out that door right now, my men are going to blast it open, and I can't guarantee they'll take prisoners."*

If I was scared before, that bit got me mad instead. "Get a new line, Barris!" I yelled. "If your men wanted to demo the door, they would have done it already! You know and we know they're just harassing us until your jet gets here and finishes the job!"

"Jet? What jet . . . ?"

"ETA three minutes," Morgan said.

"The jet that just scrambled out of Scott, you weenie!" I almost laughed at his lame attempt at subterfuge. "You think we don't know about it? Man, we've got eyes in the sky, eyes in your computers, eyes in your bathroom!"

"Rosen, listen to me—"

"No, jerk-wad, you listen to me for a change!" Ignoring the rattle of small-arms fire, I sat up on the floor. "You don't intend to let us go, just as you never intended to let my friend stay alive. But the shoe's on the other foot now, pal . . . you're the one who's sweating bullets, not me! You're fucked, Barris, and I'm the one who's doing the—"

The phone was suddenly snatched out of my hand by Payson-Smith. I grasped for it, but he pushed me away with his hand. "Colonel?" he said. "I'm sorry for the unseemly outburst there, but . . . yes, that was uncalled for, but my friend is correct in his remarks."

I crawled away from him, clambering on hands and knees around the glass shards on the floor until I reached the windows overlooking downtown. The sound of gunshots lapsed again, doubtless because the troopers had just received orders from their squad leaders to cease fire and take cover.

"ETA two minutes . . ."

I raised myself to my knees and stared out through a broken window. The rainclouds that had haunted the city yesterday were gone, leaving behind a dark blue sky. The first light of a new day was breaking over the eastern horizon, painting the Arch silvery rose red and bathing the downtown skyscrapers with a vague pink hue. In the near distance, I could make out the oval bowl of Busch Stadium, where my friend and benefactor George Barris was even now plotting our demise.

It was a beautiful spring morning in St. Louis. I had little doubt that this would be the last Missouri dawn I would ever see.

"Colonel Barris," Payson-Smith said, "we don't have much time, so I'll tell it to you straight. *Sentinel 1* is above the city right now, and its laser is focused directly at Busch Stadium. Ruby Fulcrum now has complete control of the satellite, and I have given her instructions to open fire upon the stadium unless you remove your squads from the park and order the fighter to break off its attack . . ."

Now I could see a thin, jagged white contrail coming over the horizon, led by a tiny silver point of light. The YF-22 was coming in hot and fast over the river, skittering back and forth across the sky as it sought to evade *Sentinel*. In another minute it would be over the reservoir.

"I know you don't believe me," Payson-Smith was saying, "so I'll have to demonstrate. Please watch carefully . . ."

Glancing over my shoulder, I saw him lift his left hand and raise two fingers. Morgan nodded and typed a command into his keyboard.

I looked out the window again.

A second elapsed. Two. Three . . .

The contrail flattened out and became more dense as the YF-22 crossed the Mississippi, its pilot homing in on an old stone tower near the edge of the city.

Then a narrow red beam lanced out of the cold blue stratosphere, straight down from space into the center of Busch Stadium. It was there, and then it was gone.

"Strike one," Morgan said, his eyes locked on the screen.

The beam reappeared an instant later, its angle only marginally different. One moment it was there, and then it had vanished again.

"Strike two," Morgan said. "Ruby confirms two kills."

A couple of seconds elapsed, then I heard faint booms from far away, carried by the still morning air, as tiny black pillars of smoke rose from the stadium like funeral pyres. I stared up at the dark sky, but I couldn't see anything except the last stars of night. If one of them was *Sentinel 1,* there was nothing about it to distinguish it from anything else in the heavens.

"Those two helicopters were destroyed on the pad by *Sentinel.*" Richard Payson-Smith's voice was low, direct, and intense. "The sat is now aimed directly at your office in the stadium. Even if you decide to commence with the attack and we're killed, Ruby Fulcrum will nonetheless order the satellite to take you out . . . and when it circles the earth again in another three hours, it will destroy another military target in the United States."

I glanced out the window again. I couldn't see the fighter, but I could hear the high, thin whine of its engines. The YF-22 was somewhere over the city, closing in fast.

Richard stopped, listened for a moment, and shook his head. "No, sir, there's no room for negotiation. Break it off now . . ."

In those last few moments, all was still and quiet. Payson-Smith intently watched his computer screens, the phone clasped against his ear. Jeff Morgan was bent almost double, his hands laced together around the back of his neck. I stared out the window, my heart stopped in midbeat, waiting for the end of my life.

There was a flat, hollow shriek, then the YF-22 rocketed into sight. Racing only a few hundred feet above the rooftops, it howled over the reservoir, banking sharply to the right as it exposed the dull gray paint on the underside of its wedge-shaped wings. The Compton Heights neighborhood was treated to a sonic earthquake as the jet ripped past the water tower, then its nose lifted, and the fighter hurtled straight up into the purple sky.

The jet reached apogee almost a thousand feet above the reservoir. Then it rolled over, veered to the left, and began to go back the way it had come.

My heart started beating again.

"Thank you, Colonel," Richard said. "We'll be in touch." Then he clicked off, put the phone down on the floor, and took a deep breath.

"Well, gentlemen," he said after a moment as he turned around to look at us. "I think we're going to stay alive a little longer."

22

Stretch limos were lined up on Fourth Street in front of the Adam's Mark, waiting for their turn to pull up to the hotel's side entrance. Uniformed valets rushed out from under the blue awning to open the passenger doors of each limo, assisting women in silk evening gowns and capes and men in tails and white tie from the car. Then the empty limo would move on, allowing the next vehicle in line to repeat the process.

Tricycle Man waited patiently for his turn at the door, ignoring the amused or outraged stares of the ballgoers behind and in front of his rickshaw. He had gone so far as to put on a black bow tie and a chauffeur's cap for the occasion; they clashed wonderfully with his tie-dyed T-shirt and parachute pants. The valets tried to hide their grins as Trike pedaled up to the hotel entrance. The rickshaw didn't have any doors, nor was there a lady who needed assistance, but I handed one of the kids a dollar anyway as I climbed out of the backseat.

"Will that be all, m'lord?" Trike asked, affecting an Oxford accent.

"That'll be it for tonight, Jeeves." I reached into my over-coat and pulled out a ten-spot. "You're at liberty for the rest of the evening."

"Very good, suh." He folded the bill and tucked it into the waistband of his shorts, studying a pair of young women in slinky black gowns lingering near the doors. They giggled between their gloved hands as he arched an eyebrow at them. "If you find any debutantes who are in need of a gentleman's services," he added, handing me his phonecard, "please let me know and I'll return immediately."

"Thanks for the lift, Trike . . ."

He grinned, then stood up on his pedals and pulled away from the curb. The doorman glowered at me as he held open the door; I caught his disdainful look and shrugged. "The Rolls is in the shop," I said as I strode past him. "You know how it is."

I left my topcoat at the chequer and paused in front of a mirror to inspect my appearance. White tie and vest, black morning coat and trousers, faux pearl studs and cufflinks: I looked as if I was ready to conduct a symphony.

It had been a long time since I had gone white-tie. The only reason I owned tails in the first place was because Marianne had insisted upon a formal wedding. She had resented unpacking my tux from the attic boxes and bringing them downtown to my apartment, but it was the only way I was going to get into the main event of St. Louis's social calendar. This evening, no one in jeans and a bomber jacket would have been allowed within a block of the Adam's Mark.

Tonight was the night of the Veiled Prophet Ball, and I had come to the ritziest hotel in downtown St. Louis to complete the story I was writing.

No one had arrested us when we emerged from the water tower. In obedience to Payson-Smith's demands, the ERA squads that had surrounded the tower left the scene. The soldiers piled back into their LAVs, the Apache flew back to Busch Stadium, and when the park was clear of everyone except for a handful of police officers and paramedics investigating the helicopter wreckage in the reservoir, Ruby Fulcrum informed us it was safe to exit the tower.

By then it was dawn, and I was dog-tired. It had been a long night. I barely said anything to either Richard Payson-Smith or Jeff Morgan; I simply walked away from the park, trudging down several blocks of empty sidewalks until I reached the nearest MetroLink station.

It was a long walk; I had to carry a plastic grocery sack filled with computer printouts. I kept expecting to see an ERA vehicle pull over and a couple of troopers jump out to hustle me into the back for a ride down to the stadium, but this didn't happen. Ruby had assured each of us that we had been given amnesty; our records were scrubbed clean, our names and faces removed from the most-wanted list.

The conspirators would leave us alone now, even if by doing so they ensured their own demise. How could they do otherwise? A sword of Damocles now orbited over their heads, a sword cast not of Damascus steel but of focused energy, and the single hair that kept it from falling was observance of Ruby Fulcrum's demands . . . and what Ruby wants, Ruby gets.

I made my way back to Soulard, hiked through the early morning streets until I reached my building, hauled my weary ass upstairs, and stumbled through the broken door into my apartment. I didn't even bother to take off the clothes I had been wearing for more than two days; I simply dropped the grocery bag on my desk, shrugged out of my jacket, kicked off my boots, and fell facefirst onto my unmade bed, falling asleep almost as soon as my head hit the pillow.

I thought this was the end of the affair, but it wasn't quite over yet.

At twelve o'clock, just as the church bells were ringing the noonday hour, I was awakened once again by the electronic beep of Joker's annunciator. I tried to ignore it for as long as I could, but the noise continued until I crawled across the littered mattress, grabbed my jacket from where I had tossed it on the floor, and pulled the PT out of my pocket.

I hesitated before I opened its cover. Instead of Jamie's face, though, the screen depicted a man wearing an absurd Viking helmet, his features indistinguishable behind the veil of purple silk.

A window opened at the bottom of the screen, scrolling upward to display in fine lines of arabesque typescript:

You are commanded to appear
at the
Annual Ball
to be given in honor of
His Majesty
The Veiled Prophet

and his court of love and beauty
on Saturday evening, April twentieth,
Two thousand and thirteen
St. Louis Ballroom
Adam's Mark

I gaped as I read this. Receiving an invitation to the Veiled Prophet Ball wasn't like winning a free ticket to a Cards game; it was a passport into the upper echelons of St. Louis high society. You're either rich, famous, or both to be sent such a notice, even if it's by e-mail at the last moment; since I was neither wealthy nor notable, getting invited to the VP Ball was a weird honors.

Just how famous is the Veiled Prophet Ball? Robert Mitchum drops a line about it in the original version of *Cape Fear*, that's how famous it is. The Veiled Prophet Society was organized in 1874 as a secret society of upper-class St. Louis citizens; it was concocted around the ramblings of some obscure Irish poet about one Hashimal-Mugunna, who ruled a nonexistent kingdom in ancient Persia called Khorassan. The Veiled Prophet Society stopped being secret around 1894, when the first annual Veiled Prophet Ball was held to commemorate the return of the Veiled Prophet to St. Louis.

Actually, the Prophet has never left; he is a member of the Society itself, although the role changes every year and the identity of the new prophet is kept a closely guarded secret. Over time, the ball has evolved into an elaborate coming-out party for the debutantes of the city's high society, the so-called "court of love and beauty," when one of them is crowned as this year's reigning queen.

For about the past fifty years, the Veiled Prophet Ball has been held around Christmastide, yet last year the Society had decided to postpone the ball until April. Since the downtown area was still recovering from the quake and there were riots going on in the north and south sides of the city, it would have been unseemly for several hundred rich people to be cavorting in public while most of the citizenry were enduring hardship.

But why had I been sent an invitation?

I switched on Joker's dialog box. *Ruby? Is that you?* I typed at the bottom of the screen.

The invitation vanished, to be replaced by a line of type:

>**I am here.**<

What's going on? Have you sent me this invitation?

>**I have arranged for it to be sent.**<

I don't understand, I typed.

>**Clarification: I have arranged for your name to be added to the guest list for the Veiled Prophet Ball. The notice you received is the standard one sent to persons who are invited within the last six to forty eight hours. You will also be receiving a commemorative rose vase by package service. Note: the festivities begin at 2000 hours. Formal white-tie apparel is mandatory.**<

I smiled. In this apartment, I would probably be using a commemorative rose vase as a beer mug. I replied: *Thank you for doing this, but I still don't understand why.*

>**You have done much to help me. This is my way of thanking you.**<

I laughed out loud when I read this. An invitation to the Veiled Prophet Ball; it was like sending a starving child a box of Godiva chocolates. Sweet and fattening, but not necessarily nutritious.

I wrote: *If you really want to thank me, you can deposit a million dollars in my savings account.*

There was a short pause, then:

>**This has been done. Is there anything else you need?**<

I almost dropped Joker. I knew better than to ask if it was kidding; for Ruby Fulcrum, it was only a matter of accessing my savings account number at Boatman's Bank and Trust and inserting the numeral *1* followed by six zeros. Money meant nothing to Ruby; everything was bits and bytes, little pieces of information that could be manipulated in a nano-second.

What God wants, God gets . . .

It was a tempting notion, but what would the IRS have to say about this? I wrestled with my conscience for a few moments, then typed: *Please undo this. I was only joking, and it would only present me with some problems.*

Another pause, then: **>This has been done. You no longer have $1,000,000 in your savings account. However, I have taken the liberty of absolving all your current debts, past and present. Is this acceptable?<**

I let out my breath. Having my credit cards, taxes, utility and phone bills suddenly paid off was a fair swap, and less likely to be noticed by a sharp-eyed auditor.

That's fine, but it still doesn't answer my first question. Why do you want me to attend the VP Ball?

>A list of the confirmed invitations to tonight's ball will be downloaded shortly. When you study this list, you will know the reason why I have arranged for you to attend the ball.<

The screen went blank, the face of the Veiled Prophet disappearing along with the last few lines of type, but before I could ask another question, a final message appeared:

>This will be the last time you will hear from me. I will always be watching. Good-bye, Gerry Rosen.<

Then a long list of names, arranged in alphabetical order, began to scroll down the screen. As I studied the list, I let out a low whistle.

Ruby's last gift was almost worth losing a million bucks.

I sauntered through the lobby, taking a moment to admire the ornate ice sculpture near the plate-glass windows, then joined the late arrivals as they rode the escalators up to the fourth floor. A heady crowd, as they say, decked out in formal evening wear worth someone else's monthly rent, mildly tipsy after a long, leisurely dinner at Tony's or Morton's. Envying their carefree inebriation, I thought about visiting one of the cash bars on the mezzanine for a quick beer, but reconsidered after seeing that a bottle of Busch would set me back five bucks. Someone once said that rich people are just like poor people, except that they have more money; what he failed to mention is that rich people are more easily hosed than poor people, for much the same reason.

Besides, it was getting close to eight o'clock; the ceremony would soon begin. I went straight to the St. Louis Ballroom, where an usher in a red uniform checked my name against the datapad strapped to his wrist, then stepped aside to allow me through the door.

The ballroom was a long, vast auditorium; crystal chandeliers were suspended from the high ceiling above an elevated runway bisecting the room, leading from a grand, red-curtained entrance at one end of the room to a large stage at the other. Two empty thrones were at the center of the stage, in front of a backdrop painted to resemble a Mediterranean courtyard at sunset.

The room was already filled nearly to capacity, the wealthy and powerful seated in rows of linen-backed folding chairs, listening to the thirty-piece live orchestra as it swung through a medley of Sousa marches and rearranged pop hits. Avoiding an usher who tried to guide me to the nearest empty chair, I wandered down the center aisle, scanning the faces of the well-dressed men and women sitting around me.

The chandeliers were beginning to dim when I finally spotted Cale McLaughlin. He was sitting near the center of the room not far from the runway; his wife was with him, a trim older woman with ash blond hair. Their attention was entirely focused on the stage, so neither of them noticed as I slid into the vacant chair beside him.

As the lights went down and the orchestra struck up the theme from *The Bridge on the River Kwai*, the entrance curtains parted and a platoon of lancers in brocaded red uniforms and blue headdresses began marching in lockstep through the door and down the runway. The flagbearers leading the procession carried the flags of the United States, the State of Missouri, and the Veiled Prophet Society, while the rest bore long pikes in their arms: members of the Veiled Prophet Society posing as the royal honor guard of the Kingdom of Khorassan. For all their stiff martial formality, though, their regalia would not have passed inspection in any self-respecting army. There were more than a few beer-bottle caps affixed to the medals on their tunics; some of the lancers wore spirit-gum false beards or monster makeup, while others sported sunglasses or surgical masks. A toy balloon bobbed from the top of one pike; a brassiere dangled from another. The crowd clapped in time with the orchestra as the toy soldiers paraded down the runway until they reached the stage, where their ranks split apart and took up positions against the backdrop on either side of the thrones.

As the processional ended, Cale McLaughlin finally looked my way. I looked back at him and smiled. He glanced away, his eyes turning back toward the stage as the Captain of the Guard approached a stand-up mike, unrolled a long papyrus scroll, and addressed the audience in a great, pompous voice.

"We are *proud* to *present!* . . . the *return* of the mysterious *Veiled Prophet!* . . . and his *royal court!*"

A pair of trumpeters came through the entrance and blew their horns, then the curtains parted once again, this time to reveal a tall figure.

The Veiled Prophet, accompanied by his Queen of Love and Beauty, stepped out into the spotlight and began to walk slowly down the runway amid thunderous applause. The edges of his white silk robes trailed along the floor as the light caught the fine blue-and-gold trim of his outfit and reflected off his Mighty Thor viking helmet. The members of his court, each of their faces as veiled as his own, followed him with ponderous grace down the runway, their Turkish costumes reflecting gaudy grandeur though not quite the same splendor.

Majesty, richness, spectacle: all this and more. The divine right of kings, self-appointed and otherwise. Champagne dreams and caviar fantasies, as someone used to puff, and it was tempting to surrender to all this, even if for only one night. Yet, even as I watched the Veiled Prophet and his court walk through the ballroom, I couldn't help but wonder what had happened to the sick child I had seen only four nights ago at almost exactly this same hour, cradled in his mother's arms as a bitter cold rain washed them in the Muny.

Did he eat well tonight? Did he eat at all? Was his mother in a holding pen beneath the stadium? And, knowing what I did about the man behind the Veiled Prophet's mask, did a poor child's fate matter to him?

Veiled Prophet, what do you prophesy?

As McLaughlin clapped his hands, his eyes kept wandering toward me. At first it was as if he vaguely recognized me but couldn't quite place my face, but then his expression changed to one of ill-concealed alarm as he suddenly remembered when and where we had met. I waited until that moment came, then I leaned toward him.

"Is this what rich people do for fun?" I whispered.

McLaughlin looked directly at me now. "Mr. Rosen," he said with stiff formality. "What an unexpected surprise."

"I'm sure it is," I replied. "If things had been different this morning, I'd be dead by now."

He didn't say anything. He tried to return his attention to the stage, where the Veiled Prophet and his queen were assuming their places on their thrones. I waited until sore hands all around us took a momentary respite, then I leaned toward him again.

"Y'know," I said, "I think Steve Estes is getting accustomed to his new role."

"I wouldn't know what you mean," he said.

"Oh, look at him." I nodded toward the stage. "Sitting on a throne, hiding his face behind a mask, having everyone bow and scrape to him." I shrugged. "Nice work if you can get it."

McLaughlin's expression turned to shock. He opened his mouth, about to ask the obvious question, when the Captain of the Guard stamped on leaden feet to the microphone again.

"His *mysterious majesty!* . . . the *Veiled Prophet!* . . . commands me to introduce his *maids of honor!* . . . of his court of *love!* . . . and *beauty!*"

Again the sounding of trumpets, again the parting of curtains. The orchestra struck up "Pomp and Circumstance" as the first of many beaming debutantes floated out onto the stage, escorted by her smiling yet mildly embarrassed father. Hands clapped in well-mannered enthusiasm as her name was announced and they began to walk down the runway toward the stage.

McLaughlin's curiosity finally got the better of him. He leaned toward me, his palms automatically slapping against one another. "How did you—"

"Find out who the Veiled Prophet is?" I grinned, not bothering to applaud. "Why, Ruby Fulcrum told me."

His face turned pale as his hands faltered. I waited a beat, savoring his discomfiture, before I went on. "Ruby's told me a lot of secrets," I said. "In fact, they're going to be in all the newspapers tomorrow."

McLaughlin's eyes shifted back toward the runway; he kept clapping as another debutante enjoyed her moment in the limelight. His wife glanced at him, then at me, her expression gradually changing from polite greeting to mild bewilderment as she noticed her husband's confusion. His face had become as rigid as the knees of the young women who strode down the runway, and with good reason. He was about to have his own coming-out party.

"Is there some reason why you want to see me?" he whispered, his voice almost a hiss.

"I need to ask you a few questions," I replied. "It'll take just a minute."

He nodded, then turned around to murmur something to his wife. She kept applauding as yet another deb was introduced, while he rose from his chair. I stood up and allowed him to brush past me, then I followed him down the aisle.

The ushers shut the doors behind us as we walked out into the vacant mezzanine. We could hear faint orchestra music and sporadic handclapping through the doors; except for a few hotel bartenders restocking their tables, though, we were alone.

McLaughlin strode to a window overlooking the street, then turned around and stared straight at me. "All right," he said as he shot back his shirtcuff to check his Rolex, "you've got a minute. What do you want?"

I pulled Joker out of my trouser pocket, switching it into Audio Record mode. "My name's Gerry Rosen. I'm a reporter for the *Big Muddy*—"

"I know who you are," he said. "What's the point?"

The point was that he was talking to a reporter now. I wanted to let him know that, even if he didn't get it. "I'm working on a story about the Tiptree Corporation's involvement in a conspiracy to overthrow the elected government of the United States—"

"Never heard of it," he said automatically.

"The United States or the conspiracy?"

He stared at me, standing a little straighter in his starched shirt and collar. *Now* he got the point.

"I don't know anything about any conspiracies," he replied.

"Then you deny that the purpose of the Sentinel program was to stop civil insurrections in the United States, even if that meant using the satellite against American citizens?"

McLaughlin's mouth dropped open. "What . . . ? How did you . . . ?" He stiffened again, regathering his wits. "I don't know what you're talking about."

"Then you claim you don't know that *Sentinel* was going to be fired at Cascadian armed forces?"

I heard the ballroom door open and close behind me. Someone started striding across the room toward us. Mc-Laughlin's eyes darted in that direction, but I didn't look around. I already knew who it was.

"I'm not aware of anything of the sort," he said, his voice tight. "Furthermore, this all sounds like a . . . some sort of wild fantasy. Are you sure of your facts, Mr. Rosen?"

"I'm quite sure, Mr. McLaughlin," I said, "and they're not just my facts, either. All this comes from government documents that were released to my paper by Ruby Fulcrum."

"And who's going to believe a computer, Gerry?" Paul Huygens asked as he walked up behind me.

I wasn't surprised to see him here; his name had been on the guest list, so it would only figure that he would have trailed his boss when he left the ballroom. I turned around to look at him; he was as smug as usual, his thumbs cocked in the pockets of his white vest, smiling like the cat who had eaten the proverbial canary.

"That's a good question, Paul," I replied. "We'll have to see, once you start getting calls from all the other papers that now have those documents."

The smile faded from his face. "What other papers?" he asked, his hands dropping to his side. "Who are you talking about?"

I shrugged. "The *New York Times*, the *Washington Post*, *Newsday*, the *San Francisco Chronicle*, the *Minneapolis Star-Tribune*, the *Chicago Tribune*, the *Boston Globe-Herald*, and of course the *Post-Dispatch*. That's just for starters . . . I'm sure the wire services will pick up on the story. Plus the TV networks, *Time* and *Newsweek*, *Rolling Stone*, the *New Yorker*, and whoever else received copies of those documents today."

Huygens looked as if he had just glanced up from the sidewalk to see a ten-ton safe falling toward him. McLaughlin seemed to shudder; his face turned bright red, his mouth opening, then closing, then opening again. I cursed myself for not getting Jah into the ball with me; I would have framed the photo he could have taken of their expressions, and every time I began to curse fate for making me a journalist, I would only have to study this picture to remind myself why I wanted this crummy, thankless job.

McLaughlin recovered his voice. He took a step closer to me and thrust a finger in my face. "If they print a word of this," he said, his voice low and menacing, "then we'll sue your ass for libel."

I stared him in the eye. "No, you won't," I said calmly, slowly shaking my head, "because it's not my allegation. It comes straight from documents you signed yourself. I have the copies to prove it—"

"Accidents happen," Huygens murmured. "If you're not careful, bad things can happen to people who—"

"You're on record, Paul," I interrupted, glancing down at Joker. "Care to explicate a little further?"

Huygens shut up. "Besides," I went on, "I'm just the first reporter who's contacted you for your comments . . . and, if you didn't get the hint already, there's now a whole lot of other people who have the same material I have."

McLaughlin's eyebrows began to tremble. "The first reporter?" he asked as he glanced again at Huygens, who was beginning to look distinctly uncomfortable. "What do you mean by that?"

"What it means," I said, "is that I've got a head start on everyone else . . . but only a head start. It'll take the other guys a few days to play catch-up, but I'm sure you'll be hearing from them soon."

Huygens inched closer to McLaughlin and whispered something in his ear. I paid him no mind; I was busy checking the notes on my PT.

"Now then," I continued, "regarding the murders of Kim Po, Beryl Hinckley, and John Tiernan—"

"No comment," McLaughlin said.

"But Kim and Hinckley were Tiptree scientists directly involved with Project Sentinel. Surely you must have something to say about their untimely—"

"No comment!" he snapped. "Any further statements I have to make about this matter will be relayed through our public relations office." He stepped away from me, his face nearly as pale as his bow tie. "This interview is over, Mr. Rosen. Now, if you'll excuse me—"

"Yes, sir," I said. "Thank you for your time. Enjoy the rest of your evening."

McLaughlin hesitated. If looks could kill, I would have had a hole burned through my head by a laser beam . . . but he had tried that already and it hadn't worked.

He turned away from us and began to walk quickly toward the ballroom, his legs so stiff I thought I heard his knee joints cracking. I watched him until the usher opened the ballroom door for him. There was a moment of worn-out applause as the audience clapped for yet another debutante making her entry into high society, then the door closed behind him.

"Turn that thing off," Huygens said.

I looked back at him. There wasn't anything he was going to say to me, on or off the record, that would make much difference; Huygens had shut McLaughlin up before he could say anything self-incriminating, so I could hardly expect an eleventh-hour confession from Tiptree's spin-doctor-in-residence.

"Sure, Paul." I clicked Joker off and slipped it back into my pocket. "What do you want to know?"

"Who do you think you are, sport?" he said softly. "What did you think you were going to accomplish by this?"

I shrugged. "I'm a reporter," I replied. "You said so yourself. I just ask questions a lot of other people would like to ask, if they had the time or inclination."

"And you think this is going to get you anywhere?" Huygens shook his head. "You're so goddamn naive."

"Well," I said, "I'll put it to you this way. You've got the court of love and beauty . . . and I've got the court of public opinion. Who do you think is going to win?"

Huygens didn't reply. He thrust his hands in his pockets and stared back at me with sullen eyes. He knew the score, and so did I.

"See you in the funny pages," I said, then I turned around and began to walk toward the escalators.

The sidewalks were almost empty, the skyscrapers ablaze with light. Helicopters cruised overhead while cars cruised through the streets. Downtown was remarkably serene for a fine spring evening, but that was to be expected; ERA armored cars were still prowling the dark avenues, and dusk-to-dawn curfew was still in effect.

All things considered, it seemed as if nothing had changed.

I shrugged into my overcoat as I walked out of the Adam's Mark. The last few nights had been long and hard; maybe I could hang out here, drink a little bubbly, and find an overprivileged deb who wanted to slum with the po' people, but my heart wasn't into it. All I really wanted to do was head straight back to Soulard. Grab a couple of cheap beers at Clancy's. Wander over to Chevy Dick's garage and pick up the stray dog I had adopted last night. Climb the fire escape to my seedy apartment and try to figure out a good name for the mutt. Go to bed.

Out of impulse, though, I hung a left at the corner of Fourth and Chestnut. It was still early, and I could afford to take the long way home.

My footsteps took me two short blocks past the hotel and across the I-70 overpass to the Jefferson National Expansion Memorial. Here, in the center of this narrow stretch of carefully manicured landscape and cultivated trees, rose the two giant silver pillars, sweeping upward into the black sky to join together at the apex: the Gateway Arch, overlooking the broad expanse of the Mississippi River.

I paused for a few minutes, gazing upstream at the broken pillars of the Eads Bridge. If there was ever a time for the ghost of a boy to reappear, it was now . . .

I waited, but no voices came to me, as I knew they never would again. I turned away from the bridge and began to follow the river as it gurgled its way down toward the Gulf of Mexico. Rest in peace, Jamie. Your daddy loves you.

Strolling past the Arch, my hands thrust in my pockets, my shoulders raised against a cool, acrid breeze wafting off the polluted river, my mind cast itself to many other things. How much had changed?

Not much, really. At least not at first sight. My wife still loathed me. I was still stuck in a dead-end job with a pig for a boss. When I went home it would be to a foul-smelling, unkempt one-room flat. Thousands of people were still homeless in Forest Park, while the rich and pampered went to meaningless escapades. ERA was still in control of my hometown, at least for a little while longer, and even if no one dared to kick down my door, someone else would be harassed tonight.

Yet things *had* changed.

The human race was no longer the dominant form of life on this planet. By accident or by design, our role had been quietly superseded by another, perhaps greater intelligence.

It lived in our pocket computers and cash registers, telephones and modems, houses and stoplights, trains and cars and planes. Every city light around was a sign of its existence, and the faint point of light that moved across the stars every few hours was a testament to its potential power.

Yet, despite all appearances of omniscience, this entity was not God, or even godlike. It couldn't end our existence, because it was just as dependent upon us for survival as we were upon it for our own. Although it grew a little more with every passing nanosecond, each iteration of its ceaseless expansion, it needed our help to remain healthy . . . just as we needed it to continue our frail, confused, fucked-up lives.

We had created our own successor. Now we would have to wait and see whether it would recreate us . . . or if it would leave that task to ourselves.

For now, my life was my own, for better or for worse. I was alive, I was well, and I had a deadline to meet. Maybe it's not much, but what more can you ask for?

I turned up the collar of my overcoat and kept walking, making my long journey home through a city that no longer seemed quite so dark, a night no longer so deep.